THE BRIDE'S RUNAWAY BILLIONAIRE

PIPPA GRANT

Copyright © 2024

All rights reserved. This book or any portion thereof may not be reproduced or used in any manner whatsoever, including the training of artificial intelligence, without the express written permission of the publisher except for the use of brief quotations in a book review.

This is a work of fiction. Names, characters, businesses, places, events and incidents are either the products of the author's imagination or used in a fictitious manner. Any resemblance to actual persons, living or dead, or actual events is purely coincidental. All text in this book was generated by Pippa Grant without use of artificial intelligence.

Pippa Grant is a trademark of Bang Laugh Love LLC.

Editing by Jessica Snyder/HEA Author Services
Proofreading by Emily Laughridge & Jodi Duggan
Cover Design by Qamber Designs

This book is dedicated to Beth and Jodi. Without you, it wouldn't exist.

And the campfire scene is dedicated to Connor Crais. He brought this on himself.

1

Emma Monroe, aka a normal ray of sunshine with so many, many regrets

Tripping over a body on the porch of my Fiji beach villa wasn't the way I planned to start my day, but then, what *has* gone right in the past few days?

I go down with a surprised *oof*, landing on top of the person. Pain radiates through my elbow after it smacks the wood of the porch. If there are any gods listening, *please* don't let this be a reporter.

One more thing to be filed under *things I never thought I'd worry about in my life*.

But here we are.

Also—"Don't be dead. Don't be dead. Don't be dead."

Even if this person *is* a freaking reporter.

Why can't I be the badass who'd hope the next thing on my agenda today is burying a body?

Bonus, if I were that type of badass, I wouldn't care

that I've become the world's most notorious runaway bride.

But I'm not that kind of badass.

Which means I need to find a different way to deal with this.

It has to be at least eighty degrees out here, but my teeth are chattering and I'm battling a whole-body shiver that makes me want to curl into a ball.

I'm also still sprawled across this human lump.

What would Theo do?

My brother—who is, unsurprisingly, yet again one of my favorite people in the world while simultaneously sitting at the top of my shit list—would pull a wrestling move, flip this person on their back, and use the power of his morning breath to add some extra fear when he said —something.

Probably *get the fuck off my porch before I gut you like a fish.*

No, actually, that's not Theo's style.

But then, hiding in an apparently high-end villa and ducking into closets anytime the resort staff drops by, even to leave the food you ordered from room service on the porch, also isn't Theo's style.

So how does the *new and improved, doesn't let people walk all over her* Emma want to handle this?

Do I scoot off this person, hit the porch light switch and make whoever it is think I *am* the type to not blink at starting my day with burying a body? Can I?

Can I be a warrior woman for once in my life?

I'm trying to think of another dastardly plan when the person beneath me groans.

And rolls.

And wraps a heavy arm around my waist.

"*Why*, Peyton?" moans a deep male voice that smells like dead fish steeped in whiskey. "Give me back the whalebone."

"Excuse me, sir." I poke him while I try to lift his arm off of me. "You need to leave."

"I should've known it would be you. There's never been anyone like you."

I freeze, and goosebumps erupt over my shivers while déjà vu takes hold.

I've heard this man say those words before.

Why have I heard this man say those words before?

"Sir, please *let go*," I repeat.

"Making you happy is my favorite thing in the world."

What's bigger than goosebumps? Ostrich bumps?

That's what I have now.

I've heard that sentence before too.

Am I losing my mind?

Am I actually awake?

Is this a bad dream?

Okay, yes, it's a bad dream. This whole last week has *all* been a bad dream. Except it's currently my reality, and I'm nearly certain I'm awake.

Panic has me finding strength I shouldn't have after being unable to stomach hardly anything the past few days.

And that's another thing pissing me off.

I'm having gourmet meals delivered when I call for room service, *in Fiji*, and the thought of eating them makes me feel ill.

Worse?

The person I'm most pissed at is myself.

I did this by insisting for the past *seven years* that Chandler Sullivan was the man of my dreams, even while *knowing* he wasn't Theo's favorite person and vice versa. Despite the occasional hint that my friends thought he was annoying. Including Sabrina, one of my two besties, who's his *cousin*. And despite the way his own aunts, uncles, and parents would look at him and sigh over some of his more ridiculous opinions.

The things I knew he did that I told myself he'd stop doing if I could just convince him I loved him enough.

Fuck him.

Fuck me too for doing this to me.

I manage to shove the man's arm off me, dash back inside the house, and peer through the sliding glass door that I've just locked.

I flip on the outside light, and dizziness has me leaning against the glass.

But not because of hunger.

More because my brain is trying to convince me that I know the man who's curling into a ball and wincing against the light.

"Love isn't rational, but it's not pathetic either," he moans, his voice drifting through an open window with yet *one more line* that I've heard before.

I flip the light off, plunging everything back into pre-dawn darkness.

Then I pinch myself.

Yep. That hurt.

I flip the light on again.

And he's still there.

Jonas Rutherford.

My favorite movie star on the entire planet.

The man whose movies I can recite by heart.

Number one on my *freebie list* that I only mentioned one time to Chandler, who got so offended at the joke —*who actually meets their number one celebrity crush?*—that I didn't even tell Sabrina and Laney that I'd made a list. And the three of us don't—didn't—*dammit*.

Apparently we *do* keep secrets from each other. If we truly didn't, I would've known what Chandler did to Theo *years* ago, and I wouldn't be the world's most notorious runaway bride right now.

But more important in this exact moment?

Jonas Rutherford is *here*.

Moaning and grabbing his head on the porch of the tropical villa where I'm hiding from the entire world.

Nope.

Nope nope nope. This isn't real.

I flip the lights off again.

This is a job for resort security. Not for me.

"I thought we were happy," the man who looks and sounds like Jonas Rutherford, but cannot possibly *be* Jonas Rutherford, says outside.

And my stupid, vulnerable, gullible heart wells up and sheds a tear for the sadness in his voice.

If that's really Jonas Rutherford, and not some reporter dressed up to look and act like him in some elaborate scheme to get to me—paranoia is my new BFF—then I know what he's talking about.

You basically can't get on the internet without seeing the viral video of my failed wedding right next to the reports that Jonas's movie star wife left him mere months after their wedding last summer, and that their divorce was recently finalized.

And now public.

With *allllll* of the details that mean this man should *not* be on my *freebie list*.

"Crap," he mutters.

Crap.

Like that's the worst curse word he knows for waking up hungover on a porch after someone tripped over him.

And does he even know I'm here? Does he realize he wasn't alone?

There's a shuffling on the other side of my door, and then the glass door rattles.

My heart freezes in my chest.

What is he *doing*?

The lock holds though.

"Are you freaking kidding?" he mutters.

The door rattles again but doesn't budge.

He groans, mutters, "Forget this," and then all goes quiet.

I peer into the darkness.

Can't see a thing, and pre-dawn is when I most like taking the short path down to the beach. I'm hardly *Jonas Rutherford* famous, and this *is* a gated resort with limited other guests in the half dozen or so other villas, but I still felt like I got funny looks my second day here.

Ten out of ten do not recommend starring in a viral video where you jilt your groom right before your vows after finding out there's a massive list of shitty things he did to a lot of people you love and that all of your friends and family kept from you for years.

Twenty out of ten don't recommend *knowing* that he did shitty things—though not the shittiest of the shitty things that came out just before I walked down the aisle—

and convincing yourself you could still walk down that aisle and fix him if you just loved him enough.

And a billion out of ten don't recommend living in shame, guilt, and regret for knowing what your choices have done to the people you love.

That's the one I'll have to face when I get home.

I count to five hundred, assuming that'll be enough time for the man on my porch to be long gone, and then I flip the lock and slowly slide open the door again.

I click on my flashlight app on my phone.

And I whimper.

Why is he still there?

"Wha-hm?" a froggy, sleepy, Jonas-Rutherford-sounding voice says. "Who's there? Where's there?"

I hover in the doorway. "I think you're lost. This isn't your house."

"Not my—where am I?" He pushes to sitting, groaning softly and grabbing his head. The white wicker egg swing just to my right sways lightly in the breeze, looking like a ghost. He fumbles for something in his pocket.

His phone.

He hits a button, the flashlight blinks on, and I wince and shield my face as he aims it at me.

"Oh. Sorry." His voice is still froggy, but he seems to be more aware. "I thought this was—crap. This isn't my bungalow."

"It is not," I confirm.

"Are we in Fiji?"

"Yes."

"Are you a reporter?"

"*No.*"

There's a beat of silence like he's weighing if he can believe me.

Ironic, considering I'm not sure I trust him. Nor do I think I want to if rumors about why he got divorced are true.

"Is the island having an earthquake?" he asks.

"No."

"It's not spinning?"

"No."

"Am I spinning?"

"No."

"Are you sure?"

"Absolutely positive."

"Where's my place?"

"I don't know. What villa are you staying at?"

He doesn't answer.

Because he doesn't know?

Because he forgot?

Because he fell back asleep?

He's pointing his phone's flashlight down now. Coupled with the morning light rapidly coming in, I can almost see him clearly.

Dark hair falls across his forehead. The strong nose. Rugged jawline. Stubble thick enough to make me wonder how long it's been since he shaved.

Or was sober.

He's bigger than I thought he'd be. Aren't movie stars usually short? Underwhelming in person? But even hunched over on the porch, I can tell his shoulders are broad, and he *has* to be tall. Maybe not six feet, but at least as tall as I am.

Maybe he's not really Jonas Rutherford. Maybe this is

his doppelganger.

That makes way more sense.

Yep. This is Jonas Rutherford's doppelganger, who just happens to love Razzle Dazzle films so much that he quotes them in a hungover haze.

And who was saying Jonas Rutherford's ex-wife's name in his drunken sleep-stupor.

And who's afraid of reporters.

"When did I get here?" he asks hesitantly.

"I don't know."

"Did you…see me…last night?"

"No."

"So you don't know how I got here?"

"No." I squash the urge to add *sorry*, which is what *Emma who lets people walk all over her* would do, but *Emma breaking out of bad habits* is trying *not* to do.

"Where…is here?"

"The Morinda."

His gaze flies to mine, and a soft *oh, fuck*, escapes his lips.

So Jonas Rutherford—or his doppelganger—*does* cuss.

That actually makes me smile.

He doesn't say another word.

He's too busy leaping to his feet, then swaying, and then—oh.

Oh.

Well.

Those bushes probably didn't need that kind of fertilizer, but they're getting it anyway.

And *Emma who doesn't let people walk all over her, except apparently right now when they look like her favorite movie star* makes a decision that I know I'll regret entirely too soon.

2

Jonas Rutherford, aka a man in the midst of an epic fall from grace

I THOUGHT *rock bottom* would be when the press got wind of the fact that Peyton and I had quietly gotten divorced. That *divorce in the Rutherford family* would be the biggest part of this *scandal*.

My family founded and operates an entertainment conglomerate that pumps out the warm, fuzzy romantic movies that millions and millions of people across the globe watch twenty-four seven. I've been acting in them in some capacity since before I was old enough to remember. I've also been in every holiday parade at our Razzle Dazzle-themed amusement park since babyhood.

Being the basic face of our fairy tale has made the world believe that I *live* that fairy tale off-set too.

Jonas Rutherford, *divorced* from Hollywood's sweetheart?

Scandal.

But it got worse a few days ago when my phone exploded with messages from everyone I knew that she'd gone public with *why* she filed for divorce.

During a press conference where she *also* announced she'd found a co-star for an epic project where she'd make her directorial debut.

The project that I should've said *yes* to, and that me saying *no* to, for all the reasons she just shared with the world, led to our divorce.

That tidbit going public should've been my actual rock bottom in this ordeal.

But that was before I tossed my cookies in the bushes outside the wrong villa at the wrong resort where I'm attempting to keep a low profile while everything blows over.

Someone else will have a bigger scandal any day now, and I'll get to go back to my normal life.

Not that I'm entirely sure what that is at the moment, but I'll figure it out when I can leave my house without people asking me questions that make me feel like slime.

"Here," my unexpected host says, sliding a plate of toast across the glass table to me in the small but well-stocked kitchenette with a window view of the ocean. "This might help your stomach too."

She watches me for a second, her gaze wavering. And then she takes a seat in the wire-frame chair across from me and pulls her knees to her chest.

I can't tell if she recognizes me or not.

Also can't decide if I want her to or not.

I nod my thanks and debate with myself if I can

stomach the toast and the ginger ale she poured for me while the bread was toasting.

Probably.

What's the worst that happens if I try it and I'm wrong?

Already been there, haven't we?

She takes a small sip of her own ginger ale, still studying me.

I need to get myself a ride back to my resort across the island. Back to my own villa, where I know the well-paid staff will be discreet and not tell anyone I'm there.

And where I have absolute faith that my fellow guests won't bat an eye at me either, even if they recognize me and have seen the news in the past few days.

My host, though?

There's something in the way that she's watching me that has me on edge.

But the toast smells good.

Good enough that my stomach is insisting I try it or face more consequences.

I duck my head and take a hesitant bite.

It's dry. *Super* dry.

So dry that when I inhale after I think I've swallowed it all, a speck of toast dust gets caught in my throat, and it sends me into a coughing fit that I feel in every cell in my body, from my pinky toe to my aching head.

The tabloids would love this.

Jonas Rutherford, former charming star of romantic movies who's a sexist asshole pig in secret, chokes and dies on a piece of toast.

The woman sitting across from me nudges the ginger ale closer, and I take a swig.

Cough more.

Grimace at the tenderness in my abs.

You'd think I didn't work with a personal trainer six days a week. One little *toss last night's bad decisions* moment, and everything hurts.

Maybe it's less the ralphing and more the hangover.

"I don't do this a lot," I rasp.

"If only you didn't have to go to work today," the woman across from me says, her delivery even drier than the toast.

I choke again, this time at recognizing the line.

If I've said that line once in a Razzle Dazzle film, I've said it fifty times.

Her eyes narrow. "You *are* Jonas Rutherford."

"I—"

"Please don't take this the wrong way—because I love your movies, I truly do—but you need to leave. I've had *enough* attention in the world lately, and I am *not* up for having you bring more."

I blink.

Blink again.

Eat another bite of dry toast.

Choke on it again.

Get a sigh from my hostess, who shoves my ginger ale into my hand.

"Guh toe," I say, not able to enunciate *good toast* all the way with the toast sucking all of the moisture out of my mouth.

"It's not gourmet, but it does the trick when you have an upset tummy." She glances behind me, then rises to shut the curtain on the window overlooking the sunrise over the ocean.

She's tall. At least five eight, maybe five nine.

Slender. Long arms and legs. Bony shoulders that are hunched in. Prominent collarbones. Big brown eyes over a pixie nose and a pointy chin. Ears just this side of too big holding back her blonde hair. Nearly certain she's not wearing a bra for the small breasts under that black tank top, and her loose cotton pants are hanging low on her hips.

I take another sip, watching her as she methodically closes the rest of the curtains in the sitting room beside the kitchen.

"You don't want to be seen with me," I say.

She grimaces but otherwise doesn't answer.

"What's your name?" I'd add my normal smile—tends to come easily, or it did, until my personal life imploded beyond anything I'd ever prepared myself for—but once someone sees you ruin their bushes with the contents of your stomach, *smiling* feels insignificant and unnecessary.

Or maybe *futile* is a better word.

She takes the seat across from me again, squinting at me like she doesn't trust the question. "I'm Emma."

"Lovely to meet you, Emma. I'm Jonas."

"Are you, though? Or are you someone who looks like him and knows Razzle Dazzle movies by heart so that you can sneak into an unsuspecting woman's villa to get the inside scoop on *her* disastrous life like a complete and total bastard?"

Would you look at that?

I have a smile in me after all. "I swear on my favorite Razzle Dazzle film, I'm Jonas Rutherford."

"If you were really Jonas Rutherford, wouldn't you have security?"

"Ditched them."

"Why?"

"Because I don't want to *be* Jonas Rutherford right now."

She's full-on scowling now. "Are you sure you're not using *his* situation to try to weasel your way into my life right now?"

"I—sorry?"

"You don't know who *I* am, do you?"

Ah, fuck.

My mother always said this would happen, and now, it won't be toast that kills me.

Jonas Rutherford, secret two-faced prick, dies at the hand of a stalker after refusing to listen to his mother's advice to lay low at his brother's favorite hideout while waiting for the media shitstorm to blow over. "I always warned him not to trust strangers whose porches he passed out on while he was drunk, but the child had a mind of his own," Mrs. Giovanna Rutherford is quoted as saying. And now, we have questions about his drinking habits in addition to his feelings on the place of his wife in a marriage.

"Have we met?" I ask. Nearest exit is probably the back door, but I don't know how fast I can run in my current condition.

Probably fast enough—instincts would take over, wouldn't they?—but unlike that time I got trapped with my brother in a port-a-john when I unwisely snuck off a set and got spotted by fans despite my disguise, my security team isn't close by.

"Never mind," she says quickly. Her freckled white cheeks take on a pink hue, and she ducks her head into her knees. "Just never mind."

I reach for the ginger ale, then pause.

I *don't* remember how I got here last night, but I—oh.

Oh.

This house is familiar.

The black curtains patterned with embroidered pineapples. The island sandscape painting with the weird shell in the corner that looks out of place. The layout of the kitchen and living room and the door. The sleek lines of the ivory furniture and the straw rugs on the floor.

Fiji.

The Morinda.

I've stayed in this house.

I shot a movie in this house.

With Peyton.

The headlines are getting better and better by the moment.

Rabid stalker fan tricks Jonas Rutherford into his final demise at the spot where he asked his ex-wife on their first date.

I slowly push the ginger ale back, hoping it's not poisoned. I saw her open the can. I saw her take the bread out of the bag.

I don't think any of this is poisoned.

I hope.

Emma—if that's her real name—squirms in her chair, then rises. "All I mean is that this will be a lot easier if you just leave so I don't have to deal with..." She flaps both hands in my direction, clearly indicating *so I don't have to deal with you.*

I feel like I'm reading this wrong, but then, my brain is operating on last night's whiskey and three months of divorce hell. "Is that... a threat?"

Her pale brows wrinkle together. "A—*what*?"

"Did you help me get back here last night? Were we drinking together?"

"I haven't left here since I arrived on Sunday other than to go to the beach."

Sunday.

Today's—fuck me. I don't know what day today is.

"Today's Thursday," she says.

Is it? Is it really? "Is *go to the beach* a code word?"

She squeezes her eyes shut and mutters something I can't understand as she glances at the door.

And she doesn't try to stop me when I reach into my pocket for my phone and verify that it, too, says on my home page that today is Thursday.

It also says I've missed seven text messages from my mother, three from my brother, and one from his girlfriend.

I cast a covert glance at Emma.

She's grabbing sunglasses even though it's barely light outside, and I'm realizing that paranoia is not my friend, no matter how much it claims to be when I drink too much.

She's trying to get rid of me.

Not the *bad* way though. "You don't want me here."

She grimaces. "Any other year, any other circumstances...*I'm a happy person*. I am. And here *you* are, and here *I* am, and *I cannot be happy about this*. Do you have *any* idea how aggravating it is to have your celebrity crush *sitting at your dining room table* with timing like *this*?"

"I—ah—no."

She blows a big breath out of her nose and rubs her forehead. "Of course you don't. Sorry. No, *not sorry*. Something else. Pretend I said something else that's not *sorry* but also expresses my regret—no, not my regret. My *acknowledgment* that this is *unfortunate*."

My pulse slows and the panic recedes.

She knows who I am.

She says she likes me.

And she's clearly having a rough time.

I don't think I'm in danger. I think she's having a bad day.

I *hope* she's having a bad day.

Not that I wish bad days on people. More that it's better for her to be weird because of a bad day than because she's planning on murdering me.

Also, if she'd read all of the news about me, I doubt I'd still be her celebrity crush.

Honestly, I'd probably think less of her if I still was.

My phone dings once more with another message, this one privately from Begonia instead of in the group chat.

She's the only person in that chat that I'm not related to by blood or marriage—though I know Hayes will likely propose soon enough—and she's also my favorite.

While everyone else freaked out when the tabloid coverage of Peyton's side of our divorce story blew up, Begonia simply gave me a hug and a *we all make mistakes, and it's easier to do better with support instead of judgment*.

How my brother found a woman with a heart the size of the moon who tolerates not only him, but all of the rest of us too, is one of life's greatest mysteries.

Proof of life, I type back to her. *For the moment. Tell them to call off the hunt. I'll be back when I'm back.*

The typing bubble pops up immediately, letting me know she's working on a response.

"I'm going to the beach before anyone else is up,"

Emma says. "Feel free to do whatever. And good luck with whatever it was that put you in that shape. For both of our sakes, it's probably best that I don't know details."

"You're leaving a stranger in your villa."

"It's preferable to being spotted in public with you."

I'm not a big fan of being spotted in public with myself either. "Did someone make you watch my movies under duress? Is that why you can quote them but you want me to leave? Or did you...watch the news?"

I get a side eye that suggests she's seen the news, but she's a big enough person to not judge me for it. "I've had enough attention lately. Being spotted with you would *not* help that, and you being spotted with me is probably not good for you either."

My brain is too sludgy to follow.

I hate sludgy brain.

"Who are you?" I ask her.

She grimaces.

Again.

I rise, get woozy in the head thanks to last night's activities, but I refuse to go down. "Why don't you want public attention? Who are you?"

She sighs a grumbly sigh, pulls out her phone, and after thumbing over the screen for a few seconds, she shoves it at me.

A video of what looks like a tropical wedding fills the screen.

I blink as the voices register. "I've seen this."

"You and eighty percent of the world," she mutters.

It's a train wreck on top of a plane crash on top of a mudslide on top of an earthquake during a fire tornado. There's a bride confronting the groom about setting her brother up for jail. Something about her brother being a secret adult entertainment star. The groom selling a family business out from under everyone.

At least six friends sent me this to assure me my scandal was being overtaken by some nobodies getting hitched—excuse me, *not* getting hitched in Hawaii.

I look up at Emma without finishing it, and it clicks.

She squeezes her eyes shut again. "And now my life is fully complete."

I don't think.

I just act.

And not like *acting* acting. Like *moving*.

This woman needs a hug.

She needs a hug and my security detail.

I grew up in the public spotlight. I know what it's like, but I've had training. Buffers. Publicists and media guidance and when all else failed, money talked.

And here she is, all by herself, wanting to go to the beach before the sun's fully up and anyone else spots her because she's famous for her disaster of a failed Hawaiian wedding to a guy who was apparently secretly a massive dick.

"I'm sorry." I wrap my arms around her.

Can't help myself.

But it makes sense now. *Go away. I don't want to be seen with you too.*

My brother hates the spotlight that I've mostly happily lived in my entire life. *Hates* it. Doesn't do well with publicity, and he had his own run-in with the press when they caught him and Begonia—let's just say *in a compromising position*—last summer.

Almost broke him. And not because *Rutherfords don't get caught in compromising positions.*

We've both rained down some hits to our family's reputation.

I belatedly realize I shouldn't hug strangers—*thanks again, whiskey brain*—but after the smallest hesitation, Emma's body droops against me.

"This isn't your fault," she mumbles.

"But I still know it sucks."

"I'm supposed to be on my honeymoon, and instead I'm realizing I'm an idiot who was in love with someone who didn't love me back, that I alienated my friends to the point that they didn't want to tell me, and that the whole world knows now just how stupid I am."

My mother has drilled into me the idea that the world's problems are not mine. That my fans' problems are not mine. That my staff's personal problems are not mine.

But I made myself Emma's problem when I landed drunk on her doorstep.

So maybe her situation isn't my problem.

But it's close enough to my own that I'm making her problem my problem.

Not like helping a person in need will make my life any worse.

3

Emma

JONAS RUTHERFORD SMELLS like a hungover ponderosa pine tree in the summer sun.

Like stale whiskey and yesterday's sweat and butterscotch.

And it makes him seem so real, but also, *butterscotch*? It's not enough that he's movie-star handsome *and* a billionaire by birth, he also smells like butterscotch.

"I know it doesn't seem like it, but this will pass," he tells me while he pats my back.

That's the other thing.

I'm a total stranger.

I could be planning on doing something horrible, like —like—like burying his body if he were a reporter.

And I don't think I ever *truly* believed he was a reporter. Or an imposter. Or even possibly everything his ex-wife recently painted him to be when she went public with why they got divorced.

I believed the best of him.

Which is likely half of why I ended up nearly marrying Chandler despite all of the not-great things he's done to other people I love.

My friends.

My brother.

God.

I *cannot* believe Chandler set Theo up to take the fall for something he did ten years ago. Theo *went to jail*. For something *Chandler did*.

And I'm mad at Theo for not telling me and for not fighting back in court and for just *taking* it.

For not believing in himself.

For not believing that I would've believed in him.

Jonas squeezes me tighter. Is this an act? Or is he actually a nice person?

"You can go," I say again. "Truly. I don't need help. I just want to be alone for a while."

"Have you been alone the whole time you've been here?"

He doesn't say *since your wedding*, so the man gets points for thinking on his feet while he smells like an intoxicated tree. "The airport was...uncomfortable."

"Here?"

"No, in Hawaii."

"Did people—"

"It's fine." *Don't think about it, Emma. Do. Not. Think. About. It.* "It's fine. It's over. I'm here. Everyone's leaving me alone. It's lovely on the beach." In the early mornings before anyone else is around. "And the house is very comfortable. It's a good place to—"

Nope.

Not finishing that sentence.

But my brain whispers it to me anyway.

It's a good place to think about everything you've ever done wrong in your life while you recover from a broken heart and wonder why your friends put up with someone who's as big of a backstabbing idiot as you currently feel like you are.

"To heal," Jonas says quietly.

I shudder and my eyes get hot and my nose stings. "To try."

He squeezes tighter.

And it feels so good to—no.

No.

I'm done blindly trusting people.

So I shake him off and put some distance between us. "Did you really trick your wife into getting married so she'd quit Hollywood and have designer kids with good genes with you?"

He winces, then winces harder like wincing reminded him that he has a hangover.

And I desperately try not to wince right along with him. Who asks a stranger a question like that?

You do, Emma Monroe. You do now. Don't be a sucker again. Do. Not. Be. A. Sucker.

"I changed my mind about when I wanted a family shortly after the wedding, and I don't blame her for being mad about it. The position I put her in was...not okay of me. I was wrong. And then I dug my feet in and *kept* being wrong."

There is *so* much more to this story.

But it doesn't matter. He's leaving. I'm staying here. Even if my friends would lose their minds at me meeting Jonas Rutherford—well, my friends that were my friends *last week* who rightfully might never want to see me again after I picked Chandler over them time and again for what feels like half my life—I don't need Jonas's side of things.

He steadies himself against a wall, scowls like he's trying to perfect the expression for his next role, and gingerly makes his way to the sofa to sit and put his head in his hands.

"I know I don't know you," he says, "but if it helps, from what I saw in that video, you dodged a bullet, and I'm glad you get to be somewhere quiet for a while."

I lean back against the wall. "Or I was stupid to think I could love him enough to make him change."

He squints at me, still rubbing his own temples. "You've watched one too many Razzle Dazzle films, haven't you?"

That shouldn't be funny.

It truly shouldn't.

But for the first time since I left my groom at the altar after finally confronting him about one of many things I pretended were just human imperfection instead of completely *wrong*, I laugh.

And it's an honest laugh.

I'm not faking it for him.

"Probably," I concede. "But I also…I just like to believe everyone's doing the best they can. And give them the benefit of the doubt. And—"

Dammit.

My eyes get hot again.

But I need to say it out loud. Not like *Jonas Freaking Rutherford* will remember this.

"And I thought he was the best I could do," I finish.

His head jerks up, which is clearly uncomfortable if I'm reading his face right.

It says: *Shouldn't have done that. I'm gonna puke again.*

"It's okay," I say quickly. "You don't have to tell me I can do better. I don't *want* to do better. I'm off dating. I'm off relationships. I'm off—well, honestly, I think I'm off being gaslit, except I don't think I'll notice the next time it happens either, which is why I'm off dating and relationships."

"You need to meet my brother's girlfriend," he says.

I laugh again, but this one's sheer *he does not mean that.*

"You do," he insists. "She had the balls to divorce her husband because he didn't appreciate her. Everyone thinks she's a naïve country bumpkin who can't navigate a black-tie dinner, but she slays. Every time. If Begonia and her dog can live in my world, I know you can get back into yours."

"But did she betray everyone in your world?" I whisper.

"How did you betray them?"

"I always took Chandler's side and that made my brother and one of my very best friends get hurt. Badly. And if he hurt people that close to me, he probably hurt so many more people than I can begin to guess."

He glances around the sitting area, shakes his head, grabs it like he's trying to stop his brains from sloshing around in his skull, and then blows out a short breath. "You haven't left this villa since you got here?"

"I have *really* had enough of people." The airport was

an absolute nightmare. Whispers. Weird looks. Gasps and points. I told myself I was being paranoid and nobody knew who I was. But then someone asked for a selfie with me. Someone else said Chandler's name. I walked into the bathroom and found a group of women gathered around a phone while the sound of my own voice screeching at Chandler bounced off the walls.

That's her. Did you see her? She's here. She's alone. I wonder where she's going?

The people who didn't know who I was were quickly filled in.

And the flight?

Theo is both an angel and a pain in the butt. Despite *all* the ways that my wedding week was horrible for him, he paid to upgrade my flight so I'd be in first class.

Which would've been fine if I hadn't seized on the opportunity to board first.

Boarding first meant every single other person on the plane walked past me and gawked when they boarded after me.

"There aren't people here," Jonas says.

"Oh, the staff and housekeeping crew are aliens?"

He grins that movie-star grin, and I lose my breath.

Off men and off relationships or not, knowing he's recently divorced and claiming he was an asshole or not, I can't deny that a grinning Jonas Rutherford is the stuff of heart-squeezing, panty-melting, romantic-delusion dreams.

Knowing he's here temporarily as a blip on my life radar is incredibly comforting though.

I need to *not* face that kind of smile from a man right now.

"They're paid well to keep their mouths shut," he says.

"There are other guests."

"Like twenty-three of them, total, between the two resorts on this island, and every last one of them is here to get away from the world. Nobody cares who else is here."

"Are you *sure* about that?"

"The people with the money to come here are the people who don't want to be seen any more than you and I do."

The money to come here.

The money to come here.

I'm going to murder my brother.

I *thought* this was the wrong resort. I *thought* I didn't have to take another airplane to get to my honeymoon.

But when I landed here in Fiji, there was a man waiting with a sign with my name, just as Theo said there would be when he texted to tell me he was leaving Hawaii and I should go on my honeymoon solo. And the man with the sign with my name answered the code word exactly as Theo said he would. Except instead of driving through the lush rainforest to get to my hotel, we boarded *another* plane—this one private with only two other people who didn't look at me the whole time—and flew to a smaller island.

And I was so tired that I didn't question it. I didn't even care if I was being kidnapped.

I should've asked questions.

"You okay?" Jonas asks.

"My brother accidentally got rich being a mega-star on an adult entertainment website," I whisper. "Like, *stupid* rich. I didn't realize he'd paid to take care of me here too."

"Is this bad?"

Aside from feeling like *that idiot who needs everyone else in her life to take care of her?* "My fi—my *ex* did really bad things to him, and then Theo paid for my wedding and didn't tell me, and I think he paid to upgrade my solo honeymoon. And he shouldn't have. I don't deserve this."

"All I did to earn being able to afford coming here to hide was being born into the family that created Razzle Dazzle. How about we just go with *it's okay to be here* and take it from there?"

"That was weirdly self-aware."

He grins again, and then grimaces again like grinning hurts.

We are both a mess.

There's an odd comfort in that.

"You ever toured a tropical rainforest?" he asks.

I shake my head.

"Excellent. You're doing it today. Time to come out of hiding. Trust me. It's a good thing. You think people are judgmental? Wait until you see the attitude on some of the monkeys around here. It'll make going back to the real world feel palatable."

"I'm a *stranger* and you're *Jonas Rutherford*."

"My brother was all over the tabloids last year for an unfortunately delicate public situation and he hates the spotlight with the passion of a million grumps. I can appreciate what you're going through even if the spotlight doesn't usually bother me. You can also consider this my apology for puking in your bushes and my thanks for some super dry toast."

"*Oh my god*. You know Theo. You know Theo, and he set *this* up too. He set up you meeting me, didn't he?"

"Who's Theo again?"

"My brother? The online adult entertainment star? Knits hearts while he's naked and says motivational things that I probably should've listened to a little more when it came to understanding who I should and shouldn't marry?"

Jonas points to himself. "Razzle Dazzle family-friendly sappy-romantic *but no kissing ever* film star here. Prior to my divorce, the biggest scandal I ever faced was that I wore a wet t-shirt and you could see my nipples in a movie once. Don't think your brother and I operate in the same circles."

They probably don't.

And Theo was *very* happy to be an *anonymous* adult entertainment star.

He never showed his face.

He'd be anonymous still except *Chandler outed him at my wedding*.

And now the entire world has seen the video.

The *entire world* knows Theo's biggest secret. They now know the face that goes with the penis.

He has to be absolutely miserable right now, but he's still putting me first, texting every day to ask how I am and making sure I have as much privacy as I need in a way that I couldn't provide for myself.

I shouldn't be here. I don't *deserve* to be here.

I have *so* much to make up for.

But at least I know *not* marrying Chandler was a good idea.

"C'mon, Emma," Jonas says. "I need someone to make sure I don't touch another piña colada and puke in someone else's bushes tomorrow. They'd be far less understanding."

"Why do you trust me?"

He blows out a long breath. "I don't know. But I do know I don't have much else to lose."

Well.

What's a girl supposed to say to that?

It's definitely not the *you're cute, you're friendly, I just want to help a fellow human being* that I might've expected.

But it resonates.

My favorite movie star and I have a lot in common right now.

Who saw *that* coming?

4

Jonas

"C'mon, slowpoke," Emma says with a bright smile two days after I woke up hungover on her deck. "You're almost there. And it's *adorable*."

She's maybe ten feet ahead of me on a path through a rainforest. We've seen parrots and cuckoos and iguanas and tamarins. I helped her up when she tripped over a massive root. She pulled me out of a spider web and promised not to tell anyone about the way I shrieked and danced.

Clearly, you've never had an on-set dance instructor for spider web extraction, she said. *I'll forever judge Razzle Dazzle for that oversight.*

It was such a dry, spot-on delivery that I laughed longer and harder than I thought I was capable of this week.

And now, we're apparently almost to our destination, where we'll eat the picnic the resort staff fixed for us.

Didn't see myself *enjoying* my time in Fiji when I left home. I just wanted to be away from the true-but-unflattering press coverage and all of the questions that came with it.

Instead, I found a mission to make something good out of the crap hole that I was in, and here we are.

For the first time in months, I feel like myself.

Happy. Optimistic about the future again, even if it's small optimism.

Big optimism will probably take some time.

I might even be ready to take a call from my mother sometime in the next day or so. But I'll still likely start with Begonia. Or *maybe* Hayes. He's less irritable now that he gets sunshine twenty-four seven with her in his life.

"I'm tired." I plop down on the ground five feet from Emma. "We should stop and eat here."

Her mouth forms a perfect *O*. She's in a bucket hat with her blond hair pulled up under it—I assume the hairstyle and the light pink tank top are measures against the heat—and she's also in at least a gallon of sunscreen.

I know because it took an extra half hour for her to be ready to go while she slathered more and more on.

"*Oh my god.*" She points at something in front of her. "It's *right there.*"

I grin.

She does a double take, and then she laughs.

"Okay, okay, I'll dig deep." I moan and groan and make a show of trying to get off the ground. "I'll find the energy to make it another seventy-four miles."

"How does your family tolerate you?"

"Why do you think they keep me buried in movie scripts and never visit me on set?"

She laughs again.

This is definitely the reason I'm supposed to be here.

To be her friend.

Two days of hanging out with Emma, and she's a different person.

She's *happy*. There are still moments of lingering sadness—that look on her face is haunting sometimes—but I know a few good jokes. I've pulled her out of it whenever I can.

Now, though, she's trying to pull me. "C'mon," she says, holding out a hand. "Let me get you up."

Her fingers are long and slender, much like the rest of her. When I take her hand and she tugs, there's not a lot of heft behind it.

I act like there is, leaping to my feet like she has the power to throw me over her shoulder. "Jeez. Watch it with those muscles."

She rolls her eyes with a smile. "If you think my brother hasn't tried that on me ten million times, you're mistaken."

"Brothers are the worst."

"*Older* brothers are the—no, they're the best. Except on occasion."

And there go the clouds in her expression again.

I don't know her well. We've stuck to superficial topics the past few days.

But those clouds *feel* wrong on her.

"Whoa. Hey, Emma, did you know there's an old village right there? Where did that come from?" I say, and

I do it in my best Ryan Reynolds impression for fun. Cracked her up yesterday.

She smiles again, but it's a small smile.

Still have work to do to get that full-force smile back. It disappears every time she talks about her brother. Or her friends.

We haven't touched her ex beyond the few things she said about him that first morning.

I don't want to know what that would do to her expression.

I watched the video again a few times the night after we met, and I don't like him.

Can't imagine what she's feeling right now. She almost married him.

"Oh, gosh," she says lightly, "it must've sprang up from nothing just because it knew we were here and wanted to impress us."

"Is it *sprang* or *sprung*?"

"No idea. I'm an accountant who learned grammar from Razzle Dazzle films."

"You did?"

"*No.*" She laughs, a bigger laugh this time, and heads toward the first of five bures that we can see in the small clearing on the hillside. The straw huts are all the same size, each with a plaque in front of it. Below are the brilliant green waters off the beach, complete with a line where the water turns a deep, deep blue and goes on forever with just a couple small islands dotting the horizon.

A breeze rustles through the jungle, carrying more bird songs with it. A monkey answers. And the solitude of where we are hits me.

I like my family. I don't mind the press most days. Have a job I love.

Except recently.

"I should move here," I hear myself murmur.

"To this village?"

I glance over at the five bures on either side of a dirt path cut into the clearing on the hillside. Start calculating.

One grass hut for a kitchen.

One for guests.

One for a massage room.

One for me.

One for a gathering room where my guests and I can eat inside when the storms come in, tell stories, act out old plays like I used to make Hayes do with me when we were kids.

And then I shake my head, internally laughing at myself.

Emma lifts her pale brows at me.

Just thinking about how I expect five houses and an entire village for myself isn't something I intend to admit out loud.

And then I remember I didn't even think about where my normal security detail would live.

Though at the moment, I sincerely wish I didn't need a security detail.

They're great people. Don't get me wrong.

But being here solo? Not needing protection from unfortunately real threats?

This is nice.

I like it.

"Not big enough for you?" she asks.

I blush.

My cheeks actually burn with embarrassment. "Not

sure I deserve someplace this beautiful as my home base," I improvise.

She looks back at the ocean. "I live somewhere just as beautiful for different reasons."

"Where's that?"

"Rocky Mountains."

"Ah, yes. The Rockies. Shot a few films there."

"You don't say."

"I've also gone snowboarding and climbing and rafting."

"Yes, I saw those movies too."

"You've seen them all, haven't you?"

"Multiple times. My friends and I always try to figure out when you're using stunt doubles for those dangerous, dangerous bunny hills."

"I don't have stunt doubles," I mutter.

She grins. "I'd hope not. That movie where you fell for your ski instructor? We were *well* aware you saved her on the bunny hill and not the double black diamond you all acted like it was. That's the only one we've never watched twice."

"I can ski *bigger* hills too."

Her face freezes, undoubtedly at my suddenly testy tone. "Oh, don't be mad. Please don't be mad. I was teasing. I'm sure you enjoy yourself when you're not working too."

Everything I know how to do, I learned for a role in one of my family's films.

Enjoyed it all. Don't get me wrong. If this movie star thing has completely fallen apart, I have a solid basis to learn whatever skill I want to do next.

But I don't know who I'd be or what I'd do if I hadn't

been born as a third generation heir to the Razzle Dazzle film and amusement park empire.

I loop my arm around her neck and steer her back into the village. "Not mad. Just a lot on my brain."

"Scandal and horrid publicity will do that to a person."

Doesn't matter how lightly she says it, I know it's bothering her too.

We're very different. Different worlds. Different goals, I assume, from a few hints that she's dropped. Different lives ahead of us.

But in this moment, we're both in a pile of shit in our personal lives, blasted all over the world by social media and the press.

"So if owning a Fijian village is my dream house, what's yours?" I ask while we casually stroll closer to the first bure, my arm still draped around her.

Her nose wrinkles. "I—I don't know anymore."

She's not going totally sad, so I give her a little prod. "Go on."

"When I was little, I wanted to grow up and live in my friend Sabrina's grandparents' house. It's in one of the fancier neighborhoods in town. A little more land. Creaky wooden floors. Big kitchen with the most amazing view of the mountains. And we had a treehouse there. But—"

The rainclouds take over her expression again as she cuts herself off.

I should drop it.

This is about fun. No stress.

"But?" I prompt instead.

"My—ex—is her cousin. It's technically his grandparents' house too."

Eject. Mayday. Abort mission. "Ah, look." I point to a

straw-roofed structure that doesn't quite fit. "An ancient picnic table in an ancient gazebo. It's a sign from the heavens. We're supposed to eat."

The sadness clears about eighty percent of the way, and I'm reasonably certain that's a real smile she gives me as she shakes her head. "Clearly a sign from the heavens," she agrees.

Honestly?

Watching her be happy—helping her be happy—is helping me look on the bright side in my own life again.

Everything will be okay.

I can be okay.

We set up our picnic lunch, but since we have a blanket provided by the resort in the backpack I'm carrying, Emma insists we sit on the ground.

Unlike the morning we met, when both of us could barely stomach dry toast and ginger ale, she's happily diving into pineapple, mango and passion fruit salad. She helps me eat the fish soup, and she steals more of the cassava bread than she lets me have.

We're about to dig into dessert when Emma cuts herself off with a squeak.

Except that's not Emma.

That's a chicken crossing the dirt path and clucking her way toward us.

"Oooh, *chickens*," she breathes.

"I didn't think there were chickens on this island."

"Why wouldn't there be?"

"They captured them all and relocated them to a different island so they wouldn't cluck and wake up the guests."

"*No.*"

"Yep."

"That's *crazy*."

"Welcome to very exclusive private resorts."

"Maybe it flew from another island."

It's a big chicken. Brown. Thrusting its head and clucking as it makes its way to us.

"Have you ever seen a chicken fly?" I ask.

She tips her head back and laughs, and the chicken tilts its head at us, then gives a loud *bagock*!

"Maybe it swam," she amends.

"Have you ever seen a chicken swim?"

She giggles, pauses like she's thinking about it, and giggles harder.

"I think I have to report this chicken," I tell her. "Where there are chickens, there could be roosters, and contrary to popular belief, roosters do not restrict their crowing to mornings."

"How do you know?"

"I've been in nearly a hundred Razzle Dazzle films. I've learned more than you can imagine about more things than you'd even think exist in the world."

"I don't remember seeing you in a movie with a rooster."

"They killed production after the rooster attacked one of the assistant directors."

Can't deny how much I enjoy listening to her full belly laugh.

It's worth dealing with how mad my family will be when I finally head back home.

"I want chickens," Emma says.

"For dinner?"

"*No*. As pets."

"Chickens as pets?"

"I mean, I want to get a chicken coop and raise chickens and have fresh eggs. I want chickens."

"You can probably have this one."

"*I am not taking a Fijian chicken home.*" She tips her head back and laughs again. "Can you imagine the nightmare in customs? *Ma'am, we're going to have to look in your suitcase to find out why it's clucking.*"

"They see clucking suitcases all the time."

"They do not."

"Bet they do. Look. It's a cute chicken. It would be a great starter chicken for you."

It is kinda cute. I'm not making that up.

It's also circling us like it can't decide if it wants to attack or make friends.

"Chicky-chicky want dessert?" I ask it.

"Oh, that's mean," Emma says. "Don't feed her if you're going to report her. She'll think you're friends. And friends shouldn't betray friends."

Ah, hell.

There we go again.

Her smile dips away and the clouds come back in her eyes.

"You don't seem like the type to betray your friends," I say, watching her carefully.

"But I did."

"On purpose?"

She pulls her knees back to her chest and eyes the chicken, who's watching us like we *are* the dessert. "My two best friends—they're *everything*," she says. "I love my brother, but he's...hard sometimes. Laney and Sabrina are the sisters I never had. We've been inseparable since third grade. They know me. They've protected me. They've been there for me for the very worst moments of my life, like when my mom died, but this—this was my fault. Sabrina didn't tell me everything she knew about Cha— about my ex, because she knew I didn't want to hear it."

"That was her choice. Not yours."

"But *she was right*. I didn't want to hear it. I was so in love with the idea of being married and having kids and living in their grandparents' house, but upgraded to be surrounded by the white picket fence, that I didn't want to consider that I was marrying the wrong person. And you know the worst part?"

I shake my head.

"I think I always knew he wasn't right for me, but every time I'd think about breaking up with him, I'd start calculating how long it would take me to meet someone new, fall in love, get engaged, and get married and start a family, and I'd start thinking I was already too old. And then he'd make an offhand comment about how I was too skinny, or how I was too neurotic, or how I was too naïve, and I'd question if anyone else *could* love me. *Seven years*. We spent *seven years* with me thinking I was lucky I got back together with a man who said he wanted to eventually marry me and have kids with me, all of it to end like this."

"Got *back* together?"

"We were high school sweethearts," she whispers. "Broke up in college when we went to different schools and he said he wanted to date other women. But we graduated and both moved back home and then—then I took him back. I was so stupid."

"*BaGOOOOOCK!*" the chicken yells.

"What she said," I agree. "Gotta be easier on yourself."

"I asked my other best friend to babysit my brother during my wedding week so he wouldn't fight with my ex. Who does that? Who asks a friend to babysit your adult brother so he won't accidentally upset your groom?"

I squeeze her hand. "Take it from someone who's gotten married at least two dozen times when I say no one's at their best at weddings."

She makes a strangled noise that's somewhere between a laugh and a gasp. "*You have not been married two dozen times.*"

"I have on screen. And if you think parents and the bridal party are bad at weddings, you should see how producers and directors act."

"Oh my god."

I'm being absolutely ridiculous.

But you know what?

She's smiling again. Laughing even as she wipes her eyes. "Are you always like this?"

"Absolutely."

The chicken snorts in my direction.

"Happy clucking to you too," I tell it.

It doesn't like that.

It doesn't like that *at all*.

Swear the thing bends over, lowers its head, and charges straight for me, wings flapping, *ba-gock*-ing its head off.

Emma shrieks and leaps to her feet.

I shriek and dive out of the way too.

"This is why they don't want chickens on the island here," I tell her while the chicken readjusts its course and charges me again.

"Dessert!" she cries. "Toss it some of the banana cake!"

"You're closer!"

"Here, chicky-chicky! Does Clucker want some fruit?"

It stops and tilts its head at her.

She tosses a piece of mango near it.

It fluffs its wings and looks back at me.

I've never seen a chicken with murder in its eyes before, but I think this one is contemplating my demise.

I'm frozen in place.

Having a standoff with a chicken.

"Is that a real chicken?" I whisper to Emma as quietly as I can.

"What else would it be?"

"A robot chicken sent to spy on us."

She cracks up.

"I'm serious," I whisper. "I got a script once about a post-apocalyptic world where all of the animals were actually robots spying on the humans for the robot overlord."

"That doesn't sound like a Razzle Dazzle film."

"I didn't say I *asked* for the script. I said I *got* it. Someone mailed it to me and my assistant was so amused he passed it on to me."

The chicken makes a low, threatening *baaaagoooooock*.

Emma tosses another piece of fruit at it, and this one hits it in the head.

She gasps.

I *erp*.

The chicken scratches its foot on the ground, and then it charges me again.

"No, chicky!" Emma shrieks. "Here! *Here*! Have the whole picnic! We left you fish soup!"

I'm dancing.

I'm dancing and dodging a chicken that's charging me with wings flapping.

It's *snorting*.

The chicken.

The chicken is snorting and charging and flapping and it wants to kill me.

Emma's offering it fish soup and throwing pineapple chunks at it, but it's not helping.

And it doesn't matter how I dodge and change direction or run straight, it's *keeping up with me*.

This mutant chicken is going to murder me.

Or at least my calves.

Just when I'm sure my lower legs are toast, it stops, looks back at the jungle, makes a noise like it's trying to be a rooster, and takes off running between two bures and into the underbrush.

And it doesn't come back.

The noise of leaves rattling and rustling and the chicken clucking dies away, and silence settles over the little restored village once again.

I look at Emma.

She stares back at me.

"Did that just happen?" I ask.

She doesn't answer.

Instead, she doubles over, completely losing her shit in absolute amusement. She might even be cackling, she's laughing so hard.

"Snorkeling tomorrow suddenly seems like a questionable activity," I say.

"Afraid of robot fish?" she asks through gales of laughter.

"Yes."

She tries to stop laughing. Tries again. On the third time, she manages to force a straight face.

And then do you know what she does?

Do you know what this runaway bride does? This viral runaway bride whose happiness has become my mission while I distract myself from my own problems?

She fucking *bagocks* at me.

And calls *me* the chicken.

And I'm not sure I've ever laughed so hard in my entire life either.

5

Emma

When I left home just over two weeks ago to head to Hawaii for the destination wedding of my dreams before a two-week *are you serious, we actually get to do this?* honeymoon in Fiji, I had a much different expectation of my life than where it is now.

And *now* is with me in an upgraded villa on a remote island for privacy courtesy of my brother, with Jonas Rutherford, billionaire heir to the Razzle Dazzle fortune and star of my favorite movies, sprawled on my bed while I rub aloe on his back.

The curtains are open to let in the sea breeze. Waves crash along the rockier parts of the shore that are a barrier between my private beach and the next villa's beach, providing nature's soundtrack for background noise. The entire room is lit in a soft orange glow from sunset, and the remains of our seafood dinner are packed away and ready for the resort staff to pick them up.

This would be a lovely romantic night were it my actual honeymoon.

But I think I prefer this.

Not because I'm touching my nearly lifelong celebrity crush.

More because this man has been the friend I didn't know I needed.

And he didn't have to be.

He could've walked away—and some people would likely argue he should've—yet he didn't.

That has to say something about someone's character, doesn't it?

"Does this hurt?" I ask, trying to be gentle with the aloe.

"My own fault," he replies in a husky voice. "Should've followed your lead and bathed in sunscreen before we left."

It's been three days since I woke up to him on my porch, and despite running over to his own villa once or twice, he's always come back. We've been boating. We've been hiking. We've had meals in and meals out. Spa treatments. He's crashed on my couch two of the past three nights. And today, to prove he wasn't as afraid of marine life as he apparently is of chickens now, we went snorkeling.

We saw tons and tons of tropical fish and sea life.

There were no funny looks from anyone. No press spying on us. No questions.

Nothing bad happened.

Except his sunburn.

"When do you start your next movie?" It's odd that the question rolls off my tongue easier than I ever could've expected. But Jonas is so down-to-earth and friendly, it's hard not to be relaxed.

And grateful.

So grateful for the distraction and companionship.

And the courage to leave my villa and enjoy my time here.

"Next question," he says into the pillow.

"You're not doing more movies?"

"I'm officially a has-been."

I squirt more aloe into my hand and smooth it over the chiseled plane of his back. "It wouldn't hurt for you to start playing older characters closer to your own age, but I wouldn't call you a has-been."

He barks out a laugh. "You and Begonia…"

I know who Begonia is. He's mentioned his brother's girlfriend more than he's talked about anyone else in his family. "Is she any part of why you got divorced?"

He sighs. "No. She's just my favorite person because she doesn't ask questions like that."

I laugh. Can't help it. "Not sorry," I say lightly.

"You shouldn't be," he grumbles. "And that's not honestly why she's my favorite."

"Then why?"

"She makes Hayes happy, and it's impossible not to like someone who can make the world's grumpiest asshole happy."

"Aww, you sound like me when I call Theo the world's biggest troublemaker."

"We see them for who they are, we understand why they're who they are, and we love them for who they are, no matter how hard they are some days."

"And *who they are* are those people who step up in ways no one else understands we need, right when we need it."

"Do we have the same brother?"

"I think we covered that with the porn star question."

He chuckles.

I've let Theo know a few times that I'm still alive, which I suspect he already knows from checking in with the resort staff. He might be a troublemaker, but he has a massive heart.

And my complete irritation for *not telling me my ex set him up to do jail time*.

And all of my guilt for all of the times I asked him to please get along with Chandler despite the fact that Theo was never the problem.

Never the *bigger half* of the problem, anyway.

But that's something I'll deal with when I get home.

If I want to be *new and improved Emma*, I have to.

Hiding from all of my problems and assuming that everything will turn out just fine in the end hasn't worked so well, has it?

And I actively ignore that little voice in my head that says *but the universe delivered Jonas to your doorstep*. No matter how freaking hard silencing that little voice is.

But I do it.

This is *not* a reward for bad behavior.

This is a test. Or my opportunity to be a friend to someone else in need.

Or something.

"I told Peyton I wanted her to put her career on hold so we could start a family," Jonas says into the pillow.

I almost squeeze my hands into fists. *I wanted a family.*

In my more honest moments, I can confess that's why I stayed with Chandler so long. Because he looked like the fastest path to the family I wanted. Because *starting over* didn't mean *that much longer until I get married*.

Starting over meant *that much longer until I have babies*.

No matter how much I was or wasn't actually in love with *him*, I was wholly in love with the idea of the life we could have together.

I know I don't have to want a family. I know I don't have to fit into that box that the world likes to put women in.

But *I want it*.

I crave it.

It's always been what I've wanted. Who I've seen myself being. The idea of motherhood feels as right to me as Laney running her parents' online photo gift shop feels right to her. As right as Sabrina running her family's café always felt right to her.

And here I go with the regrets again, since Chandler just sold the café out of the family.

Without telling anyone.

And all of that has nothing to do with why Jonas got divorced, and this is my time to listen.

My hands drift lower, slathering his lower back with the aloe. "So the tabloids got it right."

"They did."

"And?"

"And what?"

"And why didn't you two work it out? That can't be the whole story."

He mumbles something into the pillow.

"Oh, you have a case of the *don't wanna talk about its*, hm?"

He sighs and turns his face so I can see his profile. The strong nose. Chiseled jaw. Pouty lips. Lowered lids with thick, dark lashes under his prominent brow.

All lit by the soft glow of the dipping sun.

This man was born to be on the big screen.

"I doubled down on insisting kids before career was the right move when I should've told her the truth," he says quietly.

Hard to miss the pain and regret in his voice. I wonder if he's told anyone this yet.

I squirt more aloe in my hands and tackle his shoulders again. "Go on."

He slides one brown eye in my direction, then lets his lids close. "Before we got married, we talked about expanding beyond Razzle Dazzle. Doing bigger projects. Heavier subjects. More—more *acting*. Bigger. Stronger. Stuff that would get critical acclaim in a way Razzle Dazzle films just don't."

I make a soft noise to let him know I'm listening. I know he's won awards—like an Oscar, maybe?—but I think it was when he was a child actor. Nothing recent.

He sucks in a deep breath that makes his back move under my hands. "The first couple months we were married, we were both hip-deep in projects. Me for Razzle Dazzle. Her too, for one. But she also had one for an indie company without a lot of expectations. No one was talking about film festivals or awards or anything. For her, it was a pure passion project. A foot in the door for branching out. When she finished that up and came home talking about another new script she'd read, one that she wanted us to tackle together that *was* next-level, I—I got cold feet."

"About working with her?"

"No. About the project. It was big. It was bold. It was—it was something that needed an actor with the chops to pull it off. And I'm the guy who doesn't even have a film agent because all I've ever done is movies for my family."

I still. "That's—"

"Unheard of?" he supplies dryly.

"Absolutely fucking ridiculous."

Here's the thing.

I sugarcoat *everything*. It's a superpower and a curse.

And it's why I'm here. It's why I was able to lie to myself about Chandler being the love of my life for so long. It's why I let him gaslight me into believing no one else would want me. It's why my friends kept secrets from me.

To protect me from having my sugarcoated world view popped.

And I need to *stop*.

So I'm trying. Right here, with my favorite movie star on the entire planet.

Jonas shifts to his side and pushes up to face me. "I get the feeling you don't think me not having an agent is ridiculous for the same reason I think it's ridiculous."

He *doesn't think he has the chops* for a project.

He's *afraid*.

"You're hiding behind your family," I say.

His lips part. He holds eye contact briefly, then looks away.

"You're *Jonas Fucking Rutherford*. You were practically born on a movie set. You have all the resources to get the best teachers and coaches in the world if you're tackling something *bigger*. What can you honestly be afraid of?"

His Adam's apple bobs, and he looks me square in the eye again. "Until the past few months, I've never failed at anything."

I don't know what my face is doing, but whatever it is, it's making his face do something new too.

He's *embarrassed*.

"Did you tell her you were afraid?" I ask.

"No."

"Why not?"

He huffs out a breath. "Three guesses."

"*Jonas*."

He was afraid.

He was afraid to tell her that he was afraid.

Can it be anything else?

"I know," he mutters.

"You *married* her, and you couldn't tell her you were afraid?"

"I think she figured it out. Probably before I did, if I'm being honest. I've never…I've never been afraid of *anything* before. I didn't even know that's what it was."

I shake my head and rub the remaining aloe off my hands and on my thighs. "We're both relationship disasters, aren't we?"

"You dodged a bullet."

"About seven years too late. At least you got out fast."

He winces.

"I'm sorry." *Dumb dumb dumb*. Maybe I need to not—no. *No*. What's the worst that happens if I say something to piss off Jonas Rutherford?

He never talks to me again?

That was likely the course of my life anyway.

"Actually, I'm not sorry," I correct. "Let me go back to *you're Jonas Fucking Rutherford*. So you do a project and it bombs. Totally, completely, unequivocally. It. Bombs. People say you're a hack. They call you a nepo baby who doesn't deserve any of what you have. That you should go back to playing teenagers or stop acting entirely. You're laughed off a stage presenting at an awards show. Former fans leave dead flowers at your doorstep to mourn the loss of their perception of you. For a whole entire year, you can't go anywhere without someone clucking at you for nefarious reasons to mock you. *So what*?"

He makes a noise, but I hold up a hand.

I am *not* done. "You're still young. You're still rich. You're still handsome as sin, with a good personality to boot unless you've been faking it here with me. You can still go back to Razzle Dazzle films and *no one will care*. Or —or just *maybe*—you fail when you take a leap and then you *try again*. And you do it better. And in five years, you're accepting every major award there is to win for something you put your heart and soul into because you believed in yourself enough to go for what you want instead of hiding behind who you've always been. *Maybe that happens*."

He visibly swallows again.

His gaze dips to my lips, then back up to my eyes. "Are you talking to me or you?"

"*I'm not a freaking movie star.* I'm an accountant. A very happy accountant."

"But you put your heart and soul into a guy who didn't deserve you for too long. Like maybe I've put my heart and soul into something I outgrew years ago."

All of the breath in my body whooshes out of me. "I can't get that time back. All I can do is move forward and be smarter and stronger and—and—"

"Braver," he finishes for me. "We can both be braver."

This is going sideways, and I don't know if I like it. "We're talking about you."

"You're right. I need to be braver if I want to prove I'm more than someone who was handed this life on a silver platter. And I needed to hear that. Thank you. But who do *you* want to be?"

Who do *I* want to be? "I want to be *happy*," I whisper.

"So be happy."

Is he leaning into me?

Am I leaning into him?

What's happening here?

"You can't just wave a magic wand and suddenly give me a home and a husband and babies and pets. It's barely been a week since I left the man that I thought I would love forever."

"Do you miss him?"

"I'm too furious at him to miss him."

"*Will* you miss him?"

"No." I don't even have to think. The answer pops out like it's been lingering in there, waiting for someone to ask. So does something else that I never thought I'd hear myself say out loud. "Leaving him was almost a relief. No. Not *almost*. It—it *was*. I was *relieved* to leave him."

"Emma." He strokes my hair. "That's a sign."

"Were you glad she left you?" I whisper.

"I was more worried about how it would reflect on my family than I was about hurting her. And that's my biggest regret in my entire marriage. I wasn't a good husband. I *looked* like I'd be a good husband. The world *thought* I'd be a good husband. I *played* a husband in movies dozens of times. But I never put the energy into figuring out what it actually took to *be* a good husband in real life. She deserved better too."

"We're both disasters, aren't we?"

"We are. And I think I passed out on your porch for a reason. I think we're supposed to help each other through it."

He's going to kiss me.

Jonas is *going to kiss me*.

And fuck every warning bell in my head. Just fuck it all.

I'm going to kiss him back.

He's been the friend that I've needed this week.

"I'm not relationship material right now," I whisper as he slides both hands down my scalp to cradle my cheeks.

"I'm friend material," he whispers back. "That's all I've got."

"I can take friend material. I like friend material."

"Even if I do this?"

And then his lips are brushing mine, the sensations both magnetic and freeing.

Jonas is kissing me.

Jonas Rutherford—my celebrity crush and unexpected friend and everything I've needed here in Fiji—is kissing me.

I grip his solid forearms and lick his lower lip. "Yes," I whisper.

Maybe this is a mistake.

But some mistakes are necessary.

And tumbling into my bed, kissing Jonas, is definitely necessary.

6

Jonas

I'M KISSING EMMA.

I've kissed women since Peyton.

Hell, I kissed women *during* Peyton.

All on screen. All for movie roles. All because it was my job.

Kissing Emma is not my job, but I can't stop and I don't want to.

Be fucking brave.

I want to be brave.

The *bravest* things I've ever done are on the order of *being in public without a security detail.*

Kissing Emma isn't *brave*, though.

It's as necessary as breathing.

And she's kissing me back, her fingers tracing my jawline while she licks my lower lip, making soft noises that easily translate to *more*.

Also different from kissing a woman for my job?

I'm sprouting a raging hard-on.

For this woman that I call my friend, because that's all I can offer her, and I know that's all she can offer me.

My back is on fire.

Not as much as it was before she rubbed me down with aloe, but enough that I feel it as I move my arms to wrap them around her.

Her fingers slide up my arms to my neck, staying to my front, not bothering my sunburn.

How does this woman have no idea just how much good she deserves in her life?

She suddenly breaks free and pulls back. "Oh my god, I can't take advantage of you like this."

I want to lick her neck and bite her collarbone. "You're not taking advantage, Emma."

"Aren't I?"

"No. Am I?"

Her eyes are so wide and her breath is coming in short pants. "No."

I lift a brow.

"Promise." She licks her lower lip, then bites it. "You... were on my freebie list. But now you're my friend, and I— just *I like you*. As a person. As a friend. As *you*."

I can't stop touching her. I should pull back, slow down, give her space, but dammit, *I like her too*.

I know I shouldn't. This can't go any further.

But it feels so fucking right. "That's what makes this so easy."

She leans into me too, her nose brushing my jaw while her delicate hands settle on my chest again. "Can we keep doing what's easy?"

"You tell me when it stops being easy."

She kisses my cheek. Again. And again. Moving until she's kissing my lips, her hands making slow, easy strokes up and down my chest.

It's easy to kiss her back. Easy to take the kiss to the next level, our tongues clashing. Easy to follow her lead when she takes my hand and slides it up her leg, under her sun dress.

Easy to stroke her smooth, silky skin.

To listen to her gasp and feel her arch into me when I find her nipples under her dress.

"Okay?" I ask.

"Love—it." Her head arches back. "Sensitive. *Yes*."

It takes me a split second to pull the dress over her head, and then I'm not just touching those sweet perky nipples.

I'm sucking on them too.

She lifts her chest into my hand and my mouth and grips my hair. "Don't—deserve—"

"Yes, you do."

I don't ask the last time her ex played with her breasts.

Don't need to know.

Instead, I lick and suck and nip while her thighs fall open and she pulls me down on top of her.

Easy.

So easy to treat Emma and her body the way she deserves to be treated.

To make her feel good.

Her hips buck beneath me, and it's the most natural thing in the world to slide my hand down her belly, flicking her nipple with my tongue while my fingers drift closer and closer to her panties.

She spreads her legs more.

I brush a knuckle over her mound. "Can I touch you here?"

"Oh, *please*," she whispers. "*Please*."

I don't want to *touch* her.

I want to thrust deep inside her.

I want to show her how much it's meant to me to have a friend these past few days too.

But I'm not going anywhere. She's not going anywhere. Not tonight.

So I take it slow, stroking over her panties until she's straining so hard against my hand that her muscles quiver and her breath comes in soft bursts accompanied by *more* and *yes* and *please* and *so good*.

I swirl my tongue around her nipple and slip one finger into her panties, touching her smooth, bare, slick pussy.

"More," she whispers.

Her eyes are scrunched shut, her head tilted back, thighs straining and shifting into my touch.

I dip one finger inside her, and she bucks her hips. "Deeper. *More*."

Two fingers, then three. Her wet heat coats me as I match her rhythm while she pumps against my hand.

"Kiss me?" she gasps.

I adjust so I can kiss her and finger-fuck her at the same time, our tongues warring while her hips buck and she scratches her fingers down my tender back.

Worth it.

She gasps and breaks free of the kiss as her vagina clenches hard around my fingers, her head arched back again, the setting sun glowing against her long neck, that perfectly *Emma* jaw jutted out while she cries my name and comes hard on my fingers.

Beautiful.

No, *exquisite*.

Her entire body shudders, then sags back into the mattress. "Forgot…how good…" she murmurs.

I blink once.

Then again.

Does she—

"Oh my god, I didn't say that," she gasps.

I nuzzle her neck. "You deserve all the orgasms. Don't apologize."

"But I—*no*."

I lift my head.

She strokes my cheeks and gives me an embarrassed look. "You're right. I won't apologize."

I smile.

She smiles back.

And then her expression turns spunky. "Did you know that *someone* that I was supposed to be here with, *who knew better*, actually packed condoms in our honeymoon bag? I had them on the nightstand as a glaring reminder that I was right to leave him. I might have shoved them in the drawer when I realized it might look like…I wanted to take advantage of you."

There's entirely too much to unpack there, but for the first time since I met her, she's not retreating at the mention of why she was supposed to be here. "My dear Emma, what exactly are you saying?"

She flexes her hips under me, easily brushing my aching cock. "*I'm* satisfied, but *you're* not. We should rectify that."

My hand drifts up her side until I can brush her nipple with my thumb again. "Watching you was quite satisfying."

She bites her lip. "Shouldn't I get the satisfaction of watching you come too?"

My cock goes impossibly harder. "Only if I'm on top."

"Deal."

I grip her wrist as she reaches for the nightstand. "Emma."

She freezes and stares up at me.

"Don't *ever* let anyone convince you that you're not attractive or that you're unworthy or anything like it ever again. Understand?"

She sucks in a quick breath and blinks a few times, then stares at me like she's fully digesting every bit of meaning she can pull out of my order.

A smile slowly creeps back over her face. "Okay," she whispers. "Thank you."

I kiss her nose. "My absolute pleasure."

7

Emma

T̲H̲I̲S̲.

This is what I want my life to be.

Brave. Bold. Seize the moment.

No apologies.

Especially not as I'm rolling a condom down Jonas's erect penis, his breath coming in short pants. "Like—when you—touch me," he says.

I don't answer.

Not with words.

Instead, I wrap an arm around his neck, remember his sunburn and shift to hook my hand behind his head instead, and I kiss him.

Hard.

Deep.

Long.

I don't know how I'm flat on my back on the bed

already, but I know my body is screaming for me to part my legs for him again, to grab his ass and pull him close, to—

Holy *hell*.

I squeeze his ass.

Hello, muscles.

I knew he was fit, but—*whoa*.

His lips shift, smiling as he's kissing me.

But he doesn't stop.

Instead, he flexes his hips, bringing the broad head of his penis right to my clit, his ass muscles clenching even tighter under my hand.

This man knows what he's doing.

And I'm here for it.

Especially as he rocks that tip against my clit again, my already stimulated cells begging for more.

"Jonas," I gasp, breaking the kiss.

"You—" he starts, then shakes his head.

Smiles at me.

Kisses the tip of my nose.

And then takes my mouth again as he shifts his position and slides his cock deep, *deep* inside me.

The feel of another man inside me is foreign, but *good*.

Wrong, but right.

Necessary.

And when he pulls nearly all the way back out, then thrusts in again, I lose my words.

It's just sensations.

The way he's rocking his body against mine.

His fingers teasing my nipples again.

His tongue gliding against mine while his magnificent

cock pumps inside me, rolling his hips to hit my clit with every thrust.

I don't know if it's the novelty of a new man after *years*.

I don't know if it's the fact that he's both my celebrity crush *and* my friend in one.

Maybe it's the magic of Fiji.

The salty air. The glory of the light from the sunset.

Whatever it is, it's putting me on the precipice of losing my mind and my body falling apart in all of the best ways.

Nothing else matters beyond this connection to Jonas.

Our bodies easily finding the most natural rhythm.

There's no awkwardness.

No fumbling.

No impatience.

Time doesn't exist.

Space doesn't exist.

Troubles? Stress? What are those?

Jonas hits that spot inside me that lights me up and threatens to make my whole body explode like a firecracker.

I'm soaring.

Sucking on his tongue and squeezing his ass while he slams into me, hitting my sweet spot over and over and over until—

"Jonas, *Jonas, I'm coming*," I gasp.

Again.

I'm coming *again*.

He groans low and tenses, and I feel him pulsing inside me as he grinds down hard on my body.

"My god, Emma," he pants, his voice strained. "You're so good. *Feel so good*."

My body is out of control, spasming and coming and

squeezing him like I can hold him here forever.

Like neither of us ever have to go back to the real world.

Like this is all that matters.

The tight, hot release.

Wrapped up in each other.

Every cell in my body is glowing. I wonder if this is what the sun feels like. I could light the night sky with the power of the sensations rocking through me right now.

And in the midst of it all, there's something else.

Peace.

Jonas heaves out one last breath and collapses on top of me while the last of my orgasm is still tapering off.

I don't know where I find the strength, but I loop one leg around his hips and hold him there. "More soon," I murmur.

He huffs a laugh into the crook of my neck, one hand curling into my hair.

And he doesn't say anything, but he doesn't have to.

The soft press of his lips to my collarbone says it all.

We're friends.

Neither of us has more in us than that.

But for as long as we're both here, we are *definitely* adding *benefits* to the list of our adventures.

He doesn't say it.

I don't say it.

But I can feel it as solidly as I can feel his body against mine.

We're friends.

He's the best friend I could've asked for this week.

And the thought has me smiling as I drift off to sleep beneath him.

8

Emma

I slept with Jonas last night is the first thing in my head as I slowly come to awareness with the light of dawn.

No, not *slept with*.

We had sex. We had fun, flirty, friendly sex.

Three times. Four, if you count him getting me off with his fingers.

And as I gradually blink my eyes open, I don't know which part of last night is hitting me harder.

You've moved on and slept with someone new after Chandler. This was a good step.

Or there's that other thing.

Oh my god, I slept with Jonas Rutherford.

This, I decide, is a problem to process when I get home.

Right now, my only problem is figuring out if we'll be naked or clothed when we have breakfast.

And is that really a *problem*?

Definitely not.

I roll over and blink in the semi-darkness, reaching for him like he reached for me no more than a few hours ago. Can't help it. While I know there's nothing permanent about this, that last night didn't mean we're *involved*, he's been an unexpected friend.

I hug my friends all the time.

Having a friend with temporary sexual benefits is new, but *I like it*.

But I reach.

And reach.

And reach.

And there's nothing but emptiness in my bed.

"Jonas?" I whisper.

No answer.

Wait.

Was that a dream?

I slide a hand down my body.

Completely naked.

Pretty damn satisfied in the lady bits. I'm wet and sticky between my thighs. My lips are bruised, my nipples are tender, and there's a raw spot on my shoulder.

I *definitely* had sex with him last night.

The *good* kind of sex. Full-body sex. With multiple orgasms.

But I crawl out of bed and find my phone just to be sure.

Yep.

Today's Monday. The past few days have gone by. It's not all some weird dream since Thursday morning.

I turn on the flashlight and scan the room.

There's an indent in the pillow where his head was and the sheets are crumpled.

No, not crumpled.

The sheets are a *disaster*.

I reach up and verify the sheets aren't the only disaster. My hair is doing a *thing* too.

But there's no Jonas.

Not in the bathroom. Not in the living room. Not in the kitchen.

"Jonas?" I head to the porch and peer around.

Still no Jonas. Not on the porch, not in the pool off the porch, not on the lush winding stairway down around the boulders and limestone to the beach, and not on the beach either.

I head back to the villa.

He probably went to get us breakfast. Even though breakfast has been delivered every single day.

Maybe a run.

Yes.

Maybe he went for a run and he'll be back soon.

That's what I tell myself as I prep hot water for his morning green tea—*body is a temple and all that,* he said sheepishly Friday morning when I offered him something to drink when he showed up to check on me after we'd hung out all day Thursday.

I grab the ginger ale for me.

My nerves are making a reappearance.

It's silly.

We're friends. We agreed we'd stay friends. That neither of us is in *any* position to start a relationship.

That last night was something that just felt so natural as the next step for friends who've been through a lot and both needed to move on.

But he's still not back an hour later.

Or an hour after that.

I throw on clothes and head to the small restaurant that I initially avoided for not wanting to see other people, but where I actually had dinner with Jonas two nights ago, and I ask the hostess if she's seen my friend.

There's a small staff here. Jonas kept assuring me that they were very discreet and wouldn't say anything to anyone.

She tells me she has not and asks if I want food.

I don't have his phone number.

I don't even have pictures of us together.

My insistence. He didn't argue. Neither of us needs to be seen with new people right now, and I want *zero* reason for the press or social media or *anyone* to take more interest in me.

By mid-afternoon, I'm starting to panic.

What if he went swimming and got caught in a riptide? What if he tripped on a path while he was running and chickens that aren't supposed to be on the island pecked him to death? What if one of the other guests that he insisted were people just like us who wanted privacy and would leave us alone are secret Razzle Dazzle fans and they kidnapped him to act out weird fantasies?

"He's checked out of his resort," my massage therapist tells me when she arrives mid-afternoon, as she has every afternoon since Thursday.

Theo went above and beyond with this resort upgrade.

Which is not my primary concern at the moment. "He *what?*"

"Head down, please. Your shoulders are very tight."

"He checked out?"

"I'm not supposed to disclose personal information of guests, but he wasn't a guest *here*. And you were friends. I see you're worried. He's safe. My sister checked him out herself very early this morning at her resort and saw him off on the cart to the airstrip."

Heat stings my eyes.

Was it all a ploy?

Was it all a game just to get me to sleep with him?

Is Jonas Rutherford a gaslighting bastard too?

I suck in a breath through my nose, put my head back down in the head hole on the massage table, and I do my best to not cry.

Don't ever let anyone think you're not worthy, Emma.

That's what he said.

Don't let anyone convince you you're not worthy.

Was he talking about *himself*?

That's what I'm wondering when I flip on the TV late Monday night to live footage of some big gala where Jonas and his mom are walking the red carpet in LA as special guests.

Smiling and shaking hands and answering reporters' questions about his divorce with a charming, regretful smile and a quick *we all make mistakes*.

I almost throw the remote at the TV.

I also almost throw up.

Men suck.

The magic of Fiji is ruined.

And every day I hide here, I'm getting more behind on work at a time when I need to find *more work*.

I have to support myself solo now.

And figure out where I even fit in my own life now that I have to face the fallout of choosing Chandler over my friends and family.

9

Two and a half years later...

Emma

It's a beautiful day for a wedding.

Especially since *this* wedding is happening, and it's happening with two of my favorite people on the entire planet, and they're already kissing as man and wife.

I glance over to see Sabrina's shoulders relax too as my brother dips Laney in her gorgeous white gown, refusing to stop at a simple kiss, and I nearly giggle.

Sabrina stifles a noise too.

We're in front of Snaggletooth Creek's City Hall building. Ol' Snaggletooth was the miner who supposedly founded the town, and the statue of him we're standing beside is the one that my nearly forgotten ex-fiancé once damaged with a go-kart and blamed Theo for, sending my brother to jail for a crime he didn't commit because he didn't fight back with the truth.

Theo's committed plenty of other *indiscretions* in his time, but the indiscretion that sent him to jail wasn't actually his. He's still sitting on a promise of a *get out of jail free* card from the sheriff.

Whom I'm reasonably certain is watching this wedding from the same distance that the rest of the town is.

All of Theo and Laney's friends and neighbors would've happily come to the wedding—especially today, when it's been an unusually rainy spring and early summer, leading to dormant wildflowers blooming amidst the mountain grasses on all of the hills and valleys around us—but Laney insisted the ceremony stay small. Her parents. My dad and uncle. Sabrina and her boyfriend, Grey, who likely has his own plans to propose to her very soon too.

And not because she's five months pregnant with his baby, but because they're so utterly adorable together.

Just like Laney and Theo.

Rounding out the wedding party today is my date.

My perfect, sweet, lovable, light of my world.

"Tisses me too, Mama?" Bash says.

I squat next to my 21-month-old son and peck his cheek. "Absolutely," I whisper. "Go get kisses for you too."

Theo pulls Laney back to her feet and slides a look at me that very clearly says he heard me telling his favorite nephew—fine, his *only* nephew—to go interrupt their first kiss.

And Bash does.

He sprints as fast as his chubby little legs will carry him to my brother and my new sister-in-law, who are barely four feet from us. Theo swings him up in the air before he can charge his head into Laney's six-months-pregnant belly, which is, unfortunately, his new favorite game.

Bash squeals in delight. "Unka Deo, higher!"

Sabrina snorts softly behind me, and I know she's seeing the same thing I am.

Laney's face telegraphing *no higher! No higher! You'll drop him!*

My brother has never met a boundary he wouldn't test or a rule he wouldn't break. No matter how much Laney brings out the best in him, he will forever be a tatted bad boy at heart.

And we love him that way.

Much like we love Laney exactly as she is, whether she's braving new adventures and having fun or lapsing into her natural rule-following tendencies.

"And I now pronounce this wedding over," Zen, Grey's nibling and one of my very favorite people in all of Snaggletooth Creek, announces. Laney and Theo asked them to officiate today. "Where's the cake? We've all earned some—excuse you, sir, this is a closed wedding ceremony. If you want to—*oh my sweet baby Nora Ephron.*"

Zen's brown eyes fly to me.

Theo's brown eyes go flat and deadly.

Sabrina sucks in a breath.

Creepy-crawlies inch up my arms, over my shoulders, up my neck, and into my ears, which tickles like hell.

And then I hear someone speak behind me.

"Emma?"

Two syllables in a voice that has haunted my dreams off and on for two and a half years.

I feel like I'm trying to run through water in a dream as I turn to verify with my eyes what my ears are telling me —*Jonas Rutherford is here*.

And he is.

Oh, he is.

It's not right. He doesn't fit here. He doesn't *belong* here.

Jonas Rutherford, standing on the sidewalk at the edge of the lush green grass surrounding the statue of Ol' Snaggletooth, staring at me like *I'm* the ghost and *he's* the haunted one.

His brown eyes are saucers. His white skin has gone a mottled gray beneath his dark stubble. His dark hair looks like he's been raking his fingers through it, and his button-down shirt is mis-buttoned.

My soul suddenly feels identical. Never mind that I'm in a bridesmaid dress, heavy makeup, and a fancy updo.

My soul is just as disheveled and shocked as his entire appearance is.

His gaze moves past me to where I know Laney and Theo and Bash are standing, and panic takes over.

Bash.

Bash.

I have to—

He's there. Right where I left him, in Theo's arms.

Except Theo's handing him to Laney.

"Sorry, princess," he mutters to his new bride. "Also, worth it."

Laney's lips move but no sound comes out. Bash sticks a finger in his mouth and looks at me.

"Oh, shit," Zen whispers.

Sabrina squeaks again.

"Emma," that voice says again, and I don't know if it's wonder or disbelief, but I know I have to get out of here.

Now.

I have to take my son, and I have to run.

For his safety. For his anonymity. For my peace of mind.

Jonas Rutherford appears, and I'm suddenly a runaway bride again.

Whispers. Laughter. Pointing. Mocking.

I'm safe. I'm safe. I'm safe.

But not yet.

Not while I'm out in the open—while *Bash* is out in the open—with one of the world's most famous celebrities standing mere feet from the little boy who looks just like him.

My little boy.

There's a shuffle around me. People are moving. Theo's striding past me toward the sound of the voice.

Grey's trailing him with panic written on his face.

I'm moving too.

Straight to Laney.

To Bash.

To run.

"Not this one, Theo," Grey says. "He—*oof.*"

"Mother*fucker*," Theo grunts.

And there's another noise too.

An *urp* and a gasp that's followed by gasps from everyone watching what's going on behind me.

I'm not watching.

I'm grabbing Bash from Laney.

"Em—" she starts.

"Potty," I gasp. "We have to go potty."

Bash is months—possibly years—from being ready for potty training.

And *I have to go*.

Wherever Jonas Rutherford goes, cameras follow.

I have a good life.

I have my friends. I have my family. I have my son. And most of all, I have *privacy*.

There's no chance in hell I'm putting my son's anonymity and security at risk for a man who fucked me, disappeared, and ignored the emails I sent him two years ago.

"You okay, man?" Grey says somewhere behind me as Zen trots up next to me.

"I can run faster," they murmur.

"Mama, I run," Bash says.

He squirms.

I almost trip.

We're twelve feet from the tavern at the end of Main Street. If I can get into the tavern, I can get out the back door. "I need my car," I tell Zen.

"The bee-mobile's behind City Hall. I'll pick you up in back."

"No car seat." I parked behind the secret speakeasy most of the way down Main because that's where Theo and Laney are having their reception, and I wanted to be able to take Bash home without a long walk to my car whenever he got tired.

"You wanna hide from your baby daddy and all of his drama, or do you want a car seat?"

I almost jerk to a stop.

I've told exactly *no one* in this town who I slept with on my solo honeymoon. Who Bash's father is.

It was my secret.

Not for having a secret's sake.

Not entirely, anyway. It was just as much for *privacy's* sake.

And while I think Bash is the spitting image of his father, he's *not even two yet*. There's zero chance anyone else would see the similarity without knowing I slept with Jonas.

For fuck's sake.

Did I talk in my sleep? When were they even around while I was sleeping?

And *who believes a sleeping woman?*

"Emma, wait," Jonas calls, his voice high-pitched and pained.

"Uncle Grey racked him in the balls when he tried to get between him and Theo," Zen murmurs while they open the door to the tavern for me. "Only Uncle Grey could accomplish what Theo was trying to do more effectively while trying to stop any violence from happening. Also, Theo didn't punch Uncle Grey. He punched the flask in Uncle Grey's coat pocket. Hope he didn't break his hand, but that'd be fitting for Theo and Laney's wedding, wouldn't it?"

"Wack my balls!" Bash shrieks, drawing the attention of every single person inside the dark interior. Thankfully, it's very, *very* few people.

"You need the loo, love?" Bitsy, the proprietor's wife, says to me from her spot behind the bar.

"Back door, please," I gasp.

She looks at me, then at Zen, then back to me.

Bash squirms. "Mama, *down.*"

"What do you think happened?" someone near the front window says.

"Shh. I'm filming."

"*No filming*," Bitsy barks.

It's a standing order in Snaggletooth Creek ever since my wedding video went viral.

We don't film things that could look bad if they got posted on the internet.

It's not a fool-proof system—too many tourists for it to be completely effective—but for the most part, it's worked well.

"Filming strangers can earn you a fine of up to ten thousand dollars in this town," Zen agrees. They squeeze my shoulder and add softly, "Sabrina's got this. They're locals. Hey, Bash, my favorite little short person. You want a piece of cake?"

Bash stops squirming as we push into the kitchen.

Bitsy's husband looks up from the grill, spots us, and shrugs. "Don't want to know."

"Bash needs cake," Zen says.

He nods and jerks his head at a rack of desserts.

"Bash does *not* need cake," I mutter.

"Put it on Uncle Grey's tab," Zen says.

They grab a plate and steer me out the back door and into the alley.

We hear a roar, and then a restored old muscle car that's been painted to look like a honeybee lumbers around the corner.

"Where'd your dad get a key?" Zen mutters while they hustle me and Bash to the vehicle.

I don't answer. Less because I don't know and more because I don't care.

I swing open the heavy door and peer inside.

Dad gives me a sheepish grin. "Don't tell anyone I'm the reason Theo can hotwire a car."

"Mr. M, you're my hero." Zen tilts the front seat, takes Bash, shoves me into the car, and then deposits my little boy in the back seat with me. Once they're halfway into the front seat, pulling the door closed, Dad hits the gas.

And as we're driving away, taking the alley to the side road that will take us the back way up and around the mountains to Theo and Laney's house, something strikes me.

My dad didn't ask.

Sabrina didn't ask. Laney didn't ask.

Theo leapt into action.

Grey leapt into action to stop Theo from what he said was *worth it*.

And again—unless you know to look for it, you wouldn't draw the similarity.

Who would randomly think Jonas Rutherford was Bash's father the way Zen clearly already does?

"Oh my god," I whisper while Bash shoves cake in his face on my lap. "You *all* know."

Dad doesn't make eye contact in the rearview mirror, but Zen turns to face me. "Strongly suspected, but not until recently. Next time you have a secret baby, I highly recommend making sure they don't look exactly like their father. Especially when their father is likely to have his baby pictures shown on every entertainment news site on the entire planet when his *Who Are We?* podcast wins every award known to podcasting man."

"*Oh god.*"

"Never would've suspected without seeing the baby

pictures," Zen says. "Seriously, Em. It was a fluke that we saw his baby pictures, and I don't think anyone other than the six or eleven of us who know you best would've drawn the correlation. Nobody else looks at Bash as much as we do."

I'm going to hyperventilate.

I'm going to hyperventilate.

"Emma Monroe, listen to me," they say. "Sabrina has this. No one's breathing a word if they don't want to face her wrath."

"I should have this myself," I snap back.

Zen rocks in the seat and nearly bumps their head on the window when Dad takes a switchback curve too fast.

"Em, you are a champ at taking care of your entire life by yourself," Zen says. "Handling your baby daddy showing up after he ignored your messages for over two years? And don't tell me you were lying when you said you sent your honeymoon fling ultrasound and baby pictures. You're *Emma*. We know you did it."

"Oh my god. You all know."

Zen winces. "Full disclosure, the triplets know too. They were hanging out with us the night we had the awards show on, and you know Jack and Decker. It was immediately-to-the-keyboard-to-see-who-can-find-it-first. We know he was on the same island as you when you went on your runawaymoon. Which we *don't* think anyone else in town knows. Or would put together."

"Oh my god."

"Look, my biggest point here is, please don't deprive your friends of the chance to help the bastard see himself back out. You've done enough by yourself. *Please* let us in the sandbox with you for this one."

I bury my face in Bash's silky light brown hair and inhale his sweaty boy scent.

They're right.

Since I jilted Chandler Sullivan two and a half years ago, I've found strength I didn't know I had.

A little cynicism too. Definitely more wariness.

I wasn't alone during my pregnancy. Zen badgered me until I caved and agreed to let them help me whenever I had a craving and didn't want to drive myself out to get it. Laney and Sabrina were right there with me when I gave birth, holding my hands. I have babysitters galore and Bash and I want for nothing.

But I'm still a single mom, a small business owner, and I hope a good friend back.

And *I like it*.

"I wanted to go to my brother's wedding reception," I say.

"Unka Deo tisses!" Bash cries with a mouthful of chocolate cake.

"Still can," Zen says. "We can keep the riffraff out. They don't know the secret passcode to get in."

I meet their eyes again.

They're right.

Why should I hide?

Dad glances at me again in the rearview mirror.

Zen checks their phone. "The wedding crasher has officially been removed from public view by the sheriff."

I whimper.

If Theo gets arrested *at his wedding*—you know what?

If Theo gets arrested at his wedding, he'll post bail, he'll make it to his reception late, and Laney will laugh her ass off every time she tells the story of her wedding to anyone for the rest of her life.

She knows who she's marrying.

"And the happy couple is heading to their reception," Zen adds.

A relieved breath whooshes out of me.

Dad too. I can see his shoulders relax.

"Will everyone ask questions?" I whisper. While the wedding was small, the whole town is invited to pop in to the reception.

Provided they know the passcode for the speakeasy.

"No," Zen says.

"Because Sabrina will give them the glare?"

"Em, babe, I love you to pieces, which is why I'm here helping you instead of yelling that *you should've fucking told us*—sorry, Bash—*about your sperm donor*. So when I tell you it'll give Sabrina joy to give the gossip glare to every single person who looks at you sideways, you need to fucking listen. Sorry again, Bash."

"Duck duck goo!" Bash cries.

"My favorite game," Zen says. "Mr. M., let's get this bridesmaid to a wedding reception."

10

Jonas

U҃ntil today, the only times in my life I've been racked in the balls, it's all been staged.

Taking a blow to the nuts hurts a lot more when it happens for real.

Taking a blow to the ego might hurt more. "I met Emma Monroe on her honeymoon," I tell the sheriff for the sixth time.

"Emma Monroe didn't have a honeymoon," the stern-faced woman across from me replies.

"She took it solo after her wedding didn't happen."

"She never mentioned you."

"I don't think she wanted a lot of public attention back then."

"What makes you think she wants public attention now?"

She shoots, she scores. "Apologies. I should've thought of that. I was driving through and thought I spotted her, and figured I'd say hi."

"And interrupt a wedding."

"It was over."

I smile.

The sheriff does not smile back.

"Could I get a new bag of ice?" I ask.

I've already spent the past three days feeling like throwing up. Nothing like a new assistant searching for an email from Emma Watson, ending up in a folder of email your previous assistant marked *crazypants stalkers and AI-generated bullshit accusations* instead, and finding evidence that you might have a kid wandering around in the world that you didn't know about to throw your reality off kilter.

That hit to the gonads made it worse.

Even if I can acknowledge I probably deserve it.

The sheriff hits a button on her office phone. "Darlene, bring fresh ice for our guest's testicles, please."

"On it, boss."

The sheriff questions me for another hour. I don't ask for my lawyer. She doesn't ask for an autograph. When she releases me, she follows me to where I've parked my rental car and stands there watching while I drive out of town.

As expected, my phone's blowing up with texts from my mother and my sister-in-law.

They don't like it when I ditch my security detail.

Can't blame them, but I wanted to be low-key.

Worked fabulously well.

Until I fucked it all up.

I should've waited until the wedding was *over*-over.

But I saw Emma, and then I saw that little boy.

The little boy in a miniature tuxedo with my eyes and my nose and my chin and Emma's hair.

The little boy with the same impish grin that won me my first starring role in a Razzle Dazzle commercial at about eighteen months old.

My son.

The son Emma tried to tell me about a half dozen times two years ago.

All I've had of him from three days ago until today were two ultrasound pictures and a single newborn photo.

And now I know he's a living, breathing, perfect little human being who can *talk* and walk and probably stack blocks and sing songs and ride a bike.

Or maybe not ride a bike.

Yet.

But definitely walk.

And smile.

Oh my god.

That smile.

I saw him—saw him say something to Emma, saw *Emma*, saw him smile, saw her smile—and there was no more waiting.

I needed to talk to her.

Now.

And instead, I'm banished from town, with my car marked by the sheriff.

Easy answer.

Time to get a new car. And do this the right way.

And four hours later, that's exactly what I've accomplished.

Almost.

I'm aware that parking a brand new vehicle at a public

park a quarter mile from the back entrance to Emma's house, then hiking through pine trees and underbrush to spy and wait for her to get home, is probably not the *right* right way.

But it's righter than leaving again.

Or sending an email.

Especially after the way I left her in Fiji.

I get to her backyard, and my breath leaves me.

She has chickens.

She has chickens.

An entire decent-size penned-in coop of little cluckers next to a two-person swing that's hung from a little wooden pergola in a clearing near the coop at the back of the yard. With flowers. It's like a flower garden around a chicken coop.

Her house is cute too.

Two stories, but not large. Brown shingles. Open windows that suggest no air conditioning. There's a screen door beside a small concrete patio with a hot tub on it.

This isn't the house she told me about in Fiji. Her dream house. Her friend's grandparents' house. Her *ex's* grandparents' house.

This house is too small. The yard is too small. And I don't think it has any views.

Even if it's not her childhood dream home, it's not checking the boxes of what she wanted.

It's private though.

There are enough trees and boulders and just general mountain forest growth that I can't see her neighbors.

And I wonder if that's my fault.

The chickens cluck. A few birds chirp. I stay hidden, waiting.

Like a stalker.

Probably not wise, but *I need to see her*.

It takes forever, but finally, two cars pull into her drive shortly after nine. Dusk is settling, and I'm realizing I'm mildly fucked if she won't talk to me. In addition to the deer and elk that have wandered past the caged-in chicken coop in her cozy backyard—I'm still having reactions in my heart area to knowing she actually got her chickens—I've seen at least three foxes.

Know what else that means?

That means it's mountain lion o'clock out here now.

And if that's not dangerous enough, the tall guy who leapt between me and Theo Monroe when I thought Emma's brother was going to murder me is circling her house with a flashlight.

"See anything?" the much shorter, redheaded pregnant bridesmaid asks as she dashes along next to him, her legs moving twice as fast as his to keep up.

Something's in the water.

The bride was pregnant. The bridesmaid is pregnant. Begonia's pregnant.

Do not breathe wrong around Emma, I order myself.

Oh, fuck me.

What if she's pregnant?

What if she's seeing someone and she's pregnant too?

My gut cramps in a way it has no business cramping and that I don't want to think about too much.

"Nothing human," the tall guy says.

He sweeps his flashlight over where I'm hiding in a thick set of bushes. I close my eyes and hold my breath.

"Don't wake the chickens," the bridesmaid whispers.

"I think they'll live if they miss a little beauty rest," he mutters back.

"Aw, you're adorable when you're grumpy."

He grunts.

The light dims behind my eyes, and I open them and peer through the bushes again.

The couple is moving on to the other side of the house.

It's another hour before they leave.

Lights have flipped off and on inside the house. Two windows on the lower level are still glowing in back. I saw Emma pull the blinds, but not before I spotted a fridge and cabinets. A low light came on in one of the upstairs rooms, then shut off not long after.

Is that the boy's bedroom?

Is that where her son—our son—*holy hell*, I have a son —is sleeping?

Sebastian Nathaniel Monroe, per her email with the newborn photo attached.

My middle name is Nathaniel too.

Did she know that?

Is that why she gave it to him?

Also, am I a creepy stalker who needs to go knock on the door and quit being a spying asshole?

Yes.

It's time.

My feet are falling asleep. My balls are still tender. My stomach is in knots. My legs are tight and my ass is numb.

But I sneak out of the bushes and head for the house, debating if I should go to the front door or knock on the back door.

I make it three steps before the chickens erupt in a cacophony of squawking.

The light by the back door flips on almost immediately. Motion-activated? Or—

No.

Emma activated.

She pulls open the wooden door and stands there, staring grim-faced into the darkness behind the screen door. "So you didn't leave," she says.

"I left," I reply. "The sheriff made me. And then I came back."

"You're welcome to leave again."

"Emma—"

"There are *so* many things I could say to you right now, but they all basically end with *I fulfilled my obligations to you two years ago, I don't want you in my life, please leave.*"

No small part of me wishes her brother had gotten away with smashing my face in. It's clearly what he intended before the other guy jumped between us and got me in the nuts instead.

And it's what I deserve. "I didn't mean to leave the way I did. I'm sorry."

"Thank you. You may leave."

"My email got attacked by AI spam bots. Your notes got lost in the middle of all of them. I would've been here before if I'd—"

"Ba*gock*!" something cries at my feet.

I instinctively take a step back.

"Yolko Ono, get in the house." She opens the screen door just wide enough for a one-legged chicken to hop past her inside, then snaps it shut again like she's worried I'll force my way in.

Forty-three other chickens squawk behind me. Or maybe just ten. I don't know.

No wonder her friends were willing to leave her alone.

She has a gang of guard-chickens, and they are *loud*. I'd smile—it makes me happy that she got her chickens—but she's still glaring daggers at me.

I swallow, then have to swallow again.

This woman was my friend when I desperately needed one. I thought I was being *her* friend. But I'd be lying if I said she wasn't mine too.

And I fucked it up.

I've always known I fucked it up. I've always told myself she was better off without the limelight I'd bring into her life.

But three days ago, I discovered I fucked up on a level that goes beyond any fuck-up that I could've ever imagined.

"How are you?" I ask hesitantly.

"Tired and likely to be up early, which means it's time to say goodnight."

"Can I do anything?"

"No. Thank you, but no. Very nice to see you again, Jonas. Have a lovely life."

She shuts the door.

Flips off the light.

And leaves me without a shred of a doubt that I could offer her the world, and she still wouldn't want to talk to me.

And I don't blame her in the least.

11

Emma

I sleep like crap and wake up to a message that puts me in the kind of foul mood that I haven't felt for a very, very long time.

I don't like being cranky. It's not natural. It's not who I am.

But it's necessary today.

"What do you mean, you're postponing your honeymoon?" I hiss at Theo. I'm in the kitchen prepping industrial-strength coffee at an ungodly early hour, knowing Bash will be up within minutes because he's always awake early the mornings after he's up too late.

Today will be *brutal* if I'm not prepared.

Worth it—the reception was perfect and fun and everything it should've been, no matter how much I couldn't even contemplate what food would do to my knotted stomach—but still brutal.

Hence the coffee.

With a side of the absolute wrong news.

"We're postponing our honeymoon," my brother repeats. "Sheriff found a car parked at the Twin Ridge parking lot. You're likely to get a visitor."

"I already sent him away."

"*Why the fuck didn't you call me?*"

"Because *I can handle my own problems.*"

"*Can* and *should* and *have to* are all different things," Laney calls in the background.

These two. I know they mean well. I love that they love me enough to change their plans for me. But I can handle my life, and I don't like them coddling me when it's not necessary. "You have exactly six weeks before your doctor won't let you travel anymore. *Go on your honeymoon.*"

"Too expensive to rebook now," Theo says.

I'm gripping my phone so tightly that I might break it. Despite all of his attempts to spend and give away the cash that he made in the few years that he was the world's biggest online adult entertainment star—before giving it all up for Laney, at his insistence, which was my favorite news that I came home to after Fiji—he's accidentally made a few investments and tackled some projects that amused him which have tripled what he made as an online porn star. My brother is rich as sin.

Maybe not *Rutherford* rich, but still loaded.

Talk about things I never thought I'd hear myself say when we were growing up as *the poor kids* in Snaggletooth Creek.

And Laney's about to take the reins as CEO of her parents' online photo gift business, which is *also* a multi-million-dollar company.

They can afford to rebook their honeymoon. "I realize I have no business telling either of you how to spend your money, but *it's too expensive* is the dumbest argument I've ever heard from either one of you. Ever. Times twenty. Billion. Times twenty billion."

"Em, I hate to be the wet blanket—" Laney starts, but Theo cuts her off.

"If that asshole starts asking for paternity tests and visitation while we're gone—"

"And we've gone *so* many amazing places already," Laney continues. "Delaying our honeymoon and possibly taking the baby with us so we can be here now *just in case* makes us happy."

"And we can afford babysitters when we want private mommy-daddy time whenever we take our honeymoon," Theo adds.

"I told you not to say that to her."

He's wearing that *I love to get in trouble with my girlfriend* grin. I don't have to see him to recognize the vibe coming through the phone.

Except now, it's officially the *I love getting in trouble with my wife* grin.

I love them.

But I don't *like* them this morning.

I guzzle my coffee—doctored with so much cream and sugar that it's not hot anymore, naturally—and look out at my chicken coop, where I need to go gather a few eggs, then choke.

Jonas is asleep on my backyard swing out in the back part of my yard.

And mama instinct tells me Bash is awake a split second before I hear his little voice drift down the stairs, singing a Waverly Sweet song that I suspect he learned from Zen.

No "Baby Shark" or "Twinkle Twinkle" for my kid.

He's all pop songs.

And I adore it.

"Gotta go," I rasp. "Bash just woke up."

"We'll swing by with breakfast," Theo says.

"*You just got married*. Have breakfast just the two of you and *go on your honeymoon*."

"No."

"You think Sabrina and Grey and Zen will leave me hanging if he shows back up?" I ask, hoping Jonas is actually asleep out there and not faking it. My window is open.

He can hear me.

But I don't know if he knows who my friends are.

Grey's a scientific genius who invented self-sealing cereal bags. Licensing the patent pays him enough that he'll likely be a billionaire before long.

Never mind the research he's working on now that'll probably be even bigger once he wraps it up and goes public with it.

If I can't afford the best family law attorney, then no matter how much I hate having people take care of me, I'll ask my friends for help.

Purely for Bash's sake.

And then I'll owe them for the rest of my life.

I can't battle the Rutherford family's lawyers solo.

Which *sucks*.

All I want to do is live my simple life with my son. With our chickens and our little family-of-two-size house and good friends in our close-knit community.

When Jonas didn't reply to my emails about my pregnancy and Bash's birth—which was the only way I knew to try to get in touch with him—I thought we were safe.

That we *could* live a private, simple life.

"Knowing you have other people to help and being some of those people who help are two different things," Theo says. "We're delaying."

That's his *I'm a stubborn ass and I'm digging my heels in* voice.

He tried to break up with Laney using that voice when my wedding fell apart, but he barely made it a week before he was eating his words and groveling.

Or so the story goes.

Sort of missed witnessing it myself, and it took a while after I got home from Fiji before my friends and I found normal again.

But we found it.

Because that's what friends do. We all shared blame for hurting each other, and we're all stronger for having worked through it.

"We're absolutely delaying," Laney echoes.

Dammit.

That's *her* stubborn voice.

She's far less likely to break.

"Do what you think you have to do," I grumble. "But I still object."

"Noted," Laney says.

"We'll be over with breakfast in an hour," Theo adds.

"How's your hand?" I ask him. He insisted last night it wasn't broken, but it was definitely swollen.

"Fine. Definitely fine enough to bring you breakfast."

I roll my eyes. "I love you both, but I don't like you right now."

"We can live with that."

"Em?" Laney says. "We didn't know it was Jonas until a few weeks ago. And we didn't *know* know. We strongly suspected but didn't *know*. And that was the week Bash had strep. You had a lot on your plate that was more important."

"I told them to quit jumping to conclusions and to let you have your secret," Theo says. "My fault no one told you we suspected anything."

I growl.

Laney growls.

"Quit being the damn martyr," I tell my brother.

"Sabrina had every intention—"

"Of asking me if I wanted to know if she had accidentally found out something that she knew I wanted kept a secret," I finish for her.

She told me so last night after the reception, which would've felt very normal if I hadn't spent the entire time wondering if Jonas would sweet-talk his way into the speakeasy.

"You two are okay?" Laney asks.

"We're very okay. I told her I would've said she was wrong no matter who she guessed until the moment he showed up in town. I just—"

"Want Bash to have a normal childhood and you couldn't do that if *anyone* knew who his father was?"

"*Yes.*"

"We'll make sure he has a normal Monroe childhood," Theo says.

That makes me laugh out loud. Bash has enough of the male Monroe genes in him that I know the next forever part of my life will be filled with heart-stopping moments and probably bailing him out of jail a time or two as well.

"Thank you."

"Is it fair to ask for details now that he's here?" Laney asks.

"I'll give you details. Eventually. Promise."

"You don't have to."

"I know. But I think it's about time."

"We can put out word that I hate him because he wants to make a movie about my life," Theo says.

I almost drop my phone. "Are you serious right now?"

Laney makes a strangled noise. "We actually think it might be more believable than him being Bash's father…"

I cannot process this right now. "I need to go. Bash is awake."

"Love you, Em," they say together.

"Love you both too, even if I'm still mad you're skipping your honeymoon."

We hang up, and I look at my pet.

Not quite the dogs and cats I had in mind, but I think this is better.

"Breakfast for you," I tell Yolko Ono, who's in her favorite box in the kitchen. She's a white Silkie, which means she's tall and slender and has fluffy white feathers covering her eyes so you're never sure if she's looking at you or not.

She was born with only one leg but an attitude like she has four and can actually fly.

I love her to pieces.

So does Bash.

She clucks once and dives into yesterday's leftover fruit

salad that I set beside her. I'll let her outside to eat with the rest of the chickens later too.

Bash is singing louder to himself.

Is his window open?

I don't think I left it cracked to let in the night air, but I can't remember now.

If it's open, his voice hasn't woken Jonas. Unless he's really good at pretending he's asleep.

Which he might be.

But if I were acting like I was asleep, I wouldn't choose that position.

My lifetime-ago solo honeymoon fling has his head tilted funny on one armrest of the porch swing that's dangling from my pergola and that I only got put back up yesterday after having it cleaned and re-stained. His dark hair falls across his forehead and his legs stick out over the other armrest. His hands are tucked under his armpits like he's trying to keep them warm.

I can probably get upstairs, grab Bash, and get out of the garage and head into town before he's awake or before he realizes he needs to quit acting like he's asleep.

Or, I can face the fact that Jonas won't leave until I talk to him.

I could call the sheriff, but see again, *billionaire family who will sue me for custody and make my life miserable.*

The idea that my son would be subjected to the public limelight that follows Jonas everywhere makes my heart shrivel.

Bash deserves a normal childhood.

To know people love him for who he is, not for who he's related to or how much money he stands to inherit.

If he grows up and takes over my accounting firm and

feels like I gave him special treatment for giving him a job at the family business, I can live with that.

That's small stuff.

Growing up getting preferential treatment because his father is Jonas Rutherford?

No.

I grab my coffee and a baby monitor, which I turn down to the lowest setting. I'll still hear Bash when he's done with his slow wake-up—mama instinct and all that—but Jonas might not.

Time to fight to be able to continue raising my son in peace.

The chickens erupt in squawking the minute I open the back door. Bash will help me feed them and collect their eggs after he's up.

But now, they're doing the job I want them to do.

They're waking Jonas up.

He bolts upright, grabs his neck, sways on the porch swing, and tips off, landing on the ground with an *oof*.

But he springs right back up and smiles at me.

Smiles.

At six in the morning.

After he face-planted into two-day-old deer poop.

"Emma. You have chickens." His voice is husky with sleep, but there's a bright, happy quality to it that's impossible to miss.

Like there's no place on earth he wanted to sleep more than right there, with his body all akimbo on my porch swing where he could've been eaten by a cougar.

Like he's still the guy he was before he freaking *ran away back home* after sleeping with me.

And without a goodbye.

Or a single acknowledgment of any of my messages.

Until now.

I sip my coffee and watch him. It's a technique I've learned from Sabrina.

She's the best gossip in all of Snaggletooth Creek, and it's because she knows when to be quiet and when to tell what she knows.

Usually.

"Right. You know you have chickens." He rubs his face, then freezes for a split second like he's realized there's stuff on his face that shouldn't be there.

I point to the hose hung on the back of my house. "Deer droppings. Help yourself to the water."

Wariness sneaks into his expression. "You're mad."

"I—"

"Of course you're mad. You should be mad. I was an asshole. Didn't leave you any way to contact me. You tried. I didn't answer. And you've been doing this by yourself."

"I like doing this by myself."

Bash's voice drifts out of the baby monitor. He's moved on to his version of a Taylor Swift song. I probably have three minutes before I hear *"Mama?"* in his adorable little voice.

But the bigger problem right now is that Jonas apparently has excellent hearing.

"Is that him?" he whispers, his gaze drifting to my hip where the monitor is clipped to my pants, awe and wonder filling his face in a way that makes me both furious and light at the same time.

And that makes me even more furious.

He has *no fucking right* to show up here and look

completely smitten with the sound of my son's voice, and no fucking right to earn a soft spot in my heart again.

"I have a busy day today, so let's get right to it. What do you want?" This is *not* me.

Not the me that I like being, anyway.

I like giving people the benefit of the doubt and smiling and laughing my way through my mornings with Bash. Feeding the chickens and collecting their eggs. Washing Bash after he cracks too many eggs all over himself. Waving at my neighbors while we walk our pet chicken. Being a calming presence in my office when clients suddenly have need for me in stressful situations. Volunteering at events at Sabrina's café and other places around the community while my friends and family play with my son and give him the sense of belonging that he deserves.

I do *not* like being a grouchy mama bear who has no intention of giving this man an inch for as long as I can hold him off.

And I know being a grouchy mama bear won't get me what I want, but I'm too on guard to be *nice*.

Judging by the extra wariness settling into Jonas's eyes, he's ready for me to turn into a *feral* grouchy mama bear.

"I—I don't know," he finally says. "I didn't stop to think when I finally got your emails. I just came here."

"When you figure it out, you can have your lawyers contact my lawyers."

Dammit dammit dammit, Emma.

I'm nice. I'm too nice.

Always.

But apparently not today when it matters so damn much that I charm him.

Feral grouchy mama bear is ready to fight with everything I have in me to make the rest of my life just as peaceful and happy as it was twenty-four hours ago.

Seeing him again after all this time has apparently not only sparked overprotective instincts that I'd finally started feeling like I didn't need, but also a few latent feelings about the way he left me and ignored me after fucking me in Fiji.

Don't get me wrong. I'm eternally grateful to have Bash, and I know I wouldn't without Jonas's contribution to the whole baby-making process.

But that doesn't excuse the fact that he didn't even say goodbye.

"I'm sorry." He says it so earnestly, so easily, that I don't know if he's said it often enough in movies that it's second nature or if he means it.

But I absolutely mean my entire answer with my whole heart. "I'm not. I have a good life. I'm giving my son a good life. He's happy. He's loved. I'm happy. I'm loved. We have the best friends and family we could ask for. And we have everything else we could possibly need. So thank you for coming. Thank you for apologizing. But I sincerely mean it when I say *you can go*. We don't need any more from you than what you've already done for the past two and a half years, and I'm happy to sign anything necessary to absolve you of any responsibility here."

His lips part and move like he's working through how the script flipped when he wasn't looking.

His cheeks turn a shade of pink that I'd call honest embarrassment if I trusted him.

Bash's little voice goes whiny.

I have to get back inside.

Time for mama to rescue him from his crib and give him morning snuggles and song time and breakfast.

"Can I meet him?" Jonas asks.

My heart splits in two.

If we hadn't met in Fiji, if we hadn't had those days together, I wouldn't have Bash.

Jonas gave me a gift that I will move heaven and earth to protect.

But he also left. I tried to get in touch as soon as I found out I was pregnant.

I didn't want to. Not when I knew the same thing that I know today—that any child Jonas Rutherford publicly acknowledged would grow up under scrutiny and have to deal with the reporters and the social media rumors and the whispers that I'd already endured after my wedding video went viral.

But it was the right thing to do.

And I got silence in return.

I sent a few updates. Ultrasound pictures. Notes that I was fine and didn't need anything, but in case he hadn't seen my last messages, I wanted him to know I was pregnant, and he was the only possible father.

My last message was almost two years ago.

The day Bash was born in mid-October.

I emailed him a birth announcement.

And I got crickets in return.

"You *left*." My voice cracks and my eyes get hot. "You made me think you cared. You made me think I mattered. You made me think we were *friends*. Then you slept with me and *you left*. And I sent you at least a half dozen messages in the only way I could find to contact you. And then I started thinking that I'd been the biggest fool in the history of the world, and that someone who *looked* like you and knew all the right things to convince me that you were you had fooled me. All because I didn't want to believe that you would've fucked me and ghosted me. So please excuse me if I don't want you to see *my* son. He has excellent, *reliable* father figures in his life, and that's what he deserves. Once again, *you can go.*"

"Emma—"

I march back toward the house. Bash is ready to get up, and I'm ready to get away from Jonas Rutherford. "And if you won't go on your own, I'm calling the sheriff. *After* I call my brother. I'm sure he'd like to finish what he tried to start yesterday."

Do I mean it?

Completely.

Absolutely.

Unequivocally.

There is no room for *nice* when my son's safety, comfort, privacy, and possibly even his future are on the line.

12

Jonas

That went well.

If *well* is synonymous with *horribly*.

But she didn't have her brother waiting inside to come beat me to a bloody pulp. She didn't call the sheriff before she came outside.

She didn't wake me up with that hose she offered me.

Probably could've been more horrible.

The worst part, though?

I'm glad to see her.

Glad that she's strong. Thriving. Happy with her friends and family.

I saw the way she was smiling at her—*our* little boy at the wedding yesterday.

The sight of her robbed me of my ability to breathe. My heart quit beating. My entire life stilled to one singular thought.

My friend is even more beautiful than I remembered.

And she hates me.

As she should.

I sink onto the porch swing and drop my head in my hands, belatedly remembering that I have deer shit on my face.

"Maybe you should've called first," a surprisingly familiar voice says from the side of the house.

I jerk my head up, start to smile, and then groan and drop my head again.

"Aw, you're usually so happy to see me," Begonia says.

I don't have to look up to know she's doing the uber-pregnant-lady waddle across the small lawn to reach me.

But no matter how happy I am to see her, my shoulders and jaw are tense as an overtightened spring. "How far behind you is my mother?"

"She doesn't know where you are," Hayes answers.

Shit.

They're *both* here.

I blink in the morning light to make sure my eyes aren't playing tricks on me.

No, they're definitely both here.

My bright, happy, sunshiny sister-in-law is massively pregnant and glowing. Her white skin is clear of makeup, as always, and her hair hangs in bright pink waves at her shoulders.

She must've found pregnancy-safe hair dye.

Or Hayes did. He'd move heaven and earth to give her anything she wants, and I know he was looking for it.

And speaking of Hayes—my tall, crotchety older brother is beside his wife. Where Begonia's in a colorful shapeless dress, Hayes is in his usual casual pants and a light blue button-down.

I don't ask how they found me.

There's not a person on any of our staffs that Begonia can't charm information out of.

I also don't ask how she got permission from her doctor to travel. She's carrying twins and all I've heard for the past three months—ever since they shared the news at the beginning of her second trimester—is *she'll go into labor early so we need to be careful about everything*.

Hayes probably brought the doctor with them.

And I suddenly wonder what Emma looked like when she was pregnant.

Did she glow? Or did she get sick?

Did she love it? Did she hate it? Did she sing to him while he was growing inside her? What books did she read to him? Did she use special belly butter like Hayes says he's been getting for Begonia?

The enormity of what I've missed slaps me in the face once more.

"I'm not leaving," I inform them both.

"Maybe you can not leave but also not make a giant scene by getting arrested before you figure out how to make amends for what sounds like a pretty uncomfortable situation?" Begonia says. "We can't keep your mom from those alerts she gets on your name in the news, even if we can keep her at bay for the time being by promising we're taking care of you."

Hayes doesn't smirk, but the affectionate glance he shoots at his wife says he's amused at her diplomatic way of putting things. Although, he'd agree even if she suggested we all needed to work out my problems by going deep into the forest and doing a rain dance naked under the trees.

Which I'm pretty sure was a joke the last time she told us she and her twin sister used to do that at summer camp as kids, but I'm never completely certain with her.

"This sucks," I mutter.

The chicken closest to me in the fenced-in pen squawks in agreement.

Or possibly it's saying *this is your own fault, dumbass*.

"It'll suck a little less once you get breakfast and wash the shit off your face," Hayes says.

Begonia grabs my arm and tugs. "C'mon, Mr. *Oh, No, My World Has Had a Hiccup and That Never Happens*. We have a lovely little house just outside of town that Hayes freaking *bought* because he's ridiculous. She's not going anywhere, and even if she does, she'll come back eventually."

So they've seen the report on Emma that our family's private investigator put together for me while I was plotting how to escape from my security detail.

Or else Hayes ordered his own report from his own people.

Movement at the side of the house catches my eye, and there they are.

His security team.

Which means mine's probably also nearby to rotate in and out.

I need a little more protection than Hayes and Begonia do. Now that he's no longer single and prominently involved at the top of Razzle Dazzle's management chain, he gets to live a pretty quiet life.

As he prefers it.

"Aren't you supposed to be at summer camp?" I mutter to Begonia while she tugs harder. The two of them together manage Razzle Dazzle's summer camp division.

And they love it. Begonia because she loves everything, Hayes because nobody's beating down his door to demand updates on how the camp is impacting the bottom line for Razzle Dazzle and its stock price.

"Your mother threatened to come live with us if I didn't take early maternity leave," my sister-in-law reports.

"I would've had to actually murder her if she'd murdered Begonia, and I'd rather be around to watch my kids grow up," my brother adds.

I suck in a breath.

I have missed *so much* of my son's life already.

I know how it happened. I know why it happened. But if I'd been here sooner—

"Too soon, honey," Begonia says brightly. "C'mon, Jonas. You need to look and smell human again before you can charm the pants off of your lady friend."

Emma's watching us.

Not only can I feel it, I catch movement in one of the upper windows.

"I want to meet my son," I whisper.

"You will," Begonia insists. "But shower and food and not getting arrested first."

She's incredibly optimistic on that first point. She's also completely correct on the other three.

I follow them around the house to an SUV parked next to the garage and duck in quickly, hoping the neighbors haven't seen. Between the twisty roads and the boulders and the pine trees, there's a good amount of privacy in Emma's neighborhood.

But I still want to make sure she gets security cameras installed.

"You seriously slept with her and didn't say goodbye?" Hayes mutters to me as Begonia chats with their lead security agent about a craving while the other agent steers us around the sharply curving mountain roads.

I wince. "Wasn't the plan."

"What *was* the plan?"

"For Mom's minions to not show up and drag me away in the middle of the night."

He snorts.

Begonia glances back at us.

Hayes reaches across the space to pat her knee. "Just pineapple, or did you want kiwi and guava too?"

Her nose wrinkles. "Actually, I think I want fresh tortillas. Like the ones Françoise perfected when I was craving burritos. But only tortillas. No beans. Or lettuce. Although, I think I could eat pineapple on the tortillas. If it's cut the way Françoise cuts it."

"I'll fly her out."

"*Hayes.*"

"Contacting her now, Mr. Rutherford," his lead security agent says.

"*Nikolay.*"

Nikolay ignores her and types something on his phone.

"That's completely unnecessary," Begonia insists, and she turns her arguments to the two security guards.

"You didn't contact her again after you left?" Hayes murmurs to me, going right back to where we were.

Biggest regret of my life.

Even *before* I found out our night together had unintended consequences. "She'd gone viral for her wedding imploding—"

"We saw."

"And I thought she was better off without having my name attached to hers."

"Ah, the old *you were doing her a favor* excuse."

"Be nice," Begonia chides, clearly listening while still arguing over not needing to have her favorite chef flown in just to make tortillas. As if Françoise wouldn't come on her own if she knew Begonia had asked for anything. "As I recall, you tried the same on me."

I look back, but I can't see Emma's house anymore.

We've already taken too many curves.

Also?

I've confirmed that there's no mountain view from the front of Emma's house either.

This isn't her dream house.

At least, not the dream house she told me about in Fiji.

Hayes and Begonia are both watching me now, waiting for an explanation beyond whatever they've seen in private investigator reports.

"She was exactly the friend that I needed when my life was the biggest pile of shit that it had ever been, and look what I did to her," I say.

"Jonas Rutherford, you are a *good person*," Begonia says. "You'll work this out."

"You think *everyone* is a good person."

"Her standards have improved," Hayes assures me. "She's right. You're a good person. You've definitely fucked this up, but you're a good person."

"And you *know* it pains him to admit that," Begonia adds.

"He'd claim a serial killer was a good person if you asked him too," I reply.

Hayes shakes his head. "Not this week. Maybe last week, but I'm also suffering from improved standards. And I *still* think you're a good person."

I'm not a good person.

Last week I would've agreed with him.

But now?

Not a chance.

"Did you have a plan when you came out here, or are you winging it?" Hayes asks.

Leave it to my big brother to point out the flaw in my every action over the past three days.

I flip him off.

Affectionately.

Begonia laughs, then groans and grabs her belly.

Hayes lunges forward in his seat. "Contraction?"

That would be bad. She's only about six months along. Still massively pregnant, but only six months along.

Twins and all that.

And once again, I wish I'd learned all of these things about pregnancy from Emma.

Not from my sister-in-law.

She shakes her head at Hayes. "I have to *pee*. I laughed, so I have to pee."

"Four minutes," Nikolay reports.

"I can't wait to have my bladder back."

"I can't wait to get my head back on straight," I mutter.

She grabs my hand and squeezes. "The thing about mistakes, Jonas, is that they give you the best opportunities to learn and grow and do it better. You're going to be okay. Emma's going to be okay. Actually, I think she was already okay, but that's not helpful, is it? But don't worry. We'll work this out, and everyone will be happy. You'll see."

I'm usually happy to share in her enthusiasm.

But also, I usually haven't left a woman after sleeping with her and gone radio silent while she carried, gave birth to, and raised my kid.

I thought my divorce was a disaster.

That was nothing compared to what I'm facing here.

13

From the text messages of Emma Monroe and an unknown number

Unknown Number: Hi, Emma. This is someone who once made a fool of myself running away from a chicken during a picnic lunch with you on a hillside. And also someone who acknowledges that you probably don't want to hear from me. I'd love to have the opportunity to explain myself at your convenience. But more pressing, I'd sincerely like to take care of having security cameras put on your house. Preferably today.

Emma: That's very kind of you, but I've already installed security cameras. Have a lovely day.

Unknown Number: Are there other people causing you problems?

Emma: No. Just you.

Unknown Number: So your ex…?

Emma: Tricked into marriage with a horrible prenup by the worst gossip in town, divorced, and living the life he deserves. Which I tend to not think about at all anymore unless I happen to run into him or until someone brings it up.

Unknown Number: *wincing emoji* Is there any possibility I can properly apologize and do something right?

Emma: No.

Emma: *grumpy emoji* Sorry. I dislike being rude. But we're in a very uncomfortable position and I don't want to see you.

Unknown Number: I've been properly chastised by my sister-in-law for making the assumption that I was doing you a favor by disappearing without explanation or a way for you to contact me directly. The timing wasn't intentional. I swear. I meant to be there in the morning, but someone showed up and insisted I leave, and if I hadn't, things probably would've been even worse.

Emma: We might have different definitions of "worse."

Unknown Number: I understand. If you need me, you can reach me here anytime.

14

Emma

AFTER SEVEN YEARS of gaslighting by my former fiancé, if there's anything I dislike more than mind games, I don't know what it is.

Which is why I'm charging into Bee & Nugget, Sabrina's café, after dropping Bash off with my dad for the day on Wednesday.

She's changed a few things since we were kids coming here after school, back when her grandparents ran what was then called Bean & Nugget.

Along with the slight name adjustment, now there are plexiglass beehives in a third of the picture windows. Not the windows with the view of the lake and the mountains, but the windows facing the side street and the extra window that she and Grey put in between the café and the art gallery next door. There's also a giant fiberglass and metal bee drinking coffee hung on the outside corner of the building.

All essentially gifts for Grey after he saved the café from a money problem—also my ex's fault—right around the same time I got pregnant with Bash. They serve locally-brewed kombucha from the kombrewchery that Zen runs on the other end of Main Street. The hours have expanded since we were kids too, and the café is open for dinner now, instead of closing after the lunch rush.

But it's mostly the same old mountain building with the massive stone fireplace in the middle, wooden walls hung with local art, the bakery counter full of croissants and muffins and occasionally lemon scones, and the bar along the back wall.

It also has the same staff who have been here forever working the morning shift. As soon as they spot me, they wave Sabrina out from the kitchen.

"What is this supposed to mean?" I say, shoving my phone in her face over the bar.

Sabrina lifts her brows, which perfectly match her curly copper hair, and studies the last message Jonas sent me after our short, intermittent communications over the past few days.

He'd text. I'd sit on it. I'd eventually text him back.

He'd reply nearly immediately.

Lather, rinse, repeat.

And four days later, I need help interpreting all of it.

I have him labeled in my phone now as *Random Stalker* in case I die and anyone reads my messages, but I know Sabrina knows who it is.

She looks back to the kitchen and bites her lip before turning her green eyes back to me. "Where'd you park?"

"That's an ominous question."

"We can't talk in the kitchen."

"Is he in the kitchen?"

She doesn't answer.

Instead, she trots out from behind the bar, her pregnant belly hidden today under her apron, and grabs my hand. "C'mon. We'll sit in mine. Back in a bit, Willa."

"I'll bring coffee," Willa calls back. "Decaf, of course."

Sabrina's five two on a normal day. Five six on a good day in heels. And she knows all that goes on in Snaggletooth Creek.

"Jonas is still in town, climbing the walls with regrets, which is *not* me trying to convince you to forgive him and talk to him. It's just what I was told," she says as soon as we're tucked into her small SUV. It smells faintly like dog and more strongly like honey.

"Told by who?"

"His sister-in-law."

"The pregnant woman from my backyard." You're damn right I listened in when two more strangers popped into my backyard while two dudes in suits hung out next to a black SUV in my driveway. I've also googled Jonas's family and bodyguards to make sure I was piecing things together correctly.

"She came in this morning and completely charmed Laney to pieces before either of us caught on as to who she is. Which I don't think was intentional, by the way. She spotted Jitter and thought he was Laney's dog and asked to pet him. And she had her own dog with her and he's adorable too. So it was this dog love-fest. But as soon as Laney introduced herself, she went beet red and was like, *oh, crap, this is awkward*. They're hanging out in the kitchen right now."

"Oh my god."

"Laney's a pro. She's not letting anything slip. They're comparing pregnancy notes. I put them in the kitchen because I didn't want anyone recognizing her. She's basically due the same time as Laney, but it's twins, and she has *very* distinct hair. But she was a normal person before she married into the Rutherford family, and Laney and I both get good vibes off of her. Not that I'm saying you should listen to her. Just that she passed the first test. And we're being *very* picky about letting *anyone* who so much as listens to Jonas's podcast pass *any* tests."

"Was she sent to negotiate?" I ask.

"You know it's a really good sign that they haven't said the word *lawyers* yet, right?"

Someone knocks on my window, and we both jump.

But it's Willa with two coffee tumblers.

Sabrina hits the button to roll down my window.

"The bodyguard just told me Jonas threatened to disown his parents if they get involved," she murmurs as she passes the drinks to us.

"You know?" I squeak.

"Unfortunately, because of the scuffle at the wedding, more people than we'd like have started having suspicions," Sabrina tells me while she rolls the window back up. "We keep telling them the story about Jonas wanting to do a movie about Theo's life, and the locals aren't completely buying it. But don't worry. They're keeping their mouths shut."

I sink lower in my seat. "I hate secrets."

"We know." Sabrina squeezes my arm. "But you're in good hands. No one wants a repeat of the reporters in town after Theo was unmasked."

I wasn't here for that, but I've heard stories. Theo never showed his face on his adult entertainment channel, so when my ex called him out during our wedding that wasn't, and the whole clip went viral, apparently reporters descended on Snaggletooth Creek en masse to try to get more dirt on him.

The idea of reporters showing up because Jonas Rutherford has a secret son here makes actual goosebumps break out all over my arms. "I was secretly glad when he didn't reply to any of my messages. I didn't want Bash growing up with the world knowing who he was."

"Don't worry, Em. We're not agreeing to anything with Jonas Rutherford that involves putting you or Bash in the spotlight. As for anyone who suspects the truth here, everyone knows if they're even thinking of leaking the news, I'll spill every bit of gossip I have on them in retribution."

"Off gossip, my ass," I mutter.

She grins. "They also know that if I don't, Zen will. I think they're better than I ever was."

"Someone will leak this and you won't be able to stop it. Neither will Zen."

"Which is why I think you need to talk to Jonas."

I make a face.

The back door of the SUV opens, and Laney climbs in. "Good news and bad news, Em," she says. "Good news, Begonia claims she's on our side. Bad news, Jonas is staying here and canceling everything on his calendar to be here for you and Bash until you decide what you want, and people are going to notice he's missing again. He's even canceled a few virtual podcast recordings in case you call. Against the advice of his family, according to my sources."

My head officially hurts, but not as much as my heart.

Or my heartburn.

I haven't needed Tums like this since I was pregnant.

"Also, Sabrina, don't let Begonia's dog into your kitchen again. He, erm, opened the fridge and brought us a bottle of mustard. Also, Begonia's offered to pay for cleaning the kitchen since *brought us a bottle of mustard* isn't actually the full story, nor do I think you'd believe me if I told you."

"We're gonna need that full story," Sabrina says.

"Imagine Theo was a dog and got hold of a squeeze bottle of mustard."

They share a look, and they both crack up.

I want to, but I don't have it in me.

Which they both immediately notice. "Oh, Em," Laney whispers. "I'm so sorry you're dealing with this."

"Every time I try to talk to him, I end up yelling at him and telling him to go away."

They share another look.

I know that look.

That look says *holy shit, she's lost her marbles. She doesn't yell at anyone.*

They still don't know any details about what happened between me and Jonas in Fiji. When I told them I was pregnant, I told them I met someone on my solo honeymoon, we commiserated on our similar broken hearts, slept together, and went our separate ways.

I said I'd make sure he knew I was pregnant.

And the only thing I've done differently in our friendship since was decline the Razzle Dazzle film nights we used to have.

"He ran away," I tell the still car, staring at the lid on my coffee cup. "Ultimately, he ran away. Didn't tell me he was leaving. Just left. No warning. No goodbye. And it hurt. We'd become friends...I thought. I met him when I tripped over him passed out drunk on my porch. He was lost and thought he was at his villa, but he was at mine. It was right after the news of his divorce went public, but he'd actually been divorced for a while. Secretly. Until—until it wasn't a secret anymore."

"You were both in the middle of breakups," Sabrina murmurs.

"We were. I told him to go away that first morning because it doesn't take a lot of brain cells to know that when the world's most viral runaway bride gets spotted with a newly-divorced Jonas Rutherford, the whispers and the rumors and the press get even worse. But Theo—freaking *Theo*—had put me basically on a private island. It was safe. Jonas showed me it was safe to leave my villa. He pulled me out of what was a pretty awful funk."

"I can't even imagine, and I had my own funks then," Laney says.

I try to find a commiserating smile, and I can't. So I sum up the rest instead. "We spent three days together. We snorkeled and hiked and went on boat rides and walked on the beach. We talked. And then we slept together, and it felt right and natural to take solace in this new friend that I had who was *also* in no place for a relationship, but it was like—it was like the ultimate in *I'm not alone*, you know? But I woke up the next morning, and he'd left. Just *poof*. Gone. And I had no way to reach him. I tried. I tried at least half a dozen times, and he never answered."

"Did Theo know?" Laney asks. "Before we all saw that documentary on Jonas and realized Bash was basically his clone. Because I kinda want to punch Jonas myself now."

I shake my head. "You would've known if he knew. He doesn't keep secrets from you."

They both wince, but I'm long since over all of the secrets Chandler kept from me when we were dating and engaged.

My life is so much better without him.

Until the end of Laney's wedding, I would've said my life was perfect.

"Leaving Hawaii for Fiji was brutal." I've never told them this part either. "I didn't know half the world had seen video of the wedding until I realized everyone was staring at me and whispering. Someone asked for a selfie. Some random grandma told me I was better off without him, and someone else told me I was stupid to have even been that close to marrying him, and that they didn't feel sorry for me. A lot of people implied variations on that last one, actually."

"*I need names,*" Sabrina says.

I wave a hand. "It's over. It's done. They were strangers and they didn't matter. I have Bash. I have you. *I'm good*. But I also have *zero* intention of putting myself in that spotlight ever again. But more? Like *hell* I'll subject my son to that kind of attention. Zero. Fucking. Chance."

Maybe I'm not over it.

Not if my heart is pounding this hard and fast and my mouth is tinny and dry and my stomach is rolling over on itself.

The idea of my baby boy being suffocated by camera lights and questions and judgment from strangers?

No.

No fucking way.

Laney rubs my shoulder. "So that's what you tell him, Em."

"We'll come with you if you want us to," Sabrina says. "Backup. That's all."

"We won't say a word unless you give us the signal."

"Or unless we mistake the *be quiet* signal for the *please tell him exactly what I'm thinking* signal. We should definitely go over signals."

"I'll bring a muzzle for Sabrina."

"I'll let Laney put it on me and she'll only take it off if you give her the signal."

"The right signal. The one we've agreed on beforehand."

I laugh, but it's half panic.

Laney leans forward and hugs me from behind, even though that has to be hella awkward on her baby bump. "We won't let them put Bash in the spotlight."

Sabrina leans in too. "This might be how Grey's dream of moving to an island to hide away from people finally comes true. Except we'll all be there together. I'll tell him we need an island big enough for at least twelve. And a kombucha brewery, because I'm pretty sure Zen won't leave here without that now that they've found where they fit."

I force a laugh.

My friends squeeze me tighter.

"Do you know the very worst part?" I whisper, afraid to finally say it out loud.

"Tell us," Laney says.

"He was so easy to be friends with until he was gone."

"Oh, Em, that's the worst," Sabrina says.

My eyes get hot. "I don't know how to trust it if I start to think he's my friend again."

Laney squeezes tighter. "No matter what, we'll be here."

"For whatever you need," Sabrina agrees.

I know what I need.

But there's zero chance now that I'll get it.

"I wish I hadn't told him," I confess, even though the words taste like dirt.

"You wouldn't have been able to live with yourself if you hadn't," Laney says.

She's right.

Of course she's right.

"Em?" Sabrina says softly. "You know you've got this, right?"

I start to shake my head, but then I catch sight of a clunky beaded necklace hanging from her rearview mirror.

A gift from Bash and me after art time a few months ago.

My perfect little boy.

Who needs me to be Warrior Mommy right now.

"Yeah," I hear myself say. "I do. *I've got this.*"

15

Jonas

THIS HOUSE IS TOO SMALL.

But even a thirty-thousand square-foot mansion would be too small.

I don't want to be inside. *Anywhere.* I hate being cooped up. I hate feeling helpless. I hate knowing that *this is all my fault,* and I can't make it better if I can't leave the house.

But I can't leave the house without making things worse.

"Anyone ever tell you your body will start to break down on its own once you hit forty?" Hayes says without looking up from the parenting book he's reading in the sitting room in the more-spacious-than-I-give-it-credit-for house where he's keeping me captive.

I mean that he kindly bought to give us privacy while I'm slowly working on convincing Emma that all I want is to meet my—*our* son and have an opportunity to be involved in their—*his* life.

I got the memo loud and clear, no matter how much I hate it, that I have no place in *her* life.

That opportunity evaporated when I left her without explanation in Fiji. When I thought I was doing the right thing.

Seeing her again—this isn't regret for what I did.

It's so much deeper than that.

"So?" I reply to my older brother.

"Seven workouts a day might be too much."

"I've only done three."

"It's not even ten in the morning."

"Insomnia."

"Also bad for aging. Might get extra wrinkles and need more hair dye."

"I liked you better before you met Begonia."

One corner of his mouth hitches over his book.

I keep pacing the sitting room, letting him go back to his book instead of using him as a punching bag.

Floor-to-ceiling windows overlook mountain peaks still showing the last of the winter snow, even though it's July. A deep blue sky vaults overhead. Towering pines and rolling meadows paint the smaller peaks green.

Emma said she lived somewhere beautiful.

She undersold it.

I know there are waterfalls hiding out there. Mountain streams and creeks and rivers to be rafted. Rock formations to climb. Animals to encounter.

Things to show *my son*.

And I realize *this house* is what she described.

The views. The space. The yard.

It might not be *the* house, but this is what she wanted.

Her dream.

"You ever box?" I ask Hayes, abandoning my plans to leave him alone.

He finally looks up from his book. "I'd buy another house to get away from you, but that would probably draw more attention."

"Just tell people Mom's coming." She'll want me to demand a paternity test.

Not much point when the only difference between my toddler pictures and Emma's son's pictures are that mine were all done professionally and in makeup for auditions.

Also, I've seen pictures of Emma's ex.

That kid is *not* his. I have zero reason to doubt her messages that included the line *there's no one else who could be my baby's father*.

"I can't believe I'm about to say this," Hayes mutters, more to himself than me, "but have you tried jerking off and taking a nap?"

"Jerking off doesn't put me to sleep, asshole."

Yep.

That.

That's what I say as Begonia walks through the door with Emma on her heels.

"Well. I'll file that in my mental recycling box," Begonia says brightly. "Jonas, you have a guest. Hayes, I'm craving fried ice cream and chicken salad. The curry kind like we get in Maine."

My brother drops his book on the end table and rises with as much dexterity as if he, too, works out seven times a day and didn't hit that magic forty milestone within the past couple years. "On it, my love. Let's see what Françoise needs from the store."

"I'll introduce you two later," Begonia says to Emma and Hayes. "Marshmallow, come with me. Ooh, I forgot this room has pocket doors. Aren't they cute? Emma, if you need anything, we'll be down the hall."

She doesn't wish me good luck, but she flashes me a smile as she pulls the pocket doors closed.

Begonia-expression for *good luck, I believe in you, you've got this, and we're here for you too but won't say it out loud so your guest doesn't think I'm picking sides.*

I doubt Emma thinks Begonia would take her side.

She'd be wrong.

But I'm now alone with Emma for the first time since we talked in her backyard the other morning.

No clue what I'm supposed to say, so I settle for a small, "Hi," with what I hope is a friendly smile.

She's stressed. She doesn't smile. Doesn't say *hi* back.

Just stares at me with wary brown eyes. "What do you want?"

What do you want?

It's all I've had to think about for nearly a week now. Ever since I got her messages and got confirmation that they were true, nothing else has existed.

Just the knowledge that someone who was once the friend I needed had carried and raised our child solo since the last time I saw her, and *I haven't been here.*

I hold her gaze steadily. "I would like to be a present father."

I was an idiot for telling Peyton I wanted kids three years ago.

I *did*. I *do*.

But I put her in an awful position. Fear of failing professionally was no reason to want to immediately start a family.

Finding out I *have* a family?

Instinct has taken over. I want to be here. I want to be here for my son, and I want to be a supportive co-parent for his mother.

His mother, whom I've thought of as a friend every single day since Fiji.

As *more* than a friend.

My life wouldn't be what it is today—my *career* wouldn't be what it is today—without Emma.

I owe that to her too, and I don't think she knows it.

Nor would she likely appreciate it.

She looks away from me and rubs her hands over her bare arms beneath her short-sleeve shirt while she walks around the casual blue checkered furniture to stare out at the mountains. "I want my son to have a normal life," she says. "I don't want him in the public spotlight. And I don't want to introduce him to anyone who'll leave and disappoint him if he gets attached."

I deserved that dig. "Okay."

"You *say* okay, but how much of that is wishful thinking and how much is realistically possible?"

I nod toward the closed doors behind us. "Hayes hides from the spotlight all the time. It's easier than you might think."

"We shouldn't have to *hide from the spotlight* to live a normal life. We've been living a normal life. *You didn't want us*. That was the message I got. You didn't want me in Fiji and you didn't want your son when I tried to tell you he existed. And now you're here and you say you want to be here for him, but *how do I trust you*? How do I trust you can keep him safe? Not just physically, but mentally. Emotionally. How do I know you deserve him?"

Fuck.

She doesn't.

Hell, *I* don't know if I deserve it.

If I'm being honest, I know I don't.

Not now. Not yet. "I'm here until I've earned it. However long it takes."

She looks back at me, gnawing on her lower lip, and I feel something else.

Something I don't need right now.

Zip it up, I order myself. *Box it up and put it away.*

I was undeniably attracted to Emma when I met her in Fiji. Not just as a friend, but as *more*. And for the past couple years, I've told myself it wasn't true attraction.

That it was a knee-jerk reaction to being close to a woman who understood the pain and loneliness that went along with leaving a failed relationship that you believed in to the pit of your soul.

That it was me mistaking a friend for more because my head was in a screwed-up place.

But sometime since Fiji, I've healed.

More, I've *thrived*.

Professionally *and* personally.

Watching her now—*nope nope nope*.

Not letting that part of me have any influence in this conversation.

"People will notice you're missing from your normal life," she says, "and there's only so long before people realize you're missing because you're here. Once they realize you're here, the reporters come. My friends are telling anyone who asks that the reason you showed up here was because you want to talk my brother into letting you make a movie about his life, but the minute the reporters spot my son, they'll see you, and then this easy, comfortable life he and I have is over."

"I can sell the story about making a movie about your brother if I have to, but a guy taking a sabbatical isn't flashy. There'll be other scandals and gossip that'll overshadow me."

"You're on top of the world right now. The movie. The podcast. The awards. The documentary. You walking away from it all while you're *everywhere* is more newsworthy than you quietly ducking out for a leave of absence while things aren't going well. And *no one* will believe you're making a movie about a guy who's effectively a porn star."

She's not wrong.

Since I saw her last, I've taken risks. I've had a couple duds, but then I found my stride.

Where I fit in the entertainment world outside of my family's name.

Success. Satisfaction. Fulfillment.

The movie she's talking about is an epic biopic about Charles Darwin that came out about a month ago. It's getting Oscar buzz. My podcast—covering the topic of how we all become the people we are—is at the top of every podcast chart. A documentary that I finally relented and agreed to about my transition from Razzle Dazzle formula actor to making my own mark outside the family company is also at the top of the streaming charts.

Walking away now will cause speculation about substance abuse and my mental health. The gossip sites will be happy to say that a kid spoiled from birth who's never had to work to find success has finally cracked and fallen from grace.

Making a movie about a porn star would be viewed the same way. I've found success outside of Razzle Dazzle, but that doesn't mean people wouldn't question me lifting up the adult entertainment industry.

That's the world I live in.

My family is good at squashing press, but not as good as we were before social media made speculation and rumor spread so fast.

I can handle the rumors.

But can Emma?

And why should she have to?

"We have publicists and marketing experts to help handle the messaging," I tell her, but it's to reassure myself as much as to convince her. "We also have security teams that can operate so quietly in the background that you'll barely realize they're there after a while."

"That is *not* a normal statement in my world."

"I know. And I'm sorry."

She falls silent and looks back at the mountains for another long minute, then pulls out her phone.

My pulse kicks up.

Will she show me pictures?

She hasn't even said his name in front of me.

Is she letting me in?

She scrolls the screen, mouthing to herself, and I realize she has notes.

She brought notes to talk to me.

She's nervous.

I make her nervous.

That's a punch to the gut.

Hayes makes people nervous. He glowers and grumbles and doesn't like talking to people. He's bigger and bulkier than me. Sometimes awkward. My grandma always said we'd be mistaken for twins if he didn't wear his features so harshly.

But I'm the people person. Love crowds. Love people. Love putting them at ease.

It's a gift.

And it's not working for me right now.

Emma slides a glance my way, then back to the phone. "If I say no, if I refuse to let you see him, how long until you have an army of lawyers at my door?"

Not a surprising question, but my instant, overprotective instincts that roar at the idea of her facing a room of Rutherford lawyers catch me off-guard. "If anyone in my family sends lawyers after you, I'll disown them and go public with every dirty secret I know about them. No matter which family member it is."

She blinks, and her lips form a soft *O*.

Pink.

They're a light, glossy pink.

Sleeping with her wasn't an accident. It was the most natural thing in the world to share a night of comfort when we were both raw and vulnerable from our lives flipping inside out.

And for the past two and a half years, god only knows what she's thought of me for leaving her the way I did.

She bites her lower lip again while she studies me, and *fuck*.

Not the time for my dick to notice her lips. The way her cheeks are softer than they were in Fiji. That pointed chin.

Her slender neck and sharp collarbones, but again, not as sharp as they were in Fiji.

"If you start a Harry and Meghan war with your family, I get dragged into it too," she says quietly. "I cannot be the mother my son deserves if I'm dealing with all of that publicity again."

"They won't send the lawyers. We can keep this quiet."

"How can you be sure?"

"My family has their problems, but at the end of the day, we have each other's backs. I tell them to leave the lawyers out of it, the lawyers will get left out of it."

She narrows her eyes.

I hold up my hands. "Until we need formal paperwork, and then you lead. Nothing formal unless it's what you decide you need for yourself."

I hold my breath while she studies me like she's looking for the catch. Like she thinks this is an act and she's waiting for me to break character.

"I don't want the spotlight again," she says slowly. "I don't *ever* want to relive even a fraction of the fallout of that viral video. But make no mistake. If you hurt my son, if this is a game to you, if you're lying about your intentions, if you try to take him away from me, *I'll* go public and use every resource *I* have to make you pay, and I won't regret it for a moment. No matter what else it costs me. I will do *anything* to protect my son and give him the childhood he deserves. Are we clear?"

Mama Bear has entered the conversation, and it takes me three attempts to swallow the lump of emotions clogging my throat.

And there's not a chance I'm acknowledging what the sight of the broken and wounded bride I once knew turning into a ferocious warrior is doing to my heart and other parts of my body.

"Crystal."

She looks down at her phone again, scrolling as she reads. "You can come to my brother's house on Saturday. He's having a small family cookout. You'll be introduced as a friend in town. You will *not* tell Bash that you're his father. Any security you bring with you has to be minimal, and they have to keep their distance. If you make Bash uncomfortable, you leave. If *any* of my family thinks you're making Bash uncomfortable, you leave. If you cause harm to any of my brother's cats, you leave."

Bash. The birth announcement she emailed me welcomed Sebastian Nathaniel Monroe to the world, but she calls him Bash.

I want to deserve to call him Bash.

"Okay," I agree without hesitation.

She doesn't look up from her phone. "If you have to pee, pee in the woods. You may not ask my brother any awkward questions about his adult entertainment days. If my father offers you a piece of his artwork, accept it as the gift it is. What you do with it after you leave is none of my business, but you'll act grateful in his presence."

I wonder how many of these demands are demands she thought of, and how many she had help with. "I can do that. Anything else?"

She looks up from her list and studies me again.

There's more. There's so much more she wants to say. It's hanging between us, but it's written in a language I can't read.

Yet.

"That's all for now," she finally says. "If anything changes, I'll text you."

"Thank you."

The wariness is back. "I'm doing this because it's the right thing to do, but I still don't trust you, and I know you could attempt to ruin my life if you wanted to. Please don't make me regret this."

I step toward her, and she shies back.

So I go completely still. "I've made mistakes. I've hurt you. If I could take it back, I would. But I can't. I'd explain why I left, but it still boils down to *I was wrong*. I have a solid reason why I didn't come sooner, but again…I was wrong. I'll do better, Emma. I'll be better. I promise."

She still doesn't believe me. I can see it in every little nuance of her expression.

But she's given me an in.

I'll take it.

16

Emma

INVITING Jonas to a cookout with my family was a mistake.

A massive, huge, overwhelming, *what was I thinking?* mistake.

And he's not even here yet.

"Asking the triplets to come too was too much, wasn't it?" I murmur to Laney and Sabrina over dishes while I watch seven of my very favorite people entertain Bash on the patio. Theo has the grill ready. Grey already seasoned the burgers. Zen's kombucha is chilling in a cooler.

"You invited everyone who has a direct daily impact on Bash's life," Sabrina replies. "None of this is too much."

"You wouldn't have been out of line to invite more," Laney agrees. She turns a frown at the cats playing around the kitchen. They have each other to play with, but they still insist on being where the people are. "*Fred*. Leave your sister alone. Snaggleclaw, that's Cream Puff's toy. You don't even *like* it. *Fred. Enough.*"

"We should definitely leave him alone inside for ten minutes to see how he does with the cats," Sabrina says.

"I told him he has to pee in the woods."

"Probably best for making sure none of the cats escape," Laney says while Sabrina cackles in amusement.

For all that my destination wedding in Hawaii was a disaster, a lot of good came out of it. Theo adopted a litter of stray cats who've been his and Laney's pride and joy. He even built them an addition on to his cabin and made internet stars out of them with a paid subscription site with all proceeds going to pet shelters around the nation.

Since Laney got pregnant, they've all gotten overprotective of her and won't leave her side when she's home.

It's adorable.

And it's also half the reason they're building a larger house on their many-acres lot up here. So there's room for the two of them, the cats, *and* the baby.

Grey and Sabrina met when Chandler sold the family café to Grey, who bought it with the intention of ruining it since Chandler once tried to ruin Grey's life as well. But after a contentious battle between Sabrina and Grey over what should happen to the café, now they're expecting a baby and happily in love too, and she's back to running the café that holds her heart.

I got Bash.

Sabrina's cousins, identical triplets who were groomsmen in my wedding that wasn't, are now Bash's adopted uncles. They became a bigger part of all of our lives in the aftermath of the wedding when they took my side over Chandler's.

And also when they started suspecting at my wedding that they were Laney's half brothers.

They're not—she took a DNA test and there's no chance they're half siblings. We still don't know who their father is, but now that they've ruled out the most likely suspect locally, they're low-key curious while still keeping the secret from the dad who raised them that they're not biologically his.

But the bigger point—we're all tighter now.

I didn't think twice when I texted the triplets that I needed extra backup at a family cookout where Bash would meet his father without being told that the man visiting was his father.

"Jonas will have enough to deal with outside," I say as two different cats circle and rub my legs. "No reason to feed him to the cats. This time. We'll see how the day goes."

"Still feeling okay?" Laney asks.

This was her idea, and on the surface, it's a good one. Give Jonas a small bit of what he's asking for so he keeps thinking I'm reasonable and doesn't pull in the lawyers, but do it where I feel safe and have a lot of people on my side.

But my stomach is wrecked like it hasn't been since my stint as the world's most famous runaway bride, hiding on a solo honeymoon.

Even pregnancy heartburn wasn't that bad comparatively. And it was pretty unpleasant.

"I'm great," I lie.

Theo and Zen look at us through the window at that exact moment, like they're both listening and know I'm lying.

"Dipmuh!" Bash yells. He runs across the patio, chasing a chipmunk, his diaper hanging too low under his cute little blue shorts.

Way too low.

Someone has soiled his pants.

"Not it," Decker crows, putting his finger to his nose in the universal sign for *not it* as well.

Jack and Lucky turn to each other and have a round of rock-paper-scissors, which ends in Lucky pumping a victorious fist and Jack groaning. "C'mere, little dude. Diaper change time."

And this is why Laney, Sabrina, and I are in the kitchen.

Theo cleaned the house.

My dad set up the patio with enough chairs for everyone.

Grey brought half the food, most of it already assembled. Sabrina claims he did it himself.

Zen brought the drinks. They always let us try out the new flavors they're working on. Under normal circumstances, I would've already dug into the cooler.

And the triplets are on doody patrol, as they call it.

Mostly because they nominated Jack to be their rock-paper-scissors representative to battle me for diaper duty over kitchen prep, and Jack is notoriously unlucky at rock-paper-scissors.

Outside on the patio, Jitter and Duke both lift their heads and visibly sniff. Sabrina's St. Bernard and Grey's chocolate lab are besties. Duke's a few years older and has had a calming effect on Jitter, which is good, since Jitter weighs more than Sabrina does now that he's nearly four years old.

But both dogs lifting their heads?

And sniffing *not* in Bash's direction?

I wipe my hands, and a moment later, there's a knock at the front door.

My stomach gurgles loudly enough for Laney and Sabrina to both notice.

Fred notices too. The kitty drama king takes off with a yowl like my stomach scared him.

Both of my best friends move toward the living room and the front door, but I leap in front of them. "I've got this."

They share a look, then back off. "We'll be right here if you need us," Sabrina says.

"Yell at Fred," Laney adds. "Use that as your cue word."

I cross the living room to the front door, take one more big, deep breath, check the peephole, and then I open the wooden door to a problem I can't avoid any longer.

It's annoying that this problem isn't hard on the eyes.

Jonas has gotten a fresh haircut. He shaved. His lean arm muscles are lightly defined under his casual black T-shirt with two cats and a logo I don't recognize. His broad pecs are also outlined under the shirt. He pushes aviators off his nose and up on top of his head, then he hits me with a warm smile that I would've called *friendly* back in Fiji, but which now puts me on high alert.

He's still behind the screen door, necessary both for air flow in the summer and for cat control since Theo and Laney keep the cats inside. I know that movie-star-handsome smile will only get more potent when the screen door barrier between us is gone.

I open my mouth to say hello, or to tell him to go on

around back so we don't have to worry about the cats, but before I can utter a sound, Jack comes crashing into the living room.

"Hey, Em. Don't worry. I've got the poop monster under control."

"Poo mama!" Bash cries. "Big poopoo inna dydee!"

"It's a *massive* poo," Jack says. "I think it's the biggest poo he's ever had."

"Big big poo!" Bash says.

And through it all, Jonas sucks in a breath, looking past me as Jack side-carries a laughing Bash through the living room and down the hall toward the bathroom, where there's a permanent supply of wipes, diaper cream, and Bash-sized diapers.

I try to ignore the wonder and longing on Jonas's face as he stares at the hallway.

He'd be a good dad, a small voice whispers in the back of my head.

We don't blindly trust people anymore, I fire back.

My logic gets the message.

My heart does not.

"You can go around back," I say. "I'll meet you there."

His brown eyes flick to mine, suddenly unreadable. "Thank you."

He doesn't ask who Jack is.

And I realize he probably already knows.

He probably has people who already researched us, which is likely as necessary in his world as the two muscular guys standing just outside the black SUV that clearly delivered him here.

He probably knows all about me.

"Holy patooties, Bash," Jack exclaims down the hall. "Did you eat an entire dinosaur?"

Bash laughs.

Jonas angles his head to look in their direction through the screen door.

"Out back," I repeat, and then, like a complete and total awkward fool, I shut the door in his face.

17

Jonas

WHEN EMMA SAID FAMILY COOKOUT, I expected to see her dad and her brother and her brother's new wife.

Maybe her friend Sabrina and Sabrina's boyfriend too.

I didn't expect a patio full of people staring at me like I walked out here with my underwear on my head and my butt cheeks hanging out.

Theo's at the grill. Even if I'd only known Emma's brother was *that tatted guy who once had a popular Grippa-Peen channel*, or as the guy who tried to end me for causing a scene after his wedding, I'd recognize him. He and Emma have the same eyes and mouth, though his hair is light brown and wavy instead of blond and tucked into a neat ponytail, and they have different noses and chins. He looks me square on, silently threatens to disembowel me in very creative ways, nods once, and goes back to putting burgers on to cook.

I'm guessing the guy with the salt-and-pepper hair next to him is Emma's dad. Lots of family resemblance there too.

Two dogs, one a chocolate lab about the size of Begonia's Shiloh Shepherd, the other a significantly larger St. Bernard, sniff in my direction. Grey Cartwright rises from an Adirondack chair on the edge of the patio and heads my way the same time the older man does.

Grey, who towers over everyone else on the patio, with dark hair, a short beard, and the attention of both dogs, reaches me first and extends a hand. "Jonas. Nice to meet you. Formally. I'll try to not rack you in the balls again today. Probably. You meet Mike Monroe yet?"

I turn and shake hands with Emma's dad. "Not yet. It's a pleasure, sir."

"We'll see," he replies.

Emma tumbles out of the back door of the small cabin, and I have to remind myself to breathe.

Nerves.

All nerves.

She's the person I have to impress if I want to have a part in my—*our* son's life.

She's also the accidental friend that I didn't even know I needed when I passed out drunk on her porch in Fiji, thinking it was my own.

Today, she's in a long multicolored sundress with bare feet. She has minimal makeup on. Just enough to make her big brown eyes pop and her lips turn that soft, sparkly pink.

Her cheeks aren't as sharp as they were in Fiji, though her ears are still a little too big for her head, which is absolutely adorable.

She stumbles, and I realize she's not tumbling out alone.

Two women—easily identifiable as her best friends, Delaney and Sabrina—follow too quickly on her heels.

Both women are pregnant. Both are also forces of nature in their own ways, according to the report Hayes's security detail insisted I read before coming out here today.

"The cats wanted to come out," Emma says. The nerves in her voice make me want to hug her, but I know I lost that privilege when I left Fiji without a goodbye.

"We had to corral Fred and Panini, and then Widget tried to prove he could fly," Laney adds.

Sabrina doesn't say anything.

Hayes's security team told me not to say anything in front of her.

They also told me to read the *full* report on *everyone* in Emma's life, and I'm glad I did, since there are still at least four other people here.

Aside from Bash.

Who is *not* back out from his diaper change.

"Anyway, welcome." Emma's twisting her fingers in her dress and talking fast. Definitely nervous. "Are you thirsty? Zen brought Snaggletooth Creek-brewed kombucha. I didn't think I'd ever like kombucha, but theirs is the best."

"I drank it all," one of the Sullivan triplets lingering at the edge of the patio says. His shirt suggests he's Lucky, but the haircut says he's Decker. "Sorry, Em."

"You did not," his brother says. Haircut says Lucky. Shirt style, though, implies Jack.

I think I'm being tested. Or else the report was wrong.

Most likely, I'm being tested.

I'd be amused if my heart wasn't about to pound out of my chest.

Seeing Bash through the screen door on his way to having an honorary uncle change his diaper has me realizing what's at stake here.

I have to fit in to this family that Emma's built for herself if I want to have any role in my son's life.

If I want to have any role in *her* life.

"We have water and beer and fruit juice too." Emma's wiping her hands on her sun dress now, swaying back and forth.

She's flustered.

And I know I'm not the only one who's noticing.

This shouldn't be so hard.

We were friends.

But I have a lot of work to do if I want to be friends again. "I'm good for now. Thank you."

The back door doesn't open.

Bash doesn't come running out to meet me.

Not that I expect him to. *Want* him to, but don't expect him to.

"Whenever you change your mind, the cooler's full." She points to a red cooler next to the back door, smacking Sabrina in the chest in the process.

Delaney Kingston—no, that would be Delaney *Monroe* now, according to Begonia, who says Delaney told her herself that she took Theo's last name—steps forward like she's covering Sabrina's *oof* and Emma's horrified look at herself.

"Hi. I'm Laney. Welcome." She steers me away from where the two other women are whispering *sorry*s and *I'm* *okay*s, and points at various people and things instead. "Theo and I are in disagreement over how happy we are to have you here, but I think we'll weather this argument just fine. Hopefully you do too. Bathrooms are inside, though feel free to use the trees as long as you're out of sight. I understand that might've been one of your orders. But if you do go inside, please don't let the cats out. Also, they know how to open the bathroom door, and they don't really have any boundaries about where they like to go or what they think is a toy."

Sabrina coughs.

Emma sighs.

"This is Sabrina," Laney adds, gesturing from a safe distance to the gossip of the group. She's the shortest of the bunch, with red curly hair and bright green eyes and skin white enough that I don't know if she never goes outside or if she has excellent sunscreen.

Laney points to the largest of the men in the group next, then ticks off the people one by one. "I know you, ah, met Grey at my wedding, but this is the rest of him. Mike Monroe, Theo and Emma's dad. Zen—they're one of our favorite people, and I think they've pulled more overnight shifts with Em and the baby than the rest of us. Not to mention the craving patrol services when she was pregnant. And then we have the triplets. This is Jack and—"

She stares at the first of the two triplets out here, a comical look crossing her face.

Both of the triplets stare back straight-faced.

"Lucky," Zen, who's nearly as tall as me, slender, with short blond hair and an eyebrow ring, finishes for her. "Jack and Lucky."

"Jack and Lucky," I repeat. "Nice to meet you. All of you."

Emma's lips go flat as she slides them a look.

I'm definitely being tested.

And Emma looks like she's currently wishing I'd declined this invitation. It's like the first day I met her in Fiji. She's nervous. Uncomfortable.

Makes me want to hug her again, but she's already hugging herself, and everyone here has more of a right to comfort her than I do.

I should've made an effort to stay in touch.

This is on me.

"You grill?" Theo asks me.

One test on top of the other. Exactly what I deserve. "No, but I've always wanted to learn."

"You've never grilled?" Lucky says. The *real* Lucky, if the haircut is to be believed.

"That surprises you?" Zen replies.

I don't hear Lucky's answer.

The back door has opened, and a tiny human with light brown hair, brown eyes, a solid chunk of a body, and legs that apparently have one speed—*fast*—dashes out onto the patio. "Mama! Mama titty!"

Emma squats and catches him as he throws himself at her.

My heart tries to throw itself at both of them while my body has an instinctive need to leap to her side and make sure he doesn't bowl her over.

But she absorbs the impact like she does this a million times a day.

Which she probably does.

While I haven't been here.

"Oh, did you pet the kitty?" she asks, a real smile curving her pink lips for the first time since I knocked on the front door.

"It dick me, mama!"

"It licked you?"

"Uh-huh. Unka Deo! Titty dick me!"

"Did you lick the kitty back?" Theo asks.

"Yep!" Bash sticks his tongue out and mimics licking.

Emma shoots Theo a look.

Theo grins and goes back to putting hamburgers on the grill.

And I look back at a little boy who's staring at me with my own eyes.

The word *hi* dies in my throat, right under that rock of surprise and joy and fear and adoration and discomfort that's making it hard to swallow.

Again.

"Mama, who dat?" he says.

"That's Mama's friend, Jonas," Emma replies, still down on his level, one hand tucked around his belly while he leans against her.

This is who she was meant to be.

Not the lost, hurt bride I found in Fiji.

Not the warrior princess I found in her backyard, who appeared again when she tracked me down to lay out the terms under which I could meet my son.

She's meant to be happy. With a big family. Siblings— biological and found—and kids and joy in the little things.

She glows here.

A ghost of a smile still hovers on her lips, but her eyes —those eyes are on full alert.

And they shouldn't have to be.

I open my mouth.

Try to say *hi* again.

Fail.

Miserably.

Is that the first thing I want to say to my son? *Hi*?

Not that I'll be telling him he's my son today. Emma's instructions were clear, and I'd prefer to find a way into their lives that doesn't involve the lawyers.

No matter how much that'll give my own mother indigestion and a heart attack and probably an aneurysm too.

Bash pulls away from Emma. "I go pway side!" He takes off for a swing set between the edge of the patio and the forest behind the house, and Zen and Lucky—I *think* that's Lucky—close ranks to follow him.

The back door slams again. "Oh. You're here. Hi. I'm—"

"Decker," the real Decker answers for him. I read that report right, didn't I?

"Decker," the real Jack echoes.

"Would you three knock it off?" Emma whispers.

"No," two of them reply together.

A large spatula slaps my chest.

"Time to learn, Hollywood," Theo says.

It is.

But not how to grill.

I need to learn how to be a father.

18

Emma

I HAVE NEVER, ever, ever felt more awkward in my entire life.

Ever.

And yes, that includes the hours that I spent having total strangers stare and whisper at me when I didn't realize everyone on the planet with a smart phone or internet connection had seen me jilt my groom when I was supposed to be saying my wedding vows.

"This was a bad idea," I whisper to Laney and Sabrina when we duck inside to grab the rest of the food. Theo's holding Jonas captive at the grill. Bash is under the watchful eyes of Zen and the triplets at the swing set. Grey and my dad have re-started their ridiculous conversation about if it's possible to taxidermy a bee, which is what they always do when they want to make people uncomfortable.

They did it the first time Chandler tried to talk to me in public after our breakup.

That was funny.

This is possibly not.

"This was the best idea," Sabrina replies.

"The triplets might've been overkill," Laney says, "but even though I know you could've handled introducing Bash to Jonas all on your own, I'm glad we're able to be here for you."

Sabrina snorts. "I would've found a way to spy no matter what, so I'm glad you invited us."

I hug them both. "I don't think I could do this without you."

"Yes, you could," Laney says.

But Sabrina makes a face.

A *bad* face.

You wouldn't know it was a bad face if you didn't know her as well as I do, but I know that face.

She knows something.

"What?" I say.

"I want you to know this is one of those things that I'd prefer to not tell you, but I don't do that anymore, so please remember I'm telling you this despite knowing it's going to make today worse."

I swallow. "Maybe we can scrap that *no secrets* rule for today?"

Laney grips my hand. "We've got your back, whatever it is. You can handle it."

"You know I'm supposed to be taking care of *you two* right now, right?" I ask. "I'm ruining your first pregnancy glows and stealing the attention you should be getting. That's not fair."

"Pregnancy sucks with a side of barf. You can have it." Sabrina winces. "Dammit. I didn't mean specifically that *you* can have it. But now I'm thinking about you being pregnant again, and I need to—you know what? Please tell my brain to stop going down rabbit holes and my mouth to stop spitting them out."

"Just tell us what you know," Laney replies.

"He likes you," Sabrina whispers.

It takes a full minute to register who *he* is and who *you* is, even though it shouldn't.

Probably denial.

Full-up, willful denial.

"He does *not*." My whispered retort is at a decibel level that should only be audible to dogs. I'm honestly surprised Jitter and Duke aren't howling outside right now.

"I know he's an actor and he can fake things, but Em, I have *never* seen that look on his face before in all of the Razzle Dazzle movies I've watched. *He likes you*. And he was trying to hide it and *he couldn't*."

"He just wants to know Bash."

She *harumph*s. "He was watching you like you were a seven-course meal at the fanciest restaurant he's ever eaten at. *Before* Bash came out. *After* Bash came out, he stared at you like you're a superhero, which he damn well better, because you fucking *are*."

"Are you sick?" I put a hand to her forehead. "Hallucinating? Do I need to call Grey?"

"When the least romantic of the three of us says body language is betraying a man, I'd listen," Laney murmurs.

Sabrina rubs her belly. It seems bigger today than it was yesterday. "I *told* you I didn't want to tell you. And I wouldn't have told you if I didn't have at least ninety percent certainty about it. And if I didn't think you needed to know *all* of what you could be facing here."

She's right.

I know she's right.

But the worst part? *I felt it too.* Not just today either.

Difference is, when it's just me, I can convince myself he's acting for the sake of getting to know Bash.

If Sabrina sees it?

Screw this. I do *not* need Jonas Rutherford in my life. I'm *only* doing this because I think it's the right thing to do. For Bash first, and then for Jonas. "We need to get the food and get back outside."

Sabrina hugs me, and since she's given up heels for the duration of her pregnancy, her head rests between my boobs. "You can do this, Em. And we're here for whatever help you want along the way."

Laney wraps her arms around both of us. "Always."

We gather the food and head back outside, my brain a jumbled mess in a way it hasn't been since right before I met Jonas the first time.

I shoot a look at the grill as I hear Theo ask, "So, you pay your taxes?"

Oh my god, he did not.

Sabrina makes a strangled noise.

Laney sighs her peaceful resignation sigh.

She and Theo *hated* each other until I accidentally set them up during my destination wedding week. Actually, *hate* might not be strong enough of a word.

But they did, which means she knows better than anyone else what she's getting with my brother.

And Jonas?

He actually cracks a grin. "I pay all of my taxes," he assures Theo. "In every state. Few countries too, depending on the year and what I've been up to and where."

My shoulders drop.

"He's telling the truth," Sabrina says.

"Already has a leg up on the last guy you were this seriously involved with," Laney adds.

"We are *not*—" I start, but then I hear Bash squeal on the swing, where Jack—yes, *Jack*, despite the triplets telling Jonas wrong names for themselves—is pushing my little boy too high.

Jonas and I *are* involved.

We share a kid.

And it *is* a relief to know my baby won't one day find out that his father had to go to prison for tax evasion.

Which is likely what would've happened to the kids I would've had with Chandler if I hadn't jilted him at our wedding.

I eye Laney. "Theo keeps rubbing off on you."

She laughs, then rubs her belly. "In so many ways."

"*Ew*."

"Emma's an accountant," Theo says. "She doesn't fuck around with guys who don't pay their taxes."

"Good reason to dump a guy at the altar," Jonas replies. "These ready to be flipped?"

Dad eyes me.

He sees it too. Much as I love him, he's not a very observant man. So if he sees it too—*dammit*.

I'll just have to *not* like Jonas back.

Easy answer.

Especially when I remind myself how he left in Fiji.

"Do you know what I hate?" I whisper to Sabrina and Laney.

"Not nearly as many things and people as you should?" Sabrina quips back.

Bah. Hating people and things takes too much energy that I'd rather put to good use raising my son. "I hate that I think *I understand* why he did what he did."

"He still owes you," Laney says.

"*So* much," Sabrina agrees.

I nod. "So much. I didn't say I forgive him. I didn't say I like him. I didn't say he gets to be part of my life any more than I decide is necessary for Bash's sake. I just said I *understand*."

My two best friends eye me, then look back at Jonas.

"My standards are *much* higher now," I tell them.

Sabrina slings an arm around my waist. "For your sake, Em, I'm holding you to that."

19

Jonas

I'VE NEVER in my life wanted to crawl out of my skin the way I do today.

My son is mere feet from me.

I've had a full inquisition from Emma's brother.

I've learned how to grill an elk burger and how to tell when it's done.

I've watched other people be the parent figures that I'm supposed to be for what feels like seven centuries, even though it's probably no more than twenty or thirty minutes.

And Emma's either avoiding me or has at least one of her best friends at her side every single second.

But it's time to dig into the food, and I'm calculating every angle I need to work in order to sit next to Emma and Bash.

First stop? The cooler. "Emma, want me to grab you something?" I ask.

"Oh, no, I'll—"

"Surprise her," Sabrina interrupts her with what sounds like an order.

Yes, an *order*.

That tone isn't an accident.

I flip open the cooler and find Toothy Bee kombucha sitting on top.

Zen. Kombucha. Local.

I grab a can of raspberry and flip it around.

Brewed in Snaggletooth Creek, Colorado.

"You make this?" I ask Zen.

They arch a brow at me, then give a single nod.

I smile. "My cousin Keisha and her wife love it."

"I know. I've seen their socials."

"You know Jonas's cousin?" Grey asks them.

"Not yet, but when we're ready to expand, I will."

"If you want—" I start but stop at their eye roll the size of a mountain.

"I'll stay out of it unless you ask me for an introduction," I amend.

"Please do," Zen says. "I prefer pop stars love me for me and our kombucha, not for my connections."

"Understood." In theory. In actuality, I don't know if they're the type to bite off their nose to spite their face—if this is a subtle *you don't belong here, so I don't even want your connections*—or if they're the type to take pride in doing it all themselves.

Not a mystery for today though.

Emma's fixing Bash a plate. Watermelon, burger without a bun, carrot sticks, and baked beans.

"Little guy need anything too?" I ask her.

"Already got his juice," one of the triplets says behind me.

Emma flashes me a fake smile. "Thank you."

"Can I get your plate?" I ask.

"I've got it," Laney says.

They're brutal.

No, Jonas, we do not need you in Emma's or Bash's life. We've been taking care of them just fine for years, and we'll continue to do so. You're superfluous.

I reluctantly like it. Mostly because I don't think they're doing this for my benefit.

I think they do this for each other all the time.

One of the triplets tossed beers to his brothers and Theo already. Theo grabbed a corn cob, disappeared inside, and came back out with a pile of corn on a plate, the cob gone, and handed it to his dad. Zen's passing plates behind them to Sabrina and Grey, who are waiting in line too.

I'll be last to get lunch.

So I grab a raspberry kombucha for me and a lemon kombucha for Emma, taking my time digging around so that I can trail her to her seat.

She takes one of the Adirondack chairs and balances Bash's plate on her knees.

Both of the dogs lift their heads and sniff.

"Don't even think about it, or I'll let Fred out," she tells them.

Jitter whimpers and puts his massive head down between his paws.

Duke snorts, then also turns away.

"Who's Fred?" I ask as I take the seat beside her

and put her drink in the cupholder built into her chair.

"Fed a bad titty," Bash says.

"He's not a *bad* kitty. He's an *adventurous* kitty who thinks he's as big as a mountain lion and doesn't know boundaries."

Bash eyes her. "Dat a big wood."

"I know. *Adventurous* is a *very* big word."

"Aduwus."

"*Adventurous*. Good job."

"Booties."

"Boundaries?"

Bash grins and shoves a spoonful of beans into his own mouth with a Bash-sized orange plastic spoon, smearing bean juice at the edge of his lips. "Booties."

He's so cute it's making my heart cramp.

My stomach too.

One of the triplets—pretty sure haircut says Decker—deposits an end table next to Emma's seat.

He eyes me but doesn't say a word.

To me, anyway.

"Look at this, little bro. Table built for you. Wanna let your mama eat?"

Bash looks up at him. "Decka go 'way. I eat wif Mama."

"You can eat with Mama with your plate on the table," Emma says. "And be nice to Decker. He fixed the slide for you."

Bash eyes me.

I hold my hands up. "Can't help you, bud. I do what my mommy says too."

Decker coughs like he knows my mother doesn't yet

know that I'm off in the Colorado mountains meeting my son.

Everyone would know if my mother knew.

And by *everyone*, I mean my father. Keisha and her wife. Other relatives.

Not the general public.

But the people who matter and who'd want to be here to meet Bash too.

"My mama eat," Bash says to me.

"We should all eat," I agree.

Is that what I'm supposed to say to a kid?

Legit don't know.

Other than Begonia's sister's kids, or at appearances where it's easy to ask what's on their shirts or what their favorite color is or if they had fun doing whatever we were doing at charity or promo events, I don't have a lot of experience with kids.

This is one of those times I'd ask my mom for guidance, except I'm not talking to her right now.

She's fantastic ninety percent of the time and an overprotective bear who forgets those *boundaries* Emma was talking about the other ten percent of the time.

Ask Begonia.

Or don't.

She'd laugh too hard right now, and she sincerely hates laughing when she's pregnant. Makes her have to dash to the bathroom.

"Do you take good care of your mama?" I ask Bash.

Shit. Is that an appropriate question?

I don't know.

But he looks at Emma and grins with a mischievousness that suggests this kid is learning more from his Uncle

Theo than Emma might like. "My mama well at dick-dicks."

"Mama only yells at the chickens when they get out of their pen and try to run into the woods." Emma puts Bash's plate back on the side table as Decker pulls a juice carton from his back pocket and sets it next to the plate.

Bash leaps on the juice like it's oxygen, then dives into his plate, apparently forgetting he wanted to eat off of Emma's lap.

Laney hands Emma a plate, and they both look at me.

"Hungry?" Emma asks.

"I'm...not," I admit.

Emma looks at Bash, then down at her own plate, which holds a hamburger bun without the hamburger, a banana that I didn't see on the food line, plus plain noodles that I didn't notice on the food line.

That looks like what Begonia's sister fed her kids when they were recovering from a stomach bug.

Is Emma's stomach upset today too?

She nods. "Understandable."

I hate that I make her nervous. "How long have you had chickens?"

"About a year. Bash's daycare center got eggs for their oldest preschool class, then asked if anyone wanted the chicks. He *loved* them, and I'd been thinking about it anyway, so Dad and Theo helped me build the coop and now here we are with almost a dozen."

"Does that count the one inside?"

"Yes."

"You can look at my tax returns. I do pay my taxes."

She laughs.

Actually laughs.

And the smallest bit of tension leaves my shoulders.

"Thank you," she says.

"How long are the triplets going to pretend to be each other?"

"How do you know they're pretending to be each other?"

"Good guess."

She slides me a look.

I smile. Can't help it. "Your brother didn't run a full background investigation on me?"

"Actually, that was Grey's grandmother," Sabrina says as she lowers herself into the chair on my other side. "You're lucky she's not here today, or this would be even more uncomfortable for you. Why aren't you eating?"

"You make me nervous."

"Good. I accept that answer. Carry on. Pretend I'm not here."

"Is she always so blatant?" I ask Emma.

Emma smiles past me at her friend. "No. Most strangers have no idea how much she knows about them until it's too late."

"It's already too late, isn't it?" I murmur.

There goes the wariness again. "Most likely. I'll save your seat if you want to get food."

"I will too," Sabrina says. "I'm here for the entertainment, and I have questions about what Razzle Dazzle was thinking with redoing *That Last Summer*. Your version was fine. The new version gave me worse morning sickness."

"My version was *outstanding*," I correct.

"Passable."

Emma offers me her banana. "Here. Your stomach problems are about to get worse. This'll settle better."

"Mama? My babana?" Bash asks.

He's so fucking perfect. And absolutely irresistible. "Here you go, champ." I pass him the banana. "All yours."

I am.

I'm all his.

No matter what happens today, I'm all his.

20

Emma

BY THE TIME Bash is done eating, I'm feeling far less awkward.

Jonas keeps up a steady stream of questions that slowly put me at ease. The chickens. If there's good pho anywhere in town. How much Bash can eat. When Laney and Sabrina and I met.

He doesn't get the full story on any of his questions, and some of my friends are definitely exaggerating.

"*Ugly?*" he says to Theo. "You called them *ugly?*"

Not that part. That part is true and not exaggerated at all.

"You didn't know them when we were eight," my brother replies.

"Don't make me put Fred in the bed tonight," Laney says.

Bash has moved back to the swing set. If he hadn't, he'd be telling all of us that ugly isn't nice.

My dad's keeping an eye on him, along with Decker, who's undoubtedly absorbing all of this for his next novel.

It hasn't escaped my notice that Jonas hasn't offered to watch him. Out of respect for my boundaries? Because he doesn't *like* him? For some other reason I can't fathom?

I don't know.

I do know he keeps glancing over that way though.

Like he *wants* to be closer to Bash, but doesn't want to make one of us—me? Bash? My family?—uncomfortable by butting in.

Or maybe he's never been around kids before and doesn't know how to make friends with them.

The Jonas I thought I knew in Fiji would've bent over backwards to make sure everyone around him was comfortable. Being *normal* while understanding no one else around him thought he was normal.

Maybe he's letting all of us get used to him being here as much as he's getting used to all of us being around.

"I was ugly when I was eight too," Theo says.

"You stayed ugly until you were thirty," Sabrina replies to a round of laughter.

"Laney decided we'd be the *ugly heiress society*," I tell Jonas. "Since we all technically stood to inherit local businesses. It sort of fit."

Laney's eyes twinkle. "We *owned* that bullshit."

"And we had a clubhouse," Sabrina adds.

"Do you still?" he asks.

"We don't know you well enough to answer that question yet."

I shoot Sabrina a look—that was borderline rude—but she merely smiles back.

"Our original clubhouse is gone," I tell him. "Rightfully so. I'd have a heart attack if I thought Bash was in that treehouse in the condition it was in when we found it."

"We survived," Sabrina says. "And Laney wouldn't have let us go in it if she'd thought it was truly unsafe."

"Accurate," Laney agrees.

"Bash doesn't have a Laney yet. And he won't *be* the Laney of his group."

There's no arguing with that.

Especially as Decker's voice drifts over to us. "*Sit* to go down the slide, Bash."

"I a piwate! Piwate no sit!" Bash yells back.

Jonas's lips curve up and his entire face goes soft as he glances at them.

My stomach, meanwhile, drops to somewhere far, far beneath the mountain we're sitting on.

"Pirates sit if they want to have ice cream," Decker says.

Bash stares him down.

Decker stares right back.

I'm about to get up and intervene—Mama always gets to be the bad guy—when Bash plops down onto his butt. "Eye keem!" he yells.

"Pirate sword fight first?" Decker asks.

Bash tumbles off the bottom of the slide, rights himself, and eyes his honorary uncle. "Eye keem."

"Okay, okay, go ask your mama if you can have ice cream."

"Mama, eye keem!" Bash yells as his little legs pump at a thousand miles an hour, headed my way.

His hair sticks to his sweaty forehead. His smooth white baby cheeks are tinged with pink. And his diaper is sagging again under his shorts.

It's *nap time* more than it's *ice cream time*.

"Wash your hands first," I tell him.

He changes direction and charges to Zen. "Hewp wa han?"

"Why am I always your hand washer helper?" Zen asks.

"Wa han?" Bash repeats, waving his hands in their face.

"Are they exceptionally good at washing hands?" Jonas asks me while Zen relents, tosses Bash over their shoulder, and marches into the house.

"They've historically been around the most, and they're way more fun than I am."

"Unfortunate side effect of being the default parent," Sabrina adds. "It's gonna suck for Grey when I'm the fun one."

"Theo too," Laney deadpans.

"Quit mocking Theo while I'm not outside to enjoy it," Zen calls through the kitchen window while the rest of us laugh.

Theo's totally unfazed, as usual. He looks at Jonas. "You ever go camping?"

"And not on a movie set," Grey says.

Jonas shakes his head. "Not recently."

I wonder what he defines as *recently*. One *could* call passing out on a stranger's porch *camping*.

But that was two and a half years ago.

Theo doesn't break his concentration on Jonas. "We should go."

"Am I invited?" Grey asks.

"Naturally."

"The triplets?"

"We're sitting this one out," Jack says.

"Plausible deniability," Lucky agrees.

Decker claims Zen's open seat. "Can I watch from a distance?"

Jonas isn't breaking eye contact with Theo either. "Sure," he says. "Let's go camping."

"Has to be soon," Grey says. "I'm not leaving Sabrina's side once she hits her third trimester."

"Next week," Theo agrees.

I open my mouth, and it's like all three of them hear the motion. They all turn and look at me.

And all three of them are silently telling me to stay out of it.

Like *my son* isn't the reason they're doing this.

"Name a date," Jonas says. "I'll clear my calendar."

The back door opens, and Bash barrels out.

But instead of running straight to me, he runs to Jonas.

I freeze.

Jonas inhales an audible breath. "Hey, bud. What's up?"

Bash points to Jonas's shirt. "Dat titty wike Fwed."

Jonas looks down at his T-shirt. "You think?"

Bash nods. "You have titty?"

"No kitties. But I have a friend with a dog."

"Wike Ditta?"

Jonas nods. His fingers twitch like he wants to hug Bash, but he keeps still otherwise, arms resting on the armrests. "Like Jitter. Little smaller. He can do tricks, like opening the refrigerator."

Bash frowns.

Pretty sure that one didn't compute.

But what immediately computes for me is the look overtaking the frown.

I know that look.

I know that look *entirely* too well.

"Ba—" I start, and that's as far as I get before the inevitable happens.

Bash opens his mouth as he looks up at Jonas again, but words don't come out.

Something far, *far* worse comes out.

The beans.

How many beans did he eat? And how high was he going on the swing?

Oh my god.

Is that just *today's* beans, or has he been sneaking beans and saving them for this?

It's not stopping.

It's not stopping.

And I'm frozen.

Completely, totally, shocked, horrified frozen.

Just how fast can Jonas run while he's coated in toddler puke?

Dead silence falls on the patio aside from Bash making a low rumbly noise as he stares at what he's just finished doing.

I can tell you what every last one of my friends and family are thinking right now.

Dad: *serves the fucker right for knocking up and abandoning my daughter.*

Theo: *I wonder if I can make it look like an accident if I make Jonas eat it.*

Laney: *The fastest way to clean this mess is to throw Jonas in the shower, and Bash probably needs something for his stomach. Can toddlers have Pepto?*

Sabrina: *Oh my god, my favorite nephew just puked on my favorite movie star and I need to record every second of this in my brain forever in case I ever need to use it against the fucker who took two years to show up for his child.*

Zen: *Glad he waited that extra forty seconds.*

Decker: *Mental note, puking kids are good novel fodder.*

Jack: *How did the logistics work so that he got puke all the way up to Jonas's face? That's some physics-defying stuff. Cool.*

Lucky: *I'm off my normal nurse duties today, but for Bash and Emma, I'll give my favorite little guy a once-over and make sure he's not coming down with something.*

Bash: *Uh-oh.*

But the one person whose thought process I can't read? Jonas's.

His nose twitches. His lips too.

He doesn't look down at his shirt. Or his pants. Or his shoes.

Holy *crap*, those look like expensive shoes. I hadn't noticed his shoes until they were coated with my son's vomit.

He leans forward, closer to Bash, and puts his hands to Bash's sides. "How's your tummy, little guy? You okay? That looked like it hurt."

Fuck. Me.

He couldn't have had a more perfect and simultaneously worse reaction if he'd rehearsed it a million times.

"I'm so sorry," I gasp.

"No, she's not," Sabrina says.

Laney snorts. "Take it back, Emma. You're not sorry."

"Okay. Okay." I nod. Shake my head. Nod again. *Shit.* "I am trying very hard to not be sorry."

Bash sticks a finger in his mouth—yes, the mouth of destruction—and eyes Jonas with those big brown eyes that could talk me into nearly anything. "Eye keem?"

Jonas snorts, a smile lighting up his face.

He's sitting there covered in toddler puke and *he's smiling.*

Oh, god.

This is *not* good.

Not good at all. Not for Bash. Not for me. Not for our future.

"Made some room for it, didn't you?" Jonas asks him.

I leap out of my seat while Bash nods.

Too much. This is too much. "C'mon, Bash. Let's get cleaned up."

And then I'll talk him into the nap he needs but won't want to take.

And I'll insist I have to nap with him too.

Anything to avoid looking at Jonas any more than necessary.

"Thank you," I stutter as I grab Bash's hand. "You make a very good target. I should've told you to bring clean clothes. I always bring clean clothes."

He holds my gaze for a moment that lasts a lifetime.

"I'll be okay," is all he says.

Out loud.

The quiet part though?

He's my son too. I can be a good parent. I'll do the work. This doesn't faze me. I can handle anything. I want to handle anything.

That's the part that scares me.

"You need any help?" he adds.

Lucky appears at my side. "I'm on it. You should go hose yourself off. Bash, wanna hear your heartbeat?"

I wave a floppy hand at Jonas. "You…just take care of you. Thank you."

Not thank you.

He's not going anywhere.

And I don't know how I feel about that.

21

Jonas

DUSK IS APPROACHING as I walk around Emma's house to meet her at the chicken coop a few hours after her family cookout. I wasn't sure she'd let me come over, but she agreed to see me once Bash was in bed.

I spot her before she sees me. She's bent over, petting the tall, skinny, white chicken with the funny, light feathers and a chicken diaper on her butt. I can't tell if the bird's eyes are under the head feathers or mixed in with them, but it can clearly see, and it wants inside the pen.

"Silly girl," Emma says. "You just ate inside."

Eight or ten thick brown and red chickens with normal feathers, normal heads, and no diapers peck the ground inside the coop area. I think I spot watermelon rind. Definitely chicken feed pellets.

Emma's dress is gone, replaced with baggy black sweatpants that hang low on her hips when she stands.

Her pink crop top cuts off just above her belly button, and her small breasts sway freely underneath.

"Do the chickens get treats every night?" I ask.

"Every single night," she confirms.

She straightens and looks at me, and every nerve that's been bouncing off the walls since I took the hint that the cookout was over settles.

"How's the little guy feeling?" I ask.

"Feverish but bullheaded," she replies. There's still caution in her voice, but it's noticeably less than it was a few days ago. "He threw up three more times after we got home, but he's pretty well-trained with a bucket."

"Did I cook the burgers wrong?"

She shakes her head. "Stomach bug is going around daycare."

I had no idea something as tiny as a kid who barely stands above my knee could terrify me in so many ways.

It's a massive relief to know I didn't accidentally give him food poisoning.

I tilt my head toward the porch swing.

She nods.

We sit. I fold my hands in my lap despite wanting to drape one over the back of the swing.

She folds her hands in her lap too and pushes with one foot, making the swing sway the tiniest amount.

"Lot more comfortable to sit on than sleep on," I comment.

"I'd assume so."

"Slept on worse though."

"I'd question that, but in the number of nights I've known you, you've spent a high percentage of them not in a bed."

I smile.

She does too, though it's a nervous smile.

"You've been puked on before," she says.

"First time I met Begonia's sister and her kids. Two of the three got me. Hayes still pulls out pictures of the carnage if I get too full of myself. By his standards. Which are stupidly high."

"How high are we talking?"

"Sometimes I *breathe* too full of myself for him."

"He sounds like a good brother."

"He is."

"I like standards that high."

"Good."

I can feel her watching me, but my eyes are on her white chicken. It's hopping over on its single leg, and I think my loafers might be in danger.

Nothing compared to my heart though.

"Bash is—" I swallow. Perfect? Hilarious? Adorable? Everything I ever hoped my kid would be at his age?

"He is," she agrees softly.

Like I don't have to finish.

She just knows he's beyond normal human English words.

"Yolko Ono, do *not* peck that," she orders.

The chicken clucks at her, and my shoe lives to see another minute.

This shoe.

My other shoes are dead and buried. The clothes too. No regrets.

"Thank you for your patience with him today," Emma adds.

"I was the stranger. He had a lot of people he knew better."

"They're all family to him."

"Nice that he knows the triplets apart enough to call them on their pretend-to-be-each-other game."

She squeezes her eyes shut and suppresses a smile.

"Lucky kid," I muse. "He knows he's loved."

"He's very loved. He—thank you."

I lift a brow at her.

"He's the very best thing in my life, and I wouldn't have him without you, so…thank you. I haven't said that yet."

"My contribution was, ah, small."

"But critical."

"You don't have to thank me."

"Yes, I do. *Yolko Ono*, I said *no*."

"Bad dick-dick," a small voice drifts down from an open window of the house.

"Sing 'America's Sweetheart,' Bash," Emma says softly, jolting me back in time a few years as I realize she's talking about an old Bro Code song that I haven't heard in forever.

There's a long pause, but then he does as told.

With the words all wrong. The melody very off. Pitch off too.

Pretty horribly, actually.

Even for a kid young enough that you'd expect him to be off-key and off-melody.

And it's the cutest fucking thing I've ever heard in my entire life.

The song fades to a stop about halfway through.

But the soft smile on Emma's face lingers longer while she stares up at his window.

Birds chirp. Chickens cluck. Something rustles in the forest behind us, the breeze almost chilly against my skin as deeper shadows fall across the yard.

Emma keeps gently pushing the swing.

Her one-legged chicken keeps hopping toward my shoe.

"Mama, nigh-nigh," a little voice whispers.

"Night-night, Bash," she replies softly.

I've set foot on all seven continents. Starred in movies my whole life. Gotten critical acclaim for my more recent projects. Met the world's objectively most beautiful people. Eaten at the best restaurants money can buy. Stayed in the plushest resorts on the planet.

And all of those places have never given me the kind of peace I feel here.

The kind of peace I feel when I'm just *me*, hanging out with Hayes and Begonia or Keisha and Millie and simply *being* part of a family with no expectations and a safety that comes with knowing they'd forgive any of your fuck-ups.

Even with the overwhelming longing to be a bigger part of my son's life. To be a part of Emma's life.

To fit in as one of the family she introduced me to today.

To have my friend back.

I still have that peace despite everything that's up in the air.

"You changed my life," I tell her. "I haven't thanked you for that either."

She glances at me and pulls her legs up to her chest, letting the swing sway on its own.

"In Fiji," I clarify. "When you told me to quit being a chicken shit. I needed to hear that."

"That's what friends were for."

Were. "I'd like to be your friend again."

"I'm not the same woman I was in Fiji."

"I can see that."

"I might not be the friend you need anymore."

I smile.

"Sabrina says you like me."

That shouldn't make me smile bigger, but it does. "She's very astute."

"I like my life the way it is, Jonas."

And there goes my smile. "I know."

"*Bash* likes his life the way it is."

"Maybe most of the time. But I noticed he didn't get his—"

She lunges for me and smothers my mouth with her hand before I can finish with *ice cream*. "I swear on my brother's criminal record, if you say those words out loud, I'll give him *very* specific instructions about what I expect to happen on your camping trip."

She smells like peaches and baby shampoo, and her hand is soft and smooth and warm. My pulse ratchets up. My cock stirs.

I don't know if she realizes she's wrapped one arm around my shoulder, but I don't want to move.

Also, I lied.

I don't want to be her friend.

I want to be much, *much* more than that.

I wanted it in Fiji, but I knew I hadn't finished working through everything that happened with Peyton, and

Emma had just barely started processing what jilting her fiancé meant for her life.

But now?

Now, I've made peace with my ex-wife and Emma's a single mom. Strong. Fierce in a quiet way. Embracing the life she has.

Happy.

Except for me showing up.

I can be something she's happy about. We *were* friends. If I'd made an effort to reach out, we could've been more.

Which is one more reason I kept my distance.

I didn't want to be her rebound, and I didn't want her to think she was mine.

I inhale the scent of her hand once more. "Okay," I whisper.

She freezes. Gonna go out on a limb here and guess my breath tickling her palm just reminded her she's touching me.

And sure enough, now she's jerking back to her side of the swing. I hold it steady with one foot while she gets settled against the arm rest.

"He hears things in his sleep," she whispers.

"I guessed as much. Apologies. It won't happen again."

"Thank you."

Before Bash welcomed me to fatherhood in his special way, I watched her laughing with her friends. Listened to them reminisce. Squeal over ideas for her besties' babies and their baby shower, which they're apparently both opposed to. Picked up on the fact that both women were there in the delivery room with her when Bash was born.

Experienced simultaneous extreme relief and extreme

jealousy in a way I never could've fathomed two weeks ago.

She wasn't alone.

She hasn't been alone.

She doesn't need me.

Bash doesn't need me.

Theo has Bash's college fund—or his *explore life with reckless abandon when you graduate high school fund*, as Theo called it—already fully funded. Grey hinted at regular communication with his own lawyers, which I took as confirmation that they won't let Emma fight Razzle Dazzle lawyers on her own if I turn into a dick.

The triplets asked when they could start building Bash his own playset.

Zen made sure Emma didn't run out of drinks.

And I noticed they gave her the lemon kombucha too.

Score.

But it'll take a lot more than guessing her favorite drink flavors to get past her walls.

"I'm permanently off relationships with men," she says stiffly.

"Your friends don't hide things from you anymore."

She goes even stiffer. "Irrelevant."

Very relevant.

They'd tell her if I was doing something shitty. Or even something normal for me that could put *her* normal in jeopardy.

So I go slow.

I can go slow.

I nod to the house. "Will he be up in the middle of the night too?"

"Probably. I'm mildly surprised he hasn't puked again yet."

"You need anything?"

She shakes her head.

I don't know if it's an *I have everything I need* head shake, or a *there are other people I can call if I need things* head shake.

"Thank you for letting me come over and check on you."

She nods.

And then she makes a noise that I heard Bash make a split second before I got that very distinct welcome to fatherhood this afternoon.

"Emma?"

She doesn't answer.

She's too busy running for the back door, hand clapped over her mouth.

22

Emma

I FEEL LIKE ROADKILL.

My dad's a taxidermist. I've *seen* roadkill. I can verify it is, indeed, what I feel like.

So when I stumble downstairs to refill my and Bash's water bottles around three a.m.—seriously need to go out and get Pedialyte today—and find Jonas camped out on my couch, I'm not sure if I'm hallucinating.

If I am, the hallucination is moving.

"Hey." And it's talking. "You feeling any better?"

I subtly pinch myself.

Still feverish, but also, that hurts. "Are you actually here?" I croak out.

His grin is illuminated by the glow off the oven light carrying in from the kitchen. "Actually here," he confirms.

Did I say goodbye to him last night?

Or did I just run inside and toss my cookies?

Can't remember now. "You should go. There are germs everywhere. We'll get you sick."

"Goes with the parenthood gig, doesn't it?"

My heart absolutely cannot take this.

The hope that he means it. That he won't disappear this time.

The fear that he means it. That he'll disrupt our lives in a massive way if he stays.

"We'll be okay. Honestly. Been here, done this a couple times. And Lucky's popping in to check on us in the morning, which I couldn't stop him from doing if I tried." Having a friend who's a nurse has come in pretty handy as I've navigated snotty noses and fevers and digestive issues.

No doubt he'll arrive with—I am *definitely* hallucinating.

This time with what I'm seeing on the counters and floor in the kitchen.

"I tried not to go overboard," Jonas says sheepishly, "but I didn't want to leave, so I let my security team handle quantities."

If there's one box of crackers, there's a dozen.

Same for bottles of Pedialyte and Gatorade.

Bunches of bananas.

Industrial size cans of applesauce.

Organic. Naturally.

"Did they think an entire football team was down with the flu here?" I ask. "Is there any left at the store for anyone else?"

"They said the store is fine. They hijacked a delivery truck."

"*What?*"

"Kidding. Whatever's left, Begonia and Hayes will take. They run Razzle Dazzle's summer camp program. Most years. Not this year. My mother threatened to disinherit all of us if Begonia didn't take an extended maternity leave. And speaking of, I can't go back to their house here. Not if I want to live. Hayes would disembowel me if I shared germs with Begonia right now. And I mean *disembowel* in the *permanently dead* kind of way."

I rub my head, still staring at the mountain of stomach bug supplies.

I don't have to go to the store.

I don't have to ask one of my friends to go to the store for me and then fight with them when they refuse to let me pay them back.

"Thank you," I say quietly.

"Least I can do."

I get Bash a sippy cup filled with Pedialyte and pick the clear Gatorade for myself, and Jonas shoos me back upstairs to rest.

"Here if you need anything," he says.

He stays.

And I actually sleep.

When I wake up, the sun is streaming through my curtains, which are billowing in a soft, cool morning breeze. Birds chirp. The chickens are clucking. And Bash is chattering away downstairs.

Wait.

Wait.

How is Bash downstairs?

Fifty-fifty shot he climbed out of his crib. I've known this day was coming.

Or, Jonas got him up.

He's still here. I can hear the rumble of his voice replying to whatever Bash is saying.

I stumble through pulling on clothes that don't smell like the roadkill I resembled last night, my head still woozy but better. I'm definitely not eating anything today, but my stomach is steady enough that I can walk downstairs without the bonus extra nerves making me want to get sick again.

"Mama!" Bash is kneeling on a chair at my round oak dining room table, dressed in nothing but a diaper—clean, by the looks of it—and the applesauce that's smeared on his chest. He holds up a cracker. "I eat!"

I bury my nose in his hair and press a kiss to his head, breathing in his little boy scent—*clean*, no vomit—and avoiding looking at Jonas. "Good job. How's your belly?"

"Hungy."

"Go slow, okay?"

As if that'll be a problem. He bounces back from being sick like he's a spring.

I take a little longer these days, but I do my best to keep up with him.

"Mama babana?" He shoves a mushed banana at my face, which I expertly avoid by kissing his cheek while I pluck it out of his hand.

"Mama will eat in a bit. How are your crackers?"

"Passable."

Jonas chokes on air.

I smile and ruffle Bash's hair. *Passable* is my favorite word that he says. He reserves it for special occasions though, just as he was taught by his favorite auncle. "Good. You'll have to tell Zen later."

"Mama have boobooka?" Bash asks.

I shake my head. "Mama has Gatorade. Kombucha is for later."

"I feed dick-dicks?"

"You did already, or we still need to?"

He scrambles off the chair and dashes to the kitchen. "Feed dick-dicks!"

"We have *not* fed the chickens," Jonas says. "And I didn't get him up. I rolled over on the couch, and he was staring at me. And, ah, holding the chicken."

"Dona falled." Bash screws up his face in an expression I can't identify until he adds the noise. "*Eeeee!*"

And now *I'm* choking on a laugh.

Which hurts my poor stomach this morning, for the record.

"You scared Jonas and he squealed in terror and fell off the couch?" I ask.

"Uh-huh."

"That was a really good impression," Jonas agrees.

No irritation. No embarrassment.

That's pride.

Like he's thinking Bash will be the next generation of Rutherfords to go into showbiz as a natural.

"Don't," I mutter before I can help it.

He holds up two hands. "Actively battling every lesson from my own childhood right now. Promise. I'm not doing what you think I'm doing. Swear I'm not. You need help with that chicken food?"

I'm not the stubborn independent type. I'm the *it takes a village* type. Despite everything Jonas has seen since he got to town, my friends aren't running the *take care of Emma show*. I'm just as likely to stop at Theo and Laney's place with cookies after Bash and I had fun in the kitchen all afternoon as they are to knock on my door with diaper cream when I let it slip that I'm out.

But I *want* to feed my own chickens this morning and not depend on Jonas.

My aching body, though, would prefer that I not be a stubborn ass about my independence.

"Dick-dick food here," Bash says. He grabs Jonas's hand and pulls him toward the kitchen. "Two soops. *Two*. No more or dick-dick get sick."

Jonas looks at me like he's waiting for permission.

I pretend I don't see him blinking against his eyes going misty and his Adam's apple bobbing. And also that I have no suspicion whatsoever that he's having a reaction to Bash blindly accepting him like it's normal to wake up with him on the couch.

I shrug. "Since you're here, you might as well. Thank you."

He nods and lets Bash tug him into the next room, the smile curving his lips as he looks down at my baby—*our* son—absolutely wrecking my heart.

What happens if he stays long enough for Bash—for *both of us*—to get attached? And then leaves again?

What happens if he stays, though?

If he walked away from Hollywood entirely to be here? To be a real dad?

I follow them into the kitchen, where Bash pulls Jonas to the floor, squatting and opening the lower cabinet where we keep the chicken food near the back door. "Mama, where Dodo Nono?"

"I don't know where Yolko Ono is," I tell him. "When's the last time you saw her?"

"Dodo Nono *aaaaahhh!*" Bash says, flapping his arms. "When Dona *eeeeee!*"

"She got scared and flapped her wings?" I ask him.

He nods. "Da hoe wows!"

"The horrors," I agree. Second favorite on my list of things he says right now. And he's saying more and more every day. "Do you think she's hiding?"

"I put her in the laundry room," Jonas interrupts. "She looked like she needed some quiet time to process her feelings."

"Did you change her diaper too?" I ask.

"Not yet."

"You know how to change chicken diapers?"

"That's what YouTube is for."

Why is it so natural to smile back at him?

Caution, Emma. Caution.

Bash shoves a scoop at Jonas. "Two soops!"

"Two scoops. Got it."

Bash shows Jonas how to get the *right* scoop amount, then insists on carrying the scoop out and tossing the feed into the pen himself.

I let him tell Jonas himself that in order for this to work, Jonas has to pick him up and hold him over the top of the pen.

Takes them a few minutes to understand each other, but Jonas gets it before Bash needs help or loses his cool.

"Is Yolko Ono an inside chicken because she doesn't play well with others, or because others don't play well with her?" Jonas asks me while Bash squats in front of the pen and giggles at the show of the chickens fighting for the food that just rained down on them.

"She's afraid of her own shadow and it stresses her out

to be in the pen with them. She was a rescue a few months after the rest of the chickens. Theo keeps telling Bash that she's hiding her badass side. And for a while, he tried to convince Bash that she was actually a cat in disguise."

"You have your hands full."

"All my life. I keep telling Laney he's her problem now, but somehow, I still have to manage him too."

"Unca Deo my fabowit. Eat, dick-dick! Eat!"

He's running back for the second scoop when I notice a car door shutting out front.

Jonas frowns and looks to the side of the house.

He heard it too.

"Lucky's stopping by," I remind him.

"Mo food!" Bash dashes for the back door again. "Two soops. *Two*!"

"You're using your cameras?" Jonas asks.

I know why he's asking, and I hate that I can acknowledge that it's necessary. "My phone goes off every time someone shows up."

"Where's your phone?"

"Inside. But I'm sure it's Lucky."

"Mo food, Dona!" Bash yells.

Jonas is still frowning while he follows Bash to the back door.

His hair is perfect. His clothes aren't wrinkled. The five o'clock shadow he has going on is—*would be* sexy as hell if I were into that sort of thing.

Which I'm not.

Not when his clothes have the audacity to survive a night on the couch without wrinkling and his hair is still perfect.

And when you're off men permanently for having awful taste, I forcibly remind myself.

For good measure, I add a quick *And his life is entirely too public and complicated*.

That last message to myself should be my early warning system going off with all of its alarm bells screeching.

But, unfortunately, it isn't.

Which means when Bash and Jonas emerge from the back door the same time a tall, hefty, brown-haired man whose suit doesn't fit quite right and whom I once thought would be my world steps around the side of my house and into my backyard, I'm not nearly on guard enough.

23

Jonas

IF I THOUGHT Emma seemed pale when she walked into the dining room, that's nothing on the shade of near-translucent she's going now.

Understanding *why* is nearly instantaneous.

"Hey, Em," the man in the backyard says.

She doesn't look at me.

Doesn't acknowledge me.

But she does put her body between the man and Bash. "What do you want, Chandler?"

Emma not looking at me doesn't mean he's not though.

His gaze slides my way, and I actively resist the urge to do to him what Theo tried to do to me a little over a week ago.

"Who's this?" Chandler says.

"Distant long-lost cousin. What are you doing here?"

His eyes narrow at me.

No idea if he knows who I am or not.

And I don't mean in the *her distant cousin* kind of way.

Or in the *famous movie star and heir to the Razzle Dazzle fortune* kind of way either.

I mean in the *dude who'll kick his ever-loving ass from here to Saturn if he says anything that makes Emma or Bash uncomfortable* kind of way.

I know exactly who this assnugget is.

And I would've known even without the dossier Hayes's team gave me.

I stare back at Chandler Sullivan. Don't nod. Don't approach to shake his hand. Barely breathe.

Is this rage?

I think this is rage.

Unfamiliar feeling. Not normal. But that's undeniably what this is.

I don't even know the man.

Don't need to.

I know what he did.

He hurt Emma.

That's the only important part here.

He breaks eye contact with me and looks back at her. "I have a big appointment up in Tiara Falls. Massive business deal."

"It's Sunday."

"Best time to do business, baby."

"Mama not da baby," Bash says.

"I am definitely *not* anyone's baby," she agrees.

Chandler squats and looks past her. "Hey, Bash, little dude. Brought you a—"

"No, you didn't," Emma interrupts. "We've discussed this."

"Em—"

"I said *no*."

He rolls his eyes. "C'mon, Em. You know you're not gonna get a better offer."

"She doesn't *need* a better offer to not want you around," I growl.

Growl.

Me.

The *happy-go-lucky* guy.

I think my brother just came out of my mouth.

And I'm okay with that.

Chandler puffs his chest. "Look, you little—"

"Bash, let the chickens out," Emma says.

"Dick-dick!" my son cries in absolute glee. He drops the scoop, the feed spilling all over the yard, and dashes for the gate on the pen. "Dick-dick out!"

Chandler visibly swallows, but he's holding on to the glare he's aiming at me. "She doesn't need you talking for her."

My hands are in my pockets to keep my fists still. "You need to learn to listen when a woman tells you no."

"Emma doesn't have cousins."

"I do, actually," she says.

"I've met them all."

"Did you miss the *distant, long-lost* part?"

The dick completely ignores her. "Who are you *really*?"

Someone who would love five minutes alone with this guy in a dark alley.

But I know how that would end.

All over the news.

And that's one thing I've promised Emma I'll move heaven and earth to avoid.

It's the *only* reason I'm not following instincts that I didn't even know I had.

Squawking erupts at my feet.

"Fee, dick-dick! Dick-dick fee!"

Chandler inches back.

"Thank you, Bash," Emma says, still staring directly at the man who put her on a path to being the world's most notorious runaway bride. "Now say goodbye to Mr. Sullivan."

"Bye, Mista Suckagain!"

"Emma—" he says, the placating tone so grating that my teeth clench together.

"Aww, it's a family reunion," one of the triplets says as he strolls out through the back door.

Dude let himself into Emma's house.

He has a key.

Of course he does.

They're *family*.

"Cuz," Chandler says. "I was just—"

"Leaving," Emma interrupts firmly.

"Oh, good. I'll walk you to your car." Lucky. This one's Lucky.

Even if the haircut didn't confirm it, the small medical kit he sets on top of Emma's closed-up hot tub would.

And he's Chandler Sullivan's cousin.

As is Sabrina.

None of them actively associate with him, according to my dossier.

"I need a minute with Emma." Chandler glares at me. "*Alone*. It's about a business thing."

"Not likely, dude," Lucky says. "Sabrina and Grey are right behind me."

Chandler finally looks at Lucky. Then at me. Then at Emma.

Emma crosses her arms over her chest. "If I have to tell you to leave one more time, I'm calling the sheriff."

Lucky grabs Chandler by the collar and turns him.

I realize I'm barely breathing. My fingernails are short, but they're digging into my palms. My shoulders are tight. My jaw's clenched.

Never.

That's the last time I felt this level of rage.

I make myself breathe. Unclench my fists and jaw. Let my shoulders down.

"Dodo Ono pway!" Bash says, running to the back door. "Dodo Ono pway dick-dicks!"

"Yolko Ono needs to stay inside." She's so even-keeled, like this didn't bother her at all.

And it probably didn't.

To her, this is probably normal.

And that pisses me off all over again.

"Why don't you tell Jonas all of the other chickens' names?" she says to Bash.

"Does he do that a lot?" I ask, forcing myself to match her calm while Bash ignores the request and runs around shrieking with the chickens, scaring half of them.

"He stops by every now and again."

"Does he leave when you tell him to?"

"He's a sad, lonely narcissist who will never understand that he's the problem. He's rarely as big of a problem as he is when he thinks he has competition. And when he *is* a problem, I call Laney or Sabrina on speakerphone, and he tends to leave."

There's too much to unpack there quickly. So I hone in

on the biggest lingering question that I have. "Define *every now and again*."

"Jonas, you've been very kind to take care of us while we're sick, but *I can handle my life*. I don't have to answer to you about how I live and who I associate with."

It takes me one very deep breath before I'm calm enough to answer again. "He sets off all of my alarm bells."

"Thank you for your concern, but let me assure you, if I ever had reason to believe Bash was in danger, I'm fully capable of handling everything."

Something new flashes in her brown eyes, and it takes a minute for her full message to penetrate the fog of my fury that people like Chandler Sullivan even get to exist.

She'd handle him.

She would.

Quickly, efficiently, and with no evidence left.

I swallow.

Swallow again.

I think I'm turned on.

Yep.

Definitely turned on.

Hard not to be at realizing what my son's mother would do to protect him.

I'm also simultaneously feeling completely impotent.

Because *my* way of handling this, after I beat him to a pulp, would've been to let my security team clean it up.

Hers would likely involve calling friends with shovels and doing it herself.

"Really didn't think I'd ever see the day chickens would scare him as much as bees do," Lucky says off-handedly as he strolls back around the side of the house.

"One of them pecked him in the calf the last time he dropped by," Emma replies. "It bled. Got infected. He sent me the hospital bill. I sent Theo to give it back to him."

Lucky grins.

Emma smiles back.

I stand there feeling even more useless.

Actually, I feel worse than useless. "If he recognizes me—" I start.

Lucky snorts.

Emma sighs though. "There's approximately zero chance he'd recognize you. He always refused to watch Razzle Dazzle movies with me because he hated *dumb woman shit*, and he'd rather watch theater movies with explosions than movies that might teach him something."

"Sad but true," Lucky agrees. "If he says you seem familiar, we'll tell him you have a little podcast. He thinks those are stupid too. And if *that* fails, and he realizes you're like, *famous*"—that gets an eye roll—"then we go with Laney's plan and tell him you're studying Theo's life for the biopic about him."

My eyeball is twitching and I want to punch the douchebag all over again.

And I rarely want to punch anyone.

Bash suddenly giggles though, and all gets brighter in my world. "Dick-dicks poop! Dona soo!"

I look down.

A chicken did, in fact, just poop on my shoe.

"You know what this means, Jonas?" Lucky says.

"I've been accepted into the flock?"

"Not until you poop back on his foot."

I'm still not myself enough to do anything more than let my jaw come unhinged.

But then Bash squeals with laughter. Lucky grins. Emma laughs too.

She puts a hand to my arm, and goosebumps sweep my entire body.

"You don't have to poop on his foot," she assures me. "But I'd be incredibly grateful if you could bring me crackers and a Gatorade. And give Yolko Ono a little cup of that chicken food too, please."

"Sure. Absolutely. Be right back."

Pretty sure she wants to talk to Lucky alone.

I'm not *in* yet.

And I won't be if I act like her Neanderthal-brained ex.

So I head inside. Do what she's asked. And double down on my commitment to being here for whatever she needs.

Letting her lead.

No matter how much it scares me to know I might not ever earn my way back in.

24

Emma

JONAS RUTHERFORD IS ACTING every bit the man I thought he was when I met him in Fiji.

I like it and I hate it.

He doesn't get sick. Chandler doesn't come back, which isn't a surprise, since Chandler doesn't tend to stop by often. The security team Jonas has with him is monitoring my house cameras from about ten minutes down the road, where his family is staying, but they're not *here*.

He offers to hang out in the garage if I don't want him to be around Bash, but that would be weird.

Also weird?

He YouTubes how to change Yolko Ono's diaper, and then does it so I don't have to.

So that I can rest and relax and worry about *me*.

Just me.

As if I can help being near enough to monitor how he's interacting with Bash.

All of my initial hesitation after he watched Bash from afar at the cookout has evaporated. He was letting Bash come to him on his own time.

And now that he's here, Bash is going to him all the time.

Jonas might be the only man outside of family and honorary family to have spent any time in my house since Bash was born, but I refuse to get worked up over the idea Bash will be hurt if he gets attached.

Bash has so many people in his life who love him.

And it kills me to face this, but I know he needs to get hurt sometimes. My entire life, everyone shielded me from getting hurt.

My mom dying was the one thing they couldn't protect me from.

Losing her when I was in middle school made me cling even harder to people who didn't deserve it. I didn't want to be the reason anyone else left me or abandoned me or gave up on me.

Anyone else.

Not that it was my fault Mom died, or that I thought she left us on purpose.

My brain just went there. To that dark place of *I could lose anyone, so I have to cling to everyone*.

And it led me to almost making the biggest mistake of my life.

"Dat not dybobor," Bash says early Monday afternoon in the living room.

I'm working from home in my office on the other side of the stairwell from the living room.

When I'm not napping, that is.

I do *not* bounce back like Bash does.

Jonas is hanging out and building stuff with blocks. We've had lunch, none of us have lost the content of our stomachs in nearly twenty-four hours now, and Bash is due for naptime very, very soon.

"It is too a dinosaur," Jonas says. "Look. That's its tail."

"It no *wings*," Bash replies.

"Not all dinosaurs have wings."

"*Do too.*"

Uh-oh.

I start to rise, eyeball Jonas and Bash in the middle of a stare-down, then grab my phone instead.

EMMA: Bash is about to throw a temper tantrum all over Jonas. Do I intervene?

SABRINA: No.

LANEY: Is Bash safe?

ME: Yes.

SABRINA: I repeat, do not interfere. Let him experience the full wrath of a toddler who, if I can tell time correctly, which I think I can, would be doing his pre-nap routine right about now if he were at daycare or alone with you.

. . .

Laney: What's the temper tantrum about?

Me: If block dinosaurs have to have wings.

Sabrina: You keep talking, and I keep not changing my opinion.

Laney: I'm so proud of you for texting us when we all know you wanted to go play peacemaker.

Me: It IS naptime. Jonas doesn't know that.

Sabrina: Maybe it's time for him to figure it out.

Laney: Has he been around children before? Does he know they take naps?

Sabrina: He was around all day yesterday when Bash definitely took a nap. Remember? Emma was texting us yesterday that Jonas helped with the naptime routine? That was not long after this time yesterday, wasn't it?

. . .

A crash in the living room has me looking up from my phone. "*Dat not dybobar!*"

I should go in there.

Jonas doesn't know Bash's moods. His routines. The best way to handle temper tantrums.

Yes, he helped with the naptime routine yesterday, but also, naptimes during sick times are not the same as naptimes during normal times.

"Whoa, hey, that's not a nice way to treat friends," Jonas says. "I liked him. Now I'm sad."

I hover halfway out of my chair.

"*Not dybobar!*" Bash cries again.

"Okay. It wasn't a dinosaur."

"*Not dybobar!*"

"Agreed."

"*Dat. Not. Dybobar!*"

And I'm done being patient. Jonas hasn't done anything *wrong*. He just doesn't know what to do that's *right*.

For Bash, I mean. In this exact situation.

I stride into the living room, unsurprised to find Bash writhing about on the floor shouting about dinosaurs.

Jonas shoots me a guilty look, like he thinks this is his fault.

"Bash, want to come snuggle Mama?" I say quietly as I squat next to him.

"Mama, not dybobar," he sobs.

"I know. You're tired. And it's hard to process different perspectives when you're not even two yet, much less when you're not even two *and* tired. Come have snuggles and water and let's read a book."

"Not dybobar," he repeats.

"Okay. You didn't see the same thing Jonas saw. C'mere, Bashy-boo. Let's have hugs. We'll talk about the dinosaurs after snuggles and hugs."

Jonas is watching me. I have no idea if he thinks I'm being an asshole for not telling Bash it's not nice to wreck his friend's toys, or if he thinks I'm an angel of patience for not losing my shit right back.

Bash flops onto his stomach and army crawls the six inches to my knees then holds up one chubby little arm, a silent plea for me to do the rest of the work to pick him up and cuddle him.

I'll talk to him about being nice to friends *after* his nap.

Experience tells me if I try now, he'll go straight back into angry-land and he won't sleep well.

He'll hear the lesson better after he's had his basic needs met.

I get the little guy settled upstairs after three more books than usual for our naptime routine, then head back downstairs despite wanting a nap myself.

Jonas is squatting in the middle of my living room, picking up the blocks. He eyes me warily as I hit the bottom step.

"Sorry about that," he says quietly.

I shake my head. "It wasn't your fault. He has few enough reasoning skills when he's not approaching naptime."

"Did I do anything wrong? If there's something I can do better next time—"

"Parenthood is an experience in continuously feeling like you're wrong."

He looks down at the blocks, then back up at me. "It was too a dinosaur. Want to see a picture?"

I feel my eyes widen and a roar of *are you seriously still arguing with a two-year-old?* start to bubble up in my chest as he cracks a grin.

"Kidding. It was a really bad dinosaur. I sent the picture to Begonia and she asked if Bash made a couch out of blocks."

I sink into the fluffy recliner that saw many, *many* hours of me attempting to breastfeed Bash, followed by many, many more hours of snuggles and bottles. "I do *not* have the energy for you today."

"Take a nap. I'll do your work."

"I'd love to see how you handle the quarterly tax estimation mess my new clients got themselves into before calling me."

"Easy peasy. Just send the IRS all of the money—like, *all* of it—and straighten it out next year."

My eyes are sliding shut. They shouldn't be. I don't have time for this.

But life hasn't exactly been a bowl of cherries lately.

The blocks quit knocking together, and I hear what sounds like the lid snapping shut on the block container, and then the container being deposited back in the corner.

"You need anything?" Jonas asks quietly.

"Just to get up and do my work."

"I meant food or a blanket."

"No, thank you."

A chicken is deposited in my lap, and then the couch cushions squeak close by. "If you change your mind, I'll be right here."

I believe him.

Also, he brought me my chicken. He brought me my pet chicken, and now she's snuggling me, and everything about this feels so natural and right.

And that's terrifying.

"Do you seriously not have any work you have to do right now?" I murmur.

"Canceled nearly everything if I can't do it remotely. Except..."

"Except?"

"The press will start to spread rumors that I'm in rehab or something if I don't make an appearance here and there. So I'm doing podcast interviews again. And there's a charity dinner in New York late next week that I haven't canceled yet. It's *after* my camping trip with your family. I won't miss that."

"Charity is important." I love this recliner. It fits my body like it was born with me.

"It's just an overnight thing. If you won't be mad at me for leaving—"

"I'm not in charge of your life."

"If we were doing this parent thing the traditional way, I'd ask. So I'm asking. And I'll be back by the next morning. Promise."

There's a swirly black darkness behind my eyelids that accompanies a contented hum from Yolko Ono in my lap.

I like it.

Means sleep is close.

Since Jonas got to town, I haven't slept enough.

"Your brother and his wife have to leave eventually," I murmur.

I can't see him, but I can feel him watching me like he doesn't understand exactly where that came from.

I don't know if I understand where it came from.

Do I mean Jonas will leave when his family does?

I don't know. My brain is fogging.

"Maybe," he says. "Hayes is pretty happy in secluded houses. With maternity leave, camp isn't expecting Begonia back until next spring. Plus, Hayes bought the house. I can live in it solo even if they leave."

Oh.

That's what I meant. That he wouldn't have a place to stay without attracting more attention if his brother leaves.

But his brother owns the house.

And he said they can stay until next spring.

That's months.

Months and months.

And I have his phone number. I have phone numbers for various members of his family.

Begonia even insisted I take Keisha's phone number.

Yes, *that* Keisha.

Jonas's cousin, Keisha Kourtney. The pop star that Zen fainted over when they found out Keisha posted about loving their kombucha on her socials.

"What project are you working on now?" I ask.

"Just my podcast. Easy to do that virtually from here." His voice is getting huskier. Maybe dreamier.

Or maybe that's my ears settling deeper and deeper into that state between awake and asleep.

"Nothing else? No movies?"

"Couple options. I mean, beyond starring in a biopic about an online adult entertainment star. Want to hear about them?" he asks.

"Mm-hm."

I don't hear another word he says.

But I feel his voice wrapping around me like a solid, safe hug.

The same way it did in Fiji.

I think I'm in trouble.

25

Jonas

THERE ARE three things I know for certain today.

One, it's a bad sign when a guy's baby mama orders him to go away for a couple days.

Two, while I haven't camped like this *ever*, I have enough instincts to know I'm supposed to trust the people I'm camping with.

And three, I don't trust Theo and Grey.

I know they have Emma's best interests at heart, but I don't know how much trouble that means they'll give me.

Doubting Theo is a given.

Don't get me wrong. I respect the hell out of how much he cares about his sister. But I'm the dude who slept with her, disappeared, and didn't give her any easy way of contacting me to tell me our night together had unintended results.

I get it.

He shouldn't give me an inch. I need to earn this.

Grey, though—it's the nice ones you have to be wary of.

The ones you least expect of being ready to pounce when you show weakness.

Like now.

"Grabbed you some gear," Grey says when I meet them at Theo's place. They're loading an older model extended cab truck with bags and coolers.

"Appreciate that. What do I owe you?"

He grins.

Theo grins.

I'm fucked.

"It's on us," Theo says.

Wonder what they put in the sleeping bag. Or on the tent.

Just show up, they said.

Best way to make sure we're not missing anything is to let us handle it all.

"Pull your car around back so it's not in Laney's way," Theo says.

"We'll finish up," Grey adds.

Both of them grin again.

I didn't earn my reputation as the friendly Rutherford brother by scowling and grumbling, so I smile back, nod, and pull my car around back as requested.

Laney's nowhere in sight, but I wave at two gray tabby cats in the front window.

They stare at me like I'm a moron.

Probably am. But if Emma's family wants to put me

through trials and tests, I'll let them put me through trials and tests.

Theo and Grey have the truck loaded when I get back to the front of the house, so we hit the road.

I'm in back.

Naturally.

They humored me and gave me the location of the campsite we're going to so that I can humor my brother. He's still keeping my mother at bay. I'll also have a security team on standby somewhere close. Not that I expect to need them.

Probably.

Still not entirely certain I can reach them if I do. I've been told there's no cell signal where we're going.

I ask Grey questions about his research and Theo questions about the bigger house he and Laney are building on their land, and answer a few questions about if I've fished, hunted, or geocached.

"My brother and his wife have formally been asked to not geocache anymore by the Geocache Society of America," I tell them. "I skip it in solidarity."

Grey turns around and looks at me.

Theo slides me a look in the rearview mirror.

I shrug. "Last time they went, their dog was helping them look for a cache and caused an incident while a funeral was going on nearby."

Theo stays silent.

Grey gets a look on his face like he's contemplating how that would work. "Huh."

"You two know anything about Emma's hot tub?" I ask.

"It's broken," Theo replies.

"Figured that out. Does she use it?"

"No. It's broken."

Grey coughs, clearly hiding a laugh.

"Would she use it if it wasn't broken, or is it something she has and never used?"

Theo hits me with another glance in the rearview mirror. "Why?"

"Always wanted to learn how to fix a hot tub. Bucket list."

My two hosts share a look in the front seat.

Pretty sure at least one of them doesn't believe me. Possibly both of them.

"I won't buy her a new one if I can't fix it unless I get some indication she'd like it. And then I'll ask you to buy it and I'll pay you back so it doesn't look like it was me."

They share another look.

"Also, does her ex stop by often?"

Theo takes a curve too hard. "What?"

"Chandler. Her ex. He showed up at her house on Sunday."

Grey turns all the way around and looks at me but doesn't say anything.

"He recognize you?" Theo's voice has gone flat.

"Didn't seem to," I reply evenly. "Emma thinks it's unlikely he would."

"What did he want?" Grey asks.

"Her."

And there's one more look between my hosts.

"You know those times when you're ready to grab a shovel and a trusted friend but you know it'll piss off the one person whose opinion matters more than your gut instinct?" I ask.

Theo grunts.

Grey grimaces.

Theo grunts again.

"Yeah," I say. "Exactly that."

"You the type to do it yourself?" Theo asks.

"This time, I am."

They both look at me, and then we lapse into silence.

But not for long.

"And we're here," Theo says, pulling onto a dirt drive that quickly becomes one lane with several switchbacks. The elevation's a little higher than Snaggletooth Creek. Trees a little denser. Views unstoppable when we reach our destination in a clearing.

Grey steps out of the front seat, stretches, and stares out toward the jagged mountain peaks and fluffy white clouds floating in the brilliant blue sky. "Sabrina's right. Never gets old."

Theo heads straight for the back of the truck and pops the tailgate. "Look later, lollygagger. Time to set up camp."

Emma prepped me a little for this. Told me Theo owns some land deeper in the mountains that he and Laney sometimes disappear to. "It's very private," she told me. "You can't really find it by accident."

Theo shoves a large pack at me. "If you can't set up a tent, you're sleeping under the stars."

"Sounds pretty."

"Until the bears wander in."

"Are they cuddly? I'm a cuddler."

Grey coughs again, turning away like he can hide an amused smile.

"Your life if you want to risk it," Theo says.

He's suppressing a smile too.

But I don't count it as a win yet.

We still have hours to go before nightfall, and I've been promised I'm not eating if I don't catch my own fish.

Time to get busy fitting in with the rest of Emma's family.

26

Emma

"Do you think they'll bring him back alive?" I whisper to Zen while we sit at one of the window tables inside Bee & Nugget.

They look up from the *which hand is it in?* game they're playing with Bash. "Yes, Emma, they'll bring him back alive. Scarred, but alive."

"Too many people—namely, *us*—know he's with them," Laney says as she settles herself into the open seat with her back to the view of the lake. "Theo knows even an accident will get him in trouble. With me. In the bad way."

"Grey too. He hates being in trouble with Laney in the bad way." Sabrina deposits a massive plate of lemon scones and bacon in the center of the table, hands me five individual plates to pass around, then sits between Zen and Laney. She rubs Bash's head as he squeals at finding the Goldfish in Zen's left hand.

"Moe!" he cries.

"Turn around and don't peek," Zen replies. "You can have more if you guess which hand again."

"This feels like they're accepting him," I tell my friends.

The café isn't super busy, but it's not empty either. And while I know most of the people here, and they like keeping secrets from outsiders, I don't know *everyone*.

We're too close to ski towns and good hiking to not have tourists and visitors in town daily.

So I'm whispering basically everything.

"Are *you* accepting him?" Laney asks.

"Should I?"

"Nuh-uh, my friend," Zen says. "That's on *you*. We're not influencing this decision. Haha! Not that hand, Bash. Try again."

My son giggles and attacks Zen's other hand.

"Agreed," Sabrina says. "This is one you need to figure out on your own."

Laney nods. "Sorry, Em. But if it helps, they took him just as much to give you some breathing room, knowing he's not right around the corner for a bit, as they did to sniff out any previously unknown red flags."

There was a time I would've asked if my brother knew what a *red flag* was, but then he got stupid rich by offering sound, solid life advice to people who were going through things.

Naked.

While knitting.

On the internet.

Which is something he'll have to explain to his own kids someday.

But *he knows the things*. Despite growing up basically a total disaster—or maybe because of it—he has a pretty solid, deep understanding of boundaries and healthy relationships.

I sigh and dig into a lemon scone while Bash spots the bacon. Zen pulls him onto their lap and fixes him a plate while Laney and Sabrina grab food too.

It's the middle of the afternoon. Laney left work early. Zen left work early. Sabrina's technically still on the clock, but none of her staff will question the boss taking a break.

I left work early too.

Slow day.

February through April will be crazy, but I get breathing room in the summer.

I don't pay much attention to the doorbells jingling until I realize Sabrina and Laney are both staring at something.

Creepy-crawlies take up residence in my spine, and I carefully shift my head until I can see what they see.

"Doggie!" Bash cries. "I pet doggie!"

He pulls a Houdini and slips from Zen's grasp, and I'm a hair too slow to grab him before he's bolting across the café to throw himself at a black-and-brown dog.

"Bash," I start, unsure how to finish that.

Don't run up to dogs you don't know is what I *should* say.

It's what I've said to him a thousand times already, and what I expect to say a thousand times more before it sinks in for him.

But Begonia Rutherford has him well in hand.

Even approaching seven months pregnant with twins,

she's squatting and redirecting his hands while smiling and talking softly to him about being careful with doggies.

"I don't trust how much I like her," Zen murmurs.

"It's uncanny, isn't it?" Sabrina murmurs back.

"You two," Laney says with an affectionate sigh.

It takes me longer than it should to get out of my seat.

Mostly because Begonia and her dog aren't alone.

Her husband—Jonas's brother—is with them.

And I suddenly have butterflies in my throat. Not in my stomach. In my throat.

Jonas adores his brother the same way I adore Theo. You can hear it in his voice.

What happens if Hayes doesn't like me?

What does that mean?

And *why do I care*?

Don't answer that.

I suck in a breath and make myself leave the table to join my son, who's squealing with glee while the dog licks his fingers.

"Mama, I wan maw-mawa," he says.

Begonia winces. "I thought Marshmallow was such a good name for him, but every time I introduce him to kids... Sorry about that."

"No apology necessary," I assure her. "Bash knows he has to eat a good dinner before marshmallows, don't you?"

My son eyes me. "Mama doan."

My ears get hot. I've just been put in my place by my toddler. "Mama had a cheese stick at the office before coming for scones."

Begonia grins at me. She starts to rise, *oof*s, and then accepts the hand that Hayes has offered like he saw this coming. "I could do it on my own yesterday," she mutters. "Hayes, this is my friend Emma and her son, Bash. Emma, my husband, Hayes."

The locals are watching curiously.

The out-of-towners are oblivious.

Jonas told me Hayes is rarely recognized these days. That seems to be holding true.

"Nice to meet you," I stammer out while Hayes takes my hand and nods back.

"Likewise."

"Bring that cute doggy over here," Zen says. "We'll push the tables together."

I slide them a look.

Am I being ambushed?

Laney and Sabrina both give me the subtle headshake of *no, you're not being ambushed, but you should get your ass back over here so you have backup.*

I think.

It's either that, or they're telling me to make excuses and leave because this is a terrible idea.

"Aw, that's so sweet of you," Begonia says to Zen. "Can I have extra room between my chair and the table? Turns out, I don't fit in booths anymore. Who knew? Marshmallow. Hayes. C'mon. Let's go make friends."

"As you wish, my love," Hayes murmurs.

The resemblance between him and Jonas is remarkable. It's like they have the same eyes, chin, and nose, but if you weren't looking for the similarities, you'd miss it entirely.

Jonas is so affable. Very approachable.

Hayes looks like my statistics professor in college who'd glare at you for asking for clarification on complex mean deviation, which I still don't fully understand.

Bash trots along next to the dog, who pauses and sniffs at a clean table with nothing more than a vase of flowers on it.

"Don't even think about it," Hayes says to him.

Marshmallow whines softly and continues to our table —no, *tables*.

Zen's quick.

The two window tables are already pushed together, and Sabrina's afternoon staff is on the way with another plate of pastries.

I end up between Laney and Begonia with my back to the window. Zen takes the seat on the other side of Hayes, across from me.

They look him up and down. "You don't like people."

"Accurate."

"We'll pretend you're not here."

"For now," Sabrina agrees. "If we weren't in public, we'd have a *lot* of questions."

Hayes smiles. "Always happy when a plan comes together."

Begonia digs into her purse and hands him a thick hardcover book with an affectionate smile.

He takes a scone and settles in with his book, pausing only to glance twice at the scone after his first bite like it's way more than he expected it to be.

Understandable.

Sabrina uses her grandmother's recipe, and it's legendary.

"I heard you have chickens," Begonia says to me. "Chickens *fascinate* me. How'd you get into it?"

While I hand Bash bits of bacon, scone, and muffin as he pets the dog, I answer her questions about raising chickens, about what I do with the eggs, about the biggest hurdles to being a chicken lady, and about Yolko Ono and her unique personality. And once again, I realize just how easy it is to feel safe around Begonia.

Despite having his nose in a book while the rest of us chat, I get the impression Hayes isn't missing a single word of our conversation.

"I hope we're invited the next time you have a family cookout," Begonia whispers to me as we're finishing all of the afternoon snacks. "I'll bring my famous egg souffle."

Hayes chokes on his tea and slides her a look.

She grins and pats his hand. "Just testing if you were listening."

"You and *famous* always gets my attention." He's not grumpy.

Just reserved.

And he clearly adores his wife.

Good thing. I'd think far less of him if I had any doubts about that.

She shifts and looks down.

I look down too.

Bash is gone.

Marshmallow is gone.

And it takes a second longer than it should for their absence to register.

"Uh-oh," Zen says while Sabrina shoots to her feet and Laney catches on later than usual to a problem.

Kidnappers.

It's the first thought in my head, and it's repeating louder and louder and louder.

Not kidnappers, I tell myself while I order my misbehaving legs to *move. It can't be kidnappers. He's just —missing.*

My heart goes hollow and dips into my stomach.

He's missing.

Bash is missing.

In front of Jonas's family.

"I tied him up," Begonia says. "I swear I tied Marshmallow to the chair. With the *good* knot. The one he hasn't figured out how to undo. Yet. I thought."

"Bash," Laney and Sabrina say together.

"There's something about the Monroe boy genes," Laney adds with a sigh.

KIDNAPPERS.

Oh my god.

My baby.

My baby.

My baby is *missing* and my body is malfunctioning. I can't even force a word out of my mouth.

Get it together, Emma. Get. It. Fucking. Together.

He can't be far.

He can't.

He hasn't been kidnapped.

No one knows who he is.

But he's missing and Jonas's family is here and they know I've lost him.

Oh god. Oh god oh god oh god.

Hayes is on his feet, looking around. "Robert's not here," he murmurs to Begonia.

Zen beats Sabrina to the kitchen.

I finally get myself out of my chair to follow Sabrina and Zen toward the kitchen, my legs weighing seven thousand pounds apiece while sirens and freak-outs blare through my head. I'm stuck on the wrong side of the table to *handle the fact that my son is gone.*

I'm *never* stuck on the wrong side of the table. I know better.

I know better.

How did I get so distracted?

Because this is normal, dummy.

Anytime I'm with my friends, I let my guard down.

My friends help keep an eye on him.

And now *Bash is gone.*

Bash, who looks *so much* like Jonas that anyone who spots it will see an opportunity.

While his famous father's brother and sister-in-law are sitting right here.

Watching me lose track of my son.

Watching me—*no no no.*

Deep breaths.

I finally get myself out from behind the table, but I don't know what to do next.

I don't know what to do next.

Laney grabs my hand as Begonia turns to me. "Don't panic," Begonia says. "We have—"

She's interrupted by a chuckle.

A deep, amused chuckle. "That's a new one," Hayes says into his phone.

"A security team with us," Begonia finishes as Hayes nods to her. "They have the runaways."

They have the runaways.

Oh, god, *Bash.*

Of course. Of course he and a dog ran away.

"In the kitchen," Laney supplies. "Just like normal."

My legs collapse under me and I sit hard enough on the chair to bruise my tailbone, but I don't care.

"I don't lose him." I can't catch my breath. I know they're all telling me he's fine, but *I lost him. While Jonas's family was watching.* I know how this plays out in court. I do. "I don't. I *never* lose him."

"My sister once lost two of her kids when our whole family was out for pizza," Begonia says. "One of them crawled into the claw machine and the other was trying. It happens."

"I *don't* lose him." I can't stop saying it.

And suddenly a man who *looks* like Jonas but *isn't* Jonas is squatting in front of me. "We know," Hayes says quietly. "It's okay."

"It is *not*—"

"It is." He squeezes my shoulder. "You're a good mom. None of us are a match for Marshmallow."

I don't want to cry. I *refuse* to cry.

Not in front of these people.

"Don't take my baby," I whisper.

"If they so much as try, I will destroy all of them," Begonia says beside me.

Happily.

Cheerfully, even.

Hayes squeezes my shoulder again, clearly suppressing a smile. "It's the sunshine ones you have to be most afraid of. You never see their wrath coming."

"Mama! Mama, I sim in fower!"

Bash trots out of the kitchen, coated head to toe in white dust.

Marshmallow trots behind him, coated head to tail in white dust.

"I turned around for *three seconds*," Willa says as she exits the kitchen, mildly dusted herself. There's a man I don't recognize with her who's clearly amused, and Zen's having a facial gymnastics issue while Sabrina glares at them and rubs her belly. "Three seconds, and then there's a *whoosh* and a *thump* and the *entire fifty-pound bag of flour* pulled a cheese powder trick."

"We are *not* talking about the cheese powder incident again," Sabrina says.

"It was totally like the cheese powder," Zen replies with a grin.

"Mama, I goe!" Bash reaches me, his diaper sagging, a plume of flour trailing behind him. "Booo! I dary!"

Hayes scoots aside so I can sweep my little boy into my arms, hug him, and almost choke on the flour dust. "You're a scary ghost," I agree, my eyes getting wet all over again.

Bad idea.

Bad idea, because water and flour make glue.

Crap.

"But *do not* run and hide from mama when we're not home, okay?"

"I no hie, mama. I *goe*. Maw-mawa goe."

"I'll bet we can make you better ghost costumes." Begonia coughs.

Coughs again.

Hayes coughs.

Zen coughs.

Laney coughs.

I cough.

The only people *not* coughing from the flour dust are Bash and Marshmallow.

The culprits who *brought* the flour dust.

"Mama, maw-mawa come pway? Pway me Dodo Ono?"

"Marshmallow would eat Yolko Ono."

Bash freezes. His eyes go wide, his brown irises the only thing on him that's not white with flour. Even his *lips* are white.

"I—" I start, realizing where his brain's going.

And then he cackles. "Maw-mawa eat Dodo Ono!"

Laney chokes again, then wheezes with laughter broken with coughs. "Crap. Bathroom."

"Bathroom," Begonia agrees.

"We only have two bathrooms," Sabrina groans.

"The lady with twins has dibs," Zen announces.

I hug Bash closer. "*Please* don't leave mama's side when we're not at home, okay?"

"'Kay," he says.

I shoot a look at Laney. "And you better hope you're having a girl."

She's headed toward the bathrooms too. "We've already discussed just how much Theo will have to step up and handle things if we're having a boy. I think he's looking forward to it."

"I'm so glad Grey's a boring nerd," Sabrina says.

"He has other bad genes," Zen assures her. "Plus, he's like, twice your size. I have no idea how you'll deliver his mutantly huge baby."

Hayes takes the seat next to me and looks at me again. "My brother pulled a vanishing act once."

I sweep a glance around the room.

No one's paying attention to us.

"Did he?" I ask.

"County fair. He was about seven. Slipped away from…Mom and Dad…to go find cotton candy."

I'm pretty sure *Mom and Dad* is code for *all of our bajillionty security people*. At seven, Jonas was already starring in commercials and movies. Probably making public appearances too.

Wasn't that about how old he was when he won his Oscar?

"That must've been scary for you," I say quietly, one eye on Marshmallow. The dog has plopped down beside Hayes and has one front paw bent in.

"Wasn't the only time. Happy to send you an email detailing a few more that were worse."

Is he—

I swallow hard.

Blink again against the moisture threatening my eyes. "Will that…be necessary?"

"Better safe than sorry." He nods to Bash, who's now diving into my leftover bacon. "He's happy. That's what matters."

"Why would you do this for someone who's practically a stranger?"

"Because it's very clearly the right thing to do. And anyone in my family who doesn't understand that can deal with my wife."

"Is she really terrifying?" I can't picture it.

Not at all.

He grins again, and I see more shades of Jonas. It comes out in the way his eyes crinkle. "I hope you never have to witness the answer to that question."

"Are you talking about me getting mad again?"

Begonia stops behind him and runs her fingers through his hair, still smiling.

His smile grows as he looks up at her. "Yes."

She rolls her eyes. "I am *not* mean when I'm mad."

"That's what's so terrifying about it."

"By my calculation, that's about fifteen whole sentences from you, so it must be time to go home and take a nap. Marshmallow, come on. You need a bath. Emma, it was so good to see you again." She bends to hug me before I can get up. "And it was so nice to meet you, Bash. I hope we get to play together again sometime soon."

Hayes nods to me. "I'll email you."

"Do you need—" Duh. Of course he doesn't need my email address. "Never mind."

They take the dog and their security guy and head out, leaving me with just Zen while Laney and Sabrina finish their pregnant lady bathroom runs.

Zen looks at Bash, then at me. "That was weirdly weird but also weirdly normal."

I slowly nod. "Welcome to the past two and a half years of my life."

27

Jonas

The guys don't let me starve.

And none of us catch fish.

Pretty sure they knew that would happen. They pull a cooler out of the truck and produce packets of dehydrated backpacking meals once we get back from our trek to a stream-fed pond not far from camp.

Pretty pond, but the fish weren't biting. And we stayed until I was good and pink on my arms.

Might need better sunscreen at this elevation. Probably should've asked Emma what she uses.

Not sure what I can use to help my tongue, though.

And I'm not talking about the heat from the water that Grey boiled with a fancy miniature propane stove and that they used to rehydrate the meals in their own pouches.

"Good, isn't it?" Theo's lounging in a camp chair, slouched low, legs kicked out and crossed at the ankles.

There's a water bottle in his armrest cupholder, and he's chowing down on a packet of rehydrated pad thai.

Grey sits taller in his chair, one ankle propped over a knee, slowly sipping off a can of kombucha while enjoying his packet of red beans and rice.

"Nevah had cam foo like dis," I reply. I'm working on a packet of jambalaya, and my mouth is on fire.

Fire.

I like spicy food, but I'm starting to wonder if they doctored mine with extra hot sauce when I wasn't looking.

I can't feel my tongue.

I can't feel my teeth.

I can't feel my gums or my throat.

"Was your camp food usually catered?" Theo asks.

"Don't knock catered camp food," Grey says. "It gives you *fancier* constipation."

I'd laugh, but my tongue might be swelling. I glance at the package again as I reach for my own kombucha.

Salty Marvin's Fire In The Hole.

That's the brand.

And I picked it.

And when Theo said, *you sure?*, I doubled down.

I'm an idiot.

No doubt my two hosts are well aware.

Neither of them have Salty Marvin's meals. They both have different brands.

"You go to camp when you were a kid, Jonas?" Theo asks.

"Dee-ah—*ahem*. Theatah cam." I guzzle more kombucha. Not helping. It might actually be like gasoline to the fire that is my dinner. "Yeah. Catah-ed mees. You?"

Jesus. This is embarrassing.

I can't even *talk*.

I understand myself less than I understand Bash, and *I know what I'm trying to say*.

"Made my own summer camp. Grey?"

"Summer camp is the only academic program I was ever kicked out of."

Theo does a double take, then starts to grin. "Gonna need the rest of this story."

"Can't."

"What, you have an NDA?"

"Nope. Forgot about it until just now, and I haven't told Sabrina the story yet. She gets it first."

"I won't tell her if you tell us first."

"Yes, you will."

Theo grins again—definitely agreeing with that sentiment—and looks at me. "What about you? You ever get kicked out of theater camp?"

I shake my head.

Sweat is beading at my forehead thick enough to drip into my eyebrows.

"Okay there?" Grey asks me.

"Not eading undil you sweadin." Is that a line I said once in a script for a movie where a very similar situation played out? *Not eating until you're sweating*.

It's familiar.

Yes. Yes, I think it is a line I've said in a script.

And Grey pauses and stares at me like he knows it.

Theo notices Grey staring, but if he's aware of why, he doesn't let on.

Instead, he nods to me. "You sure you usually sweat that much when you're eating?"

"Aww da tye," I lie.

They share a look and a smile.

Uh-oh. "Ith thish when we thtart the inquithition?"

Both of them grin wickedly, this time at me.

Thought so.

"Where do you see yourself in five years?" Theo asks me.

Grey chokes on his drink and comes up laughing.

Theo shoots him a *shut the fuck up* look. "Laney's rubbed off on me. I think about the future now. Rutherford. Talk. Where are you in five years?"

Not dying from my tongue swelling up over making a very poor decision that I wouldn't be doubling down on under any other circumstances.

I gulp more kombucha and make myself concentrate on enunciating clearly. "No idea."

Both men cross their arms over their chests.

More kombucha.

More kombucha is the answer.

It still does nothing to tame the lava sitting under my tongue, but I have too much at stake to keep slurring my words for not being able to feel my mouth. "Athk me that a month ago, and I'd thay traveling the world looking for bigger and bigger thtories to tell." *Shit. Shit shit shit.* "Today?" More kombucha. Crap. Can's empty. But I make myself speak clearly anyway. "Different priorities."

"You want more kids?" Grey asks.

"If everything elthe—*else* in my life lines up to make more kids, yes."

"Tell me what happened in Fiji," Theo says.

Not just the *fire in the hole*—aka my *mouth hole*—making me sweat now. "What do you think happened in Fiji?"

"Why were you there?"

"Hiding from the preth—*press* and my own poor dethi—decisions." Talking is actually good. Talking means I don't have to eat more.

"It true you got divorced because you pulled a bait-and-switch on your wife?"

Maybe talking isn't good. "Tha's the bones of it."

"Fill out the flesh of it."

I have two options.

I can confess the worst thing I've ever done in my life and risk being left here to forage my way to survival if I pick the right direction for the nearest town.

Or I can tell them if Emma wanted them to know, she would've told them.

Which also risks me being left in the wilderness.

Good news is, fear is calming the fire in my mouth. I'm starting to get concerned for the hole it's about to burn in my stomach—pretty sure my intestines are next for dying of hot sauce poisoning—but I can talk.

"I got married because I lived a fairytale life and she was a fairytale princess and we were going to have a fairytale movie star power couple life. I've been sheltered and spoiled, and I own it. But when she suggested a project outside of Razzle Dazzle, I got cold feet. Refused to admit it was cold feet and came up with a plan to stall her by telling her I wanted a family right away instead of waiting like we'd agreed."

They're both folding their arms again.

Neither's smiling.

"I hitched the first ride I could find to the most remote spot I could think of when she went public with the news about our divorce," I say. "Landed in Fiji. Got drunk. Passed out on Emma's porch. She recognized me and told me to get lost. Didn't want the press spotting us together while she was already in the middle of publicity hell."

Theo frowns.

"Know a little about handling publicity," I tell him. Still sweating. Tongue's simultaneously still numb and also on fire, but I make my mouth work right like my life depends on it. "My family are champs at it. And I'd seen the video. She was in over her head and also didn't realize how private the island was. Didn't know it was safe to leave her house there. So I decided it was my job to help her make the most of what she had left of her honeymoon."

Grey hands me another can of kombucha.

I guzzle half of it.

Theo's glaring at me like *sleeping with my sister is not how you should've handled it*.

The kombucha fizzles on my tongue, reigniting some of the fire.

Dammit.

"Why'd you leave?" Grey asks.

"My family found out where I was, and that the press was on the verge of figuring it out too. They—they basically extracted me in the middle of the night."

They both stare at me.

I shove a hand through my hair.

This is the hard part.

"If I could go back, I would've given Emma my number the day we met. Swear I would've. But when I heard the paparazzi were on the way, I knew I needed to get out before they spotted me with her. If I was the news, all by myself, for the disaster that was my divorce, they'd leave her alone. If we were in the news together—"

I shake my head and look at Theo. "You were there.

You were at the wedding. She didn't look much better when I crashed her porch in Fiji. No chance in hell I was making it worse for her."

He's scowling.

Grey's frowning, but it looks more like he's thinking about something.

And *not* how fast he'll have to move to keep Theo from ending me.

I've heard about the get-out-of-jail-free pass.

Also pretty sure it wouldn't extend to him murdering me.

But only pretty sure.

And that might depend on how much the sheriff likes my old Razzle Dazzle films. Or my podcast.

If she's not even the tiniest bit of a fan, I could actually be fucked.

"Why didn't you answer any of her emails?" Grey asks.

Maybe it's the heat finally dying down in my mouth. Maybe it's the fact that they haven't tried to feed me to a bear or a moose. Maybe it's just getting my story off my chest.

But I'm starting to relax. "My team was fielding about three hundred emails a day with women offering to have my baby or claiming to be carrying my secret love child since the news was reporting I wanted to be a father so badly I'd fuck up my marriage for it."

"*Three hundred?*" Grey says.

I giggle.

Giggle?

Yeah.

Giggle.

Weird. "Yeah. At least. The IT team at Razzle Dazzle did some woowoo magic IT thing, and they said we were getting hit with targeted AI spam bots who were taking advantage of the keywords in the stories about my divorce and hoping I'd think one or two were real enough to convince me to send child support."

"And how many could've been real?" Theo asks.

I giggle again. *Shit*. What the fuck? "None. I mean, Emma. But otherwise, none."

"You sure about that?"

I nod. *Emphatically*. And it makes my brains catch fire a little too, on top of going a little sloshy.

The elevation is making me drunk.

On straight kombucha.

Weird.

"Why didn't you tell them to watch for emails from Emma?" Grey asks.

"I was the dick who didn't say *bye-ee*." I toast them with my kombucha can, which is a weird-ass thing to do, but it feels right. And then I guzzle the rest of this second —no, *third* can too. I had one while they were cooking. "She didn't want to hear from *meeee*."

Theo sets his trash on a folding table, tops it with a rock, and then settles back in his chair again, hands folded over his stomach. "Tell us the rest of the story but sing it."

"Like Ryan Reynolds," Grey adds. "My sources tell me you do a killer impression.

What's the rest of the story?

Oh, wait.

I have orders.

I clear my throat.

Feel the burn on my tongue.

Feel the fizzies in my brain.

I can do this. "Whaa—aat's the rest of the stoooooooooory?" I sing.

Like Ryan Reynolds would.

I honestly can do a killer Ryan Reynolds impression. It's a gift.

Grey makes a choking noise and reaches for his own drink.

Theo looks me dead in the eye without cracking a grin. "Why are you here *now*?"

"Oh, that," I start. And then I remember my orders. "Should I dance too?"

"No," Grey says. "We don't want to scare the wildlife."

"Or have them mistake your dancing for a mating ritual," Theo agrees. "Sing. Why are you here *now*?"

Yes. That. I squeeze my eyes together, and the dots behind my eyelids crisscross until they tell me I should answer with a real song.

A Bro Code song. Like Ryan Reynolds would sing it. *"Because she's my everything sweeeeeeetheeeeaaaart,"* I bellow. *"My dreeeeeeammy swweeeetheeeaaarrt."*

"You just woke up one morning, remembered she exists, and decided she's your sweetheart?" Theo is *still* not cracking a smile.

Grey's like, *whimpering*. The man can't hold his laughter. Just can't.

I have *broken* him.

Hear that sizzle?

That's the sound of my burnt tongue making a checkmark in the sky.

Jonas, one. Grey, zero.

I mean, Grey forty-three billion, because he was there

to see Emma pregnant. To watch Bash grow. To be part of their family.

And I just have one.

A measly, measly one.

"Was she—" I clear my throat. *Orders.* I have orders to perform. *"Waaaas sheeee beee-yooo-tiful when sheeee waaaas carrrrrying my baaaaaaby?"*

A bug flies in my throat, and I choke. Gag.

Spit.

Cough.

"Do *not* give him another kombucha," Grey orders Theo.

Kombucha.

"Shiiiiiiiiit," I say. No, *sing, performer.* Sing. "The kombu-uuuuucha was druuuuunk."

"You're drunk," Grey says.

"I'm *haaaappppppy* and my *mooooouth is on fiiiiii-ya!*" And the kombucha was hot.

Heavy.

Hard.

It was *hard* kombucha.

"I'm a altitude on liiiiiightweeeeeight," I sing.

"Elevation," Theo says. "It's only altitude if you're not touching the ground."

"Sabrina's gonna kill me for not recording this," Grey mutters.

"I'll kill you if you do."

"I know."

"Was an assident," I say on a sigh. "My assit—asskit—*assistant* was trying to find an email from Emma Wass—Wax—*Watson*'s people. That's know I how. Know I how. *Hew I now.* Shit."

I. Drunk. Am. So.

"Can I wakey-wakey tomorrow on Emma's porchy-porchy?" I ask my friends in my best Ryan Reynolds voice.

Yeah.

We're friends.

Friends tell friends things when they're high on the booch.

"Why would you want to do that?" Theo asks me.

"Start over. Be better. Be what she deserves."

There's a heavy sigh.

And a snore.

I don't know who's doing what.

But I know the stars are back behind my eyes, and they're pretty.

I want to show Emma the stars.

She's pretty.

And she's strong.

And she's brave.

And I like her.

28

Emma

BASH and I have just gotten home from work and daycare late Friday afternoon when there's a knock at my door.

I'm not expecting anyone, but I do know Jonas, Theo, and Grey were supposed to be getting back from their camping trip this afternoon.

I hand Bash his normal applesauce packet and ask him to go find Yolko Ono. While he scampers off to check the dining room, I pull up my camera app and check my front door.

My heart leaps. My mouth goes dry. My vagina—*nope*.

No.

She stays out of this. Permanently closed, thank you very much.

But she's *acting* like she's not at the sight of Jonas on my front porch.

He's scuffing a toe along the porch, glancing between the doorbell camera and the door like he's nervous.

I check my text messages and my phone app, and there's nothing.

He didn't call. He didn't text.

Didn't give me a heads-up that he was coming over, which is a first.

I glance at Bash, who's found Yolko Ono and is attempting to persuade her to follow him into the kitchen for afternoon snacks.

No more excuses.

Time to open the door.

"I'm taking a semi-permanent break from acting," Jonas says before I've fully opened the main door.

"I—you—*what*?" My heart isn't leaping now. It's erratically pounding like it's a drum being played by a toddler.

"Do you like your hot tub?"

"Go back to the acting thing."

"I'm taking a semi-permanent break. Do you like your hot tub?"

"Those two aren't related."

He grins.

No, he *smiles*.

A full, broad, eye-crinkling, tooth-flashing, heart-stopping Jonas Rutherford smile.

Heaven help me.

"Acting's easy. Doesn't mean it's what I'm supposed to do with the rest of my life. One more time. Do you like your hot tub?"

"It's broken."

"I know." He lifts a backpack. "Brought tools. And YouTube. Thought I'd try to fix it. But only if you like it."

I realize I'm licking my lips as I stare at him, and I suck my tongue back into my mouth so fast it makes a weird slurping noise.

He doesn't notice. Or if he does, he doesn't care or react like he thinks I'm a dork.

"It came with the house," I finally say. "I used it some when Bash was a baby, but then I didn't have time, and then the chickens broke it, so..."

"Would you use it if you had time and the chickens couldn't break it?"

I stare at him. "What's going on? What is this? What are you doing?"

"I missed you."

That's the last thing he's supposed to say.

"Not just the past couple days." His voice goes husky, and my panties go a little wet. "The past couple years. I missed you."

"I lost Bash," I blurt. "At the café. He was there one minute, playing with the dog, and then he was gone, and I've never, *ever* been afraid someone kidnapped him, but I was *terrified* someone knew he was yours and they grabbed him and I didn't know if I was going to see him again, and Begonia and Hayes were there and they saw it *all*, and I knew—I just *knew*—that that was all your family would need to take him away from me."

I haven't even finished before he's yanking the door open and striding inside, pulling me against his chest and holding me tight.

And then the very worst thing in the world happens.

I start crying.

Again.

"I can't do this, Jonas. I can't live in fear like this."

"I've got you," he murmurs into my hair. "I've got both of you."

"Stop saying all the right things."

"I'm here to *do* the right things. But if you don't want me, if you don't want this, I'll—" He cuts himself off with a shaky breath that I can feel all the way to the pit of my soul.

And not because I'm pressed so closely to him that I can feel it against my own chest.

But because I know what he's about to say.

"If you don't want me and what I bring, I'll go," he finishes.

"Stop."

"I mean it. I know my life is a lot. I know it's not simple. You don't—you don't need me. You have family. You're a fantastic mom. You have the life you wanted. I'm interfering."

I don't know if I'm holding on to him or if he's holding on to me now.

But I know there's not a chance in hell I'm letting go.

Jonas Rutherford, movie star? He can go.

But Jonas Rutherford, my friend, the man who's *here*, who went camping with my brother and has been puked on and taken care of us and wants to fix my hot tub?

"I missed you too," I whisper.

His grip on me tightens.

"And I hated you for how you left, and I hated you for not replying to my messages, and every time I got short on sleep, I hated you for having an easy life, and *I missed my friend*."

"I'm so sorry, Emma. So sorry."

"Mama kwy?" Bash whispers behind us.

I suck in a massive breath, pulling all of the snot and tears and fear back inside me, just as I've done every time I've thought I couldn't do this the past couple years. Shaking free from Jonas, I wipe my eyes, then squat down to Bash's level.

"Mama's having a moment, sweetie. I'm okay. I just need a minute with my feelings."

He stares at me with big brown eyes, that finger drifting to his mouth while he holds Yolko Ono in his other arm. "Dona make you kwy?"

"No, Jonas didn't make me cry."

Bash eyes Jonas like he knows Jonas did, in fact, make me cry.

"Hey, kiddo," Jonas says softly. "Nice chicken you got there."

Bash pulls his slobbery finger out of his mouth and grabs my hand. "I take cawe Mama."

"You're doing a fabulous job," Jonas says.

"She *my* mama."

"Best mama in the world, isn't she?"

Bash tugs on my hand. "*My* mama."

"Your mama who needs to get dinner started," I say. "What do you think? Should we have a Friday night pizza party?"

"Unka Deo!" Bash yells.

He's so firm on it, I honestly turn and peer through the screen door, wondering if Theo's here.

But he's not. "I think Uncle Theo and Aunt Laney are having a date tonight. But I can text Zen. And the triplets. What do you think?"

"Peeda pawty!"

I sniffle once more while I smile at him. "Pizza party it is. Can Jonas stay?"

"No. Dona go."

"Maybe he stays after he does a timeout?"

"No. Dona *go*."

I glance up at Jonas, and I swear he's gone into full actor mode.

No emotion at all beyond an easy smile. "It's okay," he tells me. "Begonia wants a full run-down on how much torture I was subjected to the past couple days."

"*Goooona!*" Bash cries. "*Maw-mawa!* Gona Maw-mawa peeeda pawty!"

"You…want me to invite Begonia and Marshmallow to our pizza party?" I ask Bash.

"Uh-huh."

"And Hayes too?"

"No."

"Zen and the triplets still?"

"Uh-huh."

"It's nice to include all of our friends when we can."

Bash eyes Jonas again. "Dey eat *ow-sie*."

"And you have to share Yolko Ono with Decker."

Bash grins.

Yolko Ono bagocks.

Jonas sucks in a breath and takes a half step back, and I laugh.

I actually laugh.

"Okay. Pizza party it is. Go find your pizza party pajamas, and I'll invite our guests."

Bash drops Yolko Ono, who bagocks again and startles Jonas *again*. And then my little tornado tears off up the stairs.

Jonas sighs as I rise back to my feet, watching while Bash's little legs disappear. "It's okay if he doesn't want me here. He knows I made you cry."

"Generally, leaving isn't the best way to solve a problem."

He winces.

I take his hand, realize what I've done, and drop it again, my pulse skyrocketing. "I didn't mean—"

"I will deserve that until the end of time."

If there's one thing I've learned since my failed wedding, it's that I need to not say *it's okay* quite so much. "I forgive you," I say instead, "and I understand if you can't yet forgive yourself."

He studies me, those beautiful brown eyes flickering over my face. "Bash has no idea how lucky he got with the mama lottery, does he?"

"None of us ever do. Can you invite Begonia and Hayes and Marshmallow? I need to ping Zen and the triplets, and then order pizza."

"Is there any chance you'll let me order the pizza?"

"No."

"Had to ask."

"You can fix the hot tub though. Thank you."

He smiles at me, but this isn't a *knock you off your feet with all of that movie star beauty* smile.

This is a soft smile that says *I want to hug you again*.

And it sends a full body shiver racing across my skin and down to my bones.

Something just shifted.

And I don't know if I'm ready for it.

29

Jonas

"You're planning to fix that with YouTube and willpower?" Hayes asks me as the two of us hang out by the broken hot tub while the pizza party's winding down.

And by *winding down*, I mean everyone else has left except for me, Hayes, Begonia, and Zen.

Bash has remained largely unimpressed with me tonight, choosing Zen and Begonia over everyone else. That's why they're still here. He insists that they help give him a bath and put him to bed.

Or possibly he'd do that anyway.

Even if he hadn't seen me make Emma cry.

Yep. Still feel like an absolute asshole for that.

I don't know if he remembers. I don't know how long toddler memories are. I'll have to look that up.

But I'll remember.

I hold a flashlight to study the side of the tub where it

looks like chickens pecked through the wall and into an electrical cord of some kind. "If I can't fix it, I'll replace it."

"Have you ever fixed a thing in your life?"

"I've played a mechanic *four times*."

He doesn't reply.

Likely because we both know what he'd say if he did. *I've seen the reviews on those movies, and a high number pointed out you can't change those kinds of cars' oil from the top of the engine.*

In my defense, two of those roles were as *mechanic in training*. When I was playing teenagers. And before I figured out how much I loved researching the quirks of the roles I took.

"Ready to learn new things," I mutter.

"Like how to take Mom's phone calls for yourself?"

"I've texted her."

"She's getting concerned. And Begonia's getting closer to her due date."

I know what he's saying.

I have to face my mother sooner or later. Lay out for her what I will and won't tolerate with the whole family being let in on the news about Bash.

And Emma.

Before my sister-in-law goes into labor if I want her and Hayes around for support when Mom finally figures out where I am and arrives.

Our mother doesn't worry about me the same way she worried about Hayes. But she's worried about me more since my divorce. You take a woman whose first priority is her sons' happiness followed closely by a priority to keep the family's public reputation just as perfect and happy as our amusement park and movies, and she's an unstoppable force when she thinks something's wrong.

"Thank you for sending Emma blackmail material after Bash disappeared at the café," I tell my brother.

He grunts the equivalent of a *you're welcome*.

Speaking of things we both know—we both know Emma wouldn't have freaked out at Bash disappearing in a café she goes to all the time if there wasn't the element of *me* in her life now.

A few weeks ago, she was anonymous and happy and somewhere she felt safe. Bash disappearing into the kitchen of Sabrina's café was probably normal then. Between watching how many people are in Emma's close circle who adore him, and the stories Grey and Theo told about how close-knit the community is as a whole, it wouldn't surprise me if Bash can slip into any kitchen in any restaurant in town, ask for a cookie, get it, and slip back to Emma's side before she has reason to be concerned.

Now, though, normal things are grounds for anxiety for Emma.

Because of me.

"I'm quitting acting," I tell my brother.

He doesn't respond, which could mean *duh, of course you are*, or it could mean *are you sure about that?*

"It's the right thing to do," I add.

Again, no reply.

The back door opens. Begonia's belly comes first, followed by the rest of her, and then Emma.

And I have a desperate, unquenchable desire to know what Emma looked like when she was carrying Bash.

How it felt when he kicked inside her.

If he ever got the hiccups and made her entire belly shake.

I want to have been the one fixing her a spinach and cottage cheese omelet in the middle of the night.

Or whatever *her* cravings were.

Will I miss acting?

I will. It's always come easy and I like it.

But there's a hole in my life that I can't fill with roles playing someone else, no matter how big the roles might be. I missed Bash's birth. Holding him when he was a baby. Sending Emma back to bed while I changed a diaper or gave him a bottle in the middle of the night. His first birthday.

I don't know what his first word was. What his first solid food was. When he started walking. If he's ever needed stitches. How often he gets his hair cut.

How she did it all on her own.

I'll miss acting.

But I can't miss any more of *this*.

Of *life*.

"I can't believe I'm about to say this, but I think Bash has as much energy as all of our camp kids combined," Begonia says. "He wins. Stick a fork in me. I'm done."

"I'd prefer to simply take you home," Hayes says, rising from the lawn chair beside me.

"That'll work too." Begonia hugs Emma. "Thank you for the pizza party. It's like you knew what I was craving."

"Thank you for coming. Bash had a great time."

"That's the Marshmallow effect."

Hayes grunts.

Begonia giggles.

The dog in question sticks his nose out of the back door, a chicken in his mouth.

"*Marshmallow*," Begonia chides. "Drop the chicken."

Hayes adds a throat-clear as he stares at the dog.

Yolko Ono squawks once, and Marshmallow sets her gingerly back on her one leg, then licks her.

Yolko Ono flaps her wings at him, just once, then hops under him and settles to the ground beneath the dog's chest.

Like he's her shelter from the rain that isn't falling.

All of us stare at the two of them for a second before Begonia giggles again. "That—that was not funny," she says between snickers.

Hayes smiles and loops his arm around her neck, pressing a kiss to her head. And then he snaps his fingers. "Marshmallow. Car. Now. Before you squash the chicken."

I have never been so jealous of my brother in my entire life.

Actually, I don't think I've ever been jealous of him. Everything that's come easy to me has come hard to him, and I know it.

He deserves to be happy and in love and saying volumes with grunts that his wife replies to with laughter and orders to her dog that the pup answers with whines and reluctant obedience.

I want that.

Not because I've ever felt like my life is lacking.

But because I want to laugh and have private jokes with Emma and learn how to give her chicken commands that it'll listen to.

"Need a ride?" Hayes asks me.

"Nah, I'm gonna figure out what else I need here. Thanks."

Hayes gives Emma a shoulder-hug, which is almost as startling as if he'd picked her up and swung her around in an impromptu square dance. "Thank you for dinner."

Emma smiles at him. "My pleasure. Thank you for coming."

And then my brother and his wife and their dog depart, leaving me alone with Emma and Yolko Ono.

She settles into the folding chair close to me, pulling the chicken into her lap and petting it like it's a purse dog. "Jack said to tell you to call him if you want help with the hot tub."

"Will he help, or will he pretend to help?"

She smiles. "He'll help. He's actually incapable of doing a project wrong, even to make a point. If Decker or Lucky or Zen had offered to help, though, I'd advise against taking them up on it."

Not much else I can do tonight. Not without the replacement parts.

And a fence to keep the chickens out of the hot tub area.

So instead, I open up the other chair and take a seat next to Emma.

"How was camping?" she asks me.

"Everything I expected it to be and more."

"Oh, god, what did Theo do?"

I smile. Can't help it. "Nothing I didn't respect."

"That is not the right answer."

"I'm not bloodied and bruised, so this is an improvement." Don't, ah, ask me about my intestinal tract though.

Camp food, man. It is *not* what I've been served the

few times I've visited Razzle Dazzle's camps. And the pain didn't stop with the fire in my mouth, if you know what I mean.

Emma eyes me but doesn't press for more details.

The truth here is the one thing I won't share with her.

That's a step too far.

I'd honestly hope Hayes wouldn't share details with Begonia either if the same ever happened to him.

"It was fun too," I tell her. "Would probably be *more* fun the next time."

She pulls her knees up to her chest in the chair, cradling the chicken in one arm beside her knees while the bird makes a noise that sounds strangely similar to a purr. "You'd go again?"

"Sure."

"*Sure, if I had nothing else going on,* or *sure, I hope they invite me again?*"

"I hope they invite me again, and if they don't, I'd plan something and invite them instead. Especially since I know about Theo's sneezes now. Won't be nearly so scary at four a.m. next time."

"His sneeze literally starred in my wedding video. It *opens* my wedding video."

"It's different in real life."

She shakes her head. "That I can agree with."

We both smile.

"You're serious about staying," she says slowly.

"Completely serious."

"You won't miss acting? Traveling? Being in the public spotlight?"

"I would miss being here more."

She rests her chin on one knee and stares at the chicken coop.

And it's so *peaceful*.

Soft clucks. The sun sinking lower, but not yet casting the deep shadows of dusk.

Yolko Ono purring like a cat. Swear on my lone Oscar, she's purring.

Bash's voice drifts down, singing a song I don't recognize, but Emma could probably name.

I like my life.

I've never felt like anything was missing.

But when I'm here, I feel like I've found where I'm supposed to be.

Who I'm supposed to be.

Who matters.

"Was he an easy baby?" I ask in the stillness.

"What makes an easy baby?"

Huh. "I...don't actually know."

She smiles out at the chickens again. She gathered eggs and fed them while the rest of us were picking up the pizzas and cleaning dishes, so I don't think she's worried about them.

I think she's contemplating how much she wants to share with me.

How much I've earned.

How much she believes I'm worth the time to let me a little further in.

"He was the very best baby," she finally says softly.

"He wasn't fussy?"

"Oh, he was. He loved being held. Hated being put down for even a minute the first couple months. If you put him down, he'd scream. And scream. And scream some more even when you picked him up, like he needed to tell you how terrible it was to not be held before he could settle down. But he wasn't too picky about who held him. Unless it was Decker. If Decker held him, we had to play pop music or Bash would scream some more."

"That must've made nights hard."

She shakes her head. "No, it—it's what I wanted. *He's* what I wanted. When my mom died, I lost this security that I took for granted. My dad's great, but he's not...he's not my mom."

"When did she pass?"

"I was eleven."

"Ah, Emma. I'm sorry."

"I had Laney and Sabrina. And Theo did so much more than most people would give him credit for, even though he wasn't that much older than me. And he had his own needs that weren't being met. Not that he'd admit it. But I knew. I tried my best to be what he needed too. We were in it together, you know?"

I nod like I can put myself in her shoes, but playing the part of someone who lost a parent young once or twice isn't the same as living it day in and day out.

"Since then," she continues, "I've always wanted —*needed*, maybe?—to have that dream family. To recreate what I'd missed in my own life. The family that I felt like I had stolen from me, even though I still had Dad and Theo. It's just...they weren't Mom. She was special. She was *everything*."

"You have a lot of her in you?"

There's that soft smile again. "I like to think so."

"I didn't know your mom, but I've never met a mother who wouldn't be proud of you."

"She always told me I could be anything I wanted to be. And I'm mostly living the life I always wanted. Bash was—*is*—my family. And it *was* hard, but I also knew he was getting bigger every single day. That no matter how tired I was, I didn't want to miss a second. That he'd be my only baby, ever, and one day I'd sleep again. But I wouldn't get another chance to be the mom to him that I had taken from me. And he's worth it. He's *so* worth it."

I swallow hard.

I've lost sleep for roles. For appearances. For my social life. Occasionally for heartbreak.

But never for taking care of another human being.

Not like this.

"And I didn't do it all on my own," she adds. "My friends wouldn't let me. They made sure I rested and ate enough and sometimes showered. I wasn't alone, and I wasn't too exhausted to enjoy him."

I clear my throat again, but my voice is still husky. "Good."

I missed so much.

So much.

She sucks in a soft breath and puts a hand on my arm, leaning into me. "Jonas, look," she whispers.

A mama deer and two spotted babies have just stepped into the clearing of her yard from the pine forest. Both fawns stare at the chickens while they hover behind the mama, who puts her head down, munching on the wild grass.

"Aren't they cute?" Emma whispers.

All I can do is nod.

I'm too hung up in the scent of baby shampoo and a hint of mint tickling my nose. The feel of Emma's hand on my arm. The effort of suppressing the electric shiver overtaking my skin at her touch. The heat radiating off her body.

Watching the enamored smile light up her face while she watches the animals.

I know she's lived here her entire life. This isn't the first time she's seen baby animals.

But she's soaking it in like there's nothing she wants more than the simple pleasures in life. Like she's honored that they've chosen *her* yard to visit.

Every other time I've wanted to impress a woman, I've brought exotic flowers. Had chocolates flown in fresh from Paris. There were shopping trips. Private vacations to faraway locations. Backstage passes to just about anything.

Emma doesn't want *any* of that.

She didn't in Fiji. She doesn't here.

If I want to be part of her life, I can't rely on buying her things or taking her places.

I have to be enough all by myself.

Just as I am.

Without the fame and the bank account.

That is what she sparked in Fiji. That realization that I've never had to get to know *myself*. Who I am when I'm not *Jonas Rutherford*.

She makes me want to be *more*.

She inspired my risks on bigger roles, but that's not what I'm most proud of from the past two years.

I'm most proud of my podcast.

Of finding fascinating people around the country to interview about their journey to discovering who they are and what mark they're supposed to leave on the world.

Their obstacles. Their advantages. Who they were as kids and who they choose to be as adults.

What makes them tick.

I like to think it's inspiring people all over the globe to reach deep and embrace their biggest dreams despite their biggest fears.

That it's helping them realize it's okay to contemplate the question of *who am I when it's just me?*

That this is my way of improving the world.

By encouraging the people on the planet to be a little more.

The way she encouraged *me* to be more.

"Oh, they're so little, they're still nursing," she whispers.

I'm not watching the deer.

I'm watching the absolute joy and rapture on her face.

Wondering if I can ever be the reason she glows like that.

I want *that* to be my purpose in life.

Making Emma happy. Being a person who makes every day better for her. Being what she *wants*.

I know she doesn't need me.

She doesn't need my money. My connections. My fame. My family.

She already has dreams and goals and a purpose. Happiness and joy and laughter and support.

So I have to be enough, *just me*, if I'm going to fit into her life.

"Isn't it fascinating?" She looks at me, that smile shining brighter than anything Hollywood can produce.

"I mean it," I say thickly. "I'm leaving the public spotlight."

Her lashes flutter and her smile morphs into an *O*.

"I want to be *here*. With you and Bash."

"For how long?" Her voice is barely above a whisper, and I hate that I don't know if that's longing or fear laced into her words.

Maybe it's both.

But she's still gripping my forearm.

Still leaning close enough for me to study the fascinating ring of gold around her brown irises.

"Forever," I whisper back.

"Jonas—"

"Please let me stay. Let me in. Let me try to be what you both deserve."

We had something in Fiji.

We *have* something here. I don't know if I believe in fate. If I believe in soulmates. If I believe that there's *one person* out there, and only one person, whose life I'm meant to share.

But I know that I've never been in a relationship with anyone who feels as much like everything I've been missing in my life as I've felt in the times I've been with Emma.

She squeezes my arm. "This is a massive, life-altering decision."

"And it feels *right*. I don't know if I've ever felt anything this right."

Wariness creeps into her eyes.

I cover her hand with mine. "I can keep you out of the spotlight. Both of you. You don't have to hide. You don't have to move. I won't let them attack you again."

Her chin quivers. "I am so mad at you right now," she whispers.

"Why?"

"Because you make me want to do *this*."

Before I can ask what *this* is, she's kissing me. Brushing those soft lips over mine while everything inside me stills. All of the parts of me that have been on alert, watching, worrying, waiting for some sign that she was done with me and this chance was over—all of me melts into kissing her back.

My friend. My addiction. The mother of my child.

So fragile, but so strong.

Completely irresistible.

Fuck, I've missed her.

Her fingers curling into my hair. Her nose bumping mine. Goosebumps pebbling on the smooth skin on her arms.

Her lips.

Her mouth.

Kissing her takes me back to the hillside in Fiji. The clearing in the jungle. Laughing on a picnic blanket. Grabbing her hand while we were snorkeling to point out a colorful fish.

Making love with her.

I have missed this woman so much more than I let myself feel the past two and a half years.

But now she's kissing me, and nothing has ever felt more right.

Or more worth it.

The back door bangs open, and we leap apart.

"Forgot my jacket," Zen says, striding to the swing out by the chicken coop. "Don't let me interrupt. Unless you have nefarious intentions, and then I don't care how much of a pacifist I am, I'll take you down."

"Zen-zen?" Bash says from above us.

Zen snags their coat from the swing and smirks at me before looking at Emma. "Mind if I tell the little guy goodnight one more time?"

Emma's smoothing her hair back. "Do *not* wind him up."

"Please. Who do you think I am, Theo? Text me when you're free for lunch next week. We need to finish planning the baby shower. Later, Jonas. Don't do anything that'll make me have to hurt you."

"Good to see you too," I reply.

"I need to go tuck Bash back in," Emma stutters. She's still holding the chicken. I was kissing her while she was holding her chicken. "Thank you for—for staying. But you should probably head home now."

"Can I take you to lunch sometime soon too? Or dinner. Or breakfast. Or coffee or tea or for a hike or whatever you want to do?" I'm a teenager. I am once again a rambling, bumbling, awkward teenager.

Except I think teenagers have more swagger than I do.

And I definitely had more swagger when I was a teenager than I do in this moment.

She smiles, sucks it in, then smiles again. "I—you don't have to—yes. Yes. Thank you. I—I'd like that."

I'm itching to hug her again. To kiss her. To toss her over my shoulder, carry her up to her bedroom, strip her naked, and lick her all over.

But tonight, I'm settling for sticking my hands in my pockets. "Can I come back tomorrow?"

She nods.

I smile. "Can't wait."

I truly can't.

30

Emma

"He kissed you a week ago and hasn't tried anything since?" Laney whispers to me while we hover behind Bee & Nugget the next Saturday morning. The big baby shower for her and Sabrina is today. Theoretically, Zen and I are organizing it. In actuality, all of our friends have rallied and they're doing most of the work inside.

Laney and Sabrina both objected to a baby shower, but we convinced them they could use it as an opportunity to gather baby supplies for mothers in need while letting the community celebrate their excitement about two of their favorite Snaggletooth Creek residents starting their families.

So that's what we're doing.

And we're going all out.

Except for right now, while I'm confused and needing my friends to assure me that it's normal for a guy to not try to make a move *for a week* after telling me he's changing his life to be here for me and Bash.

He's even inside helping set up.

In the kitchen. So he's not spotted.

"Maybe he's waiting for me to initiate it again?" I whisper back.

Sabrina makes a noise that sounds almost like Grey grunting his disapproval over something. "Do you want to kiss him again?"

"Yes. No. Yes. I don't know."

We're out with the dogs for a potty break and for Jitter to shake off all of his drool before we head back inside.

He's a lot more chill than he was as a puppy, but the drool will be with us until the end of time.

"Do you like him?" Laney asks.

"Yes." No hesitation there.

I do. I like him.

He's funny and he's sweet and he pays his taxes and he hasn't tried to double-cross any of my friends. He's been infinitely patient with Bash, which is a serious checkmark in the *he's a good man* column.

"But?" Sabrina prompts.

And here are the problems. "But he says he's quitting the public life, and one, I don't know if that will make him happy, and two, just because he quits the public life doesn't mean the press quits him. And three—I don't know if he's doing this for me, or if he's doing this for Bash and I'm just part of the package. Like, would he do this for *any* woman he accidentally knocked up, or does he *like* me?"

Laney wrinkles her nose while she rubs her belly. "Valid concerns."

"He likes you, Emma," Sabrina says.

"But if he liked me, and I initiated a kiss, and he's kept his hands completely to himself for the week since then, *what does that mean*?"

"Have you gotten anything out of his family?" Sabrina asks.

I shake my head. "I've seen them, but they basically treat me like I'm an old friend instead of the woman who's been hiding his secret baby for the past two years."

"Bash was *not* a secret baby and you didn't hide him. You tried to tell Jonas. He failed to get the memo." Her eyes bulge, and then she smiles while she rubs her own belly. "Oh, *hello*, little one. Rather opinionated about that pork green chili for breakfast, aren't you?"

Now that's worth smiling over. "Are they kicking? Can I feel?"

Sabrina takes my hand and puts it on her belly, where I get a little flutter against my palm.

And then I squeal.

"Here, me too." Laney grabs my other hand, and all three of us giggle and squeal while the babies kick us. "But mine's just Theo's child. They don't really care what I eat for breakfast."

We did this when I was pregnant with Bash too. All three of us feeling him kick.

With me keeping the secret about who my baby's daddy was.

"I miss this," I whisper.

My friends share a look.

Yes, the look of *she could have it again if she lets Jonas back into her life*.

I've seen him nearly every day. He declared the hot tub

dead a week ago, asked very politely if he could replace it for me so long as his name appeared nowhere on the paperwork, and also if he could add a fence with a lock that Bash and the chickens can't open.

On Monday, he patched the screens in a few windows around my house, including one in Bash's room, that I hadn't realized were the source of the increased bugs in the house.

Tuesday, while I was at work and Bash was at daycare, he tackled a deep clean of my kitchen, which I'd been meaning to get to but hadn't yet.

Wednesday, he took Bash and me for a picnic dinner behind Hayes and Begonia's house.

After sandwiches and carrot sticks and watermelon, we had fireless s'mores that he warmed up with a solar oven he made out of cardboard and aluminum foil.

YouTube can teach you the coolest stuff, he'd said, smiling like he was a kid again himself.

Thursday, we didn't see him at all. He flew back to New York for a charity dinner to put the rumors about his public absence at bay.

And while he was gone, there was a crew at my house who believed that they'd been sent by Theo to install my new hot tub and fence.

I texted Jonas pictures and updates and my appreciation.

Friday, when he got back to town, we had a smaller pizza party. Just Bash and Jonas and me.

Bash asked very politely to watch *Panda Bananda*, his favorite cartoon, which made Jonas's ears turn bright red.

When I asked if he had an issue with Panda, he winced, then very quietly did Panda's voice.

"Did you two know Jonas does Panda's voice in *Panda Bananda*?" I say suddenly.

"*What?*" Sabrina says.

"*No,*" Laney says.

"I've never watched the credits before. But he does."

"Since when?" Sabrina demands.

"The whole time. It's only in the second season. He said he auditioned on a dare not long after...we met."

"Is he giving that up too?" Sabrina whispers.

Laney's shaking her head. "The show would be *ruined* if they got a new voice."

"And how would Bash feel if he found out his father leaving was the reason his favorite TV show ended?" Sabrina adds.

"Moral dilemma," I agree. "I'm staying out of it."

"But what do you *want* him to do?" Laney asks.

I feel the ugly face coming on. "Not be famous in the first place."

It's the truth.

And it's not fair.

It's not fair to ask him to not be who he is if he wants to be part of my life and part of Bash's life.

And if he wasn't famous—well.

Life would be a lot different right now, wouldn't it?

We wouldn't be hiding in my house or around Hayes's house. We'd have lunch in the café. He'd go with me when it was time to drop off or pick up Bash at daycare. We'd paddleboard together on the lake. Take Bash on a train ride, leaving from the station at the lake.

Instead...instead, I feel like he's my dirty secret.

And I'm starting to wonder if that's how he feels too.

Laney and Sabrina share another look.

"Whatever it is, just say it," I tell them.

"If you're prepared for public attention, will it be as bad?" Laney asks.

"What you went through was awful," Sabrina adds. "I won't ever minimize that. This is not any of us making light of the impact of that video on your life and on your mental health. This is us asking if there's benefit to taking advantage of the kind of media training that you and Bash will likely both need before he's fully grown, no matter what."

"He looks so much like Jonas," Laney says. "And we know you won't hide the truth from him when he's old enough to understand. Once he's grown up...isn't it better if he's prepared too? Can you imagine if one of your parents had been even moderately famous? How that would've impacted you and Theo?"

I shudder.

The idea of Theo being Theo in the public spotlight in his teenage years...no.

Just no.

And Bash might look like Jonas, but he has that male Monroe gene through and through.

Oh god.

Oh god oh god oh god.

A teenager who looks like Jonas Rutherford and behaves like my brother—he wouldn't make it to his twenties. People will notice. The *not safe, not friends* people.

I need a paper bag.

Sabrina squeezes my hand. "We'd hide you both here forever if we could. But we know it's not realistic. Not long-term."

Laney loops her arm around my back and squeezes me

in a half hug. "Whatever you want, we're here for you. But we're not keeping our promises to always tell you the hard things if we don't speak up on this."

The door squeaks behind us. "Hate to interrupt," Theo says, "but we have a small problem."

"The food?" Sabrina says.

"Oh, no, tell me they aren't bringing us presents," Laney adds.

Theo shakes his head.

I don't like his grin.

I especially don't like that he's aiming it at me.

I cringe. "Did Bash get into the flour again?"

Jack is on Bash duty. He's sworn my baby is not getting out of his sight, and I believed him enough to sneak out here and ask my friends for advice.

Plus, the café's closed while we prep for the shower this afternoon.

No one in. No one out, except through the back door.

Theo shakes his head again, grinning bigger, and gestures all of us into the kitchen.

The first thing I notice are the balloons.

They're *everywhere*.

Pink balloons. Blue balloons. Yellow balloons. Green balloons. Purple balloons. It's a pastel rainbow of balloons that have overtaken the kitchen to the point that you can't see the floor. Most of it is buried under at least three layers of waist-high balloons.

And then I notice the shoes.

They're nice shoes. Brown leather. Large. Propped up on a stool and attached to denim-covered legs that disappear into the balloons.

"I didn't do it," Decker says. He's leaning on the edge of the metal prep table.

"Not it either," Jack says from his spot across from Decker. He's shooting glances at the dining room that tell me he's watching Bash.

I think.

I hope.

The balloons stir. "I'm okay," they say. They sound like a very wheezy Jonas. "Just a little light-headed."

Jack smirks. Decker smirks. Theo smirks.

"Where's Bash?" I ask them all.

A little giggle under the prep table, behind a bunch of balloons, answers me.

"I'm okay," Jonas says again.

He's completely covered in balloons, and he does *not* sound okay.

I cross my arms and look at Theo.

He gives me a petulant single-shoulder shrug. "Decker started it."

Decker tosses his hands up. "So you're throwing me under the bus now?"

"My wife doesn't like it when people pass out blowing up balloons for her baby shower."

"He *passed out*?" I repeat, wading through the balloons to try to find the rest of Jonas.

"I didn't know dude wasn't used to the elevation yet," Decker says. "He's been here for like a month. He should be used to the elevation."

"And we figured anybody who talks as much as he does had to have good lung capacity," Jack adds.

"Good lungs," Jonas wheezes. "Dry. But good. Big. Big lungs."

I push balloons aside to find him, but they keep falling back on themselves. "Can you four please start decorating the dining room with these?"

"Making—balloon pit—for Bash," Jonas says.

"Bawoon pit!" Bash echoes. "I die!"

"Do *not* dive in the balloon pit, please." The images flashing in my brain right now—Bash doing a header onto the floor and knocking himself out or gushing blood out of a head wound.

I shudder.

"We put cushioning on the floor first, Em," Decker says, clearly offended.

"Lucky'd basically kill us if we didn't," Jack adds.

Decker nods. "He's already pissed we're interrupting his morning to come over and check out Mr. Airhead over here."

"*So* pissed."

"My nut sack's shriveling. And I wasn't even the one who called him."

"To be fair, I had a feeling he was on a date. This isn't surprising."

"The part where he had a date is surprising."

"But him being pissed that we interrupted it isn't."

"Truer words, my brother."

Jonas giggles.

Giggles.

It's freaking adorable.

Also?

Bash giggles the exact same way.

I finally succeed in pushing enough balloons out of the way so that I can see Jonas's face.

He has his eyes closed and he's sucking in deep

breaths.

I squat next to him and put a hand to his forehead. It's automatic to check for a fever even though I know going light-headed shouldn't cause a fever.

But what if he has a fever and that's what made him pass out?

"Are you *still* light-headed?" I ask him.

No fever.

But I let my hand linger on his face while I balance on the balls of my feet beside him.

I can't help touching him.

He's absolutely adorable.

Not movie-star handsome. Not ruggedly handsome.

I mean, he's both of those things most of the time.

But right now, he's as sweet and effortlessly charming as Bash is when he's waking up in the morning.

"Small headache." His chest raises as he sucks in a big breath, displacing more balloons. "Worth it."

"Did these yahoos tell you that they have pumps for the balloons?"

Jonas slides one eye open and squints at me. "My lungs are the pumps."

I try to give him the stern mama glare, but he's clearly going to be okay, and somehow his eyes are crossed even though only one is open.

And those crossed eyes on top of that smile?

How can I *not* be completely and totally smitten with this man?

"I'm Super Lung Man," he adds.

Decker snickers.

Jack coughs.

"If you're gonna be a superhero, be a new one," Theo

says. "You want a cape? Laney. Get this man a custom cape."

"Will I be in trouble with your security team if I don't get you to a doctor?" I ask Jonas.

"Nope."

"The rest of your family?"

"Nope."

"Are you sure?"

He smiles at me. "Won't let them be mad at you."

I smile back, almost missing the fact that the balloons are moving around us again.

Jitter's coming to investigate.

He shoves against me, displacing more balloons and pushing them back over Jonas's face.

But more—Jitter's so big, he's knocking me off-balance.

"*Jitter*," I gasp as I try to grab onto him to keep from falling.

The St. Bernard snorts in my face.

In my face.

I stumble sideways.

My arms flail. I try to adjust my feet to stay upright while I'm squatting here, but it doesn't work, and I tumble.

Sideways.

With my hand connecting with denim covering—

"*Urp*," Jonas says.

Oh, god.

Oh, no no no.

I thump back onto my tailbone and snatch my hand back.

"Oh my god, I am so sorry," I whisper.

Not there, not there, not there, I silently wish. *Please tell me I didn't land directly on his penis.*

Jonas whimpers.

I can't see him anymore through the balloons.

"*Jitter*, go," I order. "Go to your house."

He ignores me and puts his massive head down into the balloons, right about where—

"*Ack*," Jonas gasps.

His body twitches next to me.

I shove the dog's backside. "Jitter, go find Grey."

Jitter's head jerks up. He gives me a massive doggy grin, then changes course, galloping through the balloons and heading toward the dining room.

Decker and Jack are watching me, their identical expressions a mixture of horrified and amused.

Theo's disappeared.

Bash pokes his head out above the balloons beneath the prep table. "Why Mama yell Ditta?"

"He *licked* me," Jonas says.

"Ditta wike you!" Bash shrieks.

Sabrina and Laney are clearly stifling laughter behind us as well.

"That's true," Sabrina forces out. "Jitter only licks the people he likes."

"Are you okay?" I whisper to Jonas.

"Might need to sit the rest of today out," he whispers back.

The back door bangs open. "I'm here," Lucky says. "Where's the ducking patient, you ack-jasses? And *why am I your personal medical professional*? Next time, find someone else."

"Hot date?" Sabrina asks him.

He flips her off, spots Bash, goes pink, and scowls harder at her.

"I'm okay," Jonas says beneath the balloons. "I'm incognito."

"Why'd you blow up this many balloons?" Lucky asks. "You don't need this many balloons."

"Social experiment," Decker replies the same time Jack says, "We were testing him."

"I'm okay," Jonas repeats.

"Did I—" I start, but he interrupts me.

"It's fine."

"Oh my god."

"I'm gonna live."

"Jonas—"

"It was an accident."

"And I am so—"

"Worth it."

I go still.

You're worth it.

I *damaged his penis*, put all of my weight on using his penis to stop my fall, and he doesn't care.

"I like you, Emma," he whispers behind the balloons.

Dammit dammit *dammit*.

My eyes are getting hot. So are my ears.

I don't know who heard that.

Not that it's a surprise to anyone.

He's offered to give up acting for me—for *us*, for me and Bash.

But I've been telling myself it's a sense of obligation. Of duty. Of guilt.

For Bash.

With me as a tag-along who sometimes oversteps boundaries and kisses him.

But *this*?

Telling me he likes me after I've basically assaulted his family jewels?

That's not obligation.

Obligation would involve the lawyers. A paternity test. Formal arrangements for child support and visitation.

He likes me.

And I can't deny it anymore.

"Can someone get these damn balloons out of the kitchen?" Lucky mutters behind me. "Scoot, Emma. Let me make sure he's gonna live."

"I'm gonna live," Jonas says. "Have to. Too much to live for not to."

"All those award shows and women fawning over you, right?" Lucky says.

I scurry out of the way and don't hear Jonas's answer over the sound of the balloons squeaking together.

Laney and Sabrina are both watching me.

So is Theo.

"C'mon, Bash." I have no idea how I'm keeping my voice normal. *He likes me.* All of me. Exactly as I am. Awkward moments and all. He's not trying to change me. He's changing his life *for me*. And Bash. For both of us. Not one over the other. "Let's go put the party balloons where the party goes."

And let my heart rate calm down.

I like you.

I don't know if he's said it before, but I *heard* it this time.

And I'm starting to truly, honestly, fully believe him.

31

Jonas

I DON'T KNOW what's on Emma's mind—once I'm upright again after what I will forever call the balloon mistake, she was busy running the baby shower, which I was forcefully invited to skip—but when she texts me and asks me to come over later that night, I don't hesitate.

It's already dark. I expect Bash is in bed, and when I follow Emma's instructions and head around back instead of coming through the house, that's confirmed.

She's standing next to the hot tub in a one-piece swimsuit, lit by the glow of little fairy lamps around the fence. Steam lifts in wispy tendrils off the top of the hot tub, also glowing in the fairy lamp light.

As soon as she spots me, she puts a finger to her lips.

She's absolutely, stunningly radiant tonight.

It's the lighting, but it's something else too.

Happiness.

That's what it is.

It's the smile illuminating her entire face. Her relaxed shoulders. The easy grace in her movements as she drapes two towels over the fence.

I walk quietly, my pulse drumming and my dick noticing just how very little material there is between her skin and the night air.

"Hi," she whispers as I stop on the other side of the new gate.

I smile, then smile broader before I whisper a soft *hi* back. I want to hook my hand around the back of her neck and pull her close for a kiss. I want to stroke her bare skin. I want to strip her out of that swimsuit and explore every inch of her.

But not until she unequivocally tells me she's ready.

Waiting for her to tell me she's ready has been absolute torture.

"Want to try out the hot tub with me?" she whispers.

Oh, *fuck yes*.

Is that my shirt practically stripping itself off of me? I believe it is. "Yes."

"The stars will be pretty tonight, and that was always my favorite thing about the old hot tub, but my text said it was undelivered when I told you to bring your swimsuit, and—oh. Okay, that works."

I look down. The shadows and my black briefs are hiding my boner, but my thighs are glowing like there's a blacklight aimed at their general pastiness. My pants, shoes, and socks are all in a pile together.

"Don't ever have a stripping contest with a theater kid. We do quick-changes like nobody's business."

She laughs, pressing her fingers to her cheeks like she's testing if they're hot.

Turned on hot?

Or embarrassed hot?

Am I doing this all wrong again?

"Last one in—" I start, but she cuts me off.

"Is on diaper duty all day tomorrow."

She flashes an impish grin and leaves me in the dust, dashing the few steps to the new salt water hot tub, swinging a leg over, and climbing in.

As if I mind.

She's just told me I get to spend the day with them tomorrow too.

Have to, if I'm on diaper duty.

Plus, I get to watch her face as she sinks into the warm water.

Her eyes slide closed, her breasts lift with a deep breath, and then she's immersed all the way up to her neck, leaning her head back against the edge with a contented sigh. "Oh my god, I forgot how much I love this."

I follow more slowly, not because I don't want to dive in headfirst, but because I don't want her spotting the reaction my body is having to her.

With any other woman, *want to come in the hot tub with me?* would be an invitation to screw around.

With Emma?

I don't know yet.

"You like the jets or not?" I ask as I step in, angled to block her view of my excited dick.

Am I embarrassed?

No.

But I don't want her thinking the only reason I'm here is to make out with a hot girl in a hot tub.

"*All* of the jets, please, Mr. Why Buy A Hot Tub If You Don't Get The Model With Jets Everywhere?"

Can't resist smiling at that. And I smile broader when I glance back and catch her watching my ass.

I don't call her on it.

I know she notices me noticing, because she jerks her gaze back up to my face, the color-changing fairy lights both inside the tub and around the fence hiding from me if she's blushing.

"You don't like people doing things for you," I say instead.

"I don't like feeling like I'm incompetent. Like I'm failing at this adulting thing."

"You are *not* failing."

"Hit the big button that looks like it could launch a spaceship into orbit, please. That's the *only hit this button if you're sure you want to get a blast of water up all of your orifices* button. And *shh*. Bash sleeps like a drunk lumberjack once he's out, but if we're loud enough, he *will* wake up."

I try—and fail—to stop laughing. "You *want* something up all of your orifices?"

"I'm playing chicken with the jets. I *think* I'm safe. But half the thrill is in not knowing."

"Emma Monroe, do your friends know you're such a daredevil?"

"Quit stalling and hit the button."

"As the lady wishes."

Never let it be said that I don't follow instructions. I hit the right button, and while the motors slowly whir to life, I slide the rest of the way into the steamy water, taking the indented seat next to Emma.

And hope I've positioned myself right too.

Might've gone overboard with the number of jets in this thing.

But I don't normally buy off-the-shelf, delivered-in-two-days-because-it's-the-floor-model-of-the-best-we-have-to-offer hot tubs.

Which is probably not the defense I'm pretending it is.

If we'd had three weeks, I could've had a mold taken of your body and made sure the jets were positioned correctly to massage you in all of the right places is more than likely overkill in her life.

As was this hot tub.

But if she's letting me buy her something, she's getting the best.

Plus, who would've believed her brother would've bought her anything less? We put his name all over the paperwork.

Emma's grinning at me, looking more alive than I've seen her since Fiji. "How long do you think it'll—*urp!*"

The jets explode to life, full-force, at least eight of them aimed at my back, six under my thighs, and two each behind my calves and under my heels.

I'm jolted forward, but Emma's flat-out flung into the middle of the hot tub.

She goes under, and I don't stop. Don't think. Just act.

I lunge for her, getting pushed by the jets that seem to be coming from the middle of the water, and I grab her arm as she starts to surface.

"Are you—" I start, but I get a face full of her hair as she flings it backward.

She's wheezing and coughing and laughing.

I swipe my face, still startled at the sting from the hair slap, my eyes wet with hot tub water.

"That's—good," she chokes out between coughs, which are between peals of laughter. "Really—strong."

"Are you okay?"

"I'm fine. Truly, I—Jonas? Are *you* okay?"

"Yep."

"What's wrong with your eyes?"

"Too much beauty. I can't look at you straight on without going blind."

"*Jonas.*"

"Just a little water."

"Let me see."

"I—"

She slides next to me, our bodies touching under the water, both of us on our knees. The jets are swirling the water hard enough that she uses my leg as leverage for hers, putting her pussy against my knee.

And then she touches my face, gently brushing water off my cheeks and eyelashes.

I blink my eyes open, knowing what I'm about to find, and still caught off-guard by how close she is.

Even with my blurred vision, I can make out the angles of her cheeks and jawline, that adorable nose, the plump lips and wide eyes. I blink again, and my vision starts to clear. My eyes still ache, but they'll live.

Her light lashes are clumped together, some still holding droplets of water. Her hair's slicked back, her ears more prominent, and she's the most beautiful thing I've ever seen.

Swear she is.

She's just so *Emma*.

And I fucking adore that about her.

"Here. I'll get you a towel."

I grip her by the waist and shake my head. "Stay."

Her hands still on my face, and she studies me like she's trying to read between the letters of that one word.

"Stay." I want to wrap my arms around her and drag her to me and kiss her until neither of us can breathe. I want—I just *want*. I want *her*. "It's dangerous out there. Tidal wave might knock you over."

Her fingers caress my cheeks. "You helped set up for my friends' baby shower."

"Had an extra set of lungs just sitting around, being useless otherwise."

She smiles, her eyes crinkling at the corners. Just a little, but it's there. Steam rises around us. The fairy lights shift from a soft blue to a soft purple.

"I was afraid you were here just for Bash," she whispers. "That you were—that you were just being nice to me because we're a package deal. That you left Fiji because I was getting too needy or clingy or—"

My heart splits itself in two. "Emma. No. I left because the paparazzi were on the way. I didn't—I should've left my phone number. I didn't think of it until I was gone, and then—then I thought you were better off without me. It's dumb. It's a stupid excuse. I—"

"I understand." She's stroking my cheeks, her gaze darting from my eyes to my lips and back to my eyes again.

I clear my throat. "If we'd met again under any other circumstance, I would've stayed just for you."

She shakes her head.

I squeeze her waist and tug her close. "I missed you, but I didn't think I was allowed to. I didn't think I deserved to. But I did. I thought about you all the time."

"Giving up your life for us—that's *massive*." It doesn't matter how loudly the jets are humming, I hear her soft voice. "Are you sure you won't regret it?"

"I get one life to make the most of. I don't want to look back in fifty years and have you be my biggest regret. I want to look back in fifty years and know that we—that *we* lived our lives with love and laughter and joy."

She bites her lower lip and watches me, not saying a word.

I'm nearly certain she's still afraid. Afraid of the public attention I bring with me. Afraid I'll have regrets. Afraid of what happened after her wedding happening all over again.

"That's very brave of you," she finally says.

Not mocking.

She's completely earnest.

She knows what it's like to have your life changed in an instant. Multiple times over.

Losing her mom. Dumping her ex. Finding out she was pregnant.

Choosing again and again to be brave on her own.

Those moments in her past required so much more bravery than I've ever had to muster, but she's still serious about understanding what a massive shift a small-town, quiet existence will be compared to the movie-star life I've led to this point.

"A very wise lady once reminded me that I don't have reason to be afraid of much," I murmur.

Her lips tip up. "She was right."

"Only about everything *outside* of here." I tap my chest. "*Inside* of here, I'm still a pretty tender guy without a lot of safety nets. Money can't buy a guard for a heart."

"Promise me you'll keep Bash safe. From—"

From the press. From rumors and whispers and judgment. From the haters.

She doesn't have to fill in the blanks lingering between us.

"I will move mountains to keep Bash safe," I say. "*That*, I can promise you."

Her shoulders drop, her breath leaves her in a rush, and then she makes all of my dreams come true.

She pushes forward and kisses me again.

Those lips on mine. Her fingers sliding back across my face to trace my ears and sink into my hair.

My entire body is on fire, and it's not the temperature of the water.

It's Emma. It's *wanting* Emma.

Drowning in her kisses. Pulling her closer. Her shifting in the water until she's wrapping her legs around my hips, my dick cradled between her thighs.

Slow, I remind myself.

So slow.

Her pace.

Whatever she wants.

But I still cradle her ass, loving the feel of her cheeks in my palms.

Her breath mingles with mine. Her tongue darts out to swipe along my bottom lip, and my already aching cock pulses against her.

Her legs tighten hard around me, and she rocks her hips against my erection.

This.

This is what I want.

Emma. In my arms. In my life. In my bed.

Every night.

"Oh, god, Jonas, we can't," she whispers as she shifts to pepper my jaw with soft kisses.

"Why?"

"No birth control. And it is *triple* or nothing with you."

That's not funny.

It's truly not.

Especially when she's raking her hands down my back and pressing her pussy against my dick and nipping at my earlobe.

I suck in a breath and have to take one more before I can talk, and even then, I'm hoarse with pent-up desperation.

Having her *this close*, with two layers of fabric all that's between my cock and her vagina, is driving me half mad. "Can I touch you?"

"Just...stay...there."

"I want you to feel good."

"I—do." She bites my neck while she tilts her hips and rubs faster against me, her breath coming in shorter and shorter pants. "You feel—so good."

"How can I help?"

"Touch—my breasts. Loved—when you—played—my nipples."

I wrap one arm around her waist, holding her tighter against me, and use the other to yank her swimsuit down and bury my face in her breast.

Her nipple is salty from the hot tub and hard as a diamond. I swirl my tongue around that perfect little point, taking my cues from the way she gasps my name, holds my head, and pumps harder against me.

"Thank you," she pants. "Oh, god, thank you."

I'm on the verge of coming. My balls ache. My cock is a steel rod. And I'm smiling against Emma's breast because she *thanked* me. "My absolute pleasure."

"Less talk. More tongue."

I suck her breast into my mouth.

She gasps and strains against me, her legs trembling and her chest lifting. "Oh, yes, *yes*—forgot—how good —*yes there yes yes yeeeessss.*"

This is the best torture I've ever experienced.

Emma straining into an orgasm in my arms while I fight back the urge to come myself.

I don't want to blow my load in a hot tub. I want to be buried deep inside her the next time I come, and I haven't earned it yet.

But holding her while trembles rack her body and she rides out the waves against my cock, holding my face to her breast—yeah.

Yeah, this is the best kind of torture.

"Oh, god, Jonas, you—bear. Bear. *Bear.*"

My brain is scrambled and my body is completely consumed with being this close to Emma, so it takes me a solid two seconds to understand why she's scrambling to her feet.

"Go!" she yells, waving her arms in the air and distracting me with one swaying breast. "Go away! Bad bear. Bad—*urp!*"

The jets.

The jets push her over, and she disappears under the water. I lunge for her again while my security team comes running, and when I realize they're pulling weapons, the first sliver of fear courses into my veins.

I look at what they're running toward as I pull Emma above the water, and *holy shit*.

That's a fucking big bear.

It's standing—yes, *standing*, on two legs, making it at least seven feet tall on the other side of the fence, watching us.

Emma pushes to her feet again. "Go away! Bad bear! *Bad*!"

"Get down, ma'am," one of the security agents orders.

"Don't shoot." If I move between Emma and the security, she's closer to the bear. If I move between her and the bear, she's closer to the guards.

The bear grunts.

Emma growls back, then howls and waves her hands in the air like one of those floppy dancing tube things that are always outside car dealerships.

"Ma'am—" the security agent says.

"If you shoot this bear and wake up my kid and I have to explain what happened to him, you'll wish you were the bear," she growls.

Goosebumps prickle up and down my skin, including on my dick, which is stubbornly insisting that he still gets to have happy playtime in Emma's lady garden.

"Ma'am—" he starts again.

"Go the frickety-frack *away*," she shouts at the bear.

It snorts, drops back down to all fours, and after one last look at us, lumbers toward the chicken coop.

"I'll let them shoot you if you go after my chickens," Emma says to it. "Even if it wakes my baby."

The bear snorts again and changes direction as the

second security agent gets between the bear and the coop and mimics Emma's wild waving.

And that's when I realize they can both see her breast.

I shove in front of her and glare at both of them while they alternate between watching us and chasing the bear away.

"Can you cover up?" I murmur to her.

She squeaks.

Lowers herself back into the water.

And is instantly blown sideways by the force of the jets.

I probably need to get those jets looked at.

But not right now.

Because now, she's once again lifting her head out of the water, flipping her hair back, and laughing.

She grabs my hand and tugs me back into the water with her.

"That was fucking terrifying," I tell her as the jets finish their cycle and shut off.

"Mama? Dona say duck?" Bash says above us.

Her eyes meet mine, wide, telegraphing *oh my god, we got caught*, and that's when I start to feel it too.

The absolute hilarity of all of this.

I cough to cover a snicker, but Emma knows.

She knows what I'm doing.

And before I realize it, we're both laughing so hard we can barely stay above water, her clinging to my shoulders, me wrapping my arms around her waist, just *being*.

"Mama?" Bash says again.

"I'll be up in a minute, sweetie. Sing a song while you wait, okay? Did Zen teach you a new Waverly Sweet song? The one about catching a case of the feels?"

"You know it's fucking hot when you stare down a bear and win, right?" I murmur to her.

"Don't fuck with *this* mama bear," she replies.

I love you.

It's on the tip of my tongue.

But I bite it back.

I don't want to move too fast and scare her.

I just want to *be here*. For her. With her.

She kisses me softly on the cheek and pulls away. "Thank you for coming over tonight."

"Can I stay?"

She pauses.

"On the couch," I clarify.

"Mama?" Bash calls once more.

Emma glances up at his window, then smiles at me. "If you'd like."

I'd like.

I would very much like.

32

Emma

Yolko Ono is sleeping on Jonas.

They're both on my couch, Jonas covered by a light quilt that my mom made me when I was a baby, the quilt serving as Yolko Ono's nest tonight.

And I finally do it.

I break my own rule, pull out my phone, and I snap a picture of Jonas.

I haven't done it yet. I haven't wanted anyone to see if I lost my phone and they hacked it, which, yes, is an abnormally ridiculous paranoid thought, but it's also the truth.

That viral video changed me.

I don't trust things the way I used to.

But I trust Jonas.

And I want a picture of him and my chicken.

Unfortunately, though, Yolko Ono is nothing if not *very*

sensitive to someone looking at her—even when she's sleeping—and I've barely hit the shutter button before she startles awake with a squawk of terror.

And I do mean a *squawk of terror*.

It's loud. It's sudden. If it could echo in here, it would.

It's like the chicken version of my brother sneezing but longer.

Weirdly more annoying too.

Theo at least stifles it the best he can if he knows he's sneezing while people are sleeping.

Yolko Ono?

She's informing the entire world that her aura has been violated, and she would please like rescue personnel to come treat her for emotional distress.

I'm used to this.

Jonas, however, is not.

Clearly.

You can tell by the way he bolts straight upright on the couch, sending the chicken tumbling beak over claws with a terrified chicken-yelp while he tosses the quilt aside, which also ends poorly for Yolko Ono.

Who falls off the couch.

Inside the quilt.

While squawking like the house is being invaded by flaming Martians who are lighting everything up with their eyeballs.

"Who—what—I'm up. I got this," Jonas gasps.

He leaps to his feet, taking the rest of the quilt with him, and trips over the fabric.

Yolko squawks in terror again.

Jonas flails on the floor.

And I—

I am not proud of what I do.

I just want to state that for the record.

Nothing about my reaction to the two of them scaring the ever-loving chicken shit out of each other is appropriate.

And it probably serves me right that I laugh so hard I pee myself a little.

Childbirth.

Ugh.

But also, as soon as Jonas realizes what's making the noise, his face goes full-on horrified. "Yolko Ono!"

He dives for the quilt.

Yolko squawks like she's possessed by the devil.

Jonas yanks the quilt, and there she is.

My pretty white silkie, rolling out of the quilt like a bowling ball.

An angry, squawking, molting, beaked bowling ball.

Jonas gapes at me through the flying feathers.

And I am not okay.

I'm not.

I'm squeezing my legs together to keep from wetting myself more while I laugh so hard that tears stream down my face.

Yolko Ono jumps to her foot, shakes out her feathers, looks at Jonas, *ba-GOCK*s once, and then—

And then my chicken charges him.

Hopping.

On one foot.

Faster than I've ever seen her move in her entire life.

"Stop," I gasp.

"I didn't mean to," Jonas yelps at the chicken as he dodges her.

"*BA-GOOOOOOOCK!*" she yells back, flapping her wings at him.

He vaults onto the couch.

She hops straight into the side of it, knocking herself over, then bounces back to her one leg and tries again.

He looks at me.

She looks at me.

I'm on the floor.

I'm absolutely dead on the floor, in the middle of a swirl of chicken feathers, unable to stop laughing.

"Mama?" Bash says behind me. "Dodo Ono otay?"

Yolko Ono answers herself with a loud squawk and a fluff of her wings.

"It's like Fiji," Jonas mutters.

I'm trying very hard to stop laughing, and I'm not quite there. "She's okay," I tell Bash.

"She *woaw*."

"Yes, she did her chicken roar." I giggle.

Giggle some more.

Glance at Jonas, who's alternately watching the bird suspiciously and me half-suspiciously. "Did you goose the chicken?" he asks.

"I took a picture!"

"Dodo Ono no wike pikker," Bash says.

Jonas raises his brows at me and crosses his arms. "So the chicken doesn't like having her picture taken, and you did it anyway?"

I giggle so hard I snort. "You were cute."

"I koot." Bash flexes an arm. "And tudwy."

Jonas blinks. "Studly?" he asks me.

"Too much Theo, but he was totally egged on by Zen and Grey."

"Pantakes!" Bash yells.

I'm finally able to speak without laughing. My cheeks hurt. My stomach hurts. I definitely need to change my pants.

And probably give my chicken a bath and smooth her ruffled feathers.

Quite literally.

Definitely change her diaper.

This is *totally* the sort of thing that would make any rational being crap themselves.

"And where are our manners?" I ask Bash.

He puffs out his chest and grins at me. "Pantakes *pwease*."

"Jonas, you know how to make pancakes?"

He steps off the couch. "Sure. I mean, I know how to google and YouTube. And I've watched Françoise do it a hundred times. Or maybe half a dozen times. She doesn't like people in her kitchen. I blame Keisha. She's a bad influence. Except for the part where it got me lessons in making pancakes when she made me go into Hayes's kitchen with her for coffee while Françoise was cooking pancakes."

Yolko Ono growls at him.

I swear, she does.

He eyes her.

She eyes him back.

"Truce?" he says.

She squawks once, then hops to me and settles on the floor beside my leg.

I giggle again. "I think you've been dismissed," I tell

Jonas.

"Better than being chicken food. How much do you know about making pancakes, Bash? Wanna help a guy out?"

"Pantakes!" Bash yells, taking off for the kitchen with all the speed he has in his adorable chunky toddler legs. "I get fower! I get pan!"

"And I'll get you happier," I tell Yolko Ono.

And then vacuum. And give her a bath. And change her diaper. And clean up from that too.

Jonas pauses on his way into the kitchen. "You took my picture."

"You were cuddling my chicken."

"That the first?"

I sincerely hope my cheeks were already red from all of the laughing. They are *definitely* hot now.

Caught.

I nod, telling myself I have nothing to be embarrassed about.

He grins back at me. "You want more, I can pose later. Pretty good at it. Natural talent."

And just like that, I'm laughing again. "Go make pancakes before I throw this chicken at you again."

He's smiling as he strides into the kitchen.

I watch his ass.

No apologies.

Not when I think last night means we're dating.

And if we're not yet—I want to.

I want to date Jonas Rutherford. I want to date the father of my child. I want to date my friend.

And I sincerely hope I'm not making a mistake.

It's not just my life—my comfort, my safety, and my heart—on the line anymore.

It's Bash's too.

It's Bash's *first*.

And that's what makes dating so much more terrifying than it should be.

33

Jonas

BASH IS A PRETTY terrible pancake batter mixer.

And I love it.

He's stripped down to his diaper and has flour all over his chest and his solid toddler belly. Milk and egg on his arm. A clump of all of it in his hair.

The bowl slides across the countertop while he stands on a chair and stirs, the spoon having more control over him than he has over the spoon.

"You need any help?" I ask him.

"I do it."

Bash isn't the only thing coated in flour. The counter, floor, chair, and window are too.

We had an incident with the measuring cup. And the flour container.

And me overestimating either his ability or his will to get the first cup into the mixing bowl.

"You're doing great," I tell him. "These are gonna be the best pancakes the world has ever seen."

He grins at me, flinging a glob of half-mixed batter up under the cabinet and making the light there go a little dimmer.

Wonder how fast I can find a housecleaner for Emma. I cleaned in here the other day, but my skills might not stand up to toddlers cooking.

And then I think about Bash in *my* house, making a mess of *my* kitchen, Emma and her chickens wandering around too, and my heart skips a beat.

I have a house near Razzle Dazzle headquarters in Albany, close to what was once Hayes's primary residence and a short helicopter ride to our parents' estate. One in Los Angeles merely for convenience, since I'm there often enough for premieres and voicework and the occasional film. One in New York City for the same reason.

But my *home* has always been an estate on a hundred acres in southeastern New Hampshire, near where most of the filming for Razzle Dazzle films is done.

I could see Emma and Bash there.

Not because I want them to move. Not because I'm changing my mind about stepping away from acting.

But because they've welcomed me into their home.

I want to share what's been mine with them too.

Bonus—the security is airtight.

"I took now," Bash says.

Took. Took. *Cook.*

I glance down to where he has the pancake mixture still goopy, the bowl resting in a soupy white slurry that'll probably turn into glue before long.

But it's close to ready for cooking.

"Can I give it a stir?" I ask him.

"No."

I stifle a grin. "Okay, then. What's next, little chef?"

"I took now," he repeats.

"Does your mama let you cook on the stove?"

"Suit up, Bash," Emma calls from the powder room down the hall where she's giving the chicken a bath in the sink.

Bash slides off the chair and runs to a cabinet across the kitchen, trailing flour and pancake goop behind him. I give half a thought to stirring the batter quickly while he has his back turned, but then remember I watched him eat canned green beans buried in mashed potatoes and honey for lunch before the baby shower yesterday and decide he's not going to care if his pancakes are lumpy.

Also, I've been inhaling parenting handbooks, and at least three of them said kids should be free to explore the world and make safe mistakes.

I assume eating lumpy pancakes falls into that category.

Even if I have no idea if the parenting books I've been reading are the right ones.

Bash nearly crawls into the cabinet, and eventually emerges with an apron, a chef's hat, and two massive oven mitts. "Tie me up, toach!" he shouts.

"Zen and Theo shouldn't be alone with him," Emma says on a sigh down the hall.

I get Bash's over-large apron tied around his waist. He plops the big white chef's hat on his own head, and then slips his arms into the oven mitts, which go all the way over his elbows.

"Up?" he says to me, lifting his arms at the chair.

"You got it, chef." His body is so little in some ways, but so solid and sturdy in others. He's warm. Messy.

Perfect.

"No, *dare*," he says, pointing to the stove. "I took *dare*."

"Oh, yes, we cook over there," I agree. "Emma? Does he get to stand at the stove?"

She strides into the kitchen with the chicken wrapped in a towel. "Yes. Here. Yolko Ono likes swaddle cuddles after bath. I've got him."

She doesn't blink at the mess.

Not much, anyway.

There's maybe a little bit of an eye twitch.

"I'm on clean-up patrol," I tell her.

"*I* tean up," Bash retorts.

"Can I help?"

He studies me while Emma wraps one arm around his belly, holding him while she scoots his chair over in front of the stove. "We wi see."

We will see.

Gonna go out on a limb and guess that means *I talk big but you'll do all of the work.*

It's what I likely would've meant at almost two.

Yolko Ono lifts her head and looks at me. She's purring —again, who knew chickens could purr? —but behind her fluffy head feathers, I can almost see her eyes. I'm nearly certain she's silently calculating how much she likes being swaddle-cuddled versus how much she hates being swaddle-cuddled by me.

I eye her right back, silently vowing to win her over too. "You and I can get along great if we agree to not scare each other first thing in the morning," I tell her.

She purrs again, then clucks dismissively.

Emma shoots me a stifled smile, amusement dancing in her big brown eyes. "She'll forgive you. Eventually."

"I'll forgive her eventually too."

Emma laughs.

"Mama, *pantake*," Bash says.

"Patience. We have to wait for the griddle to heat up. Can Mama test your batter?"

"Uh-huh."

"Thank you. Oh, look at this! You did such a good job. These will be delicious. I can tell. Did you tell Jonas thank you for helping you?"

"I do it bysef."

"You did *most* of it yourself, but you had help, didn't you?"

Bash peers around her and grins at me.

I grin back, but mine's a little more misty-eyed.

Didn't expect to find so much happiness in a disaster of a kitchen, holding a chicken and smiling at a little boy while also sneaking glances at his mama's ass, but here I am.

Happy.

Content.

And hoping it can last.

"Should we go for a hike today after breakfast?" Emma says to Bash. "With Jonas too? And have a picnic by the secret lake?"

"Secwet wake!" he yells. "Pantakes!"

"Pancakes at home. *Then* we'll pack up for a hike." She glances back at me again. "If you're up for it."

Yep, that's my heart about to burst out of my chest. "Always."

Yolko Ono clucks softly again.

I pet her head.
She doesn't try to bite my finger off.
Actually, she purrs again.
This version of my life?
I like it. And I sincerely hope it can last.

34

Emma

THE SECRET LAKE is showing off today.

It's glittering under a bright blue sky. There's a soft breeze coming off the water, rustling the pine needles and bringing a scent of ponderosa pine with them.

Butterscotch.

I haven't smelled them in almost three years without thinking about Jonas. He still smells like butterscotch too.

White fluffy clouds drift by overhead while we sit in the shade of a willow tree, and all is peaceful as Bash drifts off to sleep on the picnic blanket.

We're not the only people out here, but everyone else is local. They're friends.

While they give me a second glance after realizing exactly who Bash and I have hiked out here with, they all play it relatively cool and leave it at *nice to meet you* when I introduce Jonas. They also give us a wide berth, picking spots far enough away around the two-acre lake to give us privacy after introductions.

I know Sabrina has dirt on every single one of them, but I also know that when I request that my friends, neighbors, and acquaintances here please respect our privacy, they will.

Sabrina and Laney aren't the only people around here who feel like they need to take care of me, and *taking care of me* involves making sure I never go viral again.

Plus, the security guy trailing us at a distance is a little scary.

And not just because he saw me half-naked waving down a bear that he was ready to take out last night.

Bash sighs his *I am dead to the world, completely fast asleep for my nap* sigh, and I smile down at his little face. "Sleep well, little one," I whisper.

"Two speeds," Jonas murmurs with an amused smile as he, too, watches Bash sleep. "Stop and go."

"Were you two speeds when you were his age?"

"No idea. I know I crawled under a table of food in the middle of a shoot and fell asleep there once when I was two or three, but I don't know if I was stop and go about it."

"That must've scared everyone."

"One of the crew saw me duck under the table and made sure my mom knew I was there. Still have the pictures somewhere. Apparently I took a donut with me and cuddled it."

"Have you ever been alone?"

His expression goes thoughtful. "I don't know that I ever *wanted* to be."

"Never?"

"It's also possible I have an unusual expectation of what *alone* means."

"How so?"

"Alone to me always meant *give me an hour*. Or *I'm going home to sleep and I'll be back first thing*. But for the past twenty years, anytime Hayes says he wants to be alone, he means *I'm disappearing for at least a month and I don't want to see any of your faces or I'll claw my own eyeballs out*."

I start to smile, but he doesn't. "Seriously?"

"We are complete and total opposites. Makes me feel like my version of *alone* isn't alone at all."

"Does his wife know?"

That earns me a laugh. "She's the exception to his *leave me alone* rule."

Bash snores softly.

He is *out*.

Not really a surprise. He insisted on walking the entire trail out here himself, and then devoured two fried chicken drumsticks and an entire container of chickpea salad.

He'll probably grow two inches next week.

"Are you comfortable being alone?" I ask Jonas.

"Mostly." He flashes me a grin. "Until I don't want to be anymore."

"Has it been hard hiding from the world the past few weeks?"

He glances out at the lake. We're sitting nearly shoulder to shoulder. I could lean into him or hold his hand or rest my head against his without disturbing Bash.

"No," he finally says. "Not since you opened a door and let me in."

I'm blushing.

I can feel it, and I can't stop it.

Which is ridiculous.

I practically begged him to give me an orgasm in the hot tub last night. We have a child together. I know he likes me. I know he knows I know. I like him, and I know he knows that too.

But it's been a long, *long* time since I had full faith in anyone's insistence that my presence in their life made it better.

In a *man's* insistence that my being in their life made it better.

It's not something I thought I'd trust again after Chandler.

"I like you," I whisper, "and I'm terrified you'll get bored of us."

Those warm brown eyes shift to look at me head on. "If you could do anything in the world, what would it be?"

"Right now?"

"No. With your life. In general."

I blink. "I—I don't know."

"Lifelong dreams?"

"Being a mother."

He aims a tender smile at Bash, then back at me. "Anything else?"

There is.

There's something else I've always wanted, but I shake my head.

He lifts his brows.

I shake my head again. "I don't want you to give me things just because you can."

That doesn't ruffle his feathers in the least.

Actually, I'm not sure *anything* short of a bear

climbing into a hot tub with us or a chicken scaring the crap out of him at seven in the morning could ruffle his feathers.

"If I could do anything in the world," he says, holding eye contact without blinking, "I'd take you and Bash to Razzle Dazzle Village to watch him ride the kiddie roller coaster."

Razzle Dazzle Village has been on my *not a fucking chance* list for about two and a half years. But I've told Laney and Sabrina more than once that as soon as Bash is old enough to appreciate it, I want to take him to Universal Studios or Disneyland.

I've even been saving for it. A little here, a little there, knowing it'll take a few more years before he fully enjoys and remembers the experience.

At least.

"If I could do anything in the world, I'd buy you Sabrina's grandparents' house and build you a bigger chicken coop and install a maybe not as extreme hot tub in the backyard."

I squeak a small protest. *"Who told you?"*

Truth? I shouldn't have any interest in that house. It's also Chandler's grandparents' house.

But I loved the house before I even knew who he was. And I have so many more memories there of Laney and Sabrina and me than I do of Chandler and me.

He rarely took me there.

Sabrina did far more often.

"You did," Jonas says. "In Fiji."

"You are *not*—"

"Yet," he finishes. Smugly. "I'm not buying you a house *yet*."

I narrow my eyes at him. "Would that make *you* happy?"

"I hear it needs a lot of work."

Sabrina's family has used it as a vacation rental property since her grandmother passed away and her grandpa moved into a retirement community. And I'm guessing Grey or Theo told Jonas it's still in the family. Or possibly the triplets.

I nod at him. "It does."

And there's that smile again. That world-class, happy-go-lucky, rob-me-of-my-breath smile. "Do you know I've never had the chance to try to fix things on my own before? It's *fun*. I like it. I think that's some of what I always loved about acting. I get to learn something new with every role."

"Sounds fun."

"That part was. But the Razzle Dazzle films—they started to get old. Monotonous. Wasn't *new* anymore. Wasn't anything left to learn. Even the biopic on Darwin? Once I learned everything I could about his life, it was still just acting. The idea of renovating and fixing up an old house? Turning it into a home? For you and Bash? Yeah. That would make me happy."

My pulse cranks up to eleven. "What about when it's done?"

He glances out at the lake again, then back at me. "Seems like there might be another thing or seventy-six to learn around here. Anything in the world, Emma. Big or small. No limits. What would you do?"

I don't know what Emma of yesterday would want.

I don't know what Emma of tomorrow might dream up.

But Emma of right now wants one thing.

And I'm not ready to ask for it.

Not directly.

I look down at Bash and brush his light hair off his sleep-warmed forehead. "Can you really keep the media away?"

"Not completely, but—"

I try to suppress a small shiver and don't quite succeed.

He notices.

I know he notices because he scoots closer and links his hand in mine.

"*But*," he continues, "I have all of the resources in the world to help make it more bearable."

"Private jets and homes on every continent," I murmur.

He squeezes my hand. "Yes, but I meant media specialists and coaches and therapists."

I glance back up at him. There's no judgment, no silent *you were too weak last time* coming from him.

Just a man getting caught glancing at my lips before he lifts his gaze back up to meet my eyes.

"I've had media training since I was born," he says quietly. "My parents knew if I was going to be in the spotlight, I needed to be able to handle it mentally. They gave me all of the tools I needed. They did the same for Hayes, but we're built different. Just are. Complete opposites, the two of us. No matter where you and Bash fall on that spectrum of what you can, will, can't, and won't tolerate, I've got you covered. *We've* got you covered."

We.

I haven't met his parents, but his brother and sister-in-law have welcomed Bash and me. They've supported us too. The same way I'd expect Theo and Laney to welcome anyone into my life. The way I expect them to welcome *Jonas*.

So long as he keeps passing all of the tests and not raising red flags.

"You still ran away from it too," I whisper before I can stop myself. "You ran away from the press to hide in Fiji."

"Didn't say that's never an option. Just that it doesn't have to be the only tool in your tool kit. What you went through was awful. If it'd been me in your shoes then, even *with* a lifetime of being trained to handle that kind of attention, I would've been on a private jet going somewhere even more remote and secluded the minute I left the altar. It won't be that bad again, Emma. And if it is, we have those houses on every continent to escape to while the noise dies down."

My pulse has climbed onto a wild horse and is racing erratically.

Can it be that simple?

Not that coaching and counseling and training is *simple*. You can't just become unafraid of something because someone tells you *oh, just ignore it*.

I know it'll be a process.

It'll probably stretch and hurt my brain *and* my heart at times.

But I don't like living my life with that constant feeling in the back of my head that if I make one wrong move in front of a tourist, I'll go viral again for being that mom whose kid cried a cuss word when his ice cream fell off the cone. Or when a new friend is at my house and Yolko Ono pulls a Yolko Ono.

Not that I ever have new friends at my house.

Grey and Zen are the only two I've made since the

wedding disaster, and they came fully vetted by Sabrina, who didn't want to like them and actively tried to not let them into her life.

But the fact remains that since my wedding disaster, I've been more or less hiding.

Even when I'm out in Snaggletooth Creek, I'm cautious.

I keep secrets now. I trust less.

And I miss the version of me who believed in the best of everyone.

"No strings," Jonas says quietly. "I wish I'd offered my resources to that friend I made back in Fiji. For her sake. Not mine."

I look back at the sleeping little boy on the blanket beside me. His legs are spread wide, his shirt tugged up just enough for a sliver of his belly and his cute little outie belly button to show.

One day, he'll have to know how to navigate the public eye too.

Whether he likes it or not.

He didn't ask for us to be his parents. I owe him this.

No matter what ultimately happens between me and Jonas.

"When can Bash start?" I ask.

"Now."

"*Now*? Oh my god. Is he behind?"

"No. Not behind." He squeezes my hand again, stroking his thumb over my skin. "Just about the right age."

I look out at the clouds floating over the lake. Think about all of the places I used to tell Chandler I wanted to go.

Look at this picture of the blue grotto in Capri. Isn't that beautiful? We should go there.

We can't afford a trip to Italy, Emma. And if you get knocked up right away, who's gonna watch the kids? I'm not taking a kid to Europe. I hate people who bring kids on planes.

Oh, we can swim with dolphins in the Caribbean! And stingrays! We should take a cruise.

Cruises are nothing but floating germ boxes and you'd get seasick and puke.

Can you imagine being at the top of the Eiffel Tower?

It's just a big tourist trap.

I've always wanted to see the Canadian Rockies.

You have our Rockies right there. That's a dumb use of money to see the same thing you live with somewhere else.

And then I shed Chandler, but I took on another weight.

The weight of the world watching me.

Because I'd been dumb enough to choose Chandler.

But what if I wasn't afraid?

What if I refused to let things hold me back?

What if I hadn't gone to school to study accounting merely because I knew it would make me a solid, dependable living with minimal student debt? What if I'd gone to veterinarian school instead? Or art school?

Who would I be today?

Who could I be tomorrow if I'm brave?

My vision blurs and my sinuses burn.

"Emma?" Jonas says softly.

"If I could do anything in the world, right now, I'd kiss you."

He holds my gaze for a long, thick, heavy moment before sweeping a glance around us.

I know what he's looking for.

Who's nearby? Who can see us? Is this safe?

Those beautiful brown eyes finish their study of everything around us and meet mine again. "If I could do anything in the world right now, I wouldn't want to stop with you kissing me."

My pulse is humming a tune I know so, *so* well. My vagina aches. My clit tingles. My nipples are pointing and my heart—

My heart is bursting out of the rock wall I've hidden it behind since the disaster that was my wedding day, shedding the last of the pebbles and concrete that are still lodged around it, reminding me how much this could hurt.

"I wanted you to sleep in my bed last night," I whisper.

"I want to sleep in your bed every night."

"You scare me and make me believe there's still good in the world at the same time."

"You *are* the good in my world."

"Jonas—"

I can't finish. I don't know what I want to say.

I just know that kissing him is necessary. It's the *only* answer.

And I don't care who's watching. I don't care who could see us.

I get to choose love.

I do.

And I don't know what kind of love this is—friend love, *lover* love, forever love—but I know that what I feel for Jonas is some kind of love, and the only way—the *only* way I can say it is by kissing him.

So I lean in. Let my eyes drift closed while I stroke his rough cheek and touch my lips to his again.

A sigh shudders out of him while he grips my forearm, holding my arm in place, kissing me back.

Soft.

Gentle.

Slow.

A perfect picnic kiss under the trees while butterscotch wafts around us and our baby sleeps on the quilt next to me.

This.

This is the life I want.

The family I want.

He's the missing pieces that put my soul at ease.

He comes with complications, with hard work, with mountains between our lives that we'll have to climb, but he's worth it.

This man.

This kind, gentle, sexy, eager, funny, patient, beautiful man.

I don't know why he'd choose *me*.

But I'm done questioning my worth.

With him, I'm all in.

I can't help myself.

And I don't want to.

35

Jonas

I should not be nervous.

There's no reason to be nervous.

I eat nerves for breakfast.

Okay, fine. That's a lie. I don't. I usually have—actually, it doesn't matter, and thinking about my normal nutritionist-prepared breakfast that I've been skipping since I arrived in Snaggletooth Creek won't abate my nerves.

Not over this.

Not when it's so important.

And what is *it*?

A date.

An actual, honest date with Emma.

Before Bash woke up at our picnic, I had it planned in my head. Between the time we got signal back at the trailhead and the time we returned to Emma's house, Begonia and one of Hayes's security team had planned most of it for me.

Not that I couldn't plan it myself.

It's more that I was on a time crunch and knew Begonia could charm people faster and with fewer eyebrows raised.

"Why do I feel like I'm sixteen again?" Emma whispers to me in the back of the SUV as Robert, the other half of Hayes's security detail who's been with us all day, steers us around the lake beneath downtown.

I link my fingers through hers. "It's going around."

She smiles.

And blushes.

And looks out the window. "Why are we at the train station? It's empty this time of—*oooh*."

Exactly.

It's empty this time of day.

Passengers for the scenic route have cleared out. The paddleboarders and kayakers on the lake have all packed up and gone home.

Zen and one of the triplets are at Emma's house, taking care of Bash's bedtime for us.

And I'm taking this woman that I'm absolutely obsessed with on a privately-catered date in the middle of the historic train station on the lake.

Robert parks the SUV in the empty parking lot on the far side of the lake, hops out, scans the area, then holds the door for Emma.

I slide across the back seat and climb out on that side too.

"What did you do?" Emma breathes. "And when?"

The sun is glowing above the mountains in the distance

behind the town, making them hazy. The weather's warm. Emma's in one of her summer dresses with a shawl in case she gets cold. Her hair's in a messy ponytail, and she swapped out her hiking boots for sandals.

And she's fucking gorgeous.

Just like this.

I told her we were going somewhere casual. That she should be comfortable over dressing up for anyone.

She's eyeing the ornate train station with its large doors and old windows and potted plants near the entrance like it's a Michelin-starred restaurant and she's in her underwear.

I squeeze her hand, then use the other to gesture to the grand entrance. "Shall we?"

"What did you do?" she repeats.

I grin.

She eyes me, and then she laughs too.

Even before we get inside to find—oh, *fuck me*.

Sabrina and Laney are here.

Here.

They're both dressed in all-black, from their shoes to their aprons. One's holding a bottle of wine. The other's holding a tray of appetizers. Together, they flank the two-person table set up at the open windows overlooking the deck beyond the train tracks, the lake, and the town and mountains above.

"Welcome, madam," Sabrina says to Emma. "You look beautiful, even holding hands with the riffraff."

Laney shoots her a look, but her lips are wobbling. "Chef Bitsy will arrive shortly with your dinner. In the meantime, would you care for wine, a bread course, and deviled eggs?"

Emma's lips are having a hard time deciding what to do, but she finally smiles. "I love deviled eggs."

"The chef had a gut feeling," Sabrina replies dryly.

I carefully glance around the empty train station.

Ticket window is closed. The benches lining the windows are empty. Trash bins somewhat full, like the cleaning staff hasn't been in yet. Sun streaming through the warped glass windows, lighting dust specks in the air and putting rainbows on the old, broad-planked floor.

There's no second story. Instead, the ceiling is arched and high, held up with thick timbers.

If Theo and Grey are also here, they have to be hiding in an office or one of the bathrooms.

"Do you have dishwashers on your staff?" Emma asks her friends.

The two of them share a look, barely keeping straight faces. "You think we're washing dishes in our conditions?" Sabrina finally says.

"They're coming…later," Laney adds.

That's ominous, but after taking another look at each of them in turn, Emma laughs. "If you say so."

"We do," Laney says quickly.

"Wine?" Sabrina interjects. "We have a lovely prosecco from the Questionable Intentions river valley. It hits your nose with a fizzle and finishes with an inclination for bad decisions."

She delivers the description so dryly, I can't help but laugh along with Emma. Someone has apparently been on a wine tour she didn't fully appreciate before.

"I would love some nose-fizzle wine," Emma tells her friend.

"And remember the bread." Laney sets the plate of

deviled eggs on the table, then whips a blue checkered napkin off of a bread bowl.

Emma gasps softly, then laughs again. "*Jonas*. Have you had Sir Pretzelot pretzels yet? You have to try this."

She pulls me closer to the table, dropping my hand as she reaches for one of the giant pretzels on top of the pottery plate. She tears off a bite and holds it to my mouth. "Here. It's okay if you don't like it. I can eat enough for both of us. But don't feel obligated to *not* like it just because I'd eat all of this without regret. I know where to get more. And I do. All the time."

I don't taste the pretzel.

It's not the pretzel either.

It's the fact that Emma's feeding it to me, standing so close I can smell the baby shampoo and mint on her. So close that I can count the freckles on her nose. So close that I could pull her body against mine and kiss her until neither of us can breathe.

Why did I think a date before spending the night in her bed was a good idea?

Why didn't we stay home?

I could've ordered in pretzels.

Her eyes are sparkling as she watches me chew. "Isn't it—"

A giant sneeze from some other part of the building cuts her off.

She closes her eyes, sighs, and then looks back at her friends.

Laney's struggling to hide a wince.

Sabrina's completely straight-faced as she pours two glasses of prosecco. "Behave yourselves tonight, you two. The train station ghost is acting up."

"Bitsy's making fish and chips, isn't she?" she says to Sabrina.

"Not for you. We know you prefer the lamb."

"But for...*the ghost*?"

"You know *the ghost* can never turn down a free meal," Laney murmurs.

Emma laughs, and I barely realize I'm staring until Laney clears her throat. "Would you like to sit?"

Sit.

Crap.

First rule of taking a lady on a date. You pull out her chair.

And I'm standing here just gawking at her because she's so damn pretty when she smiles that the rest of my brain has floated away like a runaway balloon.

But Sabrina has Emma's chair and Laney has mine.

And both of them are smiling like they have a secret.

They probably do.

They know *all* of Emma's secrets.

Most of them.

They know *most* of Emma's secrets.

Not all of them. Apparently she's changed since her wedding.

"Enjoy your bread and eggs and wine," Sabrina says after we've both sat. "We'll be back with your next course soon."

"Does that mean they'll be watching us?" I ask Emma.

She laughs again, then nods. "Definitely."

I've been on dates knowing that pictures would show up online or on gossip sites. I've been on dates that have been interrupted by people wanting pictures and autographs.

But I've never been on a date while being served by my date's best friends, knowing they'll be spying on us, and excruciatingly aware that one wrong move on my part could completely wreck my plans for the rest of the evening.

Possibly the rest of my life.

Emma tears the full pretzel in half and sets the bigger piece on the bread plate in front of me. "They're not going to spy the whole night."

I raise a very suspicious brow at her, which has the effect of making her smile grow impossibly wider.

I hope Bash got some of that smile. I truly, truly hope he did. That he just hasn't grown into it yet.

"They're *not*," she insists. "Pretend they're strangers who have absolutely no interest in us whatso...ever..."

A frown overtakes her expression as she trails off.

Now I'm aiming two curious eyebrows at her.

She lifts a finger.

And then she crawls under the table.

My dick goes so hard, so fast, I feel it from the pit of my stomach all the way up to my throat.

Is she—she's not.

Is she?

Oh god. Oh fuck. Oh god.

I *cannot* take a blow job under the table from her while her *best friends and brother* are mere feet away.

I also can't squeak out the words to tell her so, because my brain has malfunctioned.

It's stuck on images of Emma's lips wrapped around my cock, gliding over my length while she plays with my balls and lifts those eyes to watch me watching her pleasure me with her mouth, and *fuck fuck fuck fuck fuck*.

Get it under control, Rutherford. You're a fucking grown man who can control his fucking urges to fantasize about sex while you're at dinner with a woman you'd like to keep up screaming your name all night long.

Nope.

Not helping.

Not helping, and the tablecloth rustles, and I feel Emma's hand on my knee, and *shit shit shit shit shit.*

"Em—" I croak out hoarsely.

If we were alone—fuck me, *why aren't we alone?*

Whose brilliant idea was this to treat her to a fancy date before I crawled into her bed with her tonight?

Mine.

My very, very, very stupid idea.

Next time she says she wants to sleep with me, we're just doing it the minute we can find the bare minimum amount of privacy.

None of this *I will treat her like she's a proper girlfriend who deserves dates first* bullshit.

She is.

She does.

But when a lady wants you, *you let the lady have you.*

"Em—" I croak again.

Her head pops up from beneath the black linen tablecloth. "Unless it's under your chair, Theo didn't tape his pho— Jonas? Are you okay? You look a little ill."

Theo didn't tape his phone.

I try to swallow and almost choke on my own tongue instead.

Grasp for water.

Don't realize I have the prosecco in my hand until the

bubbles hit my throat, then my nose, and suddenly I'm choking.

"I—fine," I rasp between coughs.

Emma's horrified.

She has no idea what's going on, but her brows are knit together and her lips are parted and she keeps darting glances to where Sabrina and Laney disappeared, like she's debating if she should call for them.

And then she glances over at Robert, standing guard just outside the glass-paned door to the train station.

I pound on my own chest and get a gulp of real water.

Emma puts a hand to my knee again, and *this time*, I know it's not with the intent of sliding that hand up my thigh, rubbing it mercilessly over my cock, then unbuttoning my pants and doing me with her mouth. Even though she's still on her knees under the fucking table.

Emma's eyes suddenly go huge, and she squeaks.

Looks at the table.

At my crotch.

At my face. "You—you thought I—"

I make a strangled noise and go for more water.

Her lips wobble. They're forming a giant O, and they're wobbling. So are her cheeks.

And her eyes.

Her eyes tell me she's pieced this all together and she's simultaneously amused and horrified and sorry for me.

"I—" she starts again before cutting herself off again.

"My bad," I rasp. "Fantasies got away from me."

She slowly closes her mouth. Still right there on the floor next to me, her hand still on my knee.

And then a wicked, delicious grin slowly spreads over her face. "Will you tell me about them?" she whispers.

"Yes. *Later*."

"Promise?"

"On my life."

Her gaze darts once more to the area of the train station where Sabrina and Laney disappeared to, where the sound of the sneeze came from.

She pinches her lips together, like that can stop her smile.

Which it can't.

And that smile?

The way her eyes have lit up?

Completely worth all of the pain. The ache in my dick. The burn in my throat and nose. The knowledge that her friends will likely tell this story for the rest of their lives if they're watching.

Which they likely are.

Definitely worth it.

She pulls her hand away from my knee, leaving a void in me at the lack of contact.

She's glowing as she re-takes her seat.

Absolutely glowing.

The way she's always deserved to glow.

It's not *me* making her glow like this. It's this whole life she's built for herself here. Bash. The friends so tight they're family. Her home and her chickens and her job.

I want to be the reason she glows brightest.

But I bring more complications than anything else in her life.

Which means I need to step up my game.

And be even better.

And deserve her.

36

Emma

My heart is a trampoline and a million different feelings are bouncing off it like they're at the world trampoline championships.

We're home from dinner.

Leftovers are in the fridge.

Bash is sleeping.

Yolko Ono is tucked in for the night.

The chickens outside are settled too.

Zen and Jack have left.

The security guard has left.

And I'm pulling Jonas up the stairs to my bedroom.

When I sold the house that was supposed to be my young bride starter home, I traded house size for lot size. Neighbors for privacy.

The four-bedroom, three-stall garage house was too much.

Especially knowing that I'd never have more than one baby.

That I wouldn't ever let a man back into my bedroom.

But here we are, with me whispering for Jonas to skip the fourth step because it squeaks, on the way to my very, very, very feminine bedroom.

Where I hope he'll tell me every detail of whatever fantasy left him unable to speak before dinner.

Bash's door is shut, and there's a soft glow coming from my bedroom.

I don't remember leaving any of my lamps on, but it's not unusual for one of my friends to do little things for me like switching on a lamp.

Or, apparently, scattering peach rose petals across my wooden floor.

My lips part as I stop in my bedroom doorway and take in the full scene.

It's not just the rose petals complementing my peach-and-white bedding. It's candles illuminating the wispy, soft, abstract painting of a woman's profile, hidden behind petals much like those scattered across my floor, rug, and bed. Soft music coming from the Bluetooth speaker on my nightstand. The fairy lights strung over my live-edge wooden headboard. My gauzy curtains billowing softly in the breeze.

More candles visible around the soaking tub in my attached bathroom.

The quilt turned down. Pillows fluffed.

Water bottles on both nightstands.

And the scent of something soft and sweet, but very, very subtle, tickling my nose.

Jonas settles a hand on my waist as he stands behind me. "Beautiful," he whispers thickly.

I swallow my instinctive *I didn't set this up*.

It doesn't matter.

The candles and the rose petals and the—oh my god.

The bowl of strawberries between the candles on the sideboard under the painting.

It doesn't matter *who* set up my bedroom.

What matters is that Jonas is snaking both of his arms around my belly as he buries his nose in my hair. "But you're still the most beautiful part of all," he whispers.

My eyes sting.

People don't call me *beautiful*. Chandler used to tell me he loved me *despite* my ears and nose. I went on three dates with someone in college who told me my personality made up for my face, but not enough. And that's why he dumped me.

Laney and Sabrina insist I'm beautiful, but they have to.

They're my best friends.

They don't see the flaws.

When Jonas says it?

When the world's most beautiful man tells you that *you're* beautiful, when you know he could've simply demanded a paternity test and sent his lawyers after you to get visitation rights with his son, when *you're* the most difficult part of this equation that's turned his life upside down, what reason do you have left to doubt him?

I turn in his arms to face him, looping mine around his neck, and pull him along as I step backwards into my bedroom.

Staring into those beautiful brown eyes that are trained

on me like he's memorizing this moment, memorizing *me*, drowning in *me*.

"Shut the door," I whisper.

He kicks it softly shut with one foot. "When you crawled under that table," he starts, and I can't help it.

I smile.

A smile so big it instantly hurts my cheeks. "When I crawled under that table?" I prompt.

"I thought you were going to have a pre-dinner snack."

"And were you ready for me to eat you?"

His pupils dilate, making his eyes dark as night. And his voice—his voice is dark as night too. "You *breathe* and you turn me on, Emma. When I thought you were going to suck on my cock? Yeah. Yeah, I was ready. Even though I don't think I've earned that yet."

The implication that's been hanging between us all evening already had my panties wet. The idea of going down on Jonas?

Yes.

Yes.

It's not enough to kiss him. It's not enough to touch him. It's not enough to dry hump him in a hot tub or anywhere else.

I want to lick him from head to toe.

I do. I can't help it, and I'm tired of trying to fight it.

But hearing him say he wants me to suck his cock?

There's now a complete and total flood happening between my thighs. It's potent enough that I can smell myself, and I have no doubt he can too.

"What do you think you have to do to earn it?" Is that *my* voice? Breathy and needy and seductive?

The things this man brings out in me…

"Be here," he says without hesitation. "Put you first. Make you come first. Always. Every time. *Multiple* times. Be an equal partner. Make up for everything I've missed. Cook. Clean. Laundry. Fix things. Make you laugh. Hold you when you cry. Listen when you need to vent. Anything. Everything. All of the things that I—that I should've been here—"

I put a finger to his lips. "You're here now. That's all I need. All I *want*."

"I swear I'll keep you safe," he whispers. "Both of you. I don't want to give you regrets. Not again."

"I will *never* regret my time with you. Ever. *Ever*."

"Emma—"

"You could leave again tomorrow, and I'd have zero regrets." Would my heart break?

Yes.

But if he left tomorrow, I'd know there was a reason.

That it was beyond his control.

That he didn't go willingly.

Or that he did it because he thought it was for the best.

That he did it to protect us. To save us from something worse than my viral wedding video.

Zero doubt.

None.

Jonas Rutherford is a good man.

The *best* man.

And I can't keep myself from going up on my toes to press a kiss to his mouth.

I want him.

I want his kisses. I want his hugs. I want his hands on my naked body.

I want my hands on his naked body. Feeling the ridges

of his muscles. Tasting his skin. Breathing in that delicious butterscotch scent of him. Losing myself in being with him.

His breath shudders out of him as he surrenders and kisses me back while he gathers my dress in his fists and lifts. Cool air rushes around my calves, my knees, my thighs.

The scent of my arousal gets stronger as he raises it to my belly, and I know he notices.

The feral growl in the back of his throat, the way he deepens the kiss, thrusting his tongue into my mouth, claiming me while he arches his hips and that thick ridge against my stomach—he notices.

We break apart just long enough for him to pull my dress the rest of the way off my body, and then we're once again attached at the mouth.

I attack the buttons on his shirt.

He unhooks my bra, slides it down my arms enough to make the cups fall away, and then he's teasing both of my nipples with his broad, flat, talented thumbs.

It's nearly enough to make me come right there, and my own fingers fumble on the buttons of his shirt.

"Can—go—slow," he says against my mouth.

"Round two."

His erection pulses against my stomach like the very idea of sex all night is a turn-on.

Like he'll never get enough of me.

Of *me*.

I finally get all of his buttons undone and shove his shirt off of his broad shoulders. My bra falls all the way off while his hands are momentarily off of my breasts.

And then my bare chest is against his while he pulls me

closer, kissing me harder, walking me backward to the bed.

The smooth, firm skin on his back radiates heat beneath my hands. I can't stop stroking him, flashing back to rubbing aloe all over him.

He's broader than he was in Fiji. Thicker. More solid.

My shield against the world.

The only thing that matters.

The backs of my thighs bump the mattress, and then Jonas's lips are gone from mine, and he's scooping me up into his arms and settling me on top of the rose petals. I hear a clink and a swoosh, and before my lust-addled brain can translate the noises, a fully naked Jonas is crawling onto the bed with me.

And he—

I swallow.

Swallow again as I stare down between our bodies, at his thick erection jutting out from a nest of dark curls, the broad, wide head, the veins wrapping around the silky skin of his cock.

I stroke him once, twice, and then he puts a hand to mine with a muffled grunt.

"Next time," he says.

And then Jonas Rutherford, my former celebrity crush, the father of my baby, my friend—and now my boyfriend?—slides down my body, peels off my panties, and settles his head between my thighs.

He presses a kiss inside my left thigh as I part my legs wider. Then he presses a kiss inside my right thigh.

And then my breath comes out in a gasp as his tongue traces my slit and ends with a flick of my clit. "*Oh my god.*"

"Delicious," he murmurs against my pussy.

And then he does it again, holding my quaking thighs that I can't spread any wider despite how hard I'm trying. I arch my hips into his mouth while he licks and sucks and feasts on me, my brain going completely blank, nothing existing except the sensations he's sparking between my legs.

He strokes my thighs with gentle fingertips, nearly tickling, but not quite, while he swirls his tongue around my clit.

I'm pumping my pelvis into his mouth. Can't stop. Don't want to stop.

I'm reaching—reaching—*reaching* for that sensation spiraling deep inside of me, so rich, so heady, so close, building heavier with every stroke of his tongue until my vagina clenches and my hips buck off the bed.

I can't speak.

Can't say his name.

Can only pant incoherent noises while the strongest orgasm of my life sweeps over me. My legs go straight up in the air. I curl my fingers into his hair, and he keeps going.

Sucking on my clit while I come.

And come.

And come.

All over his face.

I come so hard my feet cramp. My shoulder too.

And I don't care.

Not when he's making my pussy feel so gloriously loved.

Pampered.

Adored.

My body sags back into the mattress, my legs falling

again, my thighs wide open as the spasms abate. I ride out the aftershocks with Jonas slowly climbing back up my body, pressing kisses to my belly, under each breast, avoiding my nipples like he knows they're too sensitive right now, until his face is buried in the crook of my neck, breathing me in like he's never wanted to be anywhere else in his life.

Like I'm his world.

"You are so fucking beautiful," he murmurs.

"That was—*wow*."

I have bigger words.

Better words.

But not right now.

He kisses my neck once more, then shifts off me.

I whimper.

He huffs, and it sounds amused, so I let my lips fall into a smile.

But he's doing something with the covers, rolling me to my side, then onto my stomach.

"Jonas?"

"You worked hard," he murmurs, his body lining up beside mine as one broad hand sweeps down my back. "Need some pampering now if we're going another round."

He kneads a thumb into that spot between my neck and my shoulder, and *ohhhhh*.

This.

This.

I can feel his erection resting against my thigh. He's still hard as steel, and that knowledge has my vagina lifting one sleepy eye in interest. But right now? Right now, I choose to let this man treat me to a backrub.

37

Jonas

EMMA SNORES.

It's the cutest snore I've ever heard too. Just barely above loud breathing.

No windows rattling here.

Although, I'd bet they do if she ever has a cold.

There's nothing but silence coming from the rest of the house. Bash is asleep. Yolko Ono is asleep. No chicken noises drifting in from the open window.

Just the cool summer night breeze, the flicker of candles burning lower in here, and the sound of Emma's deep, soft snores.

This.

This is the peace I didn't know I wanted.

Lying here with a woman I love, our son safe in the next room, pets downstairs. Friends who would drop everything to set up what was ultimately the best date I could've dreamed of, talking and laughing with Emma over a menu custom-made for her with all of her favorites. A community that I've only just started exploring that loves her and Bash fiercely.

It's like living in one of my family's movies.

Except better.

There's no final curtain call coming on this life with *my family*.

No last scene to anticipate and dread at the same time.

No pondering where to go next.

Not that I often ended one project without knowing what was coming for at least two more projects.

I'm itching to stroke her hair, to brush that lock out of her face. Her lips are parted, and I think she's drooling.

So. Fucking. Perfect.

So fucking *real*.

She snorts suddenly, bats at her face, and her eyes pop open a split second before she pushes herself up, letting the candles illuminate her pert nipples and small breasts.

She blinks three times, looking at me, and I see the moment she registers that I'm still here.

"Hey," I say softly, giving in to the urge to stroke her hair.

She stares one more long moment, and then a sleepy smile crosses her face while she lowers herself back to the mattress. "You never get bedhead, do you?"

That makes me laugh. "Yes, I do."

"I don't believe you."

That mouth. Those dancing eyes behind sleepy eyelids. The teasing tone.

"Here. Look. I'll mess it up."

"No. No, let me." She shifts on the bed so she's facing me, reaching across me to ruffle my hair.

My eyes slide shut.

Can't help it.

I love it when she touches me.

"Have you slept?" she whispers.

"No."

"What time is it?"

"Close to midnight."

"And you haven't slept at all?"

I peek one eye open. "Didn't want to wake up and find out this was all a dream."

She stares at me like she's looking for the punchline, and it utterly kills me that she still has these moments of self-doubt.

That she questions why I'd like her.

That she doesn't fully believe me when I tell her she's beautiful.

She hasn't said it, but I can see it.

I can *feel* it.

It makes me want to disembowel her ex for the way he tore her down.

But that's for tomorrow. Or tomorrow's tomorrow.

Today, right now, all I care about is being here with her.

"You know my favorite thing about you?" I murmur.

Her cheeks go pink, and she shakes her head.

"Your massive, massive heart. The way you put everything you have into caring about everyone around you. Bash. Your friends. Your family. Your community."

"They take care of me too. It's not a one-way street."

"But you'd do the same even if they didn't."

She would.

Zero doubt.

She didn't let Zen and Jack leave without taking eggs, even though they insisted getting to hang with Bash was all that they wanted. She found a way to throw her friends a baby shower so that the community could get what they wanted while not making her friends uncomfortable for feeling like they were asking people who couldn't afford what they could to provide for the families they chose to have.

She puts everything she has into making sure Bash knows he's loved, that his needs are met, and that he knows he matters. Whether it costs her sleep, food, or patience.

And she seems to have infinite patience, which I know isn't true.

She can't.

None of us do.

But she reaches for it like she does.

"I haven't taken care of you yet," she says softly.

"Yes, you have." I put a hand to her beating heart. "You let me in here when you didn't have to. You gave me a chance when I didn't deserve it."

"*Stop*. You did too deserve it."

"No, I—"

"You need to forgive yourself," she says softly. "I don't want to spend the next fifty years with you not knowing if you're with me out of guilt or obligation or because you truly, *truly* like me as a person."

"*Love* you," I correct. "I want to spend the next fifty years of my life with you because I *love* you."

Her breath catches and her eyes go shiny, but I don't take it back.

I won't. I *can't*.

"I love you," I whisper. "I love you and you deserve to know how worthy you are of being loved for exactly who you are. I love you for being suspicious of me. I love you for giving me another chance. I love you for how you're raising Bash. I love you for all of the strength that you have that you don't give yourself credit for. I love you for being the friend I needed in Fiji and for being the friend I still don't think I deserve here. I love you for embracing your dreams and getting chickens. I love you. I just *love you*. For you. For all of who you are."

Two tears slip down her cheek and nose, and she brushes them away before I can. "Stop. I'm an ugly crier."

"No, you're not, but even if you were, I'd love you for that too."

"Oh my god, *that's a Razzle Dazzle line*."

I blink. "Oh, shit, it is. But I—Fuck. Shit. Crap. Emma, I mean it. I do. I—"

Her shoulders are shaking with laughter.

"Em—"

"I know," she gasps between peals. "I know. You're so —you can't—not your fault—I mean, it *is*, since you took the roles, but—"

I prop my head up on my fist and watch her.

Completely naked.

Laughing with her entire body.

"Don't be—don't be mad." She's still giggling as she loops a hand around my neck and pulls me down, kissing me softly. "Don't be mad. I think it's adorable. I know you didn't do it on purpose."

"I—"

"I love you too," she whispers.

Her eyes are dancing. Her mouth—I know I've seen her smile this wide before, but it feels brand new. And she's stroking my hair while she says it again. "I love you too. I didn't *want* to. But I can't help myself. I don't know anyone who could know you—*this* you, the you when all of the cameras are off—and *not* love you."

"You love entirely too easily."

She shakes her head. "Not anymore. But you? You're worth it. No matter how scary this is, you're worth it."

I don't know if I kiss her or if she kisses me.

All I know is that this is where I belong.

Here, in her bed. With her arms and legs wrapped around me, kissing me like I'm the only thing in the world that matters.

Like she never wants to let go.

I don't want to let go.

Ever.

I do—just long enough for her to grab a condom from her nightstand—but no more after that.

Never. Ever. Ever. Letting. Her. Go.

And even with the condom covering me, the moment I finally slide into her body, into her slick, hot center, surrounded by *Emma*, I'm home.

I am truly, completely, no-question where I belong.

Thrusting into her.

Kissing her.

Stroking her skin.

Teasing her breasts.

Loving her until she's coming again, squeezing my aching cock so hard that even if I wanted to keep trying to play Superman and hold out, I couldn't.

And when my own orgasm overtakes me while I'm

buried deep inside her, my eyes get hot and my heart swells so thick, I feel like it might choke me.

I love her.

I love her.

I will love her if we have more babies one day. If we don't. If she gets tired of me and sends me away. If she lets me love her every day for the rest of my life here, in her house, as part of her family.

I collapse on top of her as my orgasm fades, rolling so I don't crush her, but I don't go far.

I can't.

Not touching her—it's impossible.

"I love you," I whisper into her hair.

"I love you too," she whispers back.

And that's the last thing I hear before I tumble off the cliff into the most solid sleep I've had in weeks.

38

Emma

JONAS STAYED.

We had sex—no, *made love*, and he stayed.

I didn't realize I was still afraid he'd disappear in the morning until I feel him rubbing my arm gently as the first light of day breaks through my window.

"Emma," he whispers. "Bash is awake. I'm gonna go get him. You can go back to sleep, but I wanted you to know I've got him. And I love you."

I absolutely fall back asleep.

With a smile.

My entire body feels like I slept on a magical stress-relief cloud. There's no tension anywhere.

There's simply this sensation that all is right in my world.

Jonas loves me. He loves Bash. He has Bash. My house is overflowing with love.

And when I wake up again an hour later, it's because the two of them are laughing too loudly outside.

"Dick-dick say *gaaaawwwwk*!" Bash crows.

"I was trying to feed her," Jonas replies, softer, with definite indignation in his voice.

But he also sounds happy. Amused, even. Like he can somehow be annoyed with my chicken yet also be enjoying himself here at the same time.

"Dick-dick no wike Dona."

"I'll still feed her even if she doesn't like me. That's the job when you're a grown-up. Or a chicken owner."

"I get egg!"

I creep to my window and peer out.

Jonas and Bash are both inside the coop with the chickens. Jonas has the entire pail of chicken food with him, which feels right. There wasn't much more left than one feeding's worth. Bash is chasing the chickens, dressed in his dinosaur pajama shorts and a kitty T-shirt that he undoubtedly picked out himself, getting distracted from his plans to check for eggs.

The chickens have decided Jonas is the enemy.

Probably need to get him some good rubber boots to protect his legs from their suspicion.

But since he clearly has this, I take advantage of having time to myself for a leisurely shower. It's been a while since I haven't had to rush, knowing Bash was waiting for me, or—more recently—roaming the house since he can now climb out of his crib.

After I've stood under the hot water so long that all of my skin is pink, I dry off, pull on lounge pants and a tank top, and head downstairs to check out the breakfast situation. Kitchen's clean, but I spot evidence of a banana missing.

Yolko Ono is pecking at a chunk of it under the chair Bash usually stands on in the kitchen when he wants to help with something.

I peek outside again and verify the boys are still doing okay without me, which they are.

It's Sunday. None of us have to go anywhere today.

There's time to do something else I haven't done in even longer than it's been since I've taken a leisurely morning shower.

It takes me about fifteen minutes to prep everything and get it in the oven. Once it's baking, I slip out the back door to say good morning to my guys.

My guys.

They spot me at the same time. Jonas smiles, sweeping a glance over my body that makes every inch of my skin blush.

Bash is oblivious to the look I'm sharing with the man he still doesn't know is his father. "Mama! Mama! Dick-dick no wike Dona!"

"We're working on making friends," Jonas says. One of the chickens pecks him in the shin.

He doesn't react at all, which I take as a good sign that it was an affectionate peck and not an *I'm going to murder you* peck.

Or at least that Jonas sees it that way.

"They're friends worth making," I tell Jonas. "Especially when they all let you cuddle them."

"Do they like to have their pictures taken too?"

"Dodo Ono no wike pikkers," Bash says.

I take a seat on the porch swing near the coop and

watch as Bash chases more chickens and occasionally runs to the coop to check the boxes for eggs. Jonas has refilled the chickens' water in addition to feeding them, so he seems to be hanging out for the mere fun of it.

"Sleep okay?" His eyes twinkle like they're made of stars, which fits.

Even if he wasn't *Jonas Rutherford, movie star*, he'd still have that air.

"I did." I couldn't hold back smiling at him if my life depended on it. "You?"

"Better than I have in weeks."

"Good."

We have a lot to work out still. I know living here, in my little house, won't work long-term. Security considerations and all that. And I need to get started immediately on talking to everyone Jonas has promised can help me navigate a world where people outside of my community will know who Bash and I are.

But we have today. And soon, I'm pulling my cheat cinnamon roll bites out of the oven and bringing them outside for a peaceful breakfast on a quilt with my family, complete with Yolko Ono hopping around the yard looking for bugs.

My family.

I love the way those words feel.

Almost as much as I love the way Bash stares at me with open suspicion when I hand him a plate with three small, fluffy cinnamon pastries. "What dat?"

"This is a kind of a cinnamon roll. Like Aunt Sabrina serves at her café."

"It no wook wike cimmanin woll."

"It's a different kind."

Jonas bites into one, and his eyes cross while he flops back onto the blanket. "Oh, wow. That's delicious."

He's acting.

I am a hundred million percent certain he's acting.

But Bash looks at him, takes his own small cinnamon roll, bites into it, and does the exact same.

"Dat so good," Bash moans.

"I've never had *anything* so delicious," Jonas says.

"I no have dewisus," Bash echoes.

Jonas flops his head to one side, looking at Bash with the biggest smile. "Your mama makes the best breakfast."

"I eat evvy day!" Bash says.

Oh.

Whoops.

That was the error in my plan.

Totally forgot how this would end.

"You do eat breakfast every day," I agree. "And you eat so many good things. Oatmeal and eggs and pancakes…"

He holds up a mashed cinnamon roll in his little fist. "I eat dis evvy day."

This is a problem for tomorrow.

Just like everything else.

But none of my problems feel too big. For the first time in a very, very long time, I don't think I'm faking it when I tell myself I can handle this.

I bite into my own cinnamon roll, and I'm suddenly eight years old again, back in my mom's kitchen while she shows me how to make her fake cinnamon rolls.

Sabrina says they're technically cinnamon biscuit bites, but that's not what Mom called them.

Mom called them fake cinnamon rolls, so fake cinnamon rolls is what they will forever be.

"Your grandma taught me to make these," I tell Bash.

"Gamma Seffy?"

"Yes. Grandma Stephanie."

"I wike Gamma Seffy."

He'll never meet my mom, but I tell him stories. It's important. "Me too."

"Gamma Seffy *zoom zoom* Unka Deo," Bash tells Jonas.

I crack up.

And not just at Jonas's expression, which could mean anything from *I have no clue what that means* to *I'll bet a lot of people want to zoom zoom your Uncle Theo if it would make him behave himself.*

"My mom once chased Theo all over town on a motorbike," I tell Jonas, filling in the details of Bash's favorite story about my mom and brother. He heard it once a month or so before Theo and Laney's wedding, and he's repeated it every time anyone's mentioned my mom since. "He *borrowed* one from someone, and she happened to be sitting in the salon getting her hair cut when she saw him ride past, so she took off after him on another borrowed motorbike. With foil in her hair. She was having it dyed. The story is a little legendary around here."

"How old was he?" Jonas asks.

"Eleven."

We both look at Bash, who's grinning while shoving the last of his crumbled cinnamon roll in his mouth. His perfect every day would likely be eating fake cinnamon rolls and hearing the stories of Uncle Theo's escapades so he can plot his own fun once he's tall enough to steal a motorbike.

"Yeah," I say on a sigh as I meet Jonas's eyes again. "I

think about that sometimes, and decide I can save thinking about it more for when he's a little older."

Jonas smiles at me. "I got this one."

And there go the warm fluttery happies in my heart.

"Mama more cimmanin woll?" Bash bats his eyes at me. "Pwease?"

"I don't got this one," Jonas murmurs.

I'm laughing again as I hand Bash another cinnamon roll bite. It's a good day for a treat. Why not?

My heart is full this morning.

So full.

I never would've had morning cinnamon roll breakfast picnics if I'd stayed with Chandler. It would've been *silly*. Or we would've had *more important* things to do.

And I haven't had them often with just Bash and me, because there *is* a lot to do when you're doing it solo.

But today, we're all hanging out in the backyard, just being.

No rush.

Nowhere else to be.

Cleaning can wait. Laundry can wait. Checking the text messages that I know I'll have waiting from Laney and Sabrina can wait.

Right now, I get to just be.

But more important—I get to be with my family. I pull Bash into my lap as he's licking his fingers. "Hey, you," I murmur in his ear. "Can I tell you something?"

"Mama tell me everting."

Mama does *not* tell him everything. But I'll let him think I do. "Do you remember I told you Aunt Laney's growing a baby in her belly?"

"Uh-huh."

"And Uncle Theo is that baby's daddy?"

Jonas sucks in a breath next to me, and I swear I feel my heart swell as if it was his.

Pretty sure he knows where I'm going with this.

Bash sticks his finger in his mouth and stares at me.

"And Aunt Sabrina's growing a baby in her belly too, and Uncle Grey is her baby's daddy?"

"Everbody has daddies," Bash says like he's reciting it from a book.

Which he is.

He just hasn't reached that stage yet where he'd ask who *his* daddy is.

"Well, Jonas is your daddy," I tell him.

He stares at me with those big brown eyes that he got from his daddy, then looks at Jonas, whose breathing has gone a little uneven. "Dona my daddy?" Bash repeats.

"Yep. Jonas is your daddy."

"'Kay. I go see dick-dick."

He slides off my lap, leaps up, grabs a stick, and starts chasing imaginary pirates around the chicken coop. And Jonas slides over closer to me, his fingers linking in mine while our thighs line up.

"That's not how it goes in the movies," he says a little hoarsely.

I squeeze his hand. "It'll click eventually. And he should know. You're his family too."

"Em—if he repeats that—"

I kiss his cheek and put a finger to his mouth. "You're family, Jonas. We claim our family around here."

And Bash will repeat what I just told him. He absolutely will. Probably at daycare this week, the first chance he gets. *Dona my daddy.*

Jonas clears his throat again and drops his head to my shoulder. "This is way better than playing a role in a movie."

We spend the rest of the morning watching and playing with Bash while he battles pirates and asks for more food and drags his blocks out to tell Jonas to build a better dinosaur.

And in the middle of showing Jonas how to do it himself, Bash squints at him. "You my daddy?"

Jonas goes misty-eyed all over again, which makes me go misty-eyed too.

"I am," he tells Bash. "But you can call me Jonas or Daddy or Hey You or whatever you want, okay?"

Bash stares at him harder. "Dat a bad dibobor."

"Not all of us can build good dinosaurs," Jonas replies in his Panda Bananda voice.

Bash makes a face. "I fix it. You go 'way."

"Bash, we share with friends," I remind him.

He looks at me, and then he hands Jonas two blocks. Just two. "You pway with *dese*. I pway with *dose*."

I shouldn't laugh.

But today, smiling, laughing, and loving are all I seem capable of doing.

Eventually, Jonas and I end up sitting side by side on the quilt again. But this time, when he presses a kiss to my shoulder, he murmurs words that make me sigh.

"My mother apparently arrived in town last night. She wants to meet you two. You can say no. She's...a lot."

I slide a look at him.

Pause.

Weigh my words carefully.

And then decide if he's serious, if he loves me, he can handle this. *"You're a lot."*

His eyes flare wide for a second before he cracks up. "Not wrong."

"I have to take *media classes* just to date you. I'm aware that I'm not wrong."

"You changing your mind?"

"No. Never." I squeeze his hand back and smile. "Just realizing that this *being brave* thing is going to have to start sooner than expected."

"If she tries to imply I have to pick between the two of you, I'm picking you."

"Would she do that?"

He shakes his head. "She's overprotective, for good reason, but she's not stupid."

"Okay." I nod. Nod again. Ignore the butterflies and hummingbirds and possibly a full-size crow or two starting to flutter around my stomach. "When?"

"Whenever you're ready."

"Bash had a bath last night, and I'm already showered. So you tell me when you're—oh, wait. Let's let him finish."

Jonas finally looks away from me and out at Bash, who's gone totally still in the yard with an intense look of concentration on his face.

I put a finger to my nose and whisper, "Not it."

And when Jonas swings a raised-brow, parted-lips look back at me, I double over in laughter.

Will I happily change Bash's diaper?

Yes.

But Jonas's startled expression at losing a game he didn't even know we were playing?

I might have some of those Monroe male genes in me too.

Just a little.

And when that amused smile overtakes his handsome features again? Coupled with his sigh and his, "Only fair, isn't it?"

I swore I'd never fall in love again.

That I was over men.

But Jonas?

He's worth it.

39

Jonas

"We don't have to do this today," I tell Emma as she finishes checking the supplies in Bash's diaper bag. "Today's been good. Great. *Fantastic*. Making her wait won't make it worse. Might even make it better. Show her who has the power."

"It's like you didn't meet *my* family at an ambush cookout and let them take you camping where I hear you suffered some intestinal distress you never told me about," she replies.

"Just suffering what I deserved to prove I'm here for real. No running away. Not like last time. Also, no one wants to hear about what your brother's stash of camp food can do to a person."

"Mama, what *am-buf*?" Bash asks. He's racing cars over the bright red-patterned rug in the middle of the living room.

"Ambush? It's...a surprise. But not always a good surprise."

"Wike Unca Deo?"

"Yes. Uncle Theo is a constant ambush." She slings the large black bag over her shoulder and holds out a hand to him. "Want to go have dinner and make new friends?"

"No."

"Begonia and Marshmallow will be there."

"Aun Beebee be dare?"

"Nope, Aunt Sabrina won't be there tonight."

"Aun Waney?"

"No, sweetie. Just you, me, Jonas, Begonia, Hayes, Marshmallow, and a new friend."

"Zen-Zen?"

"No Zen-Zen either. But we'll still have fun."

"We might have different definitions of *fun*," I murmur to Emma.

Real talk though—I'm turned on as hell at how she's tackling this.

And at the way she's pursing her lips in amusement.

On a normal day, I'd smile right back.

Seeing Emma confident? Ready to tackle whatever my family throws at her? Knowing my mother will likely be looking for an opportunity to take a clip of Bash's hair for a DNA sample, and knowing Emma knows it too?

I like it.

But not as much as I would if we were tackling something less precarious.

Like rock-climbing without harnesses.

"Dodo Ono?" Bash asks.

Emma shakes her head. "Yolko Ono is staying home

tonight. What's going on here? Why don't you want to see Marshmallow and Begonia?"

He grins at her.

And while he looks just like me ninety-nine percent of the time, that grin is one hundred percent channeling his Uncle Theo.

If my family had been more like Ryan Reynolds's family and less like, well, the *Razzle Dazzle* family, I could've had some fun with Theo back in the day too.

Never really regretted not being more adventurous his way, but I'm starting to wonder what parts of life I've missed.

Emma's smiling but shaking her head at him. "C'mon, Bashy-boo. Mama's hungry. And if Mama doesn't eat—"

"Mama *woar*!" Bash finished. "Wike a *wion*."

"Exactly," Emma agrees. "Mama gets so hangry she turns into a lion."

"Mon, Dona." Bash abandons the cars on the rug and runs to me, grabbing my hand. "No mama wion. Mama go eat. *Mon*."

"Can't have Mama turning into a lion," I agree.

His chubby little fingers wrap around my thumb while he tugs on my hand, insisting I *c'mon*, and I silently vow—again—to do everything in my power to protect this little boy with my life.

He pulls me to the garage door, where Hayes's security detail has parked their van and are ready with Bash's car seat installed and waiting. Emma didn't question why we couldn't drive ourselves. Instead, she met my eyes and silently telegraphed *okay, I get it, this is your life, so this is what we'll do*.

But she still insists on making sure it's installed correctly before we load up.

If I'm being honest—I *want* to see Emma turn into a lion.

Specifically, when she meets my mother.

I like brave Emma.

I like Emma in all forms, but brave Emma?

Brave Emma is on a whole new level.

The van's seats have been turned in the back so she and Bash face me when I sit in the rear of the vehicle. Every time we take a curve, Bash throws his hands in the air and giggles. "Pass-da, Mama!"

"Mama's not driving, silly boy. And we should *not* go faster."

"Woe-wa coda!" he shrieks.

Emma smiles at him, a full-on, full-fun, amused smile. And then she fake gasps and puts a hand to her heart. "It's an out of control roller coaster! Oh, no!"

He cackles and pumps his arms higher. "Dona! Woe-wa coda!"

I throw my hands in the air too. "Help! Help! Someone stop this roller coaster!"

Robert, the security agent in the driver's seat gives me a look.

"I'm *playing*," I stage whisper.

He shifts his gaze back to the road, and suddenly the car lurches.

The tires screech.

We swerve on the windy road.

Bash screeches in utter glee, but I don't.

Not when I can see what's coming.

I register a deer.

No, not a deer. A cow. A brown cow with a llama neck charging from the hillside to the left.

Someone says *elk*—maybe me?—a split second before there's a *crunch* and a jolt and another swerve that takes us too close to the edge of the road.

My seat belt snaps hard, holding me in place as I try to lunge for Emma and Bash.

Bash is squealing and pumping his arms.

Emma holds an arm in front of him like she can keep him safe with the power of a single mom arm. Her eyes are wide.

She knows.

Danger.

Danger.

The van teeters to a stop with a steep, forested hillside inches away, waiting to swallow us whole.

Robert says a word that I know Theo and several other relatives probably say in front of Bash regularly.

The car rocks for one more long moment, and then Robert is somehow unbuckling his seat belt, whipping out his phone, and opening his door at the same time. He climbs out muttering words that are definitely a toned-down version of what I'd expect.

"What was that?" Emma gasps.

"Deer." I unbuckle too and slide forward, unsure who to check first, knowing I need to get both of them out on the road side of the van as opposed to the hillside. "You okay?"

Bash cackles. "Woe-wa coda *stop!* Go 'gain!"

Emma unbuckles and twists. "That's an *elk*, Jonas."

"Other side of the car. Don't lean that way."

She glances to her left, then lunges at Bash, unbuckling him faster than that elk was running at our car.

"Half my life," she mutters to herself while she creeps in front of Bash and pulls him down.

I inch toward the door on the road side. "Em?"

"I've been driving half my life and I've never hit an elk. Which you don't say out loud if you don't want to jinx it."

"Robert did it for you. C'mon. Out."

I pause to listen for approaching cars around the bend, and when I hear none, I take Bash from her, then grab her hand and pull her out from the driver's side. We all hustle to the back of the van.

"Woe-wa coda?" Bash asks.

"He wasn't going that fast," I say to Emma.

"I know. It's a game we play. Theo taught him. We could be going four miles an hour and Bash will play roller coaster." She glances at the van, then down the hillside, and then back at me.

And I slowly realize I'm holding Bash, and that the absolute miracle of him will never get old. No matter what he calls me.

My little boy stares at me. And then he pokes me in the cheek. "You got da suffy. Wike Unca Gay."

"He's scruffy like Uncle Grey today, hm?" Emma says.

"Get back in the car," Robert orders from the front.

"Not when it's about to fall off a cliff," I reply.

Emma clears her throat, amusement dancing back into her eyes.

Tilts her head at the car.

And the cliff.

Robert leans around the van to glare at me. "Backup is on the way. *Get back in the car.*"

There's a solid foot between the van and the edge of the road.

"Should be a guard rail," I mutter.

"This isn't the curve people fall off of around here," Emma says lightly. She leans around the van and looks at Robert. "How's the elk?"

He points down the hill. "Gone. Apologies, ma'am. I'll submit my resignation to Mr. Rutherford as soon as we arrive at the house."

"While this isn't the curve people fall off of," she says, sending me an impish grin, "it *is* the curve that has the most animal accidents per year. Even locals regularly hit wildlife here."

"It was charging us. Not the other way around," I agree.

"We're all fine," Emma adds. "It happens."

Robert stares both of us down. "Not on my watch. *Please* get back in the vehicle while we wait for backup."

Emma nods and gives me the *we need to humor him* look as another engine hums around the corner. She flings an arm in front of me, stopping me from heading to enter the van from the road side until the car passes.

But the car doesn't pass.

It slows.

Then slows more.

And more.

Until it comes to a stop right next to her.

The passenger window rolls down. "Emma? What the fuck? Are you okay?"

Chandler.

Fucking *Chandler*.

"Just fine," she replies mildly. "You shouldn't stop in

the middle of the road. Especially not here. Thanks for checking on us."

He looks at me. Then at the van. Then at Robert. Back to me. "I figured out who you are."

Emma's entire body goes stiffer than the drink I'll unfortunately be declining when we get to Hayes's house. "We're *fine*," she says again. "Thank you for stopping. Please go before someone rear-ends you."

The engine of Chandler's car shifts noises like it's been put in park. "This douchebag isn't kidnapping you, is he?"

Robert, who's halfway to the car, stops and blows out a breath.

Must've heard that one.

Emma waves her phone at Chandler. "Free to call anyone I like. I'm fine. Once again, please go."

"Emma hates the spotlight," Chandler says to me. "You know what the spotlight would do to her, don't you?"

Fuck me.

That's a threat.

I tighten my grip on Bash, who's leaning into me like he, too, is picking up on the bad vibes.

"The sheriff's on her way," she replies evenly. "Please go."

Robert steps between me and the car. "There a problem?" he says.

"Robert, this is Chandler. My ex-fiancé. He doesn't live on this road. Chandler, this is Robert. My—let's call him one of my special friends who have ways of finding out things that even Sabrina won't know."

Chandler must be angling in the car to look at me again, because Robert shifts, then shifts again.

"Are you giving me some kind of warning with that?" Chandler says to Emma.

"Do I need to?"

My ears tingle. My body tenses.

Another car is coming around the bend.

Robert hears it too. He's immediately leaping into action, flying to the back of Chandler's car to wave his arms, alerting the other driver to slow down.

I grab Emma by her shirt and yank her to me, pausing only long enough to make sure I'm not about to hurl all of us over the cliff before I drag her *and* Bash out of what I expect will be the crash zone if that car doesn't stop.

There's a squeal of brakes, and then silence.

"Move on," Robert orders.

Bash looks at me and bursts into tears.

Emma wraps her arms around both of us and buries her face in my neck.

She's shaking.

She put on a brave front, and now she's shaking.

"I'm quitting," I whisper, my voice far hoarser than I thought it would be. "In another two years, no one will even remember who I was. And until then—until then, I've got you. Okay? I've got you. I've got both of you."

She squeezes tighter. "I believe you."

Does she?

Or is this unearned optimism?

"We don't have to go," I murmur. "I'll call my mother. Tell her we'll do this tomorrow."

"Begonia needs to get home before those babies pop out here, and I know she's only here for the two of us," she replies. "We're going. We're doing this. Today. So she can go back to her normal life too. A little car accident and threats from my ex won't keep me down. I'm not that person anymore."

"If you change your mind—"

"You'll be the first person to know."

I kiss her forehead.

It's not enough. I don't know if loving her—if loving both her and Bash will ever be *enough*.

Not when I know love can't keep a person safe.

40

Emma

My heart has turned into an antelope and it is trying very hard to escape my chest.

Hitting the elk was fine.

I mean, *not* fine, but as fine as a minor accident involving a major animal can be.

Staring down Chandler was even fine enough. I've mostly tolerated him with bland kindness to his face since I broke up with him. It's remarkable what a little apathy can do to his ego.

But walking into Begonia and Hayes's house, knowing that Jonas's mother, the formidable Giovanna Rutherford, is lurking somewhere beyond the cozy foyer?

Nope.

Nope nope nope.

Not fine.

The past few weeks, I've mentally split Jonas in my

head between the Jonas *I* know, the man I met in Fiji and the man who's reappeared here, and the man the world knows as a celebrity.

Here, he's just a kind, happy, dependable, sexy man. While I've acknowledged that he comes with a public lifestyle, I've blocked those parts of him at a basic personality level.

Even when he showed up at Laney and Theo's wedding, he wasn't a *celebrity* to me. He was a normal man that I slept with once who abandoned me. It's like, knowing the world knows who he is and him behaving like he knows that he's world-famous are two different things.

But tonight?

Tonight I feel like I'm on the arm of the very most famous celebrity in the entire world, and I'm too small-town, too unworldly, too unsophisticated to be with him.

Even Begonia's tight hug and warm, "Emma! I'm so glad you're here," isn't enough to calm my nerves about the fact that I'm with a movie star and I'm about to meet his mother.

She and Jonas are the public faces of their family. His father occasionally does interviews about business topics, but for appearances, it's Jonas and his mother.

And she's Bash's grandma.

"Maw-mawa!" Bash yells. He wriggles out of my arms and takes off as he spots the Shiloh Shepherd poking his head out of the living room.

Marshmallow barks once in greeting, then trots toward the kitchen, Bash trailing behind him.

"The doors are all locked *and* Marshmallow-proofed,"

Begonia says. "We put those flippy thingies at the top, too high for either of them to reach. They're not getting out."

"Thank you."

"After the stories I've heard about how Hayes and Jonas both escaped their parents' watchful eyes as children, I assume it's likely in his nature to be part Houdini."

Jonas hugs her too. "This is why you're my favorite," he murmurs.

"I know," she replies, but it's drowned out by a tornado of a woman pushing into the foyer too.

"And what am I, chopped liver?" Keisha Kourtney, the freaking *pop star*, says.

She's about as tall as Sabrina, but where Sabrina has curves, Keisha is stick thin. Her brown skin is glowing, probably because her eyes can't contain all of her mischief, and her short, straight hair is neon green.

The last picture I saw of her, it was maroon.

"Apologies for not warning you. She just arrived," Hayes says as he, too, joins us in the foyer.

Also, he doesn't look the least bit sorry.

Keisha gives Jonas the shortest hug in the history of human hugs, then attaches to me, her head resting between my boobs just like Sabrina's does.

I have a literal pop star's head between my boobs.

"Oh my god, you're *Emma*. It is the pleasure of my life to meet you. I expect to see your little boy riding Marshmallow before you leave today, and if I don't, I'm totally teaching him." She pulls back, winks at me, and drops her voice to a whisper. "I'm on your side and I can hang out after Hayes and B leave. Aunt Giovanna doesn't stand a chance."

"I can hear you," the matriarch of the Rutherford family says.

This foyer is getting entirely too crowded.

And I'm sweating.

My armpits are perspiring, and it will be approximately half a second before they sweat enough that the entire foyer can smell my armpit sweat.

This daydream that I can love my friend Jonas will come to an end as it's determined that I'm not bright enough to use deodorant and therefore not refined enough to exist in the same world as these people.

And *refined* is not a word I use lightly.

Or frequently.

Or possibly ever before in my life.

But the size-two woman with a silver bob, on-point makeup, and ivory pantsuit that slays today and will slay for centuries to come is sophistication incarnate.

She's about my height, but her impeccable posture makes her seem taller.

"Are we having a dinner party in a room built for two?" she says. "Or are all of you going to let our guests into the rest of the house?"

Has she seen Bash? Did he pass her on his way to wherever he and Marshmallow are playing?

Has she passed judgment on both of us already?

I know Jonas said he'd take my side if it came down to it, but I get the impression he respects his mother. Loves her, actually. And I don't want to be the reason he severs an important relationship in his life.

"We're playing clown car in the foyer," Begonia says.

"And B counts for three," Keisha says, "so I think that's...not as many as we need to break a record. *Dammit.*

Hayes, call the chef and your security team. Where's my security team? Why didn't I bring Millie? Oh, right. Elevation sickness. She's getting here slower. Emma. I heard you know the owners of Toothy Bee Booch. Is that true?"

"Security," I blurt and look at Hayes. "Don't let Robert quit. And don't fire him. Please. The elk wasn't his fault. That happens on that curve all the time."

"Robert won't get fired," Begonia assures me while Jonas attempts to nudge us deeper into the house. "He's one of my two favorites."

"He would've had to intentionally murder you, and even then, if it was justified..." Hayes agrees as he also encourages the party to make its way into the formal living room.

The one with the view that I still miss from my old house.

"He'd get fired if he murdered you," Jonas assures me.

"Possibly," his mother agrees. She's waiting just beyond the foyer. "Or possibly not. Emma. Lovely to meet you. I'm Giovanna."

And this is it.

This is the moment when I find out if *lovely to meet you* secretly means *I look forward to slowly poisoning you so that I can rid my family of the most awkward new part of it*.

I take her offered hand and shake, reminding myself not to pull a Theo and grip too hard. He's somehow mastered the art of gripping too hard while not gripping so hard that you think it's on purpose. It's both annoying and inspiring in the moments of my life when I wish I understood how he does it.

"Hi. Begonia's told me all about you."

Her lips wobble.

I swear they do.

Jonas, though—he outright laughs.

And then he does the very last thing I'd expect, and he pats my ass.

Right there.

In front of his mother.

"And doesn't that say all there is to say?" he says to her.

"You've often been my favorite son, but you may not stay my favorite for long," she replies.

But where I expect daggers and brimstone, she's...amused?

"Not his fault he can't be as fab as me," Keisha says. "Also, whatever B didn't tell her about you, I will *happily* fill in the blanks."

Jonas moves his hand to the small of my back and steers me around his mom. He pauses long enough to greet her with a hug and a peck to the cheek, but then he's directing me into the living room and to a seat with a view of the mountains.

Keisha and Giovanna follow.

And then comes Bash with something red all over his face, shirt, and hands.

And Marshmallow.

Who's carrying a carton of strawberries that look like they came from the farmers market downtown yesterday.

"Mama!" Bash shrieks as he hurtles himself at me. "Maw-mawa get me *teets*!"

"Strawberry treats?" I guess as I catch him, holding him just right to keep the red bits coating him from getting onto my dress too.

I reach for the diaper bag, but Jonas is already handing me a wet wipe from inside.

"Sa-bewwy teets!" Bash agrees. "Go-na wan sa-bewwy teets?"

Begonia shakes her head. "I had three earlier, and it filled—oh. Yes. Thank you, Marshmallow."

"Me and Maw-mawa fends," Bash says.

"You and Marshmallow are good friends," I agree.

"He really does look just like him," Keisha whispers. "I thought you were exaggerating."

"I'm old, but I'm not losing my ability to accurately see family resemblances," Hayes murmurs back to her.

"You are *not* old," Begonia says.

"How old are you, Bash?" Giovanna asks.

Bash freezes.

Turns.

Looks at her.

And then he cuddles closer into me, completely forgetting about his best friends Marshmallow and Begonia. "Mama?" he whispers. "Dicka bish?"

I gulp.

And not because I know that might sound like *this a bitch?*

More because I know what he's *actually* saying.

Wicked Witch?

Okay. Close enough.

"Yes," I manage to force out, "we got the chickens clean dishes before we left."

"No, Mama, *dicka bish*," he says.

Keisha chokes on air.

Hayes grabs a book and buries his face in it.

Begonia's doing math in the air like she's trying to translate Bash-speak.

Jonas has gone completely blank-faced.

And Giovanna—technically my son's grandmother, the woman who could disinherit Jonas with a flick of her wrist, who is widely regarded as the force behind the entertainment industry's most influential family—smiles.

Smiles.

"He has quite the vocabulary, doesn't he?"

"He probably won't potty train until he's seventeen but he'll be reciting Shakespeare at four," I blurt in response.

"Very perceptive too," she says. "I've definitely been called worse."

"That's how he says *wicked witch*," I whisper.

"I'm telling you, Giovanna, you need to let your hair grow out," Begonia says. "I know everyone thought it was funny how much the witch in last year's Halloween movie looked like you, but you truly do scare small children. Oh! You could color it. You'd look fabulous in pink."

"Or *lavender*," Keisha says. "Aunt G, you'd be so hot in lavender. Like, good thing you're through menopause because these boys don't need new siblings kind of hot."

"Even Jonas didn't do Shakespeare at four," Hayes says dryly over his book, clearly done with thinking about his mother being hot.

I want to sink through this couch and never, ever, ever come back up.

But Jonas is silently shaking next to me, and I'm nearly certain he's laughing.

I slide a quick look, and—yep.

The man is about to lose his shit with complete and absolute amusement.

He slips an arm behind me and squeezes my waist.

"Although he was almost five before he was potty-trained," Giovanna muses.

"I had more important things to do," Jonas says.

"And here we go." Hayes sighs, but he, too, seems amused.

Jonas smiles bigger. "Like learning to run fast."

"Mama, dicka bish," Bash whispers again.

"Sometimes we have to give people a chance to prove our first impressions are wrong," I whisper back.

He stares at me.

That's probably a lesson too far above his cognitive skills right now.

"Do you think Marshmallow can find Mama a drink?" I ask.

He slips out of my grasp and runs to the dog, who keeps nudging the carton of strawberries closer to Hayes while Hayes occasionally reaches into the carton.

And I watch Giovanna watching him.

And as I take in the way her expression softens, and how her eyes even go a little shiny, I start to breathe.

Fully breathe.

She's seeing her grandson for the first time.

And I don't think she wants it to be the last.

41

Jonas

Dinner goes better than I expected.

Even better than I hoped.

And not because Keisha made a surprise appearance and is a master of distracting everyone from the elephant in the room, or because when Keisha pauses to actually eat or drink something, Begonia or Marshmallow fill in the blanks.

More because I can feel Emma getting more and more comfortable the whole afternoon and early evening.

Even with my mom.

Who's far more relaxed than I expected her to be.

Almost suspiciously so.

I corner her out on the patio when Emma excuses herself to use the bathroom after dessert. "What's your game here?" I quietly ask my mother.

"You only get one chance to get it right with the mother

of your grandchildren," is not the answer I expect, but it's the answer I get.

"You're not mad that I didn't call you?"

Mom sighs. "Disappointed that you didn't think you could trust me. But not mad."

"You're not demanding a paternity test?"

"While I think it would be wise, if only for his peace of mind as he gets older, looking at him is like looking at a two-year-old you."

"Huh."

"I was concerned you wouldn't handle the press well, but it seems you're just boring enough while also being on top of the world that you still have them eating out of the palm of your hand."

"*Boring*?"

She flicks a wrist like she's batting away my objection. "Your one scandal wasn't even a *scandal*. While the world at large would love to see one of us fall flat on our faces, you give them just enough *boring* to keep them at bay."

"Having a secret baby won't be boring."

"No, but I trust you've offered Emma all of the resources she'll need when word gets out. I'm honestly shocked you've been here this long without a single leak."

"This town loves her. Loves both of them."

And I haven't seen it.

Not much of it, anyway.

Don't even need to. I know I'll love it.

There are very few places I've been in this world that I haven't loved and made the most of.

"If you need backup, you have my phone number," Mom says.

Ouch. That might've been a subtle dig at how infrequently I've used it lately. "Do I? I might've lost it."

"I had your brother program it back in for me while you were sleeping. And speaking of your brother—after the number of Emmas he dated, I can honestly say I never expected to see *you* end up with one."

I suppress a snort of laughter.

She's not wrong.

Hayes dated at least four women named Emma before he went into his recluse era. "You're taking this much better than I thought you would."

She glances out at the mountains. The sun's sinking lower and casting them in hazy shadows while turning the fluffy evening clouds a deep orange. It's a beautiful evening.

"Your father and I are talking about retiring," she says, startling the hell out of me. "Hayes is settled and happy. You—you'll be happy. And we already know you've been drifting away from the family business. We've seen you *happy* drifting away. We can't run Razzle Dazzle forever, and it's best to leave while we still have some say in our successors. Living in the spotlight—it's not something we meant to do for so long. Between Begonia due soon and finding out I already have a grandchild… It's time."

My mother is apparently full of surprises tonight. "Does Hayes know?"

"I'm sure he'd suspect as much if he wanted to contemplate our plans, but I have little interest in distracting him from what makes him happy."

"He'll be happy for you."

She smiles. "I know. But it's lovely that he has someone else to be happy for first. I honestly enjoy that. There's nothing—*nothing*—as satisfying as seeing your grown children happy and at peace."

I watch her closely, looking for any tell that she's trying to subtly manipulate me into questioning my own intentions to walk away from life in the spotlight and live here with Emma and Bash.

But if she's thinking any negative thoughts, she's hiding it well.

"How extensive was your background investigation into Emma?" I ask softly.

"Oh, *very* thorough," she assures me. "I know...entirely too much...about *all* of her family."

I almost laugh.

Pretty sure my mother just told me she accidentally saw my girlfriend's brother naked.

But I manage to keep a straight face while I wait for her to fill in any other details she wants to give me.

"That wedding video was horrific," she says.

"That's never felt like a strong enough word."

"I don't know that there *is* a strong enough word."

I glance around the small patio and toward the back of the house. Begonia's chatting with her chef. Keisha's just grabbed Emma, who looked like she was possibly headed my way, and is engaging her in a full-body conversation as only Keisha can. Hayes is likely still entertaining Marshmallow and Bash.

"Her ex is a complete shithead," I tell Mom.

"Sweetheart, he's far worse than that."

"You have dirt on him?"

"Have I been shielding both of my sons from the worst that the press has to offer for years by making sure the press and gossips who couldn't be reasonable knew that I would end them if they didn't find a way to back the fuck off of insulting my children? Of course I have dirt on him."

It's official.

My mother can never meet Sabrina.

Also, she's leveled up in superhero status in my brain.

"Do you need it?" she asks.

I hate my answer. *Hate* it. But I'd hate myself more if I replied any differently. "Yes."

She pulls her phone from her pocket and dictates a text message to her assistant.

It's short.

Send Jonas the packet.

"Is there anything else I can do to help?" she asks.

"Just—be nice to Emma. Please. Don't scare her. I—she—she's my one."

"When you came back from Fiji, I knew there was something different about you. I couldn't put my finger on it, but then you called and told me you were taking that role in that dark comedy that we don't speak about. And then you started talking about a podcast. And then the Darwin movie—you came back from Fiji with a fearlessness I hadn't seen on you since you were about four years old. You never seemed *unhappy*, but you had a new zest for life. We could tell something changed you there. We just didn't know *what*."

I'd argue, but she's right and we both know it. "She was good for me from the minute we met."

"And even if she weren't, this is your life. It's not mine. You get to live it the way you want."

My heart squeezes. "Are you—are you dying?"

"Oh my *god*, right?" Keisha says. "She told me she liked my hair and I asked the same thing."

She and Emma both step out onto the patio with us as Mom sighs. "No, I'm not *dying*. Not of anything specific other than gradual old age. You likely have at least thirty more years with me."

"Good. Millie will be relieved you're just getting soft."

Emma makes eye contact with me. "We're at that critical moment where if we don't get Bash headed home for bed soon, he might get more destructive than Marshmallow."

"Oh, dear," Mom says. "Does he snoop in people's luggage when he's misbehaving too?"

"Not yet, but I'm sure if we give him a couple years, he will," Emma replies.

"I'll get better luggage locks," Mom murmurs to herself. "Lovely to meet you, Emma. If Jonas manages to talk you into a trip to New York, we look forward to seeing you there too."

"I've never been," Emma says.

"*Never?*" Keisha says.

"Never," Emma confirms.

Keisha gapes at me. "How did you *both* find women who had *never been to New York*?"

I'm smiling as I hook an arm around Emma's waist and nudge her inside. Definitely time to go. "Good taste runs in the family."

42

Emma

GOING to work while Jonas stays home with Bash is weird.

Not in a bad way.

More in a *this is the edge of my new life* kind of way.

I don't know what next week will bring. Next month. Next year.

I just know that when I get home every day to both of them, everything is utterly magic.

Hayes and Begonia have left town, taking their security team with them. Jonas's bigger team arrived, fresh off their own vacations that they'd apparently been granted the past few weeks, and I've met them all.

All very nice.

Discreet too.

And a little scary, but more in an *I don't want to be on their bad side* kind of way.

Jonas assures me there's little I can do to get on their

bad side. Except, apparently, eat the last of his lead security agent's Snickers bars. That's unlikely though since the security team has their own house and their own kitchen and their own history that makes all of them guard Graham's Snickers bar stash with their lives.

The early part of my week brings getting-to-know-you video calls with both the Rutherford family's head of public relations and their favorite PR coach, along with a celebrity therapist who's far more down to earth than the butterflies in my stomach expect her to be.

And far more compassionate too.

One more thing to give Chandler credit for, and to talk to the therapist about—his subtle messages that therapists only ever made you feel bad about yourself and ruined your life by making you ruin all of your relationships.

His way of making sure I didn't take any steps to feel better about myself enough and worse enough about him to break up with him.

Control.

Manipulation.

Whereas everyone in Jonas's family and on his staff and public relations team have made me feel valued and appreciated and worthy.

"This is so..." I pause in telling Sabrina and Laney about my week over coffee at Bee & Nugget early Friday, because I can't find the right words.

"Refreshing?" Sabrina says.

"Encouraging?" Laney suggests.

"Affirming," I decide. "It's like, even if they're gaslighting me in a good way, it makes me feel like I can take on the world, and it's *good*. I officially would rather live with false confidence than false doubts."

"You *can* take on the world," Sabrina says.

"And unless he's way more overboard in private than he is in public, I don't think he's opposite-gaslighting you," Laney says. "I think you're enjoying all of the benefits of being with someone who believes in you and wants the best for you first."

We still don't say his name in public, but we all know we're talking about Jonas. And if what he's done to me, for me, and with me in the bedroom this week is any indication, he *definitely* wants the best for me.

Laney and Sabrina both crack up.

I know I didn't say that last part out loud, but—

"Your face, Em," Laney says.

Sabrina's cackling. "This is utterly fabulous. It really is. I was ready to tear him completely apart, but I think I like this future for the two of you so much better."

"Have you talked about telling Bash who he is?" Laney asks.

I smile. "I told Bash last weekend, and when I got home last night, Bash walked up to me and said—"

I cut myself off, and not entirely because I've caught myself from saying *Bash said Jonas is his daddy, so Jonas is Daddy*. I pause just as much because Sabrina's frowning out the window.

And that's not a normal frown.

That's a *someone is going to die* frown.

I start to twist to look, but she grabs my arm. "Don't move."

Ostrich bumps erupt on every inch of my skin. Including my scalp. And my toes. "Why?" I breathe.

"Could be nothing."

"Or?"

She grips tighter. "Or it could be reporters, in which case, we've got you, okay?"

"Even if it's reporters, they probably just heard he was here," Laney murmurs. "They won't know about you."

Or they heard Keisha's here. She and her wife are using Hayes's house for a vacation, which Jonas tells me is also normal for their family.

Laney's right.

The reporters don't know about me and aren't here about me.

Except *they do* know about me.

If they remember the video, they do.

Is two and a half years long enough to forget what the star of a viral video looks like?

Breathe. Breathe. Breathe.

The bells on the door next to an old wooden bear statue jingle.

Laney's gone pale.

Not *pale*-pale, but pale enough for me to notice.

I try not to act weird while I track the movement out of the corner of my eye. I'm in the *one seat* that doesn't have a clear view of either outside or the door. But I get a glimpse of a camera on a strap slung across a guy's shoulder as he stops at the counter.

Then a glimpse of Willa coming out to help him.

We all hold our breaths and listen as he orders a cup of coffee and a muffin.

And I realize I'm being stupidly ridiculous.

Reporters will be a part of my life from here to eternity. I need to learn to handle this. I *am* learning how to handle this.

And they don't know about Jonas and me and Bash. Not together.

Plus, is this guy really a reporter, or is he a photographer stopping by on his way to get shots of the mountains?

Because we get people with cameras all the time.

I shift in my seat, pulling my phone out of my pocket and texting Jonas under the table. *Have you heard of reporters arriving in town?*

My phone vibrates with a call instantly.

I send him to voicemail and text him again. *Don't want to talk right now. At Bee & Nugget with Sabrina and Laney for a quick break.*

His reply is, again, nearly immediate, but this time over text. *Graham is across the street. Eyes on the situation. If you need him, steal Laney's scone. If he thinks you need him, he'll show up. Do whatever he says. I'm sorry. Love you. And I'm sorry.*

I text back a heart emoji and tuck my phone into my pocket. And then I lean into the table. "I heard a rumor they're taking the fish and chips off the menu at the tavern," I say quietly.

If this guy *is* a reporter, it'll look far more suspicious if we're sitting here gaping at each other like terrified morons than if we pretend all is normal.

Both of my friends look at me like I'm crazy, but only for a second before Sabrina nods. "I actually heard that too, and I didn't believe it, so we tracked Bitsy down last night. She confirmed. It's true."

"Why?"

"Apparently they can't get the right mix for the batter right now and they'd rather not serve it than serve what

Bitsy calls *utter rubbish*."

"They don't make it in-house?" Laney asks.

Sabrina cracks a weak smile. "That's a secret I'm not supposed to know."

The man's still at the counter. I think he's looking at his phone while he's waiting for his coffee.

Or possibly he's pretending to look at his phone and he's looking at us.

Is he looking at us?

Or am I letting paranoia win?

"Do you remember that time we thought the treehouse was going to fall down with us in it?" Laney suddenly says, quiet but urgent.

She has a better view of the questionable customer, and I don't like the tone in her voice.

At all.

Nor do I like that I don't remember the time the treehouse almost fell down with us in it.

This is making my heart pound and my hands shake and *I don't like it.*

"Totally hair-raising," Sabrina says. "I still wish they'd reinforced it instead of tearing it down."

My legs are trembling too.

Be strong, Emma. Be brave. They can't hurt you.

Both of my friends are watching me, casually carrying on a conversation about something I don't remember, which means they're trying to tell me something in code, and *I don't know what it is*, but I know I want out.

I don't care if that man's a tourist or a reporter. I don't care what Sabrina and Laney are trying to tell me.

I care that I *get out of this place right now.*

It's hard as hell to look Laney in the eye, say a polite,

"May I?" and reach for her scone as Jonas instructed, but I do.

I trust him.

That's what he says I need to do.

And so that's what I'm going to do.

"Of course," Laney says like this is natural.

Which it is.

We share food all of the time.

This *is* natural.

Jonas is right. He's got me.

I think.

Nothing happens immediately.

Nothing other than Willa bringing the man his coffee. And muffin.

In a ceramic mug and on a plate because *he's not leaving*.

It's not to-go.

Graham doesn't rush the front door.

I don't see him outside, but I don't have the best view.

I feel something though.

Like the hairs on the back of my neck standing up while the man takes a seat at the lone table in the café that I can see clearly.

Which means he can see me clearly.

He's still playing on his phone.

Wearing a hat that looks like a fly fisherman's hat.

Camera still slung over his shoulder.

But his phone—his phone is aimed straight at me.

I gulp.

Don't eat the scone I took off of Laney's plate.

Sabrina starts to move, but I look at her and silently beg her to not do anything.

She glares back at me.

Sabrina doesn't like being helpless, and she doesn't like sitting still when she can *do something* to fix things.

"I should get back to work," she says lightly.

It's a fake lightly.

"Oh, god, me too," Laney says. "I have a meeting in fifteen minutes."

They both look at me.

I try to feel around invisibly for Jonas's security guy.

Where is he?

It's been eighty-four minutes since I gave the signal.

Did he miss it?

Why isn't he *here*?

"I—" I start to croak, and then screams split the air.

No.

Not screams.

Sirens.

"What the *fuck*?" Sabrina leaps to her feet.

Laney puts her hands to her stomach like she's trying to shield her baby's ears from the smoke alarms.

"Clear out," Sabrina yells. "Everyone out. You! *Out!* Fire. *Out!*"

There's no smoke.

And it makes zero sense for her to grab me and Laney and haul us into the kitchen, which is where fire *should be*, but isn't, and then it all makes sense.

Graham's in the kitchen.

He's a Black man, two inches shorter than me, but built like a tank. He nods once to Sabrina, who's giving him the *I am only forgiving you for scaring the shit out of my customers because you're saving my friend* look, and then Laney and I are hustled into a black SUV waiting right outside Bee & Nugget's back door.

"Can't be late for that meeting, Mrs. Monroe," Graham says to Laney, whom he treats with absolute kid gloves while he ushers her into the SUV first.

I'm second.

Actually, I feel like an *afterthought*.

"They'll think she's more important," Graham murmurs to me while the alarm blares in the café behind us, fire truck sirens blare down the street, and my heart slams into my throat.

And then I'm tucked safely into the car with tinted windows and one of my BFFs beside me while Graham hustles around and hops into the driver's seat.

"Was that a reporter?" Laney asks him as we pull away.

He's grim-faced.

I hope that means he needs a Snickers bar.

But his answer puts that hope to rest. "The first of many."

43

Jonas

THEY KNOW.

The reporters know.

And I mean *everything*.

They know I've been here for weeks. They know Hayes bought a house and exactly where it is. They know about Fiji. They know about Emma.

They know where her house is.

They know about Bash.

They fucking know about my son.

I can't hug Emma tight enough once we're all together again at Theo and Laney's house. "Are you okay?"

"Getting there."

I'm glad she trusts me enough to give me an honest answer and pissed that there's any reason for her to *not* be okay. "I'll find the leak," I tell her. "I'll find a way to make them go away."

"Sabrina already did half of that," Laney says, holding out her phone for me to see three words in a text message.

It was Chandler.

Bubbles appear on the screen, telling me Sabrina's not done with whatever she's texting, and a second later— *No doubt. No question. I'd swear on my grandma's scone recipe in a court of law.*

I nod to Laney. "Tell her I'll handle it."

Theo's looking over Laney's shoulder. "Get in line," he tells me.

"I am in line. I'm first."

Emma sighs. "Stop. All of you. Fighting over who deals with it won't actually solve it."

It'll solve a lot for me, and I'm gonna guess based on the way Theo's jaw's working that he's in full agreement.

Laney too.

She seems a little bloodthirsty right now.

"You might want to tell Sabrina that," Laney says.

"Mama Fed titty eat Dodo Ono!" Bash suddenly shrieks.

Theo disappears like a magician while Emma pulls away and looks down the hallway like she can see the cat playing with her chicken.

"Drop the chicken, Fred," Theo orders.

Yolko Ono bagocks pathetically.

Emma squeezes her eyes shut and sighs, and Laney moves in and takes over hug duty.

I feel fucking useless.

And I *hate* feeling fucking useless.

I can take her to New Hampshire. Plenty of security there.

"When the reporters came for Theo, they left after

about a week," Laney tells me. "I have no idea if we collectively learned as a town to chase reporters away more efficiently or if you're a big enough name that we're fucked."

New Hampshire is definitely the route to go.

If Emma *wants* to go.

Her chickens are here. Bash's daycare—which may or may not be an option now—is here. Her job is here.

She doesn't have to work for money—I will absolutely make sure of that—but I know she likes having a role in the community. That's the need her job fills for her.

Belonging. Participating.

Normalcy.

And I've been fooling myself to think that this day wouldn't come.

Emma pulls back from Laney's hug. "I'm okay," she says. "I'm okay. They can't hurt us. I mean, they *can,* but they can't...destroy us."

She gulps.

And I have never, *ever* felt more impotent in my entire life.

I can't show her how to handle this fast enough. There's no four-hour seminar for building mental and emotional resilience to what people say about you. No weekend retreat that'll transform well-earned anxiety into self-confidence. She can't walk through a magic door with legit worries and fears and come out on the other side a new kind of badass wearing that rubber *whatever you say bounces off of me and sticks to you* suit.

This is when I should ask her if she wants out.

But there is no *out*.

The only thing I can do for her now if she wants out is to deny I know her and deny that Bash is mine.

Which I will do.

If she wants me to.

It'll cost me my entire heart and probably one of my lungs and definitely my happiness for the foreseeable future, but if that's what she wants, that's what I'll do.

"Emma—" I start, but she turns a glare on me that cuts me off at my knees.

"Do *not* even think about saying out loud what you're about to say," she says. "*This is part of who you are*. You're willing to turn your entire life inside out and upside down and walk away from *everything* for us, and you don't think I'd do the same for you? I don't like people knowing who I am. I don't like people knowing who Bash is. But *I chose this* when I kept him. And *I choose this now*. I choose *you*. The good and the bad. So don't go pulling a Mr. Sacrifice It All movie-hero move, okay? Just—just *be here* and show me how to get through it. Help me through it. Please?"

The knot in my heart loosens, and my eyes get hot.

I choose you.

My life has never been hard for me, but I know it's hard for other people around me.

And she knows—*she knows* what she's signing up for.

"Saved the chicken," Theo calls.

"We never had doubts," Laney calls back. "Also, *shush*. This is the good part."

Emma half smiles and rolls her eyes, which are looking a little shiny too.

"You're fucking amazing," I say hoarsely. "You know that?"

She shakes her head. "I'm a ferocious mama bear madly in love with my baby's daddy. That's all."

"I have to go somewhere and do something," I tell her.

"I'm going with him." Theo strides back into the room with Bash under one arm and the chicken in the other. I knew it was a risk, bringing Yolko Ono to a house with cats, but I couldn't leave her there. And my security team is guarding the coop at Emma's house under strict orders to take care of anyone who makes a single chicken *bagock* wrong.

"You two are *not*—" Laney starts, but Emma cuts her off.

"Let them do what they think they need to do. Much as I'd like to handle the problem my own way, a mantervention might be the only thing that solves the root of the problem."

Laney gapes at her.

But Theo puffs his chest out. "Damn right. Mantervention it is. Jonas, guess that means you're sitting this one out—ow—ow—ow—*ow*!"

"I'll mantervention you, too, if you don't do this the right way," Emma says as she lets go of his ear. She looks at Laney. "And if a mantervention doesn't work, *then* we do it our way."

"You're okay?" I slip an arm around Emma's waist and tug her closer. "You're sure you're okay?"

"I will be." She pecks my cheek. "Bash, I'll bet we can find Uncle Theo's stash of chocolate chip cookie dough if we look hard enough."

"Tookie dough!" Bash yells.

"*After* you eat watermelon and a grilled cheese for lunch."

"Oh my god, that sounds good," Laney murmurs.

Emma slips away, heading to the kitchen, but not before squeezing me back one more time.

I watch her, looking for any signs this is a mask. That she's putting on a brave front. That she's waiting for me to leave to give in to the desire to collapse in on herself the same way I found her in Fiji.

But Theo claps me on the shoulder and mutters, "She's a lot stronger than any of us give her credit for, and even if she wasn't, she's not alone," and my nerves settle.

"I'm driving," I tell him.

"Your security team's driving and we both know it."

"Semantics."

My security team drives.

The entire trip, I read over the document Mom's assistant forwarded like I'll be on camera in ten and the entire script changed overnight.

Theo stares at me without saying a word.

I ignore him until Graham tells me we're close.

"You don't strike me as the type to do this," Theo says.

"Everyone has a limit."

The fucker grins at me.

Doesn't say another word.

And he doesn't move to get out of the car when we arrive either.

But I know if I decide I need him in there with me, he'll be there.

Not that I'll need him with the little surprise my security team slips into my hand when they let me out.

The house we're stopped at is a duplex in a small mountain town not far from Snaggletooth Creek where a closed-up antique shop and a single active diner beside the gas station seem to be the only attractions. My intel says Chandler works at home, but I'm still unsurprised when my first knock goes unanswered.

So does the second.

The door finally swings open on the third though.

"What the fuck do you want?" the not-at-all charming man who belittled Emma for far too long snarls at me.

I don't know why I grab him by the neck and push him into his house. I've never done anything like this before in my life.

But I don't let go until we're in the low light of his living room, which smells like dead rodents and stale whiskey.

He tries to swing at me, but I have the advantage of adrenaline.

And rage.

Pure, unfiltered rage.

"Sit," I growl at him after ducking a second swing.

He doesn't listen.

Asshole.

So I show him the mason jar as I duck a third time. "Sit, or I let the bees out."

He freezes.

"Jar's already mostly unscrewed. You take me out, they get out. So *sit your ass down*. Now."

He's heaving from the effort of swinging at me, staring at me like he knows he's trapped.

And it takes everything inside of me to not take a swing at him.

"I know you're gambling again," I say quietly. "I know about the porn sites. And I know about the loan you got with your grandfather's forged signature. So we're going to talk about how you're moving to Nebraska and never setting foot within a hundred miles of Snaggletooth Creek,

Los Angeles, or the entire East Coast for the rest of your life."

"You don't know shit."

I know I'm so furious that I'm about to come apart at the seams, and I can't quite remember why I'm not supposed to put myself in jail for a good cause.

And crushing Chandler Sullivan's skull feels like a *very* good cause. "That business deal in Tiara Falls wasn't in Tiara Falls. Tiara Falls doesn't specialize in what's in your basement."

He goes white as a sheet.

Still not as satisfying as putting my fist through his nose.

Especially when what's in his basement is so dumb.

He's breeding hedgehogs. Part of an underground hedgehog breeding program that's illegal in Colorado.

"Moving. To Nebraska." Pretty sure there's zero chance Emma would give up her mountains for Nebraska. Pretty safe bet, and no major cities that I'd want to go are there either. Sorry, Nebraska. "And if Emma's name *ever* comes out of your mouth again, to *anyone*, I'll release everything I know to the press. When it's most convenient. Which will be about the time the press is eating out of Emma's hand because she's fucking *fabulous*, and there'll be nothing they want more than to finally see *you* get what you deserve for what you did to her."

"You think because you're a rich snooty asswipe, you can stand there and make threats? You have *no idea* who my friends are."

"The friends that aren't here?"

"One phone call—"

"Because you can't handle a snooty asswipe on your own?"

He looks about ready to lunge at me, so I wave the jar of bees again. "I'm the only thing standing between you and Theo Monroe, who probably knows even more shit than all of my money can dig up."

"Fucking all-talk asswipe."

Things after that are a bit of a blur.

I know I move.

I know something connects with my fist.

I know there's blood.

I know it's not mine.

And I know I walk out of there with the jar of bees still unopened to be returned to Grey, with zero fear that Chandler Sullivan will ever, *ever* again utter Emma's name or cause a moment's concern for her or Bash for the rest of their lives.

"He's alive," I tell Graham as I slip into the SUV.

As if they can't hear him moaning inside.

My lead security agent sighs. "Does he need medical attention?"

"Unlikely," Theo says. "Can Jonas actually throw a punch? I should go check."

"Stay," Graham orders both of us.

He doesn't knock before letting himself into the townhouse.

"Feel better?" Theo asks me.

"Mostly." My heart's still hammering like I just tried to race a horse in the Kentucky Derby. I suck in a breath that doesn't reach the bottom of my lungs. I'm too amped up. Too furious still. Too certain that there's zero punishment in the world harsh enough to compensate for what this man put Emma through. "Won't be fully better until I know he's being tortured in hell."

"Em should've been the one to put a fist through his face."

"That too. But she'd never do it."

"And he'd hit her back, and then we'd both be in jail."

I eye the man who tried to put *his* fist through *my* face the day we met, who now feels almost like a brother to me. "You're not rushing in there to do any damage yourself."

He smirks. "For once in my life, Rutherford, I'm being the responsible one who makes sure someone else doesn't get arrested. For Emma's sake. Plus, I wanted to see for myself if you surprised me and actually hit him."

Chandler yells something inside, then all goes silent. Graham slips out of the townhouse, and he's barely back in his seat before we're pulling away from the curb.

None of us say anything for a block or so.

"You fix his nose?" I ask Graham.

"Enough. He'll still think of you every time he looks in the mirror."

"Good."

Theo looks at me.

Back to Graham.

Then back to me.

"You two do this before?" he asks.

"You sure you want to know the answer to that?"

He stares at me a beat longer, and then he cracks a grin. "Does Emma know how many Razzle Dazzle lines you still use in your daily life?"

Fuck me.

He's right.

I've said that one in nearly every Razzle Dazzle movie I've ever been in.

Usually when my leading lady co-star would ask *who hurt you* or *what happened at fill-in-the-blank-based-on-the-movie-scenario* or *why do you think you could never love again?*

But I hold his gaze and spend one last long moment of my life playing a role I never want to have again.

And I end it with a line that's *not* in any Razzle Dazzle movies but could be.

"Does she know how many *you* know?"

"Would you two shut up and hand me a Snickers?" Graham mutters.

I do as the man asks.

And then Theo and I fall into another silence on our way back to his house.

My fury with Chandler Sullivan fades, and my appreciation for Emma's brother grows.

And when we get back to his house and Emma meets me in the front yard with the tightest hug I've ever had and Bash comes flying out of the house too, yelling, "*Dat my daddy!*" there's nothing left but relief and joy and love.

"Are you okay?" Emma whispers.

"Never better," I reply. "And he will *never* hurt you again."

Full truth.

No regrets.

This is the best life I could have, right here with Emma and our son.

44

Emma

For what feels like the millionth time in the past week, Jonas is once again studying me closely and saying, "Are you sure about this?"

And for the millionth time since I asked him to take Bash and me out of Snaggletooth Creek for just a week or two, while the reporters get the hint and move on, I nod. "Press the button."

Bash is napping, and even if he wasn't, Keisha and Giovanna and Millie and Jonas's chef and security team and probably a few other random people who could actually secretly live in this palatial mansion in New Hampshire without detection because it's *that big* would entertain him.

Yolko Ono is comfortably situated in a room of her own, watching *Panda Bananda* because we accidentally discovered she's a fan.

The rest of the chickens are still back home in Snaggletooth Creek, under constant care and supervision from the triplets, who have also added security cameras and *booby traps*, as they call them, to the outside of the coop.

Just in case.

Keisha and Millie and Giovanna and Jonas's chef and security team are all leaving us alone in the *business wing* of the house, probably assuming we'll use the time to get naked and have more grown-up fun.

But instead, I'm sliding into his lap in his home office, which is so very *Jonas* with the colorful, whimsical artwork on the walls, the clean glass desktop, the massive computer monitor, and the family pictures on the sideboard.

The fact that he has a home office isn't totally Jonas to me. He's motion and *what's next?* and *let's go climb a tree* so much more than he's *I need to go sit at my desk and do business work*. That probably explains why it's so clean.

Not a lot of use.

Which he fully confessed to on a laugh when I asked why he bothered with a room he spends three minutes a year in.

The house came with it. Hayes has used it more than I have, and he's only come to visit twice.

And there's zero chance that he's getting me out of my clothes until he does as I've asked.

"You're *completely* sure?" he presses. "Once it's out, there's no take-backs."

I've spent the past hour with my PR coach, and I'd be lying if I said this didn't give me a smidge of anxiety.

But it's time.

"The press wants our story," I tell him. "If I've learned

anything from your PR people so far, it's that controlling the story gives you power. And my story—*our* story—the story we recorded yesterday—is the truth. There's power in the truth too. I want to do this while we can still scoop all of those news outlets who are trying to talk everyone else out of what they know."

"Okay," he says slowly, those gorgeous brown eyes still so studious and watchful. "Let's do this."

I grab him by the cheeks. "Are *you* okay with this?"

That earns me a smile. "I'm okay with anything you're okay with."

"I'm not a delicate flower, Jonas."

"Yes, you are. But you're a tough delicate flower."

"That is not a thing."

"It's *you*. You're a thing."

"*You're* a thing," I tease back as he slips his arms around me and pulls me tight, sticking his nose in my neck and inhaling in a way that makes my nipples hum in anticipation.

"You're my favorite thing."

I laugh. "Be that as it may, hit the button. Please."

"You're absolutely, completely, one hundred percent, zero doubts sure?" he asks.

"Yes. Why? Are you not sure? Is this a bad idea? Is there something you're not telling me? Did you say too much yesterday? Are there parts you want to edit out for you?"

He leans back in the chair, tucking my head into the crook of his neck. "I'm absolutely positively completely sure about *everything* with you. Except for hitting this button without triple-quadruple checking with you first. I

THE BRIDE'S RUNAWAY BILLIONAIRE

can handle bad press for me. But I couldn't forgive myself if I had any doubt at all—if *you* have any doubts at all—that being the lead story of every gossip page around half the globe would cause you too much stress."

We've been over this six times since we finished recording our interview for his podcast yesterday.

Laney and Sabrina and Zen and Grey and Theo and the triplets listened to an early copy last night.

They're all asking the same question.

Are you sure?

But they're saying the *other* thing Jonas has said too, and the same thing that my PR coach told me just fifteen minutes ago.

If this is the absolute truth and you won't care if Bash hears it in another ten or twelve years, do it. Be in control and do it.

"Do you know what I finally realized about the wedding and Hawaii and Fiji and me?" I say as I stroke his arm.

"What's that?"

"I was the island then. I was alone. I was mad at my friends and scared they were more mad at me. I was mad at Theo and afraid I was a burden instead of the kind of family I wanted to be for him. I was mad at myself. I was mad at the world. I put up all of those barriers and I didn't want to let anyone in. I *wouldn't* have let anyone in if it weren't for you."

"I guess sometimes getting drunk and passing out on the wrong porch ends okay-ish," he murmurs with a light grin.

"Please don't ever say that in front of Bash. He'll take it as life advice." I kiss his jaw. "But my point is—I'm not alone anymore. Whatever anyone else says about me—it doesn't matter. You matter. Bash matters. My family matters. My friends matter. What the world thinks of me and you and us—it doesn't matter. I still want my version of the truth to be out there, but what happens after you hit that button—so long as you're still here and I'm still here and Bash is safe and my friends and family are still my friends and family—that's what I care about most. Not what strangers on the internet think of me."

"Okay," he says softly. "You're ready. Push the button."

"Wait, *me*?"

He scoots us closer to the desk. "Unless after all of that, you've changed your mind?"

I shake my head. "No mind-changing. I mean it. But I don't want to hit the wrong button and erase everything or—"

"You won't hit the wrong button." He jiggles the mouse, making his monitor blink on.

I don't recognize the app he has pulled up, but when he hovers the pointer over a giant yellow button that says *publish*, I get the gist of it. "That one?" I whisper.

"That's the one."

"The big yellow one right here?" I shift to take control of the mouse.

He puts his hand over mine, holding me steady. "Yep. That button controls your podcast destiny."

I snicker.

Can't help it.

He smiles at me, warm patience and easy acceptance.

"Okay," I say. "I'm doing it."

"I'm waiting."

"Right now."

"Okay."

"I'm pressing the button."

"I can see that."

"Are you sure this is the right podcast? The right files? It's going to all of the right places?"

"Checked and double- and triple-checked myself. Here. Look. *Episode one-thirty. The Guest Who Changed My Life.*"

"That's what it was called when you sent it to my friends and family last night."

"It is."

"And it's this button?"

He chuckles. "If you don't want to—"

I click it.

And then I close my eyes.

And I open them again.

"Wrong button," Jonas says.

I gasp. "*Oh my god, no.* What did I do? Did I delete it? Was it—*Jonas Rutherford, that was not funny.*"

He's laughing his little tushy off.

Right there, while I'm still sitting in his lap.

I poke him in the stomach. "*Rude.*"

"I think I just scored points with your brother."

I lean back into him, watching a progress bar at the bottom of the screen that lights up occasionally with updates about where the podcast has been submitted to. Makes sense as I'm watching the wheels turn.

"I suppose that was only fair," I murmur while I lightly run my fingers down his arm. "It's like payback for that time I convinced my chicken to be your alarm clock."

He laughs at that too, but he also sneaks a hand under

my shirt and inches it higher and higher. "Do you know what we should do?"

"Feed the chicken?" I breathe against his neck.

His fingers reach my breast and tease it lightly over my bra. "I was thinking more like scrubbing the kitchen."

"I hear there's a diaper pail that might need to go out somewhere in this maze of a house." I finish my sentence by biting his neck lightly.

He sucks in a quick breath, and a moment later, my bra is unhooked. "You give the best dirty talk," he murmurs while he rolls one of my nipples between his finger and thumb.

Electricity jolts from my breast to my vagina. I shift in the chair so I can straddle him, feeling his erection already hard and thick between my thighs. "If you like that, wait until you hear me talk about spreadsheets."

My favorite thing about Jonas?

Every time he turns me on, he makes me smile too. I'm not a burden. I'm not a big dork. I'm not crazy.

I'm just *loved*.

And *happy*.

I'm arching into his hand as he teases my nipple, his other hand hooked around the back of my head, fingers threaded through my hair while he pulls me close for a soft kiss. "I can listen to you talk about anything."

"Even when I talk about how much I want to strip you out of your shirt and lick you from your shoulders down to your thick, hard, delicious—"

"Oh my god, *you did it!*" Keisha squeals behind us. "You put it out for the world to hear!"

I squeak and jerk in the seat, making it spin. Jonas

reaches for the desk to steady us, his other hand leaving my breast to wrap around me and hold me tight.

"Exhibit A in *reasons why your wife told you to give them an hour before doing this*—you're interrupting something, Keisha," Millie says dryly. "Excuse us. We'll go. Carry on doing—ew."

"Everyone okay in here?" Giovanna says. "No hyperventilating? And Emma, I *am* asking about Jonas. I know you're stronger than the men always believe."

"I think they look okay," Keisha says. "J, you okay? Em, how about you?"

"We're good," Jonas tells them while I bury my face in his neck and stifle a laugh.

Telling my favorite movie star and my baby's daddy that I want to go down on him then being interrupted by his mother and his pop star cousin was *never* on my life bingo card.

But when I let myself think about it that way, this is even funnier.

"Mama? I sit Dada's wap too?" Bash says, much, *much* closer than the rest of our guests. "We wead books?"

I feel Jonas's heart give a hard thump beneath me, and I squeeze him tight and kiss his neck one last time before carefully untangling myself in the chair. "Later?" I whisper to Jonas.

"Later," he agrees. "Worth the interruption."

"I pway puter!" Bash shrieks as Jonas lifts him up too.

"Who wants a computer when you can have a Marshmallow?" Begonia asks.

And we've lost Bash again.

"Are you still pregnant?" I ask her.

"I'm making it to thirty-seven weeks, thank you very much," she replies with a grin.

"I bet Françoise you'd go at thirty-six weeks and two days," Keisha says.

"I think she'll make it to thirty-nine," Giovanna replies.

"Put your money where your mouth is, Aunt G."

"Françoise already has it."

"Congrats on going public, you two." Begonia gives us a finger wave and a grin while she takes Bash's hand and lets him pull her back down the hall. "Enjoy celebrating. Keisha, Hayes brought Françoise with us. She's in the kitchen complaining about the coffee selection."

"Coffee?" Keisha drifts back down the hall with Begonia too, Millie on her heels.

Giovanna leaves last, pulling the door shut behind her.

Jonas and I both stare at it like we're waiting for it to re-open and everyone to come filing back in, laughing at the idea that they'd give us any privacy right now.

"That was possibly more chaos than pizza party night at my house back home," I finally say.

"I miss home," he replies.

I blink at him. "This...is...your main home."

"*Was*," he corrects. "Until I found you again. Now—now, my heart is here"—he touches mine—"and I can't wait for the dust to settle so we can go back where you and Bash belong."

"You know it's impossible for me to keep my hands off of you when you say things like that," I whisper while I slide my hands up under his shirt.

"I mean it, Emma," he whispers back. "I love living in *your* world. I want to be part of your world. And I can't wait to explore more of it."

"I think," I say, shuffling in the seat to position myself best to press a kiss to the skin over his heart, "you'll find it's even better than the movies."

"You know what else is even better than movies?"

"What?"

"You."

EPILOGUE

Emma

"Oh my god, they actually did it," Sabrina whispers as she pokes her head into the freshly-built building at the back of my new fixer-upper home. She comes the rest of the way in with a little bundle in her arms, and I squeal just as loudly as I did when Laney arrived five minutes ago with her own little bundle.

"Can you believe this is real?" Laney's turning in a circle, taking in the pine board walls, the ceiling that looks like it's made of pine branches but is actually very sturdy above it, the plush Turkish rug under our feet, the windows overlooking the house and the yard, and the three easy chairs that take up two walls.

"It's a little posher than our first clubhouse," Sabrina replies.

I'm holding Laney and Theo's baby girl while Bash

jumps on the middle of the three easy chairs and Yolko Ono wanders around inspecting the treehouse.

Which is really a very large room supported on three sides by stilts, and reached by using the curved staircase that Jonas, Theo, and Grey built around the big pine tree that was chosen for us, leaving enough room for the tree to keep growing for years to come.

For *our* kids to use as a clubhouse.

"It's also big enough for even Grey to stand up in," I tell Sabrina.

She grins, and her little one makes a noise that has both me and Laney cooing as we cross the room to lean in and look.

Henry's only two weeks old, though he might as well be a month, considering he was a full two weeks overdue.

And almost nine pounds when he was born.

"Welcome to your best life ever," she whispers to him. "You're gonna love it here."

"I wuv it here!" Bash says.

He's made the leap to the next chair and looks like he's gearing up to jump to the third too.

"Are you getting any sleep?" Laney asks Sabrina, who nods.

"A surprising amount, actually. And when I don't, there's coffee. *All* of the coffee. All of the time. You?"

"We're up to four-hour stretches. Fred keeps sneaking into her crib and waking her up, and we *cannot* figure out how. I love that cat, and he's about to find himself with a temporary home with my parents if he doesn't get his act together."

Yolko Ono bagocks.

Possibly she's indignant on Fred's behalf, or possibly she hates him on principle.

Could go either way.

"Jonas showed me the kitchen plans," Sabrina says to me. "I thought it would be weird that you're fixing up my grandparents' house, but I love it."

"I used to feel funny about the idea of moving into Chandler's grandparents' house—anytime I'd think about it as his grandparents' house and not *your* grandparents' house—but I've realized I actually felt funny about the idea of living here with *him*. Because he wasn't right, and he would've ruined it for me eventually." I shrug. "That probably sounds weird."

"That's exactly how I felt about all of my ex-boyfriends," Laney says. "I'd think about them moving into my house, and it would be like, *this doesn't fit, we'll have to get a new house*, when really, it was them."

"All of your hundreds of ex-boyfriends," Sabrina teases.

"The hundreds," Laney agrees with a grin.

She was definitely *not* a *hundreds of boyfriends* person.

Henry makes another noise, and Sabrina looks at Bash. "Hey, little dude, I'm gonna need one of those seats to feed a baby. That okay with you?"

"You sit *dere*," he says, pointing to the chair next to him. "I hewp feed da baby."

"If Aunt Sabrina lets you," I remind him.

He scoots off his chair, grabs Yolko Ono, puts the chicken in the chair, climbs back up, lifts his shirt, and offers his nipple to the chicken.

"That's not going to end well," Laney says.

"It'll end...some way," I reply as the chicken hops into Bash's lap and sits, facing forward.

"Doko Ono, you eat," Bash says, pointing to his nipple again.

She ignores him.

"Do you need a blanket?" I ask Sabrina. "There's a closet with old blankets that all of our parents donated."

"Sure. Surprise me, please." She shuffles the baby as she sits, and Laney and I gasp at the same time.

There's something big and sparkly and *how did we miss that?* on her left ring finger.

"What—" Laney starts as I say, *"When?"*

Sabrina looks down at her finger, then grins at us while she flashes a view of her whole hand, massive diamond with an elaborate wrap and all. "Oh, this old thing?"

"Yes, *that old thing*," I squeal while Laney and I crowd into the last easy chair beside her. Laney's baby is still sleeping like an absolute angel.

"Tell us everything," Laney breathes.

"He wore me down," Sabrina says dramatically. "I was one day shy of forty-two weeks, and he was all, *you know he's not coming until we get hitched, so we might as well just do it*. Very, *very* romantic."

"Liar," Laney murmurs.

"If you don't want to tell us, just say you don't want to tell us," I agree.

Sabrina laughs. "You know him too well, don't you?"

"We do," Laney and I agree.

"He proposed in the middle of the night three days after we got home from the hospital. So...just over a week ago? I got up to feed the baby and couldn't go back to sleep, so I was avoiding the bedroom, because *one* of us should sleep, you know?"

"We know," Laney says quickly.

I smile.

I remember missing sleep.

Seeing my friends with babies makes me want to miss sleep again.

"So he found me in the kitchen staring at all of my caffeinated coffees, and he asked me if I had to choose between marrying coffee and marrying him, which one would I choose?"

Laney and I both crack up, because we know *exactly* what she told him.

"Right?" Sabrina says. "As if there was a question. But when he got down on one knee and held out the ring and said, 'But I don't see the coffee offering you this,' it was the sweetest, funniest, most perfect thing *ever*."

And this is how we all know he's her soulmate.

I love my friends' chosen partners.

Sabrina's still smiling. "So…I said yes, and I think I actually cried, and he's letting me lie and tell everyone it was the lack of sleep that made me all weepy, and we took a day trip up into the mountains yesterday with my mom and grandpa and his grandma and Zen. And now we're officially legally tied together forever, and I did *not* have sex on my wedding night, which sucks donkey balls, but also, he's never touching me with his penis again and he knows it, and he married me anyway, so here we are."

"Are you happy?" I whisper.

Her eyes go misty. "Oh my god, *yes*."

Laney squeals.

I squeal.

Sabrina laughs and lets me wipe her eyes while she feeds the baby. "I never wanted this, but *I love him so much*," she tells us.

"Welcome to the club," Laney replies with a laugh. "If you'd told me twenty years ago we'd be sitting here in a cabin that *Theo* rebuilt with *your husband* and *Jonas Rutherford* while we all fuss over our kids…"

"I can't believe you got married," I squeal again.

"I'm sorry we didn't invite you two," Sabrina says. "But it was—"

"Exactly how you needed and wanted your wedding to be," Laney interrupts. "Don't worry. We'll throw a party for you."

Sabrina smiles. "That's the best part anyway. Far less ugly crying and real emotions."

Laney slides me a look. "And how's life with our favorite movie star for you?"

"Just lacking a ring to make an engagement official," I whisper.

And now it's my two best friends who are squealing over me.

"Stop, stop." I wave a hand with a laugh, pulling Laney's little girl closer with my other arm. I can't get enough of this newborn stage, before she's figured out if she'll be like Theo and wreak havoc on the town or like Laney, quiet and reserved and rule-following, or somewhere in between. "We're enjoying you two being mothers first."

"No, we're enjoying *all* of us being happy," Laney corrects.

"And you being involved with someone who worships the ground you walk on, *as it should be*," Sabrina agrees.

"I think we've all found partners who worship the ground we walk on. And *that's* as it should be."

"When's the wedding?" Laney asks.

"*Where's* the wedding?" Sabrina corrects.

"We are *not* doing a destination wedding." I shudder. "Been there, done that."

"What if it was in Fiji?" Laney counters.

"Where you met?" Sabrina agrees.

"With chickens."

"In a restored ancient Fijian village."

"With chickens."

"I'll make sure Theo doesn't sneeze."

"Unka Theo sneeze *woud*," Bash says. "It scare Doko Ono."

I laugh. "When we figure it out, I promise you'll be among the first to know."

"How did he propose?" Laney asks.

I squeeze my lips shut, but I'm still smiling. And then I pointedly look at Bash.

Both of my friends crack up.

So you were both naked. I can hear each of them saying it, and they're not wrong.

"He, ah, asked again this morning," I say. "And I said yes…again."

They both laugh harder.

"Go, Emma," Sabrina says.

Laney squeezes my shoulders in a side hug. "I'm so thrilled for you."

"We won't breathe a word," Sabrina adds.

"It's okay. There's already speculation. We'll release an official statement sometime, and then it'll be old news until we release a wedding photo, and then it'll be old news again."

The press is not my favorite part of being involved with Jonas, but between his security team, the podcast telling our story, and an official statement from Razzle Dazzle about the Rutherford family being happy to welcome me and my son into their lives, this has been a *lot* different from the viral video that almost broke me.

I can handle the world knowing who I am.

I know there are people who are calling me a gold digger and an opportunist and a lot of worse things, but what I told Jonas when I hit *go* on that podcast is true.

I'm not alone.

I have him. I have Bash. I have family and friends and I can still mostly walk around Snaggletooth Creek without feeling like I'm on display.

Without feeling like the entire world is judging me.

And I'm so, *so* glad that Bash is already in therapy to learn all of the lessons that I wish I'd had as a kid even if I *hadn't* known I was preparing for a lifetime of having some spotlight always cast my way.

"Still not breathing a word," Sabrina repeats.

"Agreed," Laney says.

"I don't mind the attention so much now," I tell them. It's the truth. "Jonas is worth it."

They both grin.

"That is the absolute sweetest and most classic Emma thing ever, and I am *so glad* we have you back." Sabrina blinks quickly, then groans. "*Why* do I cry about everything right now?"

"Post-baby hormones," I reply. "We've got you. It's okay. You can cry."

"I hate crying."

"Okay, no more crying," Laney agrees. "Instead—I have presents for all of us."

"*Laney*," I groan.

"It's useless to argue," Sabrina tells me.

Laney flings a window open, letting in the late November air. "Bring them up, please," she says to someone below.

And a minute later, Jonas, Theo, and Grey stroll through our clubhouse door.

"*Laney*," Sabrina says again.

Each of the men have *massive* boxes.

Like, I couldn't actually carry them.

"My fault," Theo says. "I was sleep deprived and hanging out on the Kingston Photo Gifts website too late at night and my credit card fell out and landed on the keyboard."

None of us believe him.

"Dada bwing pwesents for me?" Bash asks.

"There's something for you in your mama's box," Laney tells him.

"Right on top," Theo agrees.

"This treehouse is *not* built for nine," Sabrina says.

"Not nine and presents," I agree.

"Pwesents!" Bash slingshots himself off the chair, making Yolko Ono squawk in irritation at almost being flung off too.

Jonas grabs Bash in one arm and rescues the chicken with the other, letting her down to glare at all of us from what looks to be her preferred corner of the treehouse.

Theo reclaims his daughter from me after he's set a box at Laney's feet, and after a quick reshuffle, the men are holding the kids in the seats while Laney, Sabrina, and I sit on the floor and tackle the boxes.

The first thing we pull out has all three of us doubling over in laughter, which makes me suspect Theo wasn't lying about these being his fault.

"Look, Bash," I say, handing him his T-shirt. "Aunt Laney and Uncle Theo got you a shirt."

His is yellow—his current favorite color—and it has a tractor on it—his current favorite vehicle.

It also says *Heir to the Ugly Heiress Society* in scripty font around the tractor.

The babies have matching onesies.

Complete with the tractors.

"They don't care what they wear," Theo says as Laney holds theirs up. "Why can't my daughter like tractors too?"

"Heaven help us if she tries to hotwire one someday," Laney replies, which sends all of us into a fit of laughter again.

There's a box clearly holding a coffee tumbler of some type next, and when we all open them at the same time, we once again double over.

"The *Hot Ugly Moms Club?*" Laney says.

She's the first of us able to speak.

Theo looks her square in the eye. "We have traditions to uphold."

"Should it be *Hot Ugly Moms* or *Ugly Hot Moms*?" Grey asks Theo.

Completely dead serious.

"*Ugly Hot Moms* implies menopause," Theo replies, equally staid.

"You gave this a lot of thought."

"It's what I do."

Jonas is watching all of us with that amused, quiet smile that I love so much.

I love when he's quiet. It's a peaceful, happy quiet. Like he's spent his whole life looking for something out in the wide open, only to find it in a cramped treehouse behind a fixer-upper in the mountains.

He catches my eye and smiles bigger and softer at the same time. *They know*, I mouth to him.

Good, he mouths back.

He slides a look at Theo, then back to me, and I bite my lower lip to keep from laughing at the implied statement.

You can tell him next and stand between us so he doesn't threaten to make it impossible for us to have more kids if I mistreat you. Which I will never do. Ever. EVER.

"More presents," Laney says. "Let's open this one next." She waves a square box.

Inside, we find matching jewelry boxes with the original logo Laney had made for our *Ugly Heiress Society* club, and inside the jewelry boxes are matching lockets that have matching pictures of the three of us on one side, and unique pictures on the other.

Theo, Laney, and their baby for Laney.

Sabrina, Grey, their dogs, Zen, and their baby for Sabrina.

Jonas, Bash, and me with Yolko Ono for me.

"*I said no more crying*," Sabrina moans as she wipes her eyes.

Theo starts looking guilty for the first time. "So maybe the last one can wait," he mutters.

"Eff you, Theo Monroe," she fires back. "If I'm already crying, I'm effing crying."

There's one last item to open. It's another box, about a foot and a half square and relatively flat.

I'm sniffling. Laney's sniffling. Sabrina's sniffling harder.

And on the count of three, we open the boxes together.

This time, they're all different.

All printed pieces of wood.

Mine has fairies on it and the words *Official new home of*.

Laney's is decorated with drawn kittens, and says, *the original Ugly Heiresses*.

And Sabrina's has coffee beans and bees all over it, and says *of Snaggletooth Creek, Colorado*.

We line them up, and all three of us burst into absolute sobs.

"Good job, Theo," Grey mutters.

"Every clubhouse needs a sign," Theo mutters back. "I thought they'd like it."

"They do," Jonas says.

"It's so beautiful," Sabrina wails.

"It's so *us*," Laney sobs.

"I'm so ugly when I cry," I moan.

"Why do you think I named you that?" Theo says.

"We make custom tissue packs and *you didn't think to include them*?" Laney says to him.

"Sleep deprivation," Theo says.

I crawl up to my knees and hug my brother. "Thank you for being the best worst brother ever."

He squeezes me back. "Anything for you and your ugly friends, Em."

I poke him in the gut, and then I hug Jonas, who's

handing all of my friends the tissues he hid in the closet. "And thank you for not caring that I'm ugly when I cry."

"You're not ugly when you cry," he replies with a laugh.

"Unka Theo make mama cry?" Bash says quietly.

"It's a good cry," I assure my little boy as I let Jonas go and lift up my first little joy. "Mama sometimes cries when she's happy."

"Mama cry *aww da time*." He pats my cheeks. "Mama so happy."

"Exactly right. Mama so happy."

Grey's helping Sabrina put on her locket. Theo's showing Laney where he thinks our clubhouse signs should go.

And Jonas is wrapping both me *and* Bash in a massive hug. "What do you say we all live happily ever after?"

I kiss his cheek, then Bash's cheek, then Jonas's again. "We already are."

BONUS EPILOGUE

Jonas

It's a gorgeous day to get married in the second most beautiful place in the world.

First most beautiful place?

Home, in the mountains of Snaggletooth Creek, with Emma and Bash.

Second most beautiful place?

The island where Emma and I met.

We planned a massive wedding in New Hampshire. Leaked details to the press. Booked everything.

There's a huge reception happening on my estate there right now, in fact, with all of my Hollywood friends and Emma's favorite clients and friends from Snaggletooth Creek.

While we're standing at the water below the villa where I passed out on Emma's porch with my family and hers.

Zen is officiating.

Hayes and Theo are my best men.

Sabrina and Laney are Emma's matrons of honor.

My mom is crying.

So is Emma's dad.

And I'm a little choked up myself, because my bride is smiling at me through tears as Zen finishes a beautiful speech about love, struggles, and the meaning of family.

Emma's in a soft peach summer dress. I'm in shorts.

Bash is wearing his swimsuit and inching closer and closer and closer to the water like he thinks every one of us doesn't have half an eye on him.

"And if all of that doesn't scare you," Zen says, "then Emma, it's time for you to try one last time with your vows."

Everyone laughs.

This is easily the lightest-hearted wedding I've ever been to, and that's *perfect*.

There's enough difficulty in life.

Loving Emma? Choosing Emma?

This is easy.

She squeezes my hands and looks straight into my eyes, fearless joy dancing in hers. "Jonas, I had no idea how much meeting you would save my—"

"*Aaaaaaa-ccccchhhhhhhoooooooooo!*"

The sneeze reverberates across the beach. Birds squawk and take flight. A dolphin changes direction mid-leap and dives for safety. Hayes and Begonia's twins, who recently celebrated their first birthday, simultaneously burst into sobs.

"Bless you?" my mother mutters to the offensive sneezer.

"Good *god*, I'd heard rumors, but is it really like that *all* of the time?" Keisha mutters.

Loudly.

"Stop it, Uncle Theo!" Bash yells.

I turn and look at my very-soon-to-be brother-in-law and lift my brows.

Don't miss the way Grey's nearly doubled over laughing in the small crowd gathered around us.

Or the way Mike Monroe's cringing so hard I can feel it in my own face, even though I'm actually about to laugh myself.

"Any more you're saving in there?" I ask Theo.

He stares back straight-faced. "Allergies. Never know. New pollen here."

"I'm gonna get back to marrying your sister now."

"Your wedding, man. But I strongly suggest you say your vows like you're Ryan Reynolds."

"I can take him out," Hayes murmurs to me. "Begonia's never seen me go full caveman. I think she'd like it."

I look back at Emma, who's clearly trying to stifle a laugh while she wipes more tears from her eyes.

"That shake loose any last minute things you need to say first?" I ask her.

Theo sneezes again.

Beside Emma, Laney is clearly trying to keep herself from laughing. She's three months pregnant, which I'm not supposed to know, but Sabrina and Emma both figured it out, and there aren't secrets among the six of us, so now we all know.

Sabrina's crossed her arms and is staring at Theo like she's next in line behind Hayes to go caveman on Theo's ass if he sneezes again.

"Stop scawing da birds, Uncle Theo," Bash says.

Emma grabs him by the shoulders on his little march to have words with his uncle. "Stay here with me," she whispers. "I have to say my vows and marry your daddy, okay?"

"Dat's dumb," Bash mutters.

Loudly.

Theo sneezes again.

His own daughter starts crying.

And Emma cracks up.

"Probably want to go for the short version or excuse him from his duties," Zen mutters to us.

And once more, a massive, echoing sneeze splits the air.

But this time, it's not Theo.

This time, it's Bash sneezing the sneeze of a person six times his size.

Every last person gathered at our little wedding gawks at him.

How the hell did that sound come out of his body?

"Bwess me, I get tiss-sue?" he says.

Emma whimpers, clearly stifling a laugh.

Sabrina, Laney, my mother, and one of the triplets all produce tissues for Bash.

And my bride grabs my hand again, still keeping one on Bash as she launches into her vows before anyone else sneezes. "Jonas, you are the last thing I ever wanted. *Ever*. Especially when we met, and even more so when you came back into my life. But you're also everything that's ever been missing in my life. You're my best friend. My partner. The first person to fully and completely demonstrate to me the true meaning of believing in another person. You saved me and you gave me more than I ever knew I could wish for when you chose to love me and our son, and I will love you until the end of time and back again."

"*Dammit*," Theo mutters.

"There's no objecting in this wedding, dumbass," Zen hisses at him.

"*She made me cry*," he hisses back.

"Also, this is the best wedding *ever*," Emma whispers to me. "Your turn. Maybe fast?"

She doesn't have to tell me twice. I pull her hand to my mouth and kiss it. "Emma, I spent my entire life chasing a dream with roles that weren't supposed to be mine. But when I met you, I found where I fit. You give my life meaning and purpose and more love and joy in a single minute of the day than I've ever found anywhere else. I love you more than all of the stars and planets and meteor showers that exist in the entire universe, and I give you my heart for all eternity."

Every word is true.

None come from any movie script I've ever read.

I checked.

Emma flings herself at me and kisses me. "I love you," she whispers.

"I love you too."

"You love meeeeee," Bash says.

"Fucking *dammit*," Theo mutters again. "*He* made me cry too."

"Maybe it's pregnancy hormones," Zen says.

I lift Bash up and hug him while I'm hugging Emma and she's hugging both of us.

"And I now pronounce you man and wife and child,"

Zen says. "Do the kissing and all that. Like you didn't already. Go ahead. Do the kissing again."

But Emma doesn't kiss me.

Actually, she looks at Zen and completely kiss-blocks me.

"You missed the one part," Emma whispers to Zen.

Zen rolls their eyes with a smirk that gives me pause for the first time all day. All week. Even all *month*.

"Oh, *right*. That part." They clear their throat. "I now pronounce you man and wife and child and child-on-the-way. *Now* you can do the kissing thing."

Squeals and gasps and *are they serious* zip around us.

I blink at Emma.

Blink again.

"Are they—" I murmur.

She grins, and then she kisses me, again, this one longer and slower and sweet and spicy and *everything*, and I know.

She is.

We are.

"Only my friends got the announcement last time," she whispers as she pulls out of the kiss. "I thought it was only fair your friends and family got to be included at the same time this time."

"More babies," my mom says, sounding a little choked up.

"Way to *go*, J," Keisha crows.

"I still know where you live," Theo says behind me.

"I can always find where *you* live," Hayes mutters back to him.

"Awww, this is the *best wedding ever*. After ours." Begonia reaches us the same time as Laney and Sabrina, all of them hugging us and laughing and asking questions while I keep stealing kisses from my new wife, who's glowing with love and happiness.

Best day of my life.

Hands down.

Until our little girl comes along about eight months later. And her and Bash's baby brother eighteen months after that. And one last surprise girl four years after that.

This is my life.

And living it day in and day out with Emma is better than all of the fame and fortune in the world.

PIPPA GRANT BOOK LIST

The Girl Band Series (Complete)

Mister McHottie

Stud in the Stacks

Rockaway Bride

The Hero and the Hacktivist

The Thrusters Hockey Series

The Pilot and the Puck-Up

Royally Pucked

Beauty and the Beefcake

Charming as Puck

I Pucking Love You

The Bro Code Series

Flirting with the Frenemy

America's Geekheart

Liar, Liar, Hearts on Fire

The Hot Mess and the Heartthrob

Copper Valley Fireballs Series (Complete)

Jock Blocked

Real Fake Love

The Grumpy Player Next Door

Irresistible Trouble

Three BFFs and a Wedding Series (Complete)

The Worst Wedding Date

The Gossip and the Grump

The Bride's Runaway Billionaire

The Tickled Pink Series

The One Who Loves You

Rich In Your Love

Standalones

The Last Eligible Billionaire

Not My Kind of Hero

Dirty Talking Rival *(Bro Code Spin-Off)*

A Royally Inconvenient Marriage *(Royally Pucked Spin-Off)*

Exes and Ho Ho Hos

The Bluewater Billionaires Series (Complete)

The Price of Scandal by Lucy Score

The Mogul and the Muscle by Claire Kingsley

Wild Open Hearts by Kathryn Nolan

Crazy for Loving You by Pippa Grant

Co-Written with Lili Valente

Hosed

Hammered

Hitched

Humbugged

Happily Ever Aftered

Pippa Grant writing as Jamie Farrell:

The Misfit Brides Series (Complete)

Blissed

Matched

Smittened

Sugared

Merried

Spiced

Unhitched

The Officers' Ex-Wives Club Series (Complete)

Her Rebel Heart

Southern Fried Blues

ABOUT THE AUTHOR

Pippa Grant wanted to write books, so she did.

Before she became a USA Today and #1 Amazon best-selling romantic comedy author, she was a young military spouse who got into writing as self-therapy. That happened around the time she discovered reading romance novels, and the two eventually merged into a career. Today, she has more than 30 knee-slapping Pippa Grant titles and nine published under the name Jamie Farrell.

When she's not writing romantic comedies, she's fumbling through being a mom, wife, and mountain woman, and sometimes tries to find hobbies. Her crowning achievement? Having impeccable timing for telling stories that will make people snort beverages out of their noses. Consider yourself warned.

Find Pippa at…
www.pippagrant.com
pippa@pippagrant.com

Printed in the USA
CPSIA information can be obtained
at www.ICGtesting.com
JSHW022017141223
53788JS00002B/7